Babylon by Grant Allen

In Three Volumes

Charles Grant Blairfindie Allen was born on February 24th, 1848 at Alwington, near Kingston, Canada West (now part of Ontario).

Home schooled until 13 when his family moved to England, Grant was to become a highly regarded science writer who branched out to a fiction career and became enormously popular.

His work helped propel several genres of fiction and whilst his career was short it was enormously productive.

Grant's scientific background enabled him to root much of his work in a plausibility that was denied to others. He had little fear in challenging a society that treated women as second class citizens and creating best sellers from such works.

On October 25th 1899 Grant Allen died at his home in Hindhead, Haslemere, Surrey, England. He died just before finishing Hilda Wade. The novel's final episode, which he dictated to his friend, doctor and neighbour Sir Arthur Conan Doyle from his bed appeared under the appropriate title, The Episode of the Dead Man Who Spoke in 1900.

Index of Contents

VOLUME I

CHAPTER I

RURAL AMERICA

Whar's Hiram, Het?' Deacon Zephaniah Winthrop asked of his wife, tartly. 'Pears to me that boy's allus off somewhar, whenever he's wanted to do anything. Can't git along without him, any way, when we've got to weed the spring peppermint. Whar's he off, I say, Mehitabel?'

Mrs. Winthrop drew herself together from the peas she was languidly shelling, and answered in the dry withered tone of a middle-aged northern New Yorker, 'Wal, I s'pose, Zeph, he's gone down to the blackberry lot, most likely.'

'Blackberry lot,' Mr. Winthrop replied with a fine air of irony. 'Blackberry lot, indeed. What does he want blackberryin', I should like to know? I'll blackberry him, I kin tell you, whenever I ketch him. Jest you go an' holler for him, Het, an' ef he don't come ruther sooner'n lightnin', he'll ketch it, an' no mistake, sure as preachin'. I've got an orful itchin', Mis' Winthrop, to give that thar boy a durned good cow-hidin' this very minnit.'

Mrs. Winthrop rose from the basket of peas and proceeded across the front yard with as much alacrity as she could summon up, to call for Hiram. She was a tall, weazened, sallow woman, prematurely aged, with a pair of high cheekbones, and a hard, hungry-looking, unlovable mouth; but she was averse to the extreme and unnecessary measure of cowhiding her firstborn. 'Hiram,' she called out, in her loudest and shrillest voice: 'Hiram!

Drat the boy, whar is he? Hiram! Hi-ram!' It was a dreary and a monotonous outlook altogether, that view from the gate of Zephaniah Winthrop's freehold farm in Geauga County. The homestead itself, an unpainted frame house, consisted of planed planks set carelessly one above the other on upright beams, stood in a weedy yard, surrounded by a raw-looking paling, and unbeautified by a single tree, creeper, shrub, bush, or scented flower. A square house, planted naked in the exact centre of a square yard, desolate and lonely, as though such an idea as that of beauty had never entered into the human heart. In front the long straight township road ran indefinitely as far as the eye could reach in either direction, beginning at the horizon on the north, and ending at the horizon on the south, but leading nowhere in particular, that anyone ever heard of, meanwhile, unless it were to Muddy Creek Dépôt (pronounced deepo) on the Rome, Watertown, and Ogdens-burg Railroad. At considerable intervals along its course, a new but congenitally shabby gate opened here and there into another bare square yard, and gave access to another bare square frame house of unpainted pine planks. In the blanks between these oases of unvarnished ugliness the road, instead of being bordered by green trees and smiling hedgerows, pursued its gaunt way, unrejoicing, between open fields or long and hideous snake fences. If you have ever seen a snake fence, you know what that means; if you haven't seen one, sit down in your own easy chair gratefully and comfortably, and thank an indulgent heaven with all your heart for your happy ignorance.

Beyond and behind the snake fences lay fields of wheat and meadows and pasture land; not, as in England, green and lush with grass or clover, but all alike bare, brown, weedy, and illimitable. There were no trees to be seen anywhere (though there were plenty of stumps), for this was 'a very fully settled section,' as Mr. Winthrop used to murmur to himself complacently: 'the country thar real beautiful: you might look about you, some parts, for a mile or two right away togither and never see a single tree a-standin' anywhar.' Indeed, it was difficult to imagine where on earth a boy could manage to hide himself in all that long, level, leafless district. But Mrs. Winthrop knew better: she knew Hiram was loafing away somewhere down in the blackberry lot beside the river.

'Lot' is a cheap and nasty equivalent in the great American language for field, meadow, croft, copse, paddock, and all the other beautiful and expressive old-world names which denote in the tongue of the old country our own time-honoured English inclosures. And the blackberry lot, at the bottom of the farm, was the one joy and delight of young Hiram Winthrop's boyish existence. Though you could hardly guess it, as seen from the farm, there was a river running in the hollow down yonder-Muddy Creek, in fact, which gave its own euphonious name to the naked little Dépôt; not here muddy, indeed, as in its lower reaches, but clear and limpid from the virgin springs of the Gilboa hillsides. Beside the creek, there stretched a waste lot, too rough and stony to be worth the curse of cultivation; and on that lot the blackberry bushes grew in wild profusion, and the morning-glories opened their great pink bells blushingly to the early sun, and the bobolinks chattered in the garish noontide, and the grey squirrels hid by day among the stunted trees, and the chipmunks showed their painted sides for a moment as they darted swiftly in and out from hole to hole amid the tangled brushwood. What a charmed spot it seemed to the boy's mind, that one solitary patch of undesecrated nature, in the midst of so many blackened stumps, and so much first-rate fall wheat, and such endless, hopeless, dreary hillocks of straight rowed, dry leaved, tillering Indian corn!

'Hiram! Hiram! Hi-ram!' cried Mrs. Winthrop, growing every moment shriller and shriller.

Hiram heard, and leaped from the brink at once, though a kingfisher was at that very moment eyeing him with head on one side from the half-concealing foliage of the basswood tree opposite. 'Yes, marm,' he answered submissively, showing himself as fast as he was able in the pasture above the blackberry lot. 'Wal! What is it?'

'Hiram,' his mother said, as soon as he was within convenient speaking distance, 'you come right along in here, sonny. Where was you, say? Here's father swearin he'll thrash you for goin' loafin'. He wants you jest to come in at once and help weed the peppermint. I guess you've bin down in the blackberry lot, fishin', or suthin'.'

'I ain't bin fishin',' Hiram answered, with a certain dogged, placid resignation. 'I've bin lookin' around, and that's so, mother. On'y lookin' around at the chipmunks an' bobolinks,'cause I was dreadful tired.'

'Tired of what?' asked his mother, not uncompassionately.

'Planin',' Hiram answered, with a nod. 'Planks. Father give me forty planks to plane, an' I've done'em.'

'Wal, mind he don't thrash you, Hiram,' the sallow-faced woman said, warningly, with as much tenderness in her voice as lay within the compass of her nature. 'He's orful mad with you now, 'cause you didn't answer immejately when he hollered.'

'Then why don't he holler loud enough?' asked Hiram, in an injured tone, he was an ill-clad boy of about twelve—'I can't never hear him down lot yonder.'

'What's that you got in your pocket, sir?' Mr. Winthrop puts in, coming up unexpectedly to the pair on the long, straight, blinking high-road. 'What's that, naow, eh, sonny?'

Hiram pulls the evidence of guilt slowly out of his rough tunic. 'Injuns,' he answers, shortly, in the true western laconic fashion.

Mr. Winthrop examines the object carelessly. It is a bit of blackish stone, rudely chipped into shape, and ground at one end to an artificial edge with some nicety of execution.

'Injuns!' he echoes contemptuously, dashing it on the path: 'Injuns! Oh yes, this is Injuns! An' what's Injuns? Heathens, outlandish heathens; and a drunken, p'isonous crowd at that, too. The noble red man is a fraud; Injuns must go. It allus licks my poor finite understandin' altogether why the Lord should ever have run this great continent so long with nothin' better'n Injuns. It's one o' them mysteries o' Providence that 'taint given us poor wums to comprehend daown here, noways. Wal, they're all cleared out of this section naow, anyway, and why a lad that's brought up a Chrischun and Hopkinsite should want to go grubbin' up their knives and things in this cent'ry is a caution to me, that's what it is, a reg'lar caution.'

'This ain't a knife,' Hiram answered, still doggedly. 'This is a tommyhawk. Injun knives ain't made like this 'ere. I've had knives, and they're quite a different kinder pattern.'

Mr. Winthrop shook his head solemnly.

'Seems to me,' he said with a loud snort, ''taint right of any believin' boy goin' lookin' up these heathenish things, mother. He's allus bringin' 'em home—arrowheads, he calls 'em, and tommyhawks, and Lord knows what rubbish—when he ought to be weedin' in the peppermint lot, an' earnin' his livin'. Why wasn't you here, eh, sonny? Why wasn't you? Why wasn't you? Why wasn't you?'

As Mr. Winthrop accompanied each of these questions by a cuff, crescendo, on either ear alternately, it is not probable that he himself intended Hiram to reply to them with any particular definiteness. But Hiram, drawing his sleeve across his eyes, and wiping away the tears hastily, proceeded to answer with due deliberation: ''Cause I was tired planin' planks. So I went down to the blackberry lot, to rest a bit. But you won't let a feller rest. You want him to be workin' like a nigger all day.'Taint reasonable.'

'Mother,' Mr. Winthrop said again, more solemnly than before, 'it's my opinion that the old Adam is on-common powerful in this here lad, on-common powerful! Ef he had lived in Bible times, I should hev been afeard of a visible judgment on his head, like the babes that mocked at Elijah. (Or was it Elisha?' asked Mr. Winthrop to himself, dubitatively. 'I don't'zackly recollect the pertickler prophet.) The eye that mocketh at its father, you know, sonny; it's a dangerous thing, I kin tell you, to mock at your father. Go an' weed that thar peppermint, sir; go an' weed that thar peppermint.' And as he spoke the deacon gave Hiram a parting dig in the side with the handle of the Dutch hoe he was lightly carrying.

Hiram dodged the hoe quickly, and set off at a run to the peppermint lot. When he got there he waited a moment, and then felt in his pocket cautiously for some other unseen object. Oh joy, it wasn't broken! He took it out and looked at it tenderly. It was a bobolink's egg. He held it up to the light, and saw the sunshine gleaming through it.

'Aint it cunning?' he said to himself, with a little hug and chuckle of triumph. 'Ain't it a cunning little egg, either? I thought he'd most broke it, I did, but he hadn't, seems. It's the first I ever found, that sort. Oh my, ain't it cunning?' And he put the egg back lovingly in his pocket, with great cautiousness.

For a while the boy went on pulling up the weeds that grew between the wide rows of peppermint, and then at last he came to a big milk-weed in full flower. The flowers were very pretty, and so curious, too. He looked at them and admired them. But he must pull it up: no room in the field for milk-weed (it isn't a marketable crop, alas!), so he caught the pretty thing in his hands, and uprooted it without a murmur. Thus he went on, row after row, in the hot July sun, till nearly half the peppermint was well weeded.

Then he sat down to rest a little on the pile of boulders in the far corner. There was no tree to sit under, and no shade; but the boy could at least sit in the eye of the sun on the pile of ice-worn boulders. As he sat, he saw a wonderful and beautiful sight. In the sky above, a great bald-headed eagle came wheeling slowly toward the corner of the fall wheat lot. From the opposite quarter of the sky his partner circled on buoyant wings to meet him; and with wide curves to right and left, crossing and recrossing each other at the central point like well-bred setters, those two magnificent birds swiftly beat the sunlit fields for miles around them. At last, one of the pair detected game; for an instant he checked his flight, to steady his swoop, and then, with wings halffolded, and a rushing noise through the air, he fell plump on the ground at a vague spot in the midst of the meadow. One moment more, and he rose again, with a quivering rabbit suspended from his yellow claws. Presently he made towards the corn lot. It was fenced round, like all the others, with a snake fence, and, to Hiram's intense joy, the eagle finally settled, just opposite him, on one of the two upright rails that stand as a crook or stake for the top rail, called the rider. Its big white head shone in the sunlight, its throat rang out a sharp, short bark, and it craned its neck this way and that, looking defiantly across the field to Hiram.

'I reckon,' the boy said to himself quietly, 'I could draw that thar eagle.'

He put his hand into his trousers pocket, and pulled out from it a well-worn stump of blacklead pencil. Then from another pocket he took a small blank book, an old account book, in fact, with one side of the pages all unwritten, though the other was closely covered with rows of figures. It was a very precious possession to Hiram Winthrop, that dog-eared little volume, for it was nearly-filled with his own tentative pencil sketches of beast and birds, and all the other beautiful things that lived together in the blackberry bottom. He had never seen anything beautiful anywhere else, and that one spot and that one book were all the world to him that he loved or cared for.

He laid the book upon his knee, and proceeded carefully to sketch the grand whiteheaded eagle in his boyish fashion. 'He's the American eagle, I guess,' the lad said to himself, as he looked from bird to paper with rapid glances; 'on'y he ain't so stiff-built as the one upon the dollars, neither. His head goes so. Aint it elegant? Oh my, not a bit, ruther. And his tail! That's how. The feathers runs the same as if it was shingles on the roof of a residence. I've got his tail just as true as Genesis, you bet. I can go the head and the tail, straight an' square, but what licks me is the wings. Seems as if you couldn't get his wing to show right, nohow, agin the body. Think it must be that way, pretty near; but I don't know. I wish thar was some feller here in Geauga could show me how the folks that draw the illustriations in the books ud draw that thar wing. It goes one too high for me, altogether.'

Even as Hiram thought that last thought he was dimly aware in a moment of an ominous shadow supervening behind him, and of a heavy hand lifted angrily to cuff him about the head for his pesky idleness. He knew it was his father, and with rapid instinct he managed to avoid the unseen blow. But, alas, alas, as he did so, he dropped the precious account book from his lap and let it fall upon the heap of boulders. Deacon Winthrop took the mysterious volume up, and peered at it long and cautiously. 'Wal,' he said slowly, turning over the pages one by one, as if they were clear evidence of original sin unregenerated—'wal, this do beat all, really. I've allus wondered what on airth you could be up to, sonny, when you was sent to weed, and didn't get a furrer or two done, mornings, while I was hoein' a dozen rows of corn or tomaters. Wal, this do beat all. Makin' figgers of chipmunks, and woodchucks, and musk-rats, and—my goodness, ef that thar aint a rattlesnake! Hiram Winthrop, it's my opinion that you was born to reprobation, that's jest about the size of it!'

If this opinion had not been vigorously backed by a box on the ears and a violent shaking, it isn't likely that Hiram in his own mind would have felt deeply concerned at it. Reprobation is such a very long way off (especially when you're twelve years old), whereas a box on the ears is usually experienced in the present tense with remarkable rapidity. But Hiram was so well used to cuffing (for the deacon was a God-fearing man, who held it prime part of his parental duty to correct his child with due severity) that he didn't cry much or make a fuss about it. To say the truth, too, he was watching so eagerly to see what his father would do with the beloved sketch-book that he had no time to indulge in unnecessary sentiment. For if only that sketch-book were taken from him, that poor, soiled, second-hand, half-covered sketch-book, Hiram felt in his dim inarticulate fashion that he would have solved the pessimistic problem forthwith in the negative, and that life for him would no longer be worth living.

The deacon turned the leaves over slowly for some minutes more, with many angry ejaculations, and then deliberately took them between his finger and thumb, and tore the book in two across the middle. Next, he doubled the pages over again, and tore them a second time across, and so on until the whole lot was reduced to a mass of little fluttering crumpled fragments. These he tossed contemptuously among the boulders, and with a parting cuff to Hiram proceeded on his way, to ruminate over the singular mystery of reprobation, even in the children of regenerate parents. 'You jest mind you go in right thar an' weed the rest of that peppermint, sonny,' he said as he strode away. 'An' be pretty quick about it, too, or else you'll be more scar't when you come home to-night than ever you was scar't in all your life afore, you take my word for it.'

As soon as the deacon was gone, poor Hiram sat down again on the heap of boulders and cried as though his little heart would fairly break. In spite of his father's vigorous admonition, he couldn't turn to at once and weed the peppermint. ''Taint the lickin' I mind,' he said to himself ruefully, as he gathered up the scattered fragments in his hand, ''tain't the lickin', it's the picturs. Them thar picturs was pretty near the on'y thing I liked best of anything livin'. Wal, it wouldn't hev mattered much ef he'd on'y tore up the ones I'd drawed: but when he tore up all my paper, so as I can't draw any more, that does make a feller feel reel bad. I never was so mad with him in my life afore. I reckon fathers is the onaccountablest and most mirac'lous creeturs in all creation. He might hev tore the picturs ef he liked, but what for. did he want to go tearin' up all my paper?'

As he sat there on the boulders, still, with that gross injustice rankling impotently in his boyish soul, he felt another shadow approaching once more, and looked up expecting to see his father returning. But it wasn't the gaunt long shadow of the deacon that came across the pile: it was a plump, round, thickset English shadow, and it was closely followed by the body of its owner, his father's hired help, late come from Dorsetshire. Sam Churchill leant down in his bluff, kindly way, when he saw the little chap crying, and asked him quickly if he was ill.

'Sick?' Hiram answered, through his sobs, unconsciously translating the word into his own dialect. 'Sick? No, I aint sick, Mr. Sam; but I'm orful mad with father. He kem right here just now and tore up my drawin' book, an' that drawin' book was most everything to me, it was, and he's tore it up, a ravin' an' tearin' like all possest, this very minnit.'

Sam looked at the fragments sympathetically. 'I tell'ee, Hiram,' he said gently, 'I've got a brother o' my own awver yonder in Darsetshire, about your age, too, as is turble vond of drawin'. I was turble vond of it myself when I was a little chap at 'Ootton. Thik ther eagle is drawed first-rate,'e be, an' so's the squir'l. I've drawed squir'ls myself, many's the time, in the copse at 'Ootton, I mind: an' I've gone mitching, too, in summer, birds'-nestin' and that, all over the vields for miles around us. Your faather's a main good man, Hiram;'e's a religious man, an' a 'onest man, and I do love to 'ear 'un argify most turble vine about religion, an''ell, an' reprobation, an''Enery Clay, and such like: but'e's a'ard man, tiler's no denyin' of it.'E's took'is religion 'ot an' 'ot, 'e 'as; an' I do think'e do use 'ee bad sometimes, vor a little chap, an' no mistake. Now, don't 'ee go an' cry no longer, ther's a good little vulla; don't 'ee cry, Hiram, vor I never could abare to zee a little chap or a woman a-cryin'. Zee 'ere, Hiram,' and the big hand dived deep into the recesses of a pair of very muddy corduroy trousers, ''ere's a sixpence for'ee, what do 'ee call it awver 'ere, ten cents, bain't it? 'Ere, take it, take it young un; don't 'ee be aveard. Now, what'll 'ee buy wi' it, eh? Lollipops, most like, I sim.'

'Lollipops!' the boy answered quickly, taking the dime with a grateful gesture. 'No, Mr. Sam, not them: nor toffy, nor peanuts neither. I shall go right away to Wes' Johnson's store, next time father's in the city, an' buy a new book, so as I can make a crowd more drawin's. That's what I like better'n anything. It's jest splendid.'

Sam looked at the little Yankee boy again with a certain faint moisture in his eyes; but he didn't reflect to himself that human nature is much the same all the world over, in Dorsetshire or in Geauga County. In fact, it would never have occurred to Sam's simple heart to doubt the truth of that fairly obvious principle. He only put his hand on Hiram's ragged head, and said softly: 'Well, Hiram, turn to now, an' I'll help 'ee weed the peppermint.'

They weeded a row or two in silence, and then Sam asked suddenly: 'What vor do un grow thik peppermint, Hiram?'

'To make candy, Mr. Sam,' Hiram answered.

'Good job too,' Sam went on musingly. 'Seems to me they do want it turble bad in these 'ere parts. Sight too much corn, an' not near enough candy down to 'Murrica; why can't deacon let the little vulla draw a squir'l if 'e's got a mind to? That's what I wants to know. What do those varmers all around 'ere do? (Varmers they do call 'em; no better nor labourers, I take it.) Why, they buy a bit 'o land, an' work, an' slave thesselves an' their missuses, all their lives long, what vor? To raise pork and corn on. What vor, again? To buy more land; to raise more corn an' bacon; to buy more land again; to raise more corn an' bacon; and so on, world without end, amen, for ever an' ever. An' in the tottal, what do ur all come to? Pork and flour, for ever an' ever. Why, even awver yonder in old England, we'd got something better nor that, an' better worth livin' vor.' And Sam's mind wandered back gently to Wootton Mandeville, and the old tower which he didn't know to be of Norman architecture, but which he loved just as well as if he did for all that: and then he borrowed Hiram's pencil, and pulled a piece of folded paper from his pocket (it had inclosed an ounce of best Virginia), and drew upon it for Hiram's wondering eyes a rough sketch of an English village church, with big round arches and dog-tooth ornament, embowered in shady elm-trees, and backed up by a rolling chalk down in the further distance. Hiram looked at the sketch admiringly and eagerly.

'I wish I could draw such a thing as that, he said with delight. 'But I can't, Mr. Sam; I can only draw birds and musk-rats and things, not churches. That's a reel pretty church, too: reckon I never see such a one as that thar anywhere. Might that be whar you was raised, now?'

Sam nodded assent.

'Wal, that does beat everything. I should like to go an' see something like that, sometime. Ef I git a book, will you learn me to draw a church same as you do, Mr. Sam?'

'Bless yer 'eart, yes,' Sam answered quickly, and turned with swimming eyes to weed the rest of the peppermint. From that day forth, Sam Churchill and Hiram Winthrop were sworn friends through all their troubles.

CHAPTER II

RURAL ENGLAND

It was a beautiful July morning, and Colin Churchill and Minna Wroe were playing together in the fritillary fields at Wootton Mandeville. At twelve years old, the intercourse of lad and maiden is still ingenuous; and Colin was just twelve, though little Minna might still have been some two years his junior. A tall, slim, fair-haired boy was Colin Churchill, with deep-blue eyes more poetical in their depth and intensity than one might have expected from a little Dorsetshire peasant child. Minna, on the other hand, was shorter and darker; a gipsy-looking girl, black-haired and tawny-skinned; and with two little beady-black eyes that glistened and ran over every moment with contagious merriment. Two prettier children you wouldn't have found anywhere that day in the whole county of Dorset than Minna Wroe and Colin Churchill.

They had gathered flowers till they were tired of them in the broad spongy meadow; they had played hide-and-seek among the eighteenth-century tombstones in the big old churchyard; they had quarrelled and made it up again half a dozen times over in pure pettishness: and now, by way of a distraction, Minna said at last coaxingly: 'Do 'ee, Colin, do 'ee come down to the lake yonder and make I a bit of a vigger-'ead.'

'Don't 'ee worrit me, Minna,' Colin answered, like a young lady who refuses to sing, half-heartedly (meaning all the time that one should ask her again): 'Don't 'ee see I be tired? I don't want vor to go makin' no vigger-'eads vor 'ee, I tell 'ee.'

But Minna would have one: on that she insisted: 'What a vinnid lad 'ee be,' she cried petulantly, 'not to want to make I a vigger-'ead. Now do 'ee, Cohn, ther's a a good boy; do 'ee, an' I'll gee 'ee 'arf my peppermint cushions, come Saturday.'

'I don't want none o' your cushions, Minna,' Colin answered, with a boy's gallantry; 'but come along down to the lake if 'ee will: I'll make 'ee dree or vower vigger-'eads, never vear, an' them vine uns too, if so be as you want 'em.'

They went together down to the brook at the corner of the meadow (called a lake in the Dorsetshire dialect); and there, at a spot where the plastic clay came to the surface in a little cliff at a bend of the stream, Colin carved out a fine large lump of shapeless raw material from the bank, which he forthwith proceeded to knead up with his hands and a sprinkling of water from the rill into a beautiful sticky consistency. Minna watched the familiar operation with deepest interest, and added from time to time a word or two of connoisseur criticism: 'Now thee'st got it too wet, Colin;' or, 'Take care thee don't putt in too much of thik there blue earth yonder; or, 'That's about right vor the viggeread now, I'm thinkin'; thee'd better begin makin' it now avore the clay gets too dried up.'

As soon as Colin had worked the clay up to what he regarded as the proper requirements of his art, he began modelling it dexterously with his fingers into the outer form and fashion of a ship's figure-head: 'What'll 'ee 'ave virst, Minna?' he asked as he roughly moulded the mass into a bold outward curve, that would have answered equally well for any figure-head in the whole British merchant navy.

'I'll 'ave the Mariar-Ann,' Minna answered with a nod of her small black head in the direction of the mouth in the valley, where the six petty fishing vessels of Wootton Mandeville stood drawn up together in a long straight row on the ridge of shingle. The Mariar-Ann was the collier that came monthly from Cardiff, and its figure-head represented a gilded lady, gazing over the waves with a vacant smile, and draped in a flowing crimson costume of no very particular historical period.

Cohn worked away at the clay vigorously for a few minutes with fingers and knife by turns, and at the end of that time he had produced a very creditable figure-head indeed, accurately representing in its main features the gilded lady of the Mariar-Ann.

'Oh, how lovely!' Minna cried, delighted. 'Thik's the best thee'st made, Colin. Let's bake un and keep un always.'

'Take un 'ome an' bake un yourself, Minna,' the boy answered. 'We ain't got no vire 'ere. What'll I make 'ee now? 'Nother vigger-'ead?'

'No!' Minna cried, with a happy inspiration.

'Make myself, Colin.'

The boy eyed her carefully from head to foot. 'I don't s'pose I can do 'ee, Minna,' he answered after a pause. 'Howsonedever, I'll try;' and he took a fresh lump of the kneaded clay, and began working it up loosely into a rough outline of the girl's figure. It was his first attempt at modelling from life, and he went at it with careful deliberation. Minna posed before him in her natural attitude, and Colin called her back every minute or two when she got impatient, and kept his little sitter steadily posed till the portrait statuette was fairly finished. Critical justice compels the admission that Colin Churchill's first figure from life was not an entirely successful work of sculpture. Its expression was distinctly feeble; its pose was weak and uncertain; its drapery was marked by a frank disregard of folds and a bold conventionalism; and, last of all, it ended abruptly at the short dress, owing to certain mechanical difficulties in the way of supporting the heavy body on a pair of slender moist clay legs. Still, it distinctly suggested the notion of a human being; it remotely resembled a little girl; and it even faintly adumbrated, in figure at least, if not in feature, Minna Wroe herself.

But if the work of art failed a little when judged by the stern tribunal of adult criticism, it certainly more than satisfied both the young artist and the subject of his plastic skill. They gazed at the completed figure with the deepest admiration, and Minna even ventured to express a decided opinion that anybody in the world would know it was meant for her. Which high standard of artistic portraiture has been known to satisfy much older and more exalted critics, including many ladies and gentlemen of distinction who have wasted the time of good sculptors by 'having their busts taken.'

Meanwhile, down in the village by the shore, Geargey Wroe, Minna's father, was standing by a little garden gate, where Sam Churchill the elder was carefully tending his cabbages and melons. 'Zeen our Minna, Sam!' he asked over the paling. 'Wher's 'er to, dost know? Off zumwhere with yer Colin, I'll be bound, Sammy. They're always off zumwhere together, them two is, I vancy. 'E's up to 'is drawin' or zummat down to lake there. Such a lad vor drawin' an' that I never did zee. 'Ow's bisness, Sammy?'

'Purty good, Geargey, purty good. Volks be a-comin' in now an' takin' lodgin's, wantin' garden stuff and such like. First-rate family from London come yesterday down to Walker's. Turble rich volk I should say by the look o' un. Ordered a power o' fruit and zum vegetables.'Ow's vishin', Geargey?'
'Bad,' Geargey answered, shaking his head ominously: 'as bad as ur could be. Town's turble empty still: nobody come 'ceptin' a lot o' good-vor-nothin' meetingers. 'Ootton ain't wot it 'ad used to be, Sammy, zince these 'ere rail-rawds. Wot we wants is the rail-rawd to come 'ere to town, so volks can get 'ere aisy, like they can to Sayton. Then we'd get zum real gintlevolk who got money in their pockets to spend, an'll spend it vree and aisy to the tradesmen, and the boatmen, and the vishermen; that's wot we wants, don't us, Sammy?'

'Us do, us do,' Sam Churchill assented, nodding.

'Ah, I do mind the time, Sammy,' Geargey said regretfully, wiping his eyes with the corner of his jersey, 'w'en every wipswile I'd used to get a gintleman to go out way, who'd gi' us share an' share alike o' his grub, and a drap out o' his whisky bottle: and w'en we pulls ashore, he sez, sez'e: "I don't want the vish, my man," sez'e; "I only wants the sport, raly." But nowadays, Lard bless 'ee, Sam, we gets a pack o' meetingers down from London, and they brings along a hunk o' bread and some fat pork, or a piece o' blue vinny cheese, as 'ard as Portland stone. Now I can't abare fat pork without a streak o' lean in it, 'specially when I smells the bait; and I can't tackle the blue vinny, 'cos I never 'as my teeth with me: thof my mate, Bill-o'-my-Soul, 'e can putt 'isself outside most things in the way o' grub at a vurry short notice, as you do well know, Sam, and I never seed as bate made no difference to 'e nohow. But these 'ere meetingers, as I was a sayin' (vor I've got avore my story, Sammy), they goes out an' haves vine sport, we'll say; and then, w'en we comes 'ome they out and lugs out dree or vower shillin's or so, vor me an' my mate, an' walks off with 'arf-a-suvren's worth o' the biggest vish, quite aisy-like, an' layves all the liddle fry an' the blin in the boat; the chattering jackanapes.'

''Ees,'ees, lad, times is changed,' Sam murmured meditatively, half to himself; 'times is changed turble bad since old Squire's day. Wot a place 'Ootton 'ad used to be then, 'adn't ur, Geargey? Coach from Darchester an' 'bus from Tilbury station, bringin' in gurt folks from London vor the sayson every day; dinner party up to vicarage with green paysen an' peaches, an' nectarines, "An' a 'ole turbat,' Geargey put in parenthetically. 'Ay, lad, an' a 'ole turbot every Saturday. Them was times, Geargey; them was times. I don't s'pose they ther times ull never come again. Ther ain't the gentry now as ther'd used to be in old Squire's day. Pack o' trumpery London volk, with one servant, comin' down 'ere vor the sayson, short sayson, six week, or murt be seven, an' then walkin' off agin, without so much as spending ten poun' or so in the'ole parish. I mind the times, Geargey, when volks used to say 'Ootton were the safety valve o' the Bath sayson. Soon as sayson were over up to Bath, gentlevolk and ladies a-comin' down 'ere to enj'y thesselves, an' spendin' their money vree and aisy, same as if it were water. Us don't see un comin' now, Geargey: times is changed turble: us don't see un now.'

'It's the dree terms as 'as ruined 'Ootton,' Geargey said, philosophically, the research of the cause being the true note of philosophy.

'It's they dree terms as 'as done it, vor sartin.'

'Why, 'ow's that, Gearge?'

'Well, don't 'ee see, Sam, it's like o' thik. W'en they used to 'ave 'arf-years at the schools, bless 'ee, volks with families 'ad used to bring down the children vrom school so soon as the 'arf-year were over. Then the gurt people ud take the young gentlemen out vishin', might be in June, or July may-be, and gee a bit o' work to honest visher-people in the off-sayson. Then in August, London people ud come an' take lodgin's and gee us a bit more work nice and tidy. So the sayson 'ad used to last off an' on vrom June to October. Well, bime-by, they meddlesome school people, they goes an' makes up these 'ere new-vangled things o' dree terms, as they calls 'em, cuttin' up the year unnat'ral-like into dree pieces, as 'adn't used to be w'en we was children. Wot's the consequence? Everybody comes a-rushin' and a-crushin' permixuous, in August, the 'ole boilin' o' 'em together, wantin' rooms an' boats and vishermen, so as the parish baint up to it. Us 'as to work 'ard vor six or seven week, and not give satisfaction nayther; and then rest o' the year us 'as to git along the best us can on the shart sayson. I can't abare they new-vangled ways, upsettin' all the constitooted order of things altogither, an' settin' poor vishermen at sixes and sevens for arf their lifetime.'

'It's the march of intellect, Geargey,' Sam Churchill answered, deprecatingly (Sam understood himself to be a Liberal in politics, and used this convenient phrase as a general solvent for an immense number of social difficulties). 'It's the march of intellect, no doubt, Geargey: there's a sight o' progress about; board-schools an' sich like: an' if it cuts agin us, don't 'ee see, w'y us 'as got to make the best of it, however.'

'It murt be, an' agin it murtn't; and agin it murt,' Geargey murmured dubiously.

'But any way, wher's Minna to, Sammy?—that's wot I comed vor to ax 'ee.'

'Down to vield by lake, yander, most like,' Sam answered with a nod of his head in the direction indicated.

'I'll go an' vetch her,' said Geargey; 'dinner's most ready.'

'An I'll come an' zee wot Colin's up to,' added Sam, laying down his hoe, and pulling together his unbuttoned waistcoat.

They walked down to the brook in the meadow, and saw the two children sitting in the corner so intent upon their artistic performances that they hardly noticed the approach of their respective fathers. Old Sam Churchill went close up and looked keenly at the clay figure of Minna that Colin was still moulding with the last finishing touches as the two elders approached them. 'Thik ther vigger baint a bad un, Colin,' he said, taking it carefully in his rough hand.

"ee'aven't done it none so ill, lad; but it don't look so livin' like as it 'ad ought to. Wot do 'ee think it is, Geargey, eh? tell us?'

'Why, I'm blowed if that baint our Minna,' Geargey answered, with a little gasp of open-mouthed astonishment. 'It's her vurry pictur, Colin: a blind man could see that, of course, so soon as 'e set eyes on it. 'Ow do 'ee do it, Colin, eh? 'Ow do 'ee do it?' 'Oh, that baint nothin',' Colin said, colouring up. 'Only a little bit o' clay, just made up vor to look like Minna.'

'Look 'ee 'ere,' Colin,' his father went on, glancing quickly from the clay to little Minna, and altering a touch or two with his big clumsy fingers, not undeftly. 'Look 'ee 'ere; 'ee must putt the dress thik way, I should say, with a gurt dale more flusterin' about it; it do zit too stiff and starchy, somehow, same as if it wur made o' new buckram. 'ee must put in a fold or two, 'ere, so as to make un sit more nat'ral. Don't 'ee see Minna's dress do double itself up, I can't rightly say 'ow, but sununat o' tkik there way?' And he moulded the moist clay a bit with his hands, till the folds of the drapery began to look a little more real and possible.

'I'd ought to 'ave drawed it first, I think,' Colin said, looking at the altered dress with a satisfied glance. "ave 'ee got such a thing as a pencil about 'ee, father?'

Old Sam took a piece of pencil from his pocket, and handed it to Colin. The boy held it tightly in his fingers, with a true artistic grasp, like one who knows how to wield it, and with a few strokes on a scrap of paper hit off little Minna far better than he had done in the plastic material. Geargey looked over his shoulder with a delighted grin on his weatherbeaten features. 'I tell 'ee, Sam,' he said to the old gardener, confidentially, 'it's my belief that thik ther boy'ull be able one o' these vine days to paint rale picturs.'

CHAPTER III

PERNICIOUS LITERATURE

When winter came, Hiram Winthrop had less to do and more time to follow the bidding of his own fancy. True, there was cordwood to split in abundance; and splitting cordwood is no child's play along the frozen shores of Lake Ontario. You go out among the snow in the wood-shed, and take the big ice-covered logs down from the huge pile with numbed fingers: then you lay them on a sort of double St. Andrew's cross, its two halves supported by a thwart-piece, and saw them up into fit lengths for the kitchen fireplace: and after that you split them in four with a solid-headed axe, taking care in the process not to let your deadened hands slip, so as to cut off the ends of your own toes with an ill-directed blow glancing off the log sideways. Yes, splitting cordwood is very serious work, with the thermometer at 40° below freezing; and drawing water from the well when the rope is frozen and your skin clings to the chill iron of the thirsty bucket-handle is hardly better: yet in spite of both these small drawbacks, Hiram Winthrop found much more to enjoy in his winters than in his summers. There was no corn to hoe, no peas to pick, no weeding to do, no daily toil on farm and garden. The snow had covered all with its great white sheet; and even the neighbourhood of Muddy Creek Dépôt looked desolately beautiful in its own dreary, cold, monotonous, Siberian fashion.

The flowers and leaves were gone too, to be sure; but in the low brushwood by the blackberry bottom the hares had turned white to match the snow; and the nut-hatches were answering one another in their varying keys; and the skunks were still busy of nights beneath the spreading walnuts; and the chickadees were tinkling overhead among the snow-laden pine-needles of the far woodland. All the summer visitors had gone south to Georgia and the gulf: but the snow-buntings were ever with Hiram in the wintry fields: and the bald-headed eagles still prowled around at times on the stray chance of catching a frozen-out racoon. Above all there was ease and leisure, respite from the deacon's rasping voice calling perpetually for Hiram here, and Hiram there, and Hiram yonder, to catch the horses, or tend the harrow, or mind the birds, or weed the tomatoes, or set shingles against the sun over the drooping transplanted cabbages. A happy time indeed for Hiram, that long, weary, white-sheeted, unbroken northern New York winter.

Sam Churchill was with the deacon still, but had little enough to do, for there isn't much going on upon an American farm from November to April, and the deacon would gladly have got rid of his hired help in the slack time if he could have shuffled him off; but Sam had been well advised on his first hiring, and had wisely covenanted to be kept on all the year round, with board and lodging and decent wages during the winter season. And Hiram initiated Sam into the mysteries of sliding on a bent piece of wood (a homemade toboggan) down the great snowdrifts, and skating on the frozen expansion of Muddy Creek, and building round huts, Esquimaux fashion, with big square blocks of solid dry snow, and tracking the white hare over the white fields by means of the marks he left behind him, whose termination, apparently lengthening itself out miraculously before one's very eyes, marked the spot where the hare himself was hopping invisible to human vision. In return, Sam lent him a few dearly-treasured books: books that he had brought from England with him: the books that had first set the Dorsetshire peasant lad upon his scheme of going forth alone upon the wide world beyond the ocean.

Hiram was equally delighted and astonished with these wonderful charmed volumes. He had seen a few books before, but they were all of two types: Cornell's Geography, Quackenboss's Grammar, and the other schoolbooks used at the common school; or else Barnes's Commentary, Elder Coffin's Ezekiel, the Hopkinsite Confession of Faith, and other like works of American exegetical and controversial theology. But Sam's books, oh, gracious, what a difference! There was Peter Simple, a story about a real live boy, who wa'n't good, pertickler, not to speak of, but had some real good old times on board a ship, somewhere, he did; and there was Tom Jones (Hiram no more understood the doubtful passages in that great romance than he understood the lucubrations of Philosopher Square, but he took it in, in the lump, as very good fun for all that), Tom Jones, the story of another real live boy, with, most delightful of all, a reg'lar mean sneak of a feller, called Blifil, to act as a foil to Tom's straightforward pagan flesh-and-bloodfulness; the Buccaneers of the Caribbean Sea, a glorious work of fire and slaughter, whar some feller or other got killed right off on every page a'most, you bet; Jake the Pirate, another splendid book of the same description; and half a dozen more assorted novels, from the best to the worst, all chosen alike for their stirring incidents which went straight home to the minds of the two lads, in spite of all external differences of birth and geographical surroundings. Hiram pored over them surreptitiously, late at nights, in the room that he and Sam occupied in common, a mere loft at the top of the house and felt in his heart he had never in his life imagined such delightful reading could possibly have existed. And they were written by growed-up men, too! How strange to think that once upon a time, somewhile and somewhere, there were growed-up men capable of thus sympathising with, and reproducing the ideas and feelings of, the natural mind of boyhood!

One evening, very late, eleven nearly, the deacon, prowling around after a bottle or something, spied an unwonted light gleaming down from the trap-door that led up to the loft where the lads ought at that moment to have been sleeping soundly. Lights in a well-conducted farmhouse at eleven o'clock was indeed incomprehensible: what on earth, the deacon asked himself wonderingly, could them thar lads be up to at this hour? He crept up the step-ladder cautiously, so as not to disturb them by premonitions, and opened the trap-door in sedulous silence. Sam was already fast asleep; but there was Hiram, sot up in bed, as quiet as a 'possum, 'pearin' as if he was a-readin' something. The deacon's eyes opened with amazement! Hiram reading! Had his heart been touched, then, quite sudden-like? Could he have took up the Hopkinsite Confession in secret to his upper chamber? Was he meditatin' makin' a public profession afore the Assembly?

The deacon glowered and marvelled. Creeping, still quite silently, up to the bedhead, he looked with an inquiring glance over poor Hiram's unsuspecting shoulder. A sea of words swam vaguely before his bewildered vision; words, not running into long orthodox paragraphs, like the Elder's Ezekiel, but cut up, oh horror, into distinct sentences, each indicating a separate part in a conversation. The deacon couldn't clearly make it all out; for it was a dramatic dialogue, a form of composition which had not largely fallen in the good man's way: but he picked up enough to understand that it was a low pothouse scene, where one Falstaff was bandying improper language with a person of the name of Prince (given name, Henry)—language that made even the deacon's sallow cheek blush feebly with reflected and vicarious modesty. For a moment he endeavoured, like a Christian man, to retain his wrath; and then paternal feeling overcame him, and he caught Hiram such a oner on his ears as he flattered himself that boy wouldn't be likely to forgit in any very partickler hurry.

Hiram looked round, amazed and stunned, his ear tingling and burning, and saw the gaunt apparition of his father, standing silent and black-browed by the bare bed-head. For a moment those two glared at one another mutely and defiantly.

At last Hiram spoke: 'Wal!' he said simply.

'Wal!' the deacon answered, with smothered wrath. 'Hiram, I am angry and sin not. What do you go an' take them bad books up to read for? Who give 'em you? Whar did you get 'em? Oh, you sinful, bad boy, whar did you get 'em?' And he administered another sound cuff upon Hiram's other ear.

Hiram put his hand up to the stinging spot, and cried a minute silently: then he answered as well as he was able: 'This aint a bad book: this is called "The Complete Dramattic Works of William Shakespeare." Sam lent it to me, an' it's Sam's book, an' ther ain't no harm in it, anyhow.'

The deacon was plainly staggered for a moment, for even he had dimly heard the name of William Shakespeare; and though he had never made any personal acquaintance with that gentleman's works, he had always understood in a vague, indefinite fashion that this here Shakespeare was a perfectly respectable and recognised writer, whose books were read and approved of even by Hopkinsite ministers edoocated at Bethabara Seminary. So he took the volume in his hand incredulously and looked it through casually for a few minutes. He glanced at a scene or two here or there with a critical eye, and then he flung the volume from him quickly, as a man might fling and crush some loathsome reptile. By this time Sam was half-awake, and sat up in bed to inquire sleepily, what all thik ther row could be about at thik time of evenin'?' The deacon answered by going savagely to Sam's box, and taking out, one by one, for separate inspection, the volumes he found there. He held up the candle (stuck in an empty blacking-bottle) to each volume in succession, and, as soon as he had finally condemned them each, he flung them down in an untidy pile on the bare floor of the little bedroom. Most of them he stood stoically enough; but the Vicar of Wakefield was at last quite too much for his stifled indignation. Sitting down blankly on the bed he fired off his volley at poor Hiram's frightened head, with terrible significance.

'Hiram Winthrop,' he said solemnly, 'you air a son of perdition. You air more a'most 'n I kin manage with. Satan's openin' the door for you on-common wide, I kin tell you, sonny. It makes me downright scar't to see you in company along of sech books. Your mother'll be awful took back about it. I don't mind this 'ere about the Pirates of the Caribbean Sea, so much; that's kinder hist'ry, that is, and mayn't do you much harm: but sech things as this Peter Simple, an' Wakefield, and Pickwick's Papers—why, I wonder the roof don't fall in on 'em an' crush us in the lot altogether. I'm durned ef I could have thought you'd bin wicked enough to read 'em, sech on-principled literatoor. I sha'n't chastise you to-night, sonny; it's late, now, and we've read chapter: but to-morrer, Hiram, to-morrer, you shall pay for them thar books, take my word for it. You shall be chastened in the manner that's app'inted. Ef I was you, I should spend the rest of the evenin' in wrestlin' for forgiveness for the sin you've committed.'

And yet in the chapter the deacon had read at family worship that evening there was one little clause which said: 'Quench not the Spirit.'

Hiram slept but little that night, with the vague terror of to-morrow's whipping overshadowing him through the night watches. But he had at least one comfort: Sam Churchill had got out and gathered up his books, and locked them carefully in his box again.

'If the boss tries to touch they books again, I tell 'ee, Hiram,' he said bi-lingually (for absorbent America was already beginning to assimilate him), "'e'll vind 'isself a-lyin' longways on the vloor, afore he do know it, I promise 'ee.' Hiram heard, and was partly comforted. At least he would still have the books to read, somehow, at some time. For in his own heart, unregenerate or otherwise, he couldn't bring himself to believe that there could be really anything so very wicked in Henry the Fourth or Peter Simple.

CHAPTER IV

PROFESSIONAL SOCIETY

The deacon's cowhide cut deep; but the thrashing didn't last long: and after it was all over, Hiram wandered out aimlessly by himself, down the snowclad valley of Muddy Creek, and along to the wooded wilds and cranberry marshes near the Ontario debouchure, to forget his troubles and the lasting smart of the weals in watching the beasts and birds among the frozen lowlands. He had never been so far from home before, but the weather and the ice were in his favour, enabling him to get over an amount of ground he wouldn't have tried to cover in the dry summer time. He had his skates with him, and he skated where possible, taking them off to walk over the intervening land necks or drifted snow-sheets. The ice was glare in many places, so that one could skate on it gloriously; and before he had got half-way down to Nine-Mile Bottom he had almost forgotten all about the deacon, and the sermon, and the beating, and the threatened ten chapters of St. John (the Gospel of Love the deacon called it) to be learned by heart before next Lord's day, in expiation of the heinous crime of having read that pernicious work the 'Vicar of Wakefield.' It was the loveliest spot he had ever seen in all his poor unlovely little existence.

Close under the cranberry trees, by a big pool where the catfish would be sure to live in summer, Hiram heard men's voices, whispering low and quiet to one another. A great joy filled his soul. He could see at once by their dress and big fur caps what they were. They were trappers! One piece of romance still survived in Geauga County, among the cranberry swamps and rush beds where the flooded creek flowed sluggishly into the bosom of Ontario; and on that one piece of romance he had luckily lighted by pure accident. Trappers! Yes, not a doubt of it! He struck out on his skates swiftly but noiselessly toward them, and joined the three men without a word as they stood taking counsel together below their breath on the ice-bound marshland.

'Hello, sonny!' one of the men said in a low undertone. 'Say whar did you drop from? What air you comin' spyin' out a few peaceable surveyors for, eh? Tell me.'

'I didn't think you was surveyors,' Hiram answered, a little disappointed. 'I thought you was trappers.' And at the same time he glanced suspiciously at the peculiar little gins that the surveyors held in their great gauntleted hands, for all the world like Oneida traps for musk-rats.

The man noticed the glance and laughed to himself a smothered laugh, the laugh of a person accustomed always to keep very quiet. 'The young un has spotted us, an' no mistake, boys,' he said, laughing, to the others. 'He's a bit too 'cute to be took in with the surveyor gammon. What do you call this 'ere, sonny?'

'I calc'late that's somewhar near a mink trap,' Hiram answered, breathless with delight.

'Wal, it is a mink trap,' the trapper said slowly, looking deep into the boy's truthful eyes. 'Now, who sent you down here to track us out and peach upon us; eh, Bob?'

'Nobody sent me,' Hiram replied, with his blue eyes looking deep back into the trapper's keen restless grey pair. 'I kem out all o' my own accord, 'cos father gave me a lickin' this mornin', an' I've kem out jest to get away for a bit alone somewhar.'

'Who's your father?' asked the man still suspiciously.

'Deacon Winthrop, down to Muddy Creek Deepo.'

'Deacon Winthrop! Oh, I know him, ruther. A tall, skinny, dried-up kind of fellow, ain't he, who looks as if most of his milk was turned sour, an' the Hopkinsite Confession was a settin' orful heavy on his digestion?'

Hiram nodded several times successively, in acknowledgment of the general accuracy of this brief description. 'That's him, you bet,' he answered with unfilial promptitude. 'I guess you've seed him somwhar, for that's him as like as a portrait. Look here, say, I'll draw him for you.' And the boy, taking his pencil from his pocket, drew as quickly as he was able on a scrap of birch-bark a humorous caricature of his respected parent, as he appeared in the very act of offering an unctuous exhortation to the Hopkinsite assembly at Muddy Creek meeting-house. It was very wrong and wicked, of course, a clear breach of the Fifth Commandment, but the deacon hadn't done much on his own account to merit honour or love at the hands of Hiram Winthrop.

The man took the rough sketch and laughed at it inwardly, with a suppressed chuckle. There was no denying, he saw, that it was the perfect moral of that thar freezed-up old customer down to the Deepo. He handed it with a smile to his two companions. They both recognised the likeness and the little additions which gave it point, and one of them, a Canadian as Hiram conjectured (for he spoke with a dreadful English accent, so stuck-up), said in the same soft undertone: 'Do you know where any mink live anywhere hereabouts?'

'A little higher up stream,' Hiram answered, overjoyed, 'I know every spot whar ther's any mink stirrin' for five miles round, anyhow.'

The Canadian turned to the others.

'Boys,' he said, 'you can trust the youngster. He won't peach on us. He's game, you may be sure. Now, youngster, we're trappers, as you guessed correctly. But you see, farmers don't love trappers, because they go trespassing, and overrunning the fields: and so we don't want you to say a word about us to this father of yours. Do you understand?'

Hiram nodded.

'You promise not to tell him or anybody?'

'Yes, I promise.'

'Well, then, if you like, you can come with us. We're going to set our traps now. You don't seem a bad sort of little chap, and you can see the fun out if you've a mind to.'

Hiram's heart bounded with excitement. What a magnificent prospect! He promised to show the trappers every spot he knew about the place where any fur-bearing animal, from ermine to musk-rat, was likely to be found. In ten minutes, all four were started off upon their skates once more, striking up the river in the direction of the deacon's, and setting traps by Hiram's advice as they went along, at every likely run or corner.

'You drew that picture real well,' the Canadian said, as they skated side by side: 'I could see it was the old man at a glance.'

Hiram's face shone with pleasure at this sincere compliment to his artistic merit. 'I could hev done it a long sight better,' he said simply, 'ef my hands hadn't been numbed a bit with the cold, so's I could hardly hold the pencil.'

It was a grand day, that day with the trappers, the gipsies of half-settled America; the grandest day Hiram had ever spent in his whole lifetime. How many musk-rats' burrows he pointed out to his new acquaintance along the bank of the creek; how many spots where the mink, that strange water-haunting weasel, lurks unseen among the frozen sedges! Here and there, too, he showed them the points where he had noticed the faint track of the ermine on the lightly fallen snow, and where they might place their traps across the path worn by the 'coons on their way to and from the Indian corn patch. It was cruel work, to be sure, setting those murderous snapping iron jaws, and perhaps if Hiram had thought more about the beasts themselves (whom after all he loved in his heart) he wouldn't have been so ready to aid their natural enemies in thus catching and exterminating them:

but what boy is free from the aboriginal love of hunting something? Certainly not Hiram Winthrop, at least, to whom this one glimpse of a delightful wandering life among the woods and marshes, a life that wasn't all made up of bare fields and fall wheat and snake fences and cross-ploughing, seemed like a stray snatch of that impossible paradise he had read about in 'Peter Simple' and the 'Buccaneers of the Caribbean Sea.'

'Say, Bob,' the Canadian muttered to him as they were half-way through their work (in Northern New York every boy unknown is ex officio addressed as Bob), 'we shall be back in these diggings in the spring again, looking after the summer furs, you see. Now, don't you go and tell any other trappers about these places we've set, because trappers gener'ly (present company always excepted) is a pretty dishonest lot, and they'll poach on other trappers' grounds and even steal their furs and traps as soon as look at 'em. You stand by us and we'll stand by you, and take care you don't suffer by it.'

'When'll you come?' Hiram asked in the thrilling delight of anticipation.

'When the first spring days are on,' the Canadian answered. 'I'll tell you the best sign: it's no use going by days o' the month, we don't remember 'em mostly;—but it'll be about the time when the skunk cabbage begins to flower.'

Hiram made a note of the date mentally, and treasured it up in safety on the lasting tablets of his memory.

At about one o'clock the trappers sat down upon the frozen bank and ate their dinner. It would have been cold work to men less actively engaged; but skating and trapping warms your blood well. 'Got any grub?' one of the men asked Hiram, still softly. Your trapper seems almost to have lost the power of speaking above a whisper, and he moves stealthily as if he thought a spectral farmer was always dogging his steps close behind him.

'No, I ain't,' Hiram answered.

'Then, thunder, pitch into the basket,' his new friend said encouragingly.

Hiram obeyed, and made an excellent lunch off cold hare and lake ship-biscuit.

'Are you through?' the men asked at last.

'Yes,' Hiram replied.

'Then come along and see the fun out.'

They skated on, still upward, in the general direction of the blackberry bottom. When they got there, Hiram, now quite at home, pointed out even more accurately than ever the exact homes of each individual mink and ermine. So the men worked away eagerly at their task till the evening began to come over. Then Hiram, all aglow with excitement and wholly oblivious of all earthly considerations, became suddenly aware of a gaunt figure moving about among the dusky brushwood and making in the direction of his friends the trappers. 'Hello,' he cried to his new acquaintances in a frightened tone, 'you'd best cut it. Thar's the deacon.'

The Canadian laughed a short little laugh. 'All right, Bob,' he said coolly; 'we ain't afraid of him. If he touches you to hurt you, I surmise he'll find himself measuring his own height horizontally rather quicker than he expected.' The deacon overheard the alarming prediction, and, being a wise man in his generation, prudently abstained from making any hostile demonstration to Hiram in the presence of his self-constituted protectors. 'Good evenin', gents all,' he said, advancing blandly.

'I'd lost my son, d'ye see, an' I'd kem out right here to look after him. Hiram, you come along home, sonny; your mother's most out of her mind about you, I kin tell you.'

'Good evening, Colonel,' the Canadian answered in a determined fashion. 'We're sorry business has compelled us to trespass on your property; but the fur trade, Colonel, the fur trade is a pretty exacting profession. The Lord Chief Justice of England insists upon his ermine, you see, Colonel, and the demand compels the supply. We're all instruments, sir, instruments merely. Your boy's a pretty smart lad, and if he concentrates his mind upon the subject, I surmise that he'll grow up to be a pretty accomplished trapper.' (The deacon's disgust spoke out volubly at this suggestion even upon his lantern-jawed impassive countenance.) 'Well, sir, he's been very useful to us, and we particularly request that you won't lick him for it. We don't wish him to be hurt. We're law-abiding citizens, Colonel, but we won't let that boy be hurt. You understand, sir—precisely so. Bob, we'll clear them traps on Saturday morning. You come then and report proceedings.'

'All right,' Hiram answered defiantly; 'I'll be along.'

'Good evenin', Colonel,' the three men said.

'Good evenin', gents all,' the deacon answered, boiling over with wrath, but smothering his rage till they were well off the premises.

Hiram turned and walked home in perfect silence by the side of his father. They had got inside the house before the deacon ventured to utter a single word, then he closed the door firmly, cuffed Hiram half a dozen times over about the head, and cried angrily, 'I was afeard, sonny, you'd got drownded in the creek, reely: I was afeard you was cut off in your sin this time; I was afeard of a judgment, I was: for I've reproved you often, sonny; you can't blame it agin me that I hain't reproved you often: and he that bein' often reproved hardeneth his neck shall suddenly be destroyed.'

'Wal,' Hiram cried through his tears (he was a stubborn un, some), 'it's you that hardens it, ain't it? What do you go allus hittin' it for?'

''Tain't that neck, you scoffin' sinner,' the deacon answered savagely, dealing him another cuff or two about the head. ''Tain't that neck, you know as well as I do: it's the sperritooal neck the prophet is alloodin' to. But you shall have some cow-hide, again, Hiram; don't you be afeard about it: you shan't go to reprobation unhindered ef I kin help it. 'The rod an' reproof give wisdom: but a child left to himself bringeth his mother to shame. Mis' Winthrop, I'm afeard this son o' yours'ull bring you to shame yet, marm, with his sinful onregenerate practices. What's he bin doin'?

Now, you jest guess: why, bringin' a whole crowd of disrepootable trappers a-settin' mink-traps an' ermine-springes on his own father's blackberry lot. He ain't satisfied with the improvin' company he kin get to home, he ain't, but he must go consortin' and associatin' with a lot of no-account, skulkin', profane trappers, a mean crowd, a mob, a set of low fellers I wouldn't hold no intercourse with, anyhow. Hiram Winthrop, it's my belief you hev got no sense of the dignity of your persition.'

'I beg pardon, Colonel,' the Canadian interposed, lifting the latch of the front door lightly (it opened into the living room), 'but I wish gently to protest against them opprobrious epithets being out of thoughtlessness applied to the exacting perfession of the fur trade. The fur trade, sir, is a most noble perfession. The honourable Hudson Bay Company, for whose deepo at Kingston I trade, is a recognised public body, holding a charter from Queen Victoria, and reckoning among its officials several prominent gentlemen of the strictest probity. I should be sorry, Colonel, and my mates'ud be sorry, to cause any unpleasantness as a sequel to this little excursion: but we can't stand by and hear them opprobrious epithets applied to the noble per-fession of the fur trade, or to ourselves as its representatives in Geauga County. I'll trouble you, Colonel, to withdraw them words, right away, with a candid apology, and to give us your word of honour that you ain't going to thrash this little chap for the exertions he has made to-day on behalf of the noble perfession which me and my mates has the pleasure and honour of representing. Otherwise, I don't hesitate to say, Colonel, I surmise there'll be a little unpleasantness somewhere between us.'

CHAPTER V

EMANCIPATION

Churchill,' said the vicar, pulling up his cob opposite the gate of the little market garden, 'I want to speak to you a minute about that boy of yours. He's twelve years old and more, I should say, by the look of him, and he's hanging about the village all his time, doing nothing. Do you want a place to put him to? What are you going to do with him?'

'Wull, passon,' Sam Churchill answered, touching his hat in a semi-deferential manner (as a liberal politician, Sam was constitooshionally agin the passon), 'Us did think o' zendin' un to school a bit longer, and tryin' vor to prentice un to zum trade zumwhere; but if a good place at sarvice was goin' a beggin', wy, me an' 'is mother wouldn't stand in the way of 'is takin' it, sartinly, noways.'

'Don't send the boy to school any more, Churchill,' the vicar said decisively. 'This education business is being overdone. You allowed your other boy, Sam I think you called him, to read a pack of nonsensical books about going to sea and so forth, and what's the result? He's gone off to America and left you alone, just as he was beginning to be fitted for a useful assistant. Depend upon it, Churchill, over-education's a great error.'

'That's just what my missus do zay, zur,' Sam chimed in respectfully. 'If us 'adn't let Sam read them Cap'n Marryat books, 'ur do zay,' e 'ouldn't never 'ave gone off a-zeekin' 'is fortune awver yander to 'Murrica. Howsom-dever, what place 'ave 'ee got in yer eye vor our Colin, passon?'

'Let him come to the vicarage,' the parson said, 'and I'll train him to be my own servant. Then he can get to be a gentleman's valet, and take a good place by-and-by in London. The boy's got good manners and good appearance, and would make a capital servant in time, I don't doubt it.'

'Wull, I'll talk it awver wi' the missus,' old Sam replied dubiously.

When Colin was asked whether he would like to go to the vicarage or not, he answered, with the true west-country insouciance, that he didn't much care where he went, so long as the place was good and the work was aisy: and so, before the week was out, he had been duly installed as the vicar's buttons and body-servant, and initiated into the work of brushing clothes, opening doors, announcing visitors, and all the other mysteries of his joint appointment.

The vicar of Wootton was a very great person indeed. He was second cousin to the Earl of Beaminster, the greatest landowner in that part of Dorset; and he never for a moment forgot that he was a Howard-Russell, the inheritor of two of the noblest names in England, and of nothing else on earth except a remarkably narrow and retreating forehead. The vicar was not clever; to that he had no pretensions: but he was a high-minded, honourable, well-meaning English gentleman and clergyman of the old school; not much interested in their new-fangled questions of High Church, and Low Church, and Broad Church, and all the rest of it, yet doing his parochial duty as he conceived of it in a certain honest, straightforward, perfunctory, official fashion. 'In my young days, my dear,' he used to say to his nieces (for he was a bachelor), 'we didn't have all these high churches, and low churches, and mediumsized churches, that people have nowadays.

We had only one church, the Church of England. That's the only church that I for my part can ever consent to live and die in.'

In the vicar's opinion, a clergyman was an officer charged with the maintenance of spiritual decorum in the recognised and organised system of this realm of England. His chief duty was to dispense a decorous hospitality to his friends and equals, to display a decorous pattern of refined life to his various inferiors, to inculcate a decorous morality on all his parishioners, and to take part in a decorous religious service (with the assistance of his curates) twice every Sunday. The march of events had latterly compelled him to add morning prayer on Wednesdays and Fridays in Lent to this simple list of functions; but further than that the vicar resolutely refused to go. When anyone talked to him about matins and evensong, or discussed the Athanasian Creed, or even spoke of the doings of Convocation, the vicar sniffed a little with his aristocratic nose, and remarked stiffly that people didn't go in for those things in his young days, thank goodness. So far as his opinion went, he hated innovations; the creeds were very good creeds indeed, and people had got along very well with them, and without matins or convocations, ever since he could remember.

Still, the vicar was a man of taste. A cousin of Lord Beaminster's and a vicar of Wootton Mandeville ought, he felt, in virtue of his position, to be a man of taste. Not an admirer of new fads and fancies in art: oh, no, no; by no means: not a partisan of realism, or idealism, or romanticism, or classicism, or impressionism, or any other of their fashionable isms; certainly not: but in a grand, old-fashioned, unemotional, dignified sort of way, a man of taste. The vicar had two Romneys hanging in his dining-room; graceful ancestresses with large straw-hats and exquisitely highborn eighteenth-century Howard faces (the Russell connection hadn't then got into the family); and he had good engravings from originals in the Vatican and the Pitti Palace well displayed in his drawingroom: and he had even a single small Thorwaldsen, a Thetis rising from the sea, which fronted him as he sat in the oak-wainscoted study, and inspired his literary efforts while engaged on the composition of his three annual new sermons. It was impossible to enter the vicarage, indeed, without feeling at once the exact artistic position of its excellent occupant. He was decorously æsthetic, just as he was decorously religious and decorously obedient to the usages of society. The Reverend Philip Howard-Russell, in fact, hated enthusiasm in every form. He hated earnest dissent most of all, of course; it was an irregular, indecorous, unauthorised way of trying to get to heaven on one's own account, without the aid of the duly constituted ecclesiastical order: but he hated all nonsense about art almost equally. He believed firmly in Raffael and Michael Angelo, as he believed in church and state: he thought Correggio and Guido almost equally fine; but he had a low opinion of the early Italian masters, and would have looked askance at Botticelli or Era Angelico, wherever he found them, even in a ducal mansion. He didn't live (as good fortune would have it) to see the extremely ill-balanced proceedings of Mr. Burne Jones and his school: indeed the vicar could never have consented to prolong his life into such an epoch of 'movements' and 'earnestness' as our own: but he distinctly recollected, with a thrill of horror, that when he was a tutor at Christ Church there were two or three young men who got up something they called a Preraphaelite Brotherhood, which ultimately came to no good. 'One of them, by name Millais,' he used to say, 'got rid of all that nonsense at last, and has become a really very promising young painter: but as to the others, that fellow Hunt, and a half-Italian man they call Rossetti, well, you know the things they paint are really and truly quite too ridiculous.'

On the whole, Colin Churchill liked his place at the vicarage fairly well. To be sure, passon was exacting sometimes; he had a will of his own, the Reverend Philip, and knew what was becoming from the lower classes towards their natural superiors, but, for all that, Colin liked it. The work wasn't very hard; there was plenty of time to get out into the fields still and play with Minna at odd minutes; the vicarage was pretty and prettily furnished; and above all, it was full of works of art such as Colin had never before even imagined. He didn't know why, of course, but the Romneys and the Thorwaldsen in particular took his fancy immensely from the very first moment he saw them. The Thetis was his special adoration: its curves and lines never ceased to delight and surprise him. An instinctive germ of art which was born in all the Churchill family was beginning to quicken into full life in little Colin. Though the boy knew it not, nor suspected it himself, he was in fact an artistic genius. All the family shared his gifts more or less: but in Colin those gifts were either greater by original endowment, or were more highly developed by the accidents of place and time, who shall say which? Perhaps Sam, put where Colin was, might have become a great sculptor: perhaps Colin, put where Sam was, might have become a respectable American citizen. And perhaps not. These are mysteries which no man yet can solve, least of all the present biographer.

The vicar had a large collection of prints in his study; and when visitors came who were also men of taste with no nonsense about them, it was his custom to show them his collection on a little frame made for the purpose. On such occasions, Colin had to perform the duty of placing the prints one after another upon the frame: and while the vicar and his guests looked at them critically, the boy, too, would gaze from behind them, and listen open-mouthed to their appreciative comments. There was one picture in particular that Colin especially admired, a mezzotint from a fresco of the Four Seasons, by a nameless Renaissance artist, in an out-of-the-way church at Bologna. Perhaps it was the classical bas-relief air of the picture that struck the boy's fancy so much; for the native bent of Colin Churchill's genius was always rather sculpturesque than pictorial: but at any rate he loved that picture dearly, and more than once the vicar noticed that when they came to it, his little page lingered behind abstractedly, and didn't go on to the next in order as soon as he was told to.

'Churchill,' the vicar once said to him sharply on such an occasion, 'why don't you mind when you're spoken to? I said "Next!" Didn't you hear me?'

'I beg your pardon, zur, sir, I mean,' Colin answered, relapsing for the moment into his original barbarism: 'I heer'd you, but—but I was a-lookin' at it and forgot, sir.'

The vicar gazed at the boy for a moment in mute astonishment. 'Looking at it!' he murmured at last, half to himself, with a curious curl about the corner of his mouth; 'goodness gracious, what are we coming to next, I wonder! He was looking at my mezzotints! Extraordinary. Young Churchill looking at my mezzotints!—The next, you see, Colonel, is a very rare print by Cornelius Bloemart after Mieris. Exquisitely delicate engraving, as you observe; very remarkable purity and softness. A capital conjunction in fact: no burin but Bloemart's could render so finely the delicate finish of Frans Mieris. The original is almost worthy of Gerard Douw; you've seen it, I dare say, at Leyden. Next, boy: next.—Looking at it! Well, I declare! He says he was looking at it! That man Churchill always was an ill-mannered, independent, upstanding sort of fellow, and after all what can you expect from his children?

In spite of occasional little episodes like this, however, Colin and the parson got on fairly well together in the long-run. The parson's first task had been, of course, to take care that that boy's language should be reduced to something like the queen's English: and to that effect, Capel, the butler (better known in Wootton as the Dook, on account of his distinguished and haughtily aristocratic manners) had been instructed to point out to Colin the difference in pronunciation between the letters hess and zud, the grammatical niceties of this, these, those, they and them, and the formalities necessary to be used by men of low estate in humbly addressing their duly constituted pastors and masters. Colin, being naturally a quick boy, had soon picked up as much of all this as the Dook was able to teach him; and if there was still a considerable laxity in the matter of aspiration, and a certain irregularity in the matter of moods and tenses, that was really more the fault of the teacher than of the pupil. The Dook had been to London and even to Rome, and had picked up the elegant language of the best footmen in west-end society. Colin learnt just what the Dook taught him; he had left behind the crude West-Saxon of the court of King Alfred, on which he had been nurtured as his mother-tongue, and had almost progressed to the comparatively cultivated and cosmopolitan dialect of an ordinary modern English man-servant.

At first, little Minna was in no small degree contemptuous of Colin's 'vine new-vangled talkin'.' '"Don't you," indeed,' she cried one day in her supremely sarcastic little manner, when Colin had ventured to use that piece of superfine English in her very ears, instead of his native West-Saxon 'don't 'ee;' 'vine things we're comin' to nowadays, Colin, wen the likes o' thee goes sayin' "don't you." I s'pose 'ee want to grow up an' be like the Dook, some o' these vine days. Want to be a butler, an' 'old theeself so stiff, and talk that vine that plain volk can't 'ardly tell what thee's talkin' about. Gurt stoopid, I do call 'ee.' But Colin, in spite of ridicule, continued on his own way, and Minna, who had her pride and her little day-dreams on her own account, too, at last began to think that perhaps after all Colin might be in the right of it.

So, being a west-country girl with a mind of her own (like most of them), Minna set to work on her part also to correct and get rid of her pretty, melting native dialect. She went to school at the British National School (the vicar had carefully warded off that last disgrace of the age, the blatant board school, from his own village); and even as Colin set himself to attain the lofty standard of excellence afforded him by the Dook, so did Minna do her best to follow minutely the voice and accent of the head pupil-teacher, who had actually been for three terms at the Normal College in London. There she had picked up a very noble vulgar London twang, learnt to pronounce 'no' as 'na-o,' and acquired the habit of invariably slurring over or dropping all her short unaccented syllables.

In all these splendid characteristics of the English language as currently spoken in the great metropolis, Minna endeavoured to the best of her ability to follow her leader; and at the end of a year she had so far succeeded that Colin himself complimented her on the immense advance she had lately made in her new linguistic studies.

Colin's greatest delight, however, was still to go down in the afternoon, when the vicar was out, to the brook in the meadow, and there mix up as of yore a good big batch of plastic clay with which to model what he used to call his little images. The Dook complained greatly of the clay, 'a nasty dirty mess, indeed, to go an' acshally bring into any gentleman's house, let alone the vicar's, and him no more nor a page neither!' but Colin managed generally to appease his anger, and to gain a grudging consent at last for the clay to be imported into the house under the most stringent sumptuary conditions. The vicar must never see it coming or going; he mustn't be allowed to know that the Dook permitted such goings-on in the house where he was major-domo. On that point Mr. Capel was severity itself. So when the images were fairly finished, Colin used to take them out surreptitiously at night, and then hand them over to Minna Wroe, who had quite a little museum of the young sculptor's earliest efforts in her own bedroom. She had alike the Thetis after Thorwaldsen (a heathenish, scarce half-clad huzzy, who shocked poor Mrs. Churchill's sense of propriety immensely, until she was solemnly assured that the original stood in the vicar's study), and the Infant Samuel after the plaster cast on the cottage mantelpiece; as well as the bust of Miss Eva, the vicar's favourite niece, studied from life as Colin stood behind her chair at night, or handed her the potatoes at dinner. If Miss Eva hadn't been eighteen, and such a very grand young lady, little Minna might almost have been jealous of her. But as it was, why, Colin was only the page boy, and so really, after all, what did it matter?

For three years Colin continued at the vicarage, till he was full fifteen, and then an incident occurred which gave the first final direction to his artistic impulses.

One afternoon he had been down to the brook, talking as usual with his old playmate Minna (even fifteen and thirteen are not yet very dangerous ages), when he happened, in climbing up that well-known clay cliff, to miss his foothold on the sticky slippery surface, and fell suddenly into the bed of the stream below. His head was sadly cut by the flints at the bottom, and two neighbours picked him out and carried him between them up to the vicarage. There he was promptly laid upon his own bed, while Capel sent off hurriedly for the Wootton doctor to staunch the flow of blood from the ugly cut.

When the vicar heard of the accident from the Dook, he was sitting in the drawing-room listening to Miss Eva playing a then fashionable gavotte by a then fashionable composer. 'Is he badly hurt, Capel?' the vicar asked, with decorous show of interest.

'Pretty bad, sir,' the Dook answered in his official manner. 'I should judge, sir, by the look of it, that the boy had cut a artery, sir, or summat of that sort; leastways, the wownd is bleeding most uncommon profusely.'

'I'll come and see him,' the vicar said, with the air of a man who decorously makes a sacrifice to Christian principles. 'You may tell the poor lad, Capel, that I'll come and see him presently.'

'And I will too,' Eva put in quickly.

'Eva, my dear!' her uncle observed with chilling dignity. 'You had better not. The sight would be a most unpleasant one for you. Indeed, for all of us. Capel, you may tell Churchill that I am coming to see him. Eva, I'm afraid I interrupted you: go on, my dear.'

Eva played out the gavotte to the end a little impatiently, and then the vicar rose after a minute or two of decent delay (one mustn't seem in too great a hurry to sympathise with the accidents which may befall one's poorer neighbours), and walked in his stately leisurely fashion towards the servants' quarters. 'Which is Churchill's room, Capel?' he asked as he went along. 'Ah, yes, this one, to be sure. Poor lad, I hope he's better now.'

But as soon as the vicar stood within the room, which he had never entered before since Colin had used it, he had hardly any eyes for the boy or the surgeon, and could scarcely even ask the few questions which decorum demanded as to his state and probable recovery.

For the walls of Colin Churchill's bedroom were certainly of a sort gravely to surprise and disquiet the unsuspecting vicar. All round the room, a number of large sheets of paper hung, on which were painted in bright water-colours cartoon-like copies of the engravings which formed the chief decoration of the vicar's drawing-room.

'Who did these?' he asked sternly.

'Me, sir,' the boy answered, trembling, from the bed.

The Reverend Philip Howard-Russell started visibly. He displayed astonishment even before his own servants. In truth, he was too good a judge of art not to see at a glance that the pictures were well drawn, and that the colouring, which was necessarily original, had been harmonised with native taste. All this was disquieting enough; but more disquieting than all was another work of art which hung right on the top of Colin's bed-head. It was a composition in clay of the Four Seasons, reproduced in bas-relief from the mezzotint in the vicar's portfolio, over which he now at once remembered Colin had so often and so constantly lingered.

Though he ought to have been looking at the boy, the vicar's eyes were fixed steadily during almost all the interview on this singular bas-relief. If the water-colours had merit, the vicar, as a man of taste, could not conceal from himself the patent fact that the bas-relief showed positive signs of real genius. It was really most untoward, most disconcerting! A lad of that position in life to go and model a composition in relief from an engraving on the flat, and to do it well, too! The vicar had certainly never heard of anything like it!

He said a few words of decorously conventional encouragement to Colin, told the surgeon he was delighted to hear the wound was not a serious one, and then beckoned the Dook quietly out of the room as he himself took his departure.

'Capel,' he said, in a low voice on the landing, 'what on earth is the meaning of that, ur, that panel at Churchill's bedside?'

'Well, sir, the boy likes to make a mess with mud and water, you see,' the butler answered submissively, 'and I didn't like to prevent him, because he's a well-conducted lad in gen'ral, sir, and he seems to have took a awful fancy to this sort of imaging. I hope there ain't no harm done, sir. I never allows him to make a mess with it.'

'Not at all, not at all, Capel,' the vicar continued, frowning slightly. 'No harm in the world in his amusing himself so, of course; still', and this the vicar added to himself as though it were a peculiarly aggravating piece of criminality, 'there's no denying he has reproduced that mezzotint in really quite a masterly manner.'

The vicar went back to the drawing-room with a distressed and puzzled look upon his clean-shaven clear-cut countenance. 'Is he badly hurt, uncle?' asked Eva. 'No, my dear,' the vicar replied, testily; 'nothing to speak of; but I'm afraid he has made himself a very singular and excellent bas-relief.'

'A what?' cried Eva, imagining to herself that she had overlooked the meaning of some abstruse medical term which sounded strangely artistic to her unaccustomed ears.

'A bas-relief,' the vicar repeated, in a disgusted tone. 'Yes, my dear, I'm not surprised you should be astonished at it, but I said a bas-relief. He has reproduced my Bologna Four Seasons in clay, and what's worse, Eva, he has really done it extremely well too, confound him.'

It was only on very rare occasions that the vicar allowed himself the use of such doubtful expressions, and even then he employed them in his born capacity as a Howard-Russell rather than in his acquired one as a clergyman of the Church of England.

'Eva, my dear,' he said again after a long pause,'the boy's head is bandaged now, and after all there's really nothing in any way in his condition to shock you. It might be as well, perhaps, if you were to go to see him, and ask Mr. Walkem whether the cook ought to make him anything in the way of jelly or beef-tea or any stuff of that sort, you know. These little attentions to one's dependents in illness are only Christian, only Christian. And, do you know, Eva, you might at the same time just glance at the panel by the bed-head, and tell me by-and-by what you think of it. I've great confidence in your judgment, my dear, and after all it mayn't perhaps be really quite so good as I'm at first sight inclined to believe it.'

When niece and uncle met again at dinner, Eva unhesitatingly proclaimed her opinion that the bas-relief was very clever (a feminine expression for every degree of artistic or intellectual merit, not readily apprehended by the ridiculous hair-splitting male intelligence). The vicar moved uneasily in his chair. This was most disconcerting. What on earth was he to do with the boy? As a man of taste, he felt that he mustn't keep a possible future Canova blacking boots in his back kitchen; as a Christian minister, he felt that he must do the best he could to advance the position of all his parishioners; yet finally, as a loyal member of this commonwealth, he felt that he ought not to countenance people of that position in life in having tastes and occupations above their natural station. Old Churchill's son, too! Could anything be more annoying? 'What on earth ought we to do with him, Eva?' he asked doubtfully.

'Send him to London to some good artist, and see what he can make of him,' Eva replied with astonishing promptitude. (It's really wonderful how young people of the present day will undertake to solve the most difficult practical problems off-hand, as if there were absolutely nothing in them.)

The vicar glanced towards the Dook uneasily. 'It's a very extraordinary thing,' he said, 'for a lad of his class to go and dream of going and doing. I may be old-fashioned, Eva, my dear, but I don't quite like it. I won't deny that I don't quite like it.'

'Haven't I read somewhere,' Eva went on innocently, 'that Giotto or somebody was a peasant boy who fed sheep, and that someone or other, Cimabue, I think (only I don't know how to pronounce his name properly), saw some drawings he'd made with a bit of charcoal on some rock, and took him for his pupil, and made him into, oh, such a great painter?

I know it was such a delightfully romantic story, wherever I read it.'

The vicar coughed drily. 'That was in the thirteenth century, my dear,' he said, in his coldest and most repressive tone. 'The thirteenth century was a very long time ago, Eva. Society hadn't organised itself then, as it has done in our own day. Besides, the story has been critically doubted. Ci-ma-bu-e,' and the vicar dwelt carefully on each syllable of the name with a little distinct intonation which mutely corrected Eva's faulty Italian without too obtrusively exciting the butler's attention, 'had probably very little to do with discovering Giot-to. Capel, this is not the green seal claret. Go and decant some green seal at once, will you. My dear, this is a discussion which had better not be carried on before the servants.'

In three days more the Dook was regaling the gossips of the White Lion with the whole story how the vicar, with his usual artistic sensibility, had discovered merit in that lad of Churchill's, and had found out as the thing the lad had made out of mud were really what they call a bas-relief, 'which I've seen 'em, of course,' said the Dook, loftily, 'in lots of palaces in Italy, carved by Jotter, and Bonnomey, and Jamberty, and all them old swells; but I never took much notice of this one o' young Churchill's, naterally, till the vicar came in; and then, as soon as ever he clapped eyes on it, he says at once to me, "Capel," says he, "that's a bas-relief." And then, I remembered as I'd seen just the same sort of things, as I was sayin', over in Italy, by the cart-load; but, Lord, who'd have ever thought old Sam Churchill's son could ever ha' done one! And now the vicar's asted Sam to let him get the boy apprenticed to a wood-carver: and Sam's give his consent; and next week the boy's going off to Exeter, and going to make his fortune as sure as there's apples in Herefordshire.'

The idea of the wood-carver may be considered as a sort of compromise on the vicar's part between his two duties, as a munificent discoverer of rising talent, and a judicious represser of the too-aspiring lower orders. A wood-carver's work is in a certain sense artistic, and yet it isn't anything more, as a rule, than a decent handicraft. The vicar rather prided himself upon this clever sop to both his consciences: he chuckled inwardly over the impartial manner in which he had managed to combine the recognition of plastic merit with the equal recognition of profound social disabilities. Eva, to be sure, had stood out stoutly against the wood-carving, and had pleaded hard for a sculptor in London: but the vicar disarmed her objections somewhat by alleging the admirable precedent of Grinling Gibbons. 'Gibbons, you know, my dear, rose to the very first rank as a sculptor from his trade as a wood-carver. Pity to upset the boy's mind by putting him at once to a regular artist. If there's really anything in him, he'll rise at last; if not, it would only do him harm to encourage him in absurd expectations.' Oh, wise inverted Gamaliels! you too in your decorous way, with your topsyturvy opportunism, cannot wholly escape the charge of quenching the spirit.

CHAPTER VI

ENTER A NEW ENGLANDER

Hiram Winthrop's emancipation had come a little earlier, and it had come after this fashion.

It was early spring along the lake shore, and Hiram had wandered out, alone as usual, into the dense marshy scrub that fringed the Creek, near the spot where it broadens and deepens into a long blue bay of still half-frozen and spell-bound Ontario. The skunk-cabbage was coming into flower! It was early spring, and the boy's heart was glad within him, as though the deacon, and the cord-wood, and the coming drudgery of hoeing and weeding had never existed. Perhaps, now, he should see the trappers again. He wandered on among the unbroken woods, just greening with the wan fresh buds, and watched the whole world bursting into life again after its long wintry interlude; as none have ever seen it waken save those who know the great icy lake country of North America. The signs of quickening were frequent in the underbrush. The shrill peep of the tree-frog came to him from afar through the almost silent woodland. The drumming of the redheaded woodpecker upon the hickory trunks showed that the fat white grubs were now hatching and moving underneath the bark Close to the water's edge he scared up a snipe; and then, again, a little farther, he saw a hen hawk rise with sudden flappings from the clam-shell mound. Hark, too; that faint, swelling, distant beat! surely it was a partridge! He looked up into the trees, and searched for it diligently: and there true enough, settling, after the transatlantic manner, on a tall butternut (oh, heterodox bird!), he caught a single glimpse of the beautiful fluttering creature, as it took its perch lightly upon the topmost branches.

It was so delightful, all of it, that Hiram never thought of the time or his dinner, but simply wandered on, as a boy will, for hour after hour in that tangled woodland. What did he care, in the joy of his heart, for the coming beating? His one idea was to see the trappers. At last, he saw an unwonted sight through the trees, two men actually pushing their way along beside the river. His heart beat fast within him: could they be the trappers? Spurred on by that glorious possibility, he crept up quickly and noiselessly behind them. The men were talking quite loud to one another: no, they couldn't be trappers: trappers always go softly, and speak in a whisper. But if they weren't trappers, what on earth could they be do down here in the unbroken forest? Not felling wood, that was clear; for they had no axes with them, and they walked along without ever observing the lie of the timber.

Not going to survey wild lands, for they had none of those strange measuring things with them (Hiram was innocent of the name theodolite) that surveyors are always peeping and squinting through. Not gunning either, for they had no guns, but only simple stout walking-sticks. 'Sech a re-markable, on-common circumstance I never saw, and that's true as Judges,' Hiram said to himself, as he watched them narrowly. He would jest listen to what they were sayin', and see if he could make out what on airth they could be doin' down in them woods thar.

'When I picked him up,' one of the men was saying to the other, in a clear, distinct, delicate tone, such as Hiram had never heard before, 'I saw it was a wounded merganser, winged by some bad shot, and fallen into the water to die alone. I never saw anything more beautiful than its long slender vermilion bill, the very colour of red sealing wax; and its clean bright orange legs and feet; and its pure white breast just tinged at the tip of each feather with faint salmon, or a dainty buff inclining to salmon. I was sorry I hadn't got my colours with me: I'd have given anything to be able to paint him, then and there.'

Hiram could hardly contain himself with mingled awe, delight, and astonishment. He wanted to call out on the spur of the moment 'I know that thar bird. I know him. 'Tain't called that name you give him, down our section, though. We call him a fisherman diver.' But he didn't dare to in his perfect transport of surprise and amazement. It wasn't the strange person's tone alone that pleased him so much, though he felt, in a vague indefinable way, that there was something very beautiful and refined and exquisitely modulated in it, the voice being in fact the measured, clearly articulate voice of a cultivated New England gentleman, such as he had never before met in his whole lifetime: it wasn't exactly that, though that was in itself sufficiently surprising: it was the astounding fact that there was a full-grown, decently clad man, not apparently a lunatic or an imbecile, positively interesting himself in such childish things as the very colours and feathers of a bird, just the same as he, Hiram Winthrop, might have done in the blackberry bottom. The deacon never talked about the bill of a merganser! The deacon never noticed the dainty buff on the breast, inclining to salmon! The deacon never expressed any burning desire to pull out his brushes and paint it! All the men he had ever yet seen in Geauga County would have regarded the colours on the legs of a bird as wholly beneath their exalted and dignified adult consideration. Corn and pork were the objects that engaged their profound intellects, not birds and insects. Hiram had always imagined that an interest in such small things was entirely confined to boys and infants. That grown men could care to talk about them was an idea wholly above his limited experience, and almost above what the deacon would have called his poor finite comprehension.

'Yes,' the other answered him, even before Hiram could recover from his first astonishment. 'It's a lovely bird. I've tried to sketch him myself more than once. And have you ever noticed, Audouin, the peculiar way the tints are arranged on the back of the neck? The crest's black, you know, glossed with green; but the nape's white; and the colours don't merge into one another, as you might expect, but cease abruptly with quite a hard line of demarcation at the point of junction.'

'Jest for all the world as ef they was sewed together,' Hiram murmured to himself inaudibly, still more profoundly astonished at this incredible and totally unexpected phenomenon. Then there were two distinct and separate human beings in the world, it seemed, who were each capable of paying attention to the coloration of a common merganser. As Hiram whispered awestruck to his own soul, 'most mirac'lous!'

He followed them up a little farther, hanging anxiously on every word, and to his continued astonishment heard them notice to one another such petty matters as the flowering of the white maples, the twittering of the red-polls among the fallen pine-needles, the wider and ever wider circles on the water where the pickerel had leaped, nay, even the tracks left upon the soft clay that marked the nightly coming and going of the stealthy wood-chuck. Impossible: unimaginable: utterly un-diaconal: but still true! Hiram's spirit was divided within him. At last the one who was addressed as Audouin said casually to his companion, 'Let's sit down here, Professor, and have our lunch. I love this lunching in the open woods. It brings us nearer to primitive nature. I suppose the chord it strikes within us is the long latent and unstruck chord of hereditary habit and feeling. It's centuries since our old English ancestors lived that free life in the open woods of the Teutonic mainland; but the unconscious memory of it reverberates dimly still, I often think, through all our nature, and comes out in the universal love for escape from conventionality to the pure freedom of an open-air existence.'

'Perhaps so,' the Professor answered with a laugh: 'but if you'll leave your Boston philosophy behind, my dear unpractical Audouin, and open your sandwich-case, you'll be doing a great deal more good in the cause of hungry humanity than by speculating on the possible psychological analysis of the pleasure of picnicking.'

Hiram didn't quite know what all that meant; but from behind the big alder he could, at least, see that the sandwiches looked remarkably tempting (by the way, it was clearly past dinner-time, to judge by the internal monitor), and the Professor was pouring something beautifully red and clear into a metal cup out of the wicker-covered bottle. It wasn't whisky, certainly; nor spruce beer, either: could it really be that red stuff, wine, that people used to drink in Bible times, according to the best documentary authorities?

'Don't, pray, reproach me with the original sin of having been born in Boston,' Audouin answered, with a slight half-affected little shiver. 'I can no more help that, of course, than I can help the following of Adam, in common with all the rest of our poor fallen humanity.' (Why, that was jest like the deacon!) 'But at least I've done my very best to put away the accursed thing, and get rid, forever, of our polluted material civilisation. I've tried to flee from man (except always you, my dear Professor), and take refuge from his impertinent inanity in the bosom of my mother nature. From the haunts of the dry-goods man and the busy throng of drummers, I've come into the woods and fields as from a solitary desert into society. I prefer to emphasise my relations to the universe, rather than my relations to the miserable toiling ant-hill of petty humanity.'

'Really, Audouin,' the Professor put in, as he passed his friend the claret, 'you're growing positively morbid; degenerating into a wild man of the woods. I must take you back for a while to the city and civilisation. I shall buy you a suit of store clothes, set you up in a five-dollar imported hat, and make you promenade State Street, afternoons, keeping a sharp eye on the Boston ladies and the Boston fashions.'

'No, no, Professor,' Audouin answered, with a graceful flourish of his small white hand: (Hiram noticed that it was small and white, though the dress the stranger actually wore was not a 'store suit.' but a jacket and trousers of the local home-spun); 'no, no; that would never do. I refuse to believe in your civilisation. I abjure it: I banish it. What is it? A mere cutting down of trees and disfiguring of nature, in order to supply uninteresting millions with illimitable pork and beans. The object of our society seems to be to provide more and more luxuriously for our material wants, and to shelve all higher ideals of our nature for an occasional Sunday service and a hypothetical future existence. I turn with delight, on the other hand, from cities and railroad cars to the forest and the living creatures. They are the one group of beautiful things that the great Anglo-Saxon race, in civilising and vulgarising this vast continent, has left us still undesecrated. They are not conventionalised; they don't go to the Old Meeting House in European clothes Sunday mornings; they speak always to me in the language of nature, and tell me our lower wants must be simplified that the higher life may be correspondingly enriched. The only true way of salvation, after all, Professor, lies in perfect fidelity to one's own truest inner promptings.'

Hiram listened still, all amazed. He didn't fully understand it all; some of it sounded to him rather affectedly sentimental and finnikin; but on the whole what struck him most was the strange fact that this fine-spoken town-bred gentleman seemed to have ideas about the world and nature, differently expressed, but fundamentally identical, such as he himself felt but never knew before anybody else in the whole world was likely to share with him. 'That's pretty near jest what I'd have said myself,' the boy thought wonderingly, 'if I'd knowed how: only I shouldn't ever have bin able to say it so fine and high-falutin.' They finished their lunch, and sat talking a while together under the shadow of the leafless hickories. The boy still stopped and watched them, spell-bound. At last Audouin pulled a head of flowers from close to the ground, and looked at it pensively, with his head just a trifle theatrically on one side. 'That's a curious thing, Professor,' he said, eyeing it at different distances in his hand: 'what do you call it now? I don't know it.'

'I'm sure I can't tell you, the Professor answered, taking it from him carelessly. I don't pretend to be much of a botanist, you see, and I'm out of my element down here among the lake-side flora.'

Hiram could contain himself no longer.

'It's skunk-cabbage,' he cried, in all the exultation of boyish knowledge, emerging suddenly from behind the big alder. 'Skunk-cabbage, the trappers call it. Ain't it splendid? You kin hear the bees hummin' an' buzzin' around it, fine days in spring, findin it out close to the ground, and goin' into it, one at a time, before the willows has begun to blossom. I see lots as I kem along this mornin', putting out their long tongues into it, and scarin' away the flies as they tried to get a bit o' the breakfast.'

Audouin laughed melodiously. 'What's this?' he cried. 'A heaven-born observer dropped suddenly upon us from the clouds!

You seem to know all about it, my young friend. Skunk-cabbage, is it? But surely the bees aren't out in search of honey already, are they?'

''Tain't honey they get from it,' the boy answered quickly. 'It's bee-bread. Jest you see them go in, and watch 'em come out again, and thar you'll find they've all got little yaller pellets stickin' right on to the small hairs upon their thighs. That's bee-bread, that is, what they give to the maggots. All bees is born out of maggots.'

Audouin laughed again. 'Why, Professor,' he said briskly, 'this is indeed a phenomenon. A country-bred boy who cares for and watches nature! Boston must have set her mark on me deep, after all, for I'm positively surprised to find a lover of nature born so far from the hub of the universe. Skunk-cabbage, you call it; so quaint a flower deserves a rather better name. Do you know the tassel-flower, my young fellow-citizen? (we're both citizens of the woods, it seems). Do you know tassel-flower? is it out yet? I want to find some.'

'I know it, some,' Hiram answered, delighted, 'but it ain't out yet; it comes a bit later. But I kin draw it for you, if you like, so's you can know it when it comes into blossom.' And he felt in his pocket for some invisible object, which he soon produced in the visible shape of a small red jasper arrowhead. The boy was just beginning to scratch a figure with it on a flat piece of water-rolled limestone when Audouin's quick eye caught sight, sideways, of the beautifully chipped implement.

'Ha, ha,' he cried, taking it from Hiram suddenly, 'what have we here, eh? The red man: his mark: as plain as printing. The broad arrow of the aboriginal possessor of all America! Why, this is good; this is jasper. Where on earth did you get this from?'

'Whar on airth,'Hiram echoed, astonished anew; 'why jest over thar: I picked it up as I kem along this morning. Thar's lots about, 'specially in spring time.'Pears as if the Injuns shot 'em off at painters and bars and settlers and things, and missed sometimes, and lost 'em. Then they lie thar in the ground a long time till some hard winter comes along to uncover 'em. Hard winters, the frost throws 'em up; and when the snow melts, the water washes 'em out into the furrers. I've got crowds of 'em to home; arrowheads and tommyhawks, and terbacker pipes, an' all sorts. I pick 'em up every spring, reglar.' Audouin looked at the boy with a far more earnest and searching glance for a moment; then he turned quickly to the Professor. 'There's something in this,' he said, in a serious tone, very different from his previous half-unreal banter. 'The bucolic intelligence evidently extends deeper than its linguistic faculties might at first lead one to suspect.' He spoke intentionally in hieroglyphics, aiming his words above the boy's head; but Hiram caught the general sense notwithstanding, and flushed slightly with ingenuous pride. 'Well, let's see your drawing,' Audouin went on, with a gracious smile, handing the boy back his precious little bit of pointed jasper.

Hiram took the stone weapon between finger and thumb, and scratching the surface of the waterworn pebble lightly with its point in a few places, produced in a dozen strokes a rough outline of the Canadian tassel-flower. Audouin looked at the hasty sketch in evident astonishment. It was his turn now to be completely surprised. 'Why, look here, Professor,' he said very slowly: 'this is, yes, this is, actually a drawing.'

The Professor took the pebble from his hands, and scanned it closely. 'Why, yes,' he said, in some surprise. 'There's certainly a great deal of native artistic freedom about the leaf and flower. It's excellent; in fact, quite astonishing. I expected a diagrammatic representation; this is really, as you say, Audouin, a drawing.'

Hiram looked on in perfect silence: but the colour came hot and bright in his cheek with very unwonted pleasure and excitement. To hear himself praised and encouraged for drawing was indeed a wonder. So very unlike the habits and manners of the deacon.

'Do you ever draw with a pencil?' Audouin asked after a moment's pause, 'or do you always scratch your sketches like this on flat bits of pebble?'

'Oh, I hev a pencil and book in my pocket,' Hiram answered shyly; 'only I kinder didn't care to waste the paper on a thing like that; an' besides, I was scar't that you two growed-ups mightn't think well of my picturs that I've drawed in it.'

'Produce the pictures,' Audouin said in a tone of authority, leaning back against the trunk of the hickory.

Hiram drew them from his pocket timidly.

'Thar they are,' he murmured, with a depreciatory gesture. 'They ain't much, but they're all the picturs I knowed how to draw.'

Audouin took the book in his hand, Sam Churchill's ten-cent copybook, and turned over the well-filled pages with a critical eye. The Professor, too, glanced at it over his shoulder. Hiram stood mute and expectant before them, with eyes staring blankly, and in the expressive uncouth attitude of a naïf shamefaced American country boy.

At last Audouin came to the last page.

'Well, Professor'—he said inquiringly.

'Something in them, isn't there, eh? This boy'll make a painter, I surmise, won't he?' The Professor answered only by opening a small portfolio, and taking out a little amateur water-colour drawing. 'Look here, my son,' he said, holding it up before Hiram. 'Do you think you could do that sort of thing?'

'I guess I could,' Hiram answered, with the unhesitating confidence of inexperienced youth. 'ef I'd on'y got the right sort of colours to do it with.'

The Professor laughed heartily. 'Then you shall have them, anyhow,' he said promptly. 'Native talent shall not go unrewarded for the sake of a paltry box of Prussian blue and burnt sienna. You shall have them right off and no mistake. Where do you live, Mr. Melibous?'

'My name's Hiram,' the boy answered, a little smartly, for he somehow felt the unknown nickname was not entirely a courteous one: 'Hiram Winthrop, and I live jest t'other side of Muddy Creek deepo.'

'Winthrop,' Audouin put in gaily. 'Winthrop. I see it all now. Good old Massachusetts name, Winthrop: connected with the hub of the universe after all, it seems, in spite of mere superficial appearances to the contrary. But it's a pretty far cry to Muddy Creek dépôt, my friend. You must be hungry, ain't you? Have you had your dinner?'

'No, I ain't.'

'Then you sit down right there, my boy, and pitch into those sandwiches.'

Hiram lost no time in obeying the seasonable invitation.

'How do you find them?' asked Audouin.

'Real elegant,' Hiram answered.

'Have some wine?'

'I never tasted none,' the boy replied:

'But it looks real nice. I don't mind ef I investigate it.'

Audouin poured him out a small cupful. The boy took it with the ease of a freeborn citizen, very unlike the awkwardness of an English plough-boy, an awkwardness which shows itself at once the last relic of original serfdom. 'Tain't bad,' he said, tasting it. 'So that's wine, then! Nothing so much to go gettin' mad about either. I reckon the colour's the best thing about it, any way.'

They waited till the boy had finished his luncheon, and then Audouin began asking him a great many questions, cunningly devised questions to draw him out, about the plants, and the animals, and the drawings, and the neighbourhood, and himself, till at last Hiram grew quite friendly and confidential. He entered freely into the natural history and psychology of the deacon. He told them all his store of self-acquired knowledge. He omitted nothing, from the cuffs and reprobation to Sam Churchill and the bald-headed eagles. At each fresh item Audouin's interest rose higher and higher. 'Have you gone to school, Hiram?' he asked at last.

'Common school,' Hiram answered briefly. 'Learnt much there?'

'Headin', writin', spellin','rithmetic, scrip-tur', jography, an' hist'ry an' const'tooshun of the United States,' Hiram replied, with the sharp promptitude begotten of rote learning.

Audouin smiled a sardonic Massachusetts smile. 'A numerous list of accomplishments, indeed,' he answered, playing with his watch-chain carelessly. 'The history of the United States in particular must be intensely interesting. But the Indians, you learnt about them yourself, I suppose, that's so, isn't it, Hiram? What we learn of ourselves is always in the end the best learning. Well, now look here, my boy; how'd you like to go to college, and perhaps in time teach school yourself?'

'I'd like that fust-rate,' Hiram answered; 'but I think I'd like best of all to go to sea, or to be a painter.'

'To be a painter,' Audouin murmured softly; 'to be a painter. Our great continent hasn't produced any large crop of prominent citizens who wanted to be painters. This one might, after all, be worth trying. Well, Hiram, do you think if I were to ask your father, there's any chance that he might possibly be willing to let you go to college?'

'Nary chance at all,' Hiram answered vigorously. 'Why, father couldn't spare me from the peppermint an' the pertaters; an' as to goin' to college, why, it ain't in the runnin' any way.'

'Professor,' Audouin said, 'this boy interests me. He's vital: he's aboriginal: he's a young Antæus fresh from the bare earth of the ploughed fields and furrows. Let's till him; without cutting down all the trees, let's lay him out in park and woodland. I'll have a try, anyhow, with this terrible father of yours, Hiram. Are you going home now?'

'I reckon I must,' the boy answered with a nod. 'He'll be mad enough with me as it is for stopping away so long from him.'

'You'll get a thrashing, I'm afraid, when you go home?'

'I guess that's jest the name of it.'

'Professor,' Audouin said, rising resolutely, 'this means business. We must see this thing right through immediately to the very conclusion. The boy must not have his thrashing. I'll go and see the father, beard the Geauga County agriculturist in his very lair: dispute his whelp with him: play lambent lightning round him: save the young Antæus from sinking in the natural course of things into one more pickier of pork and contented devourer of buttered buckwheat pancakes. There's a spark in him somewhere: I'm going to try whether I can manage to blow it up into a full-fed flame.'

CHAPTER VII

THE DEACON FALTERS

Boston has worn itself out. The artificial centre of an unnatural sickly exotic culture ever alien to the American soil, it has gone on studying, criticising, analysing, till all the vigour and spontaneity it may ever have possessed has utterly died out of it from pure inanition. The Nemesis of sterility has fallen upon its head in the second generation. It has cultivated men, fastidious critics, receptive and appreciative intellects by the thousand; but of thinkers, workers, originalities, hardly now a single one.

Lothrop Audouin was the very embodiment of the discontent and mocking intellectual nihilism begotten of this purely critical unoriginative attitude. Reaction against American materialism was the mainspring of his inner being. He felt himself out of harmony with the palace cars on the New York Central Railroad; jarring and conflicting with the big saloons of the Windsor Hotel; unappreciative of the advertising enterprise on the rocks of the Hudson River; at war with mammoth concerns, gigantic newspapers, Presidential booms, State legislatures, pop corn, saw mills, utilisation of water power, and all the other component elements of the great American civilisation. Therefore, being happily endowed by fate and his ancestors with a moderate competence, even as moderate competences go on the other side of the Atlantic, he had fled from Boston and the world to take refuge in the woods and the marshes. For some years he had hidden himself in the western hill district of Massachusetts; but being driven thence by the march of intellect (enthroned on a steam plough), he had just removed to a new cottage on the shore of Muddy Creek, not far from its entry into Lake Ontario. There he lived a solitary life, watching the birds and beasts and insects, sketching the trees and shrubs and flowers, and shunning for the most part his fellow-man, save only his friend, the distinguished ornithologist, Professor Ezra P. Hipkiss, of Harvard College, Massachusetts.

The Professor had left them, intending to return home by himself; and Audouin walked back alone with the boy, noticing at every step his sharp appreciation of all the natural signs and landmarks around him. At last a sudden thought seemed to strike Hiram. He drew back a second in momentary hesitation.

'Say,' he said falteringly, 'you ain't one of Father Noyes's crowd at Oneida, are you?'

Audouin smiled half contemptuously.

Father Noyes is a New Haven fanatic who has established an Agapemone of his own in northern New York; and to Hiram, who had heard the Oneida community spoken of with vague horror by all the surrounding farmers from his babyhood upward, the originally separate and distinct notions of Father Noyes and the Devil had so coalesced that even now in his maturer years they were not completely differentiated or demarcated. 'No, no,' Audouin answered reassuringly: 'I'm not one of the Oneida people, my boy: I'm quite free from any taint of that sort. I'm a Boston man; a Boston man, I said; even in the woods that sticks to me. "Patriæ quis exul," I think the line runs, "se quoque fugit."' Hiram didn't understand exactly what he was driving at, but he went along satisfied at least that his strange acquaintance, though he spoke with tongues, was not directly connected either with Father Noyes or the Devil.

By-and-by they reached the high-road, and came at last opposite the bare gate that gave access to Deacon Winthrop's yard. Audouin gazed about him drearily at the dreary prospect. 'A very American view, Hiram,' he said slowly: 'civilisation hard at work here; my boy, we must try to redeem you out of it.'

Hiram looked up in the stranger's face curiously. He had grown up among his native surroundings so unquestioningly, after the fashion of boys, that, though he knew it was all very ugly, hopelessly and hideously ugly, it would never even have occurred to him to say so in so many words. He took it for granted that all the world was of course dull and uninteresting, except the woods, and the weeds, and the marshes, and the vermin. He expected always to find all man's handicraft a continuous course of uglification, and he never suspected that there could by any possibility be anything beautiful except untouched and unpolluted nature. If you had told him about the wonders and glories of art, he would simply have listened to you then in mute incredulity.

Audouin lifted up the latch of the gate and walked into the yard; and the deacon, seeing him approach, strode to meet him, in no very amiable frame of mind, thinking it probable that this was only another one of Hiram's undesirable trapper acquaintances. To say the truth, the misapprehension was a natural one. Audouin was coarsely dressed in rough country clothes, and even when he spoke a nature like the deacon's was hardly of the sort to be much impressed by his quiet cultivated manner. 'Wal, cap'n,' the deacon said, coming towards them, 'what might you be lookin' after this mornin', eh? I presume you air on the look-out for horses?'

Audouin smiled and bowed with a dignity which suited strangely with his rude outer aspect. 'No, sir,' he answered in his bland voice. 'I'm not looking out for horses. I met your son here, a very interesting boy, down by the Creek, and I have come up here with him because his individuality attracted me. I wanted to have a talk with you about him.' As it happened, to speak well of Hiram, and before his face too (the scapegrace!), wasn't exactly the surest path to the deacon's esteem and affection. He coughed nervously, and then inquired in his dry manner, 'Trapper?' 'No, not exactly a trapper,' Audouin replied, smiling again faintly. The faint smile and the 'exactly' both misled and exasperated the deacon.

'Farmer, then?' he continued laconically, after the fashion of the country.

'No, nor farmer either,' the New Englander answered in his soft voice. 'I am Mr. Audouin, of Lakeside Cottage.'

The deacon scanned him contemptuously from head to foot. 'Oh, Mister Audouin,' he said significantly. 'Wal, Mister Audouin, so you've bought up that thar ramshackle place of Hitchcock's, hev you? And what air you goin' to dew with it naow you've got it? Clear off the timber, I reckon, and set up rafting.'

'God forbid,' Audouin replied hastily. (The deacon frowned slightly at such obvious profanity.) 'I've taken the place just because of its very wildness, and I merely wish to live in it and watch and sympathise with nature. I see your son loves nature, too, and that has formed a bond of union between us.'

'Wal,' the deacon murmured meditatively, 'that's all accordin' to taste. Hiram is my own son, an' if the Lord has bin pleased to afflict us in him, mother an' me ain't the ones to say nothin' agin him to casual strangers, anyway. But I don't want to part with him, Mister Audouin; we ain't lookin' out for a place for him yet. Thar's work enough for him to do on this farm, I kin tell you, ef on'y he'd do it. You wasn't in want of any butter or eggs now, was you?'

'No, Mr. Winthrop,' Audouin answered seriously, leaning against the gate as he spoke. 'I see you quite misunderstand me. Allow me a moment to explain the position. I'm a Boston man, a man of independent means, and I've taken Lakeside because I wish to live alone, away from a world in which I have really very little interest. You may possibly know, by name at least, my uncle, Senator Lothrop, of Syracuse;' (that was a horrid bit of snobbery, worthy almost of the old world, Audouin thought to himself as he uttered it; but it was necessary if he was to do anything for Hiram). 'Well, that's my card, some use in civilisation after all, Lothrop Audouin; and I was wandering in the woods by the Creek this morning with my friend, Professor Hipkiss of Harvard, when I happened to fall in quite accidentally with your son here. He charmed us by his knowledge of nature all around, and, indeed, I was so much interested in him that I thought I would just step over and have a little conversation with you about his future.'

The deacon took the little bit of pasteboard suspiciously, and looked with slowly melting incredulity at Audouin's rough dress from head to foot. Even upon his dense, coarse, materialised mind the truth began to dawn slowly that he was dealing with a veritable gentleman. 'Wal, Mr. Audouin,' he said, this time without the ironical emphasis upon the 'Mister,' 'what do yer want to dew with the boy, eh, sir? I don't see as I kin spare him; 'pears to me, ef he's goin anywhar, he may as well go to a good farmer's.'

'You mistake me still,' Audouin went on. 'My meaning is this. Your son has talked to the Professor and myself, and has shown us some of his sketches.' The deacon nodded ominously. 'Now, his conversation is so intelligent and his drawings so clever, that we both think you ought to make an effort to give him a good education. He would well repay it. We have both a considerable influence in educational quarters, and we would willingly exert it for his benefit.'

The deacon opened his eyes with astonishment. That lad intelligent? Why, he was no judge at all of a bullock, and he knew scarcely anythin' more about fall wheat'n a greenhorn that might hev kem out from Ireland by the last steamer. However, he contented himself upon that head with smiling sardonically, and muttered half to himself, 'Edoocation; edoocational influence; not with members of the Hopkinsite connection, I reckon.'

Audouin carefully checked the smile that threatened to pull up the corners of his delicate mouth. He was beginning to understand now what manner of man he had got to deal with, and for Hiram's sake he was determined to be patient. Fancy such a lad living always exposed to the caprices of such a father!

'No,' he said gravely, 'not with the Hopkin-sites, but with the Congregationalists and others, where your boy would not be interfered with in his religious convictions.'

"Tain't entirely satisfactory,' the deacon continued. 'Consider my persition as one set in authority, as it were, in the Hopkinsite connection. Hiram ain't bin nowhar so far, 'ceptin' to common school, an' I dunno as I hev made up my mind ever to send him any-whar else. Boys loses a lot o' time over this here edoocation. But ef I was to, I guess I should send him to Bethabara Seminary. We hev a seminary of our own, sir, we of the Believin' Church, commonly known as the Hopkinsite connection, at Athens in Madison County, which we call Bethabara, because we surmise it's the on'y place in America whar the Gospel is taught on thorough-goin' Baptist principles. We air not only for immersion as agin sprinklin', mister, but also for scriptooral immersion in runnin' water as agin the lax modern practice of or'nary immersion in tanks or reservoyers. That's why we call our seminary Bethabara, Athens bein' sitooated on the Musk-rat river close above its junction with the Jordan; an' that's why, ef I was goin' to send Hiram any whar, I should send him whar he could hear the Gospel expounded accordin' to the expositions an' opinions of Franklin V. Hopkins, of Massachusetts, which air the correck ones.'

'This question will take a little time to thrash out,' Audouin answered with unruffled gravity. 'May I ask, deacon, whether you will courteously permit me to take a chair in your house and talk it over fully with you?'

'Why, certainly,' the deacon answered with a doubtful look that clearly belied his spoken words. 'Hiram, you jest go an' drive up the cows, sonny, an' mind you put up the fence behind you, jest the same as you find it.'

They went together into the dreary living-room, a room such as Audouin had seen in duplicate ten thousand times before, with a bare wooden floor, bare walls, a white pine table, a rocking-chair, a bunk, some cane seats, a stove, and a cheap lithograph of a vacant-looking gentleman in a bag-wig and loose collar, whom an inscription surmounted by a spread eagle declared largely to have been first in war, first in peace, and first in the hearts of his countrymen. (Lithographs of the sort are common in American farmhouses, and are understood to be posthumous libels on the intelligence and personal appearance of George Washington.) Audouin seated himself humbly on the bunk, and the deacon took his accustomed place in the rocking-chair, where he continued to sway himself violently to and fro during the whole interview.

Audouin began by pleading hard for education for Hiram, and suggesting, as delicately as he was able, that if pecuniary difficulties barred the way, they might perhaps be easily smoothed over. (As a matter of fact, he would willingly have given freely of that dirty paper, stamped with the treasury stamp, that they call money, to free such a lad as Hiram Winthrop from the curse of that material civilisation that they both so cordially detested.) He praised Hiram's intelligence and his wonderful talent for drawing: spoke of the wrongfulness of not allowing full play to his God-given faculties: and even condescended to point out that Hiram educated would probably make a much larger fortune (ugh! how he shuddered over it) than Hiram set to do the drudgery of a farm which he hated and always would hate. The deacon listened, half-wrathful; such open aiding and abetting of sinful rebelliousness and repining was almost too much for him; his only consolation was that Hiram wasn't along to listen to it all and drink in more unfilial sentiments from it.

But Audouin soon made one convert at least. Mrs. Winthrop, with her hard unlovable face, sat silently listening beside the stove, and picking over the potatoes for the spring planting. In her shrivelled mother's heart, she had always been proud of Hiram; proud even of his stubbornness and rebellion, which in some dim, half-unconscious fashion she vaguely knew to be really a higher, nobler sort of thing at bottom than the deacon's stern, unbending fidelity to the principles of Solomon and the Hopkinsite Confession. Somewhere away down in the dark unfathomed depths of Mehitabel Winthrop's stunted personality there lay a certain stifled, undeveloped, long-since-smothered germ of human romance and feminine sympathy which had blossomed out in Hiram into true love of art and of nature. Deadened as it was in her by the cruel toilsome life of Muddy Creek, with its endless round of dull monotonous labour, as well as by the crushing defeat experienced by all her girlish ideals in the awful reality of the married state with Zephaniah Winthrop, the deacon's wife still retained in some half-buried corner of her soul a little smouldering spark of the divine fire which enabled her in a doubtful half frightened fashion to sympathise with Hiram. It was very wrong and weak of her, she knew: father was right, and Hiram was a no-account, idle loiterer: but still, when he spoke up to father, to his very face, about his novel-reading, and his birds-nesting, and his drawing, Mrs. Winthrop was somehow aware of a sneaking admiration and pride in him which she never felt towards the deacon, even during his most effective and unctuous exhortation. And now, when she heard Audouin praising and speaking well of her boy for those very, things that the deacon despised and rejected, she felt that here was somebody else who could appreciate Hiram, and that perhaps, after all, her own instinct had not in the end entirely misled her.

'Zeph,' she said at last, it was many years since she had called him 'Zeph' habitually, instead of 'Father' or 'Deacon'—'Zeph, I think we might manage to send Hiram to college.'

The deacon started. Et tu, Brute! This was really almost too much for him. He began to wonder whether the universe was turned upside down, and all the powers that be were hereafter to be ranged on the side of rebelliousness and opposition. To say the truth, his godly horror was not altogether feigned. According to his lights, his dusky and feeble lights, the deacon wished and believed himself to be a good father. He held it his clear duty, as set forth in his reading of the prophets and apostles, to knock this idle nonsense out of Hiram, and train him up in the way he should go, to be a respectable corn-raising farmer and shining light of the Hopkinsite connection. These habits of hunting 'coons and making pictures of rattlesnakes, into which the boy had lapsed, were utterly abhorrent to the deacon's mind as idle, loitering, vagabond ways, deserving only of severe castigation His reading of English classics appeared as a crime only one degree less heinous than frequenting taverns, playing cards, or breaking the Sabbath. The boy was a bad boy, a hopelessly bad boy, given him as a thorn in the flesh to prevent spiritual boasting: on that hypothesis alone could the deacon account for such a son of perdition being born of such believing and on the whole (as poor worms go) extremely creditable parents.

And now, here was this fine-spoken, incomprehensible Boston critter, who had took that ramshackle place of Hitchcock's, and didn't even mean to farm it, here was this unaccountable phenomenon of a man positively interested in and pleased with Hiram, just because of these very self-same coon-hunting, snake-drawing, vagabond proclivities. The Deacon's self-love and selfrespect were deeply wounded. Audouin had already been talking with the boy: no doubt he had set him even more agin his own father than ever. No doubt he had told Hiram that there was something fine in his heathenish love for Injun tommy-hawks, in his Bohemian longings for intercourse with ungodly trappers (men to whom the Sabbath was absolutely indifferent), in his wicked yearning after Pickwick's Papers, and the Complete Dramatic Works of William Wakefield. The deacon couldn't bear to stultify himself after all, by sending Hiram to school at the request of this favourer of rebellion, this vile instigator of revolt against paternal authority, this Ahithophel who would lure on a foolish Absalom with guileful counsel to his final destruction.

'Wal, Het,' the Deacon said slowly, 'I dunno about it. We must take time to consider and to wrastle over it.'

But Audouin, now thoroughly in earnest, his sense of plot-interest vividly aroused, would hear of no delay, but that the question must be settled that very evening, he saw the deacon wouldn't entertain the idea of Hiram being sent somewhere to prepare for Yale or Harvard, where Audouin would have liked him to go: and so, with a diplomatic cleverness which the deacon, if he could have read his visitor's mind, would doubtless have characterised as devilish, he determined to shift his ground, and beg only that Hiram might be sent to Bethabara. In a year or two, he said to himself, the boy would be older and would have a mind of his own; and then it would be possible, he thought, to send him to some college where his intellectual and artistic nature might have freer development than at the Hopkinsite Seminary. Bit by bit, the Deacon gave way: he couldn't as a consistent church member and a father with the highest interests of his son at heart, refuse to let him go to Bethabara, when a mere stranger declared he saw in him signs of talent. He yielded ungraciously at last, and told Audouin he wouldn't stand in the way of the boy's receivin' a good edoocation, purvided allus it wa'n't contrary to the principles of Franklin P. Hopkins.

'Very well,' Audouin said with a sigh of relief. 'I'll write and inquire about the matter myself this very evening.'

'Address the Secatary,' Mr. Winthrop put in officially, 'Bethabara Seminary, Athens, N.Y.' Audouin made a note in his memorandum book of the incongruous address with a stifled sigh.

'Mother,' the deacon said, 'call in Hiram.' Mrs. Winthrop obeyed. Hiram, who had been loitering about the wood-shed in wonder at what this long interview could portend, slunk in timidly, and stood with his ragged hat in his hand beside the table.

'Hiram,' said the deacon, solemnly, with the voice and air of a judge publicly addressing a condemned criminal, 'that gentleman thar has been conversin' with mother an' me relatively to the desirability of sendin' you to an edoocational establishment, whar you may, p'raps, be cured from your present oncommonly idle and desultory proclivities. Though you hev allus bin, as I confess with shame, a most lazy lad, sonny, an' hev never done anything to develop your nat'ral talents in any way, that gentleman thar, who has received a college edoocation hisself at one of our leadin' American Universities, an' who is competent by trainin' an' experience to form an opinion upon the subjeck, believes that you dew possess nat'ral talents of which you ain't yet giv any open indication. 'Tain't for me to say whether you may hev inherited them or not: it is sufficient to point out that that thar gentleman considers you might, with industry and application, dew credit in time to an edoocational institoot. Such an institoot of our own denomination is Bethabara Seminary, located at Athens, New York. Thar you would receive instruction not at variance with the religious teachin' you hev enjoyed in your own residence an' from your own parents. An eminent Hopkinsite pastor is installed over that institoot as President; I allood to Elder Ezra W. Coffin, with whose commentary on the prophet Ezekiel you air already familiar. Mother an' me has decided, accordingly, that it will be for your good, both temporal and sperritooal we hope, to enter junior at Bethabara Seminary. That gentleman thar will make inquiries relatively to the time when you kin be received into the institootion.

We trust that when you he ventered upon this noo stage in your career, you will drop them habits of idleness an' insubordination for which it has been my dooty on a great many occasions to correck you severely.' Hiram stood there dazed and trembling, listening with blank amazement to the deacon's exhortation (the same as if it was conference), and only vaguely taking in the general idea that he was to be sent away shortly to some school or other somewhere. Andouin saw at a glance the lad's timid hesitation, and added kindly: 'Your father and mother think, Hiram, that it would be well to send you to Bethabara' (he suppressed his rising shudder), 'so that you may have opportunities of learning more about all the things in which you're already so much interested. You'll like it, my boy, I'm sure; and you'll get on there, I feel confident.'

The boy turned to him gratefully: 'That's so, I guess,' he answered, with his awkward country gratitude; 'I shall like it better'n this, anyhow.'

The deacon frowned, but said nothing.

And so, before a week was over, Hiram had said good-bye to his mother and Sam Churchill, and was driving over in the deacon's buggy to Muddy Creek deepo, ong rowt for Athens, Madison County.

CHAPTER VIII

WOOD AND STONE

Colin Churchill's first delight at the wood-carver's at Exeter was of the sort that a man rarely feels twice in a lifetime. It was the joy of first emancipation. Hitherto, Colin had been only a servant, and had looked forward to a life of service. Not despondently or gloomily, for Colin was a son of the people, and he accepted servitude as his natural guerdon, but blankly and without eagerness or repining. The children of the labouring class expect to walk through life in their humble way as through a set task, where a man may indeed sometimes meet with stray episodes of pleasure (especially that one human episode of love-making), but where for the most part he will come across nothing whatsoever save interminable rules and regulations. Now, however, Colin felt himself free and happy: he had got a trade and a career before him, and a trade and a career into which he could throw himself with his utmost ardour. For the first time in his life Colin began dimly to feel that he too had something in him. How could he possibly have got up an enthusiasm about the vicar's boots, or about the proper way to deliver letters on a silver salver? But when it came to carving roses and plums out of solid mahogany or walnut, why, that of course was a very different sort of matter.

Even at Wootton Mandeville, the boy had somehow suspected, in his vague inarticulate fashion (for the English agricultural class has no tongue in which to express itself), that he too had artistic taste and power. When he heard the vicar talking to his friends about paintings or engravings, he recognised that he could understand and appreciate all that the vicar said; nay, more: on two or three occasions he had even boldly ventured to conceive that he saw certain things in certain pictures which the vicar, in his cold, dry, formal fashion, with his coldly critical folding eyeglass, could never have dreamt of or imagined. In his heart of hearts, even then, the boy somehow half-knew that the vicar saw what the vicar was capable of seeing in each work, but that he, Colin Churchill the pageboy, penetrated into the very inmost feeling and meaning of the original artist. So much, in his inarticulate way, the boy had sometimes surprised himself by dimly fancying; but as he had no language in which to speak such things, even to himself, and only slowly learnt that language afterwards, he didn't formulate his ideas in his own head for a single minute, allowing them merely to rest there in the inchoate form of shapeless feeling.

Now, at Exeter, however, all this was quite altered. In the aisles of the great cathedral, looking up at the many-coloured saints in the windows, and listening to the long notes of the booming organ, Colin Churchill's soul awoke and knew itself. The gift that was in him was not one to be used for himself alone, a mere knack of painting pictures to decorate the bare walls of his bedroom, or of making clay images for little Minna to stick upon the fisherman's wooden mantelshelf: it was a talent admired and recognised of other people, and to be employed for the noble and useful purposes of carving pine-apple posts for walnut bedsteads or conventional scrolls for fashionable chimneypieces. To such great heights did emancipated Colin Churchill now aspire. Even his master allowed him to see that he thought well of him. The boy was given tools to work with, and instructed in the use of them; and he learnt how to employ them so fast that the master openly expressed his surprise and satisfaction. In a very few weeks Colin was fairly through the first stage of learning, and was set to produce bits of scroll work from his own design, for a wainscoted room in the house of a resident canon.

For seven months Colin went on at his wood-carving with unalloyed delight, and wrote every week to tell Minna how much he liked the work, and what beautiful wooden things he would now be able to make her. But at the end of those seven months, as luck would have it (whether good luck or ill luck the future must say), Colin chanced to fall in one day with a strange companion. One afternoon a heavy-looking Italian workman dropped casually into the workshop where Colin Churchill was busy carving. The boy was cutting the leaves of a honeysuckle spray from life for a long moulding. The Italian watched him closely for a while, and then he said in his liquid English: 'Zat is good. You can carve, mai boy. You must come and see me at mai place. I wawrk for Smeez and Whatgood.'

Colin turned round, blushing with pleasure, and looked at the Italian. He couldn't tell why, but somehow in his heart instinctively, he felt more proud of that workman's simple expression of satisfaction at his work than he had felt even when the vicar told him, in his stiff, condescending, depreciatory manner, that there was 'some merit in the bas-relief and drawings.' Smith and

Whatgood were stonecutters in the town, who did a large trade in tombstones and 'monumental statuary.' No doubt the Italian was one of their artistic hands, and Colin took his praise with a flush of sympathetic pleasure. It was handicraftsman speaking critically and appreciatively of handicraftsman.

'What's your name, sir?' he asked the man, politely.

'You could not pronounce it,' answered the Italian, smiling and showing his two fine rows of pure white teeth: 'Giuseppe Cicolari. You cannot pronounce it.'

'Giuseppe Cicolari,' the boy repeated slowly, with the precise intonation the Italian had given it, for he had the gift of vocal imitation, like all men of Celtic blood (and the Dorsetshire peasant is mainly Celtic). 'Giuseppe Cicolari! a pretty name. Da you carve figures for Smith and Whatgood?'

'I am zair sculptor,' the Italian replied, proudly. 'I carve for zem. I carve ze afflicted widow, in ze classical costume, who bends under ze weeping willow above ze oorn containing ze ashes of her decease husband. You have seen ze afflicted widow? Ha, I carve her. She is expensive. And I carve ze basso-rilievo of Hope, gazing toward ze sky, in expectation of ze glorious resurrection. I carve also busts; I carve ornamental figures. Come and see me. You are a good workman. I will show you mai carvings.'

Colin liked the Italian at first sight: there was a pride in his calling about him which he hadn't yet seen in English workmen, a certain consciousness of artistic worth that pleased and interested him. So the next Saturday evening, when they left off work early, he went round to see Cicolari. The Italian smiled again warmly, as soon as he saw the boy coming. 'So you have come,' he said, in his slow English. 'Zat is well. If you will be artist, you must watch ozzer artist. Ze art does not come of himself, it is learnt.' And he took Colin round to see his works of statuary.

There was one little statuette among the others, a small figure of Bacchus, ordered from the clay by a Plymouth shipowner, that pleased Colin's fancy especially. It wasn't remotely like the Thorwaldsen at Wootton; that he felt intuitively; it was a mere clever, laughing, merry figure, executed with some native facility, but with very little real delicacy or depth of feeling. Still, Colin liked it, and singled it out at once amongst all the mass of afflicted widows and weeping children as a real genuine living human figure. The Italian was charmed at his selection. 'Ah, yes,' he said; 'zat is good. You have choosed right. Zat is ze best of ze collection. I wawrk at zat from life. It is from ze model.' And he showed all his teeth again in his satisfaction.

Colin took a little of Cicolari's moist clay up in his hand and began roughly moulding it into the general shape of the little Bacchus. He did it almost without thinking of what he was doing, and talking all the time, or listening to the Italian's constant babble; and Cicolari, with a little disdainful smile playing round the corners of his full lips, made no outward comment, but only waited, with a complacent sense of superiority, to see what the English boy would make of his Bacchus. Colin worked away at the familiar clay, and seemed to delight in the sudden return to that plastic and responsive material. For the first time since he had been at Begg's wood-carving works, it sudddenly struck him that clay was an infinitely finer and more manageable medium than that solid, soulless, intractable wood. Soon, he threw himself unconsciously into the task of moulding, and worked away silently, listening to Cicolari's brief curt criticisms of men and things, for hour after hour. In the delight of finding himself once more expending his energies upon his proper material (for who can doubt that Colin Churchill was a born sculptor?) he forgot the time, nay, he forgot time and space both, and saw and felt nothing on earth but the artistic joy of beautiful workmanship. Cicolari stood by gossiping, but said never a word about the boy's Bacchus. At first, indeed (though he had admired

Colin's wood-work), he expected to see a grotesque failure. Next, as the work grew slowly under the boy's hands, he made up his mind that he would produce a mere stiff, lifeless, wooden copy. But by-and-by, as Colin added touch after touch with his quick deft fingers, the Italian's contempt passed into surprise, and his surprise into wonder and admiration. At last, when the boy had finished his rough sketch of the head to his own satisfaction, Cicolari gasped a little, open-mouthed, and then said slowly: 'You have wawrked in ze clay before, mai friend?'

Colin nodded. 'Yes,' he said, 'just to amuse myself, don't ee see? Only just copyin the figures at the vicarage.'

The Italian put his head on one side, and then on another, and looked critically at the copy of the Bacchus. Of course it was only a raw adumbration, as yet, of the head and bust, but he saw quite enough to know at a glance that it was the work of a born sculptor. The vicar had half guessed as much in his dilettante hesitating way; but the workman, who knew what modelling was, saw it indubitably at once in that moist Bacchus. 'Mai friend,' he said decisively, through his closed teeth, 'you must not stop at ze wood-carving. You must go to Rome and be a sculptor. Yes. To Rome. To Rome. You must go to Rome and be a sculptor.'

The man said it with just a tinge of jealousy in his tone, for he saw that Colin Churchill could not only copy but could also improve upon his Bacchus. Still, he said it so heartily and earnestly, that Colin, now well awakened from his absorbing pursuit, laughed a boyish laugh of mingled amusement and exultation. 'To Rome!' he cried gaily. 'To Rome! Why, Mr. Cicolari, that's where all the pictures are, by Raffael and Michael Angelo and them that I used to see at the vicarage. Rome! why isn't that the capital of Italy?' For he put together naively the two facts about Rome which he had yet gathered: the one from the vicar's study, and the other from the meagre little geography book in use at the Wootton national school.

'Ze capital of Italy!' cried the Italian contemptuously. 'Yes, mai friend, it is ze capital of Italy. And it is somesing more zan zat. I tell you, it is ze capital of art.'

Colin Churchill was old enough now to understand the meaning of those words; and from that day onward, he never ceased to remember that the goal of all his final endeavours must be to reach Rome, the capital of art, and then learn to be a sculptor.

CHAPTER IX

CONSPIRACY

After that, Colin went many days and evenings to see Cicolari: and the more he talked with him and the more he watched him, the more dissatisfied did the boy get with the intractability of wood, and the more enamoured did he become of the absolute plasticity of clay and marble. How could he ever have been such a fool, he thought to himself, after having once known what he could do with the kneaded mud of Wootton lake, as to consent, nay, to consent gladly, to work in stupid, hard, irresponsive walnut, instead of in his own familiar, plastic, all potential material? Why, wood, do what you would to it, was wood still: clay, and after clay marble, would answer immediately to every mood and fancy and idea of the restless changeable human personality. The fact was the ten or twelve months Colin Churchill had spent at Exeter had made a vast difference to his unfolding intellect. He was going to school now, to the university of native art; he was learning himself and his own powers; learning to pit his own views and opinions against those of other and less artistic workmen. Every day, though he couldn't have told you so himself, the boy was beginning to understand more and more clearly that while the other artificers he saw around him had decent training, he himself had instinctive genius. He ought to have employed that genius upon marble, and now he was throwing it away upon mere wood. When one of the canons called in one day patronisingly to praise his wooden roses, he could scarcely even be civil to the good man: praising his wooden roses, indeed, when he saw that fellow Cicolari engaged in modelling from the life a smiling Bacchus! It was all too atrocious!

'Mai friend,' Cicolari said to him one day, as he was moulding a bit of clay in his new acquaintance's room, into the counterfeit presentment of Cicolari's own bust, 'you should not stop at ze wood wawrk. You have no freedom in ze wood, no liberty, no motion. It is all flat, stupid, ungraceful. You are fit for better sings. Leave ze wood and come, here and wawrk wiz me.'

Colin sighed deeply. 'I wish I could, Mr. Cicolari,' he said eagerly. 'I was delighted with the wood at first, and now I'm disgusted at 'un. But I can't leave 'un till I'm twenty-one, because I'm bound apprentice to it, and I've got to go on with the thing now whether I like 'un or not.'

Cicolari made a wry face, expressive of a very nasty taste, and went through a little pantomime of shrugs and open hand-lifting, which did duty instead of several vigorous sentences in the Italian language. Colin readily translated the pantomime as meaning in English: 'If I were you, I wouldn't trouble myself about that for a moment.'

'But I can't help it,' Colin answered in his own spoken tongue; 'I'm obliged to go on whether I choose to or not.'

Cicolari screwed himself up tightly, and held his hands, palms outward, on a level with his ears, in the most suggestive fashion. 'England is a big country,' he observed enigmatically.

Colin's face flushed at the vague hint, but he said nothing.

'You see,' Cicolari went on quickly, 'you are a boy yet. When you come to Exeter, you are still a child. You come from your own village, your country, and you know nossing of ze wawrld. Zis master and ze priest of your village between zem, zey bind you down and make you sign a paper, indenture you call it, and promise to wawrk for zem zese six years. It is ridiculous. When you come here, you do not know your own mind: you do not understand how it differs, wood and marble. Now you are older: you understand zat; it is absurd zat you muss stand by ze agreement.'

Cohn listened and took in the words eagerly. 'But what can I do, Mr. Cicolari?' he asked in suspense. 'Where can I go to?' 'England is a big country,' the Italian repeated, with yet another speaking pantomime. 'Zere are plenty railways in England. Zere is wawrk for clever lads in London. I have friends zere who carve in marble. Why should you not go zere?''

'Run away?' Cohn said, interrogatively.

'Run away, if you call it zat,' Cicolari replied, bowing with his curved hands in front of his breast, apologetically. 'What does it matter, ze name? Run away if zey will not let you go. I care not what you call it. Zey try to keep you unjustly; you try to get away from zem. Zat is all.'

'But I've got no money to go with,' Colin cried, faltering

'Zen get some,' Cicolari answered with a shrug.

Colin thought a good deal about that suggestion afterwards, and the more he thought about it, the more did it seem to him just and proper. A week or two later, little Minna came over to Exeter for a trip, nominally to do a few errands of household shopping, but really of course to see Colin; and to her the boy confided this difficult case of conscience. Was the signature obtained from him when he first came to Exeter binding on him now that he knew more fully his own powers, and rights, and capabilities?

Colin was by this time a handsome lad of sixteen, while little black-eyed gipsy-faced Minna, though two years younger than him, was already budding out into a pretty woman, as such dark types among the labouring classes are apt to do with almost Oriental precocity.

'What should you do, Colin?' she repeated warmly, as the boy propounded his question in casuistry to her for her candid solution. 'Why, just you go and do what Mr. Chickaleary tells you, won't 'ee, sure?'

'But would it be right, Minna?' Colin asked. 'You know I signed the agreement with them.'

'What's the odds of that, stupid?' Minna answered composedly. 'That were a year ago an' more, weren't it? You weren't no more nor a boy then, Lord bless 'ee.'

'A year older nor you are now, Minna,' Colin objected.

'Ah, but you didn't know nothing about this sculpturin' then, you see, Colin. They tooked advantage of you, that's what they did. They hadn't ought to have done it.'

'But I say, Minna, why shouldn't I wait till I'm twenty-one, an' then take up the marble business, eh?'

'What rubbish the boy do talk,' Minna cried, imperiously. 'Twenty-one indeed! Talk about twenty-one! Why, by that time you'd 'a' got fixed in the wood-carving, and couldn't change your trade for marble or nothin'. If you're goin' to change, you must do it quickly.'

'I hate the wood-carving,' Colin said, gloomily.

'Then run away from it and be done wi' it.'

'Run away from it! Oh, Minna, do you know that they could catch me and put me in prison?'

'I'd go to prison an' laugh at 'em, sooner nor I'd be bound for all those years against my will,' Minna answered firmly. 'Leastways I would if I was a man, Colin.'

That last touch was the straw that broke the camel's back with poor Colin. 'I'll go,' he cried; 'but where on earth can I go to? It's no use goin' back to Wootton. Vicar'd help 'em to put me in prison.'

'I'd like to see 'em,' Minna answered, with her little eyes flashing. 'But why can't you go to London like Mr. Chickaleary told you?' 'Cicolari, Minna,' Colin said, correcting her as gravely and distinctly as the vicar had corrected Miss Eva. 'The Italians call it Cicolari. It's as well to be right whenever we can, ain't it? Well, I can't go to London, because I've got no money to go with. I don't know as I could get any work when I got there; but I know I can't get there without any money; so that settles it.'

Minna rose from the seat in the Northernhay where they were spending Colin's dinner-hour together and walked slowly up and down for a minute or two without speaking. Then she said, with a little hesitation, 'Colin!'

'Well, Minna.'

'I could lend 'ee, lend you, nine shillin'.' 'Nine shillings, Minna! Why, where on earth did you get 'em from?'

'Saved 'em,' Minna answered laconically. 'Fish father give me. In savin's bank.'

'What for, Minna?'

Minna hesitated again, still more markedly. Though she was only fourteen, there was a good deal of the woman in her already. 'Because,' she said at last timidly,' 'I thought it was best to begin savin' up all my money now, in case, in case I should ever want to furnish house if I was to get married.'

Country boy as he was, and child as she was, Colin felt instinctively that it wouldn't be right of him to ask her anything further about the money. 'But, Minna,' he said, colouring a little, 'even if I was to borrow it all from you, all your nine shillings, it wouldn't be enough to take me to London.'

Minna had a brilliant idea. 'Wait for a 'scursion,' she said simply.

Colin looked at her with admiring eyes. 'Well, Minna,' he cried enthusiastically, 'you are a bright one, and no mistake. That's a good idea, that is. I should never have thought of that. I could carve you, Minna, so that a stranger anywhere'd know who it was the minute he set eyes on it; but I should never have thought of that, I can tell you.' Minna smiled and nodded, the dimple in her brown cheek growing deeper, and the light in her bright eye merrier than ever. What a vivacious, expressive little face it was, really! 'I'll tell you what I'd do,' Minna said, with her sharp determination as if she were fifty. 'I'd go first and ask Mr. What's-his-name to let me off the rest of my 'prenticeship. I'd tell him I didn't like wood, an' I wanted to go an' make statues. Then if he said to me: "You go on with the wood-carvin' an' don't bother me," I'd say: "No, I don't do another stroke for you." Then if he hit me, I'd leave off, I would, an' refuse to work another turn till he was tired of it. But if he hardened his heart then, an' wouldn't let 'ee go still, I'd wait till there was a 'scursion, I would, and then I'd run away to Mr. Chick-o-lah-ree's friends in London. That's what I'd do if I was you, Colin.'

'I will, Minna,' Colin faltered out in reply; 'I will.'

'Do 'ee, Colin,' Minna cried eagerly, catching his arm. 'Do 'ee, Colin, and I'll send 'ee the money. Oh, Colin, I know if you'd only get 'prenticed to the sculpturin', you'd grow to be as grand a man, as grand as parson.'

'Minna,' Colin said, taking her hand in his as if it were a lady's, 'thank you very much for the money, an' if I have to work my fingers to the bone for it, I'll send it back to 'ee.'

'Don't 'ee do that, Colin, oh don't 'ee do that,' Minna cried eagerly. 'I'd a great deal rather for you to keep it.'

When Colin told Cicolari of this episode (suppressing so much of it as he thought proper), the Italian laughed and showed all his teeth, and remarked with a smile that Colin was very young yet. But he promised staunchly to keep the boy's secret, and to give him good introductions to his former employer in London.

The die was cast now, and Colin Churchill resolutely determined in his own mind that he would abide by it. So a few days later he screwed up courage towards evening to go to Mr. Begg, his master, and for form's sake, at least, ask to be let off the remainder of his apprenticeship. 'At any rate,' he thought to himself, 'I won't try running away till I've tried in a straightforward way to get him to cancel the indentures I signed when I didn't really know what I was signing.'

Mr. Begg, that eminently respectable Philistine cabinet-maker, opened his eyes in blank astonishment when he actually heard with his two waking ears this extraordinary and unprecedented request. 'Let you off the rest of your time, Churchill!' he cried, incredulously. 'Was that what you said, boy? Let—you—off—the rest—of—your—time?'

'Yes,' Colin answered, with almost dogged firmness, 'I said that.'

'And why, Churchill?' Mr. Begg asked again, lost in amazement. 'And why?'

'Because, sir, I don't like wood-carving, and I feel I could do a great deal better at marble.'

Mr. Begg gazed up at him (he was a little man and Colin was tall) in utter surprise and hesitation. 'You're not mad, are you, Churchill?' he inquired cautiously. 'You're not mad, are you?'

'No, sir,' Colin replied stoutly; 'but I think I must have been when I signed them indentures.'

The cabinet-maker went into his little office, called Colin in, and then sat down in a dazed manner to hear this strange thing out to its final termination. Colin burst forth, then, with his impassioned pleading, astonishing himself by the flood of native eloquence with which he entreated Mr. Begg to release him from that horrid wood-carving, and let him follow his natural calling as a sculptor in clay and marble. He didn't know what he was doing when he signed the indentures; he had only just come fresh from his life as a servant. Now he knew he had the makings of a sculptor in him, and a sculptor alone he wished to be. Mr. Begg regarded him askance all the time, as a man might regard a stray dog of doubtful sanity, but said never a single word, for good or for evil. When Colin had worn himself out with argument and exhortation, the cabinet-maker rose from his high seat, unlocked his desk mechanically, and took out of it his copy of Colin's indentures. He read them all through carefully to himself, and then he laid them down with the puzzled air of one who meets for the first time in his life with some inexplicable practical enigma. 'This is very strange, Churchill,' he muttered, coolly, half to himself; 'this is really most remarkable. There's no mistake or flaw of any sort in those indentures; nothing on earth to invalidate 'em or throw doubt upon them in any way. Your signature's there as clear as daylight. I can't understand it. You've always been a good workman, the best apprentice, take you all round, I've ever 'ad 'ere; and Canon Melville, he's praised your carving most uncommonly, and so they all do. A good, honest-working, industrious lad I've always found you, one time with another; not such a great eater neither; and I was very well satisfied altogether with you till this very evening. And now you come and say you want to cancel your indentures, and go to the stone-cutting! Never heard anything so remarkable in all my life! Why, you're worth more than a hundred pounds to me! I couldn't let you go, not if you was to pay me for it.'

Poor Colin! how he wished at that moment that he had been idle, careless, voracious and good-for-nothing! His very virtues, it seemed, were turning against him. He had thrown himself so heartily into the wood-carving at first that his master had found him worth half a dozen common apprentices. He fumbled in his pocket nervously at little Minna's poor nine shillings which he had changed that very morning from her post-office order.

'Can't you understand, Mr. Begg,' he said at last, despairingly, 'that a fellow may change his mind? He may feel he can do one thing a great deal better than another, and he may have a longing to do that thing and nothing else, because he loves it?'

Mr. Begg gazed at him stolidly. 'Cabinetmaking's a very good trade,' he said in his dull methodical bourgeois tone; 'and so, no doubt,'s stone-cutting. But these indentures 'ere bind you down to the cabinet-making, Churchill, and not to the sculpture business.

There's your signature to 'em; and you've got to stick to it. So that's the long and the short of it.'

'But it's not the end of it,' Colin answered in his most stubborn voice (and your Dorsetshire man can be very stubborn indeed when he pleases): 'if you don't let me off my indentures as I ask you, you'll have to put up in future with what you can get out of me.'

Next morning, when it was time to begin work, Colin marched as usual into the workshop, and took up a gouge as if to continue carving the panel on which he was engaged. But instead of doing anything to the purpose, he merely kept on chipping off small splinters of wood in an aimless fashion for half an hour. After a time, Mr. Begg observed him, and came up to see what he was doing, but said nothing. All through the day Cohn went on in the same manner, and from time to time Mr. Begg looked in and found the work no further advanced than it had been last evening; still, he said nothing. When the time came to shut up the shop, Mr. Begg looked at him sternly, but only uttered a single sentence: 'We shall have the law of you, Churchill; we shall have the law of you.'

Colin stared him back stolidly and answered never a word.

For a whole week, this passive duel between the man and boy went on, and towards the end of that time Mr. Begg began to grow decidedly violent. He shook Cohn fiercely, he boxed his ears, he even hit him once or twice across the head with his wooden ruler; but Colin was absolutely immovable. To all that Mr. Begg said the boy returned only one answer: 'I mean to be a sculptor, not a wood-carver.' Mr. Begg had never seen anything like it.

'The obstinacy and the temper of that boy Churchill,' he said to his brother-tradesmen, 'is really something altogether incredulous.' (It may be acutely conjectured that he really meant to say 'incredible.')

Sunday came at last, and on Sundays Cohn went round to visit Cicolari. The Italian listened sympathetically to the boy's story, and then he said, 'I have an idea of mai own, mai friend. Let us both go to London together. I have saved some money; I want to set up on mai own account as a sculptor. You will go wiz me. I have quarrelled wiz Smeez. We will start tomorrow morning. I will pay you wages, good wages, and you will wawrk for me, and be mai assistant.'

'But I've only got nine shillings,' Colin answered.

'I will lend you the rest,' Cicolari said.

Cohn closed with the offer forthwith, and went home to Mr. Begg's trembling with excitement.

Early next morning, he tied up his clothes in his handkerchief, crept downstairs noiselessly and let himself out by the backdoor. Then he ran without stopping all the way to the St. David's station, and found Cicolari waiting for him in the booking office. As the engine steamed out of the station, Colin felt that he was leaving slavery and wood-carving behind him for ever, and was fairly on his way to London, Rome, and a career as a sculptor.

Mr. Begg, when he found that Colin was really gone, didn't for a moment attempt to follow him. It was no use, he said, to throw good money after bad: the boy had made up his mind not to work at woodcarving; he was as stubborn as a mule; and nothing on earth would ever make him again into a good apprentice. So, though he felt perfectly sure that that nasty foreigner fellow had enticed away the boy for his own purposes, he wouldn't attempt to bring him back or take the trouble to have him punished. After all, he reflected to himself philosophically, as things had lately turned out it was a good riddance of bad rubbish. Besides, it would be rather an awkward thing to come out before the magistrate that he had hit the boy more than once across the head with a wooden ruler.

Two days later, it was known in Wootton Mandeville that that lad o' Churchill's had gone and broke his indentures and runned away from Exeter along of a furrener chap o' the name of Chickaleary. The vicar received the news with the placid contentment of a magnanimous man, who has done his duty and has nothing to reproach himself with, but who always told you so from the very beginning. 'I quite expected it, Eva,' he said loftily; 'I fully expected it. Those Churchills were always a bad radical lot, and this boy's just about the very worst among them. When I discovered his slight taste for carving, I feared it was hardly right to encourage the lad in ideas above his station: but I was determined to give him a chance, and now this is how he goes and repays us. I did my best for him: very respectable man, Begg, and well recommended by Canon Harbottle.

But the boy has no perseverance, no application, no stability. Put him to one thing, and he runs away at once and tries to do another. Quite what I expected, quite what I expected.'

'Perhaps,' Eva ventured to say suggestively, 'if you'd sent him to a sculptor's in London at first, uncle, he might have been perfectly ready to stop there. But you see his natural taste was for sculpture, not for woodcarving; and I'm not altogether surprised myself to hear he should have left Exeter.'

The vicar put up his double eyeglass and surveyed Eva from head to foot, as though she were some wild animal, with a stare of mingled amazement and incredulity. 'Well,' he said slowly, opening the door to dress for dinner. 'Upon my word! What the young people of this generation are coming to is really more than I can answer for.'

CHAPTER X

MINNA IMPROVES HERSELF

Five years is a long slice out of a young man's life, but the five years that Colin Churchill spent with Cicolari in London were of a sort that he need never have regretted; for though the work he learnt to do in the Italian's little shop and studio in the Maryle-bone Road was mainly self-taught, he found Cicolari always sympathetic and anxious to help him, and he had such opportunities of study and improvement at the British Museum, and the South Kensington, and the great houses in the suburban counties, as he could never have obtained in the artless wilds of his native west country. It was a grand day for Colin, the day when he first entered the smoky galleries in Great Russell Street and feasted his eyes on those magnificent Hellenic torsos, carved by the vivifying chisel of Pheidias himself. Cicolari was an easy master: he had an Italian's love of art for art's sake and he was proud of 'mai Englishman,' as he used to call him; the boy whom he had himself discovered in the midst of a profoundly inartistic race, and released from the petty drudgery of an uncongenial vulgar calling. He felt a genuine interest in Colin's success; so he allowed the boy as much time as possible for visiting the places where he could see the finest works of art in England, and helped him to see those which are usually locked up in rich men's tasteless houses from the eyes of all who would most appreciate them.

Colin's own taste and love for art, too, were daily developing. He saw all that he could see, and he read about all that he couldn't see, spending every penny of his spare money (after he had repaid poor little Minna's nine shillings) on books about sculpture and painting; and making frequent visits to the reading-room and galleries at the great Museum. Now and then, too, when the trade in mourning widows was slack, when busts were flat and statuettes far from lively, Cicolari would run down into the country with him, and explore the artistic wonders of the big houses. At Deepdene they could look at Thorwaldsen's Jason and Canova's Venus: at Knole they gazed upon Vandycks, and Rey-nolds's, and Constables, and Gainsboroughs; in London itself they had leave to visit the priceless art collections at Stafford House, and half a dozen other great private galleries. So Colin Churchill's mind expanded rapidly, in the midst of the atmosphere it should naturally have breathed. Not books alone, but the mighty works of the mightiest workers, were the documents from which he spelt out slowly his own artistic education. Later on, men who met Colin Churchill at Rome, men who had gone through the regular dull classical round of our universities, were astonished to find that the Dorsetshire peasant-sculptor, of whom they had heard so much, was a widely cultivated and well-read man. They expected to see an inspired boor wielding a sculptor's mallet in a rude labourer's hand: they were surprised to meet a handsome young man, of delicate features and finely-stored mind, who talked about Here and Aphrodite, and the nymphs who came to visit the bound Prometheus, as if he had known them personally and intimately all his life long in their own remote Hellenic dwelling places.

And indeed, though the university where Colin Churchill took his degree with honours was not one presided over by doctors in red hoods and proctors in velvet sleeves, one may well doubt whether he did not penetrate quite as deeply, after all, into the inmost recesses of the great Hellenic genius as most men who have learnt to write iambic trimeters from well-trained composition masters, with the most careful avoidance of that ugly long syllable before the cretic in the two last feet, to which the painstaking scholar attaches so much undue importance. Do you think, my good Mr. Dean, or excellent Senior Censor, that a man cannot learn just as much about the Athens of Pericles from the Elgin Marbles as from a classical dictionary or a dog-eared Thucydides? Do you suppose that to have worked up the first six Iliads with a Liddell and Scott brings you in the end so very much nearer the heart and soul of the primitive Achæans than to have studied with loving care the vases in the British Museum, or even to have followed with a sculptor's eye the exquisite imaginings of divine John Flaxman?

Why, where do you suppose Flaxman himself got his Homer from, except from the very same source as poor, self-taught Colin Churchill, Mr. Alexander Pope's correctly colourless and ingenious travesty? Do you really believe there is no understanding the many-sided essentially artistic Greek idiosyncrasy except through the medium of the twenty-four written signs from alpha to omega? Colin Churchill didn't believe so, at least: and who that has seen his Alcestis, or his Agamemnon and Clytemnestra, or his Death of Antigone, can fail to admit that they are in very truth the direct offshoots of the Hellas of Sophocles, and Æschylus, and Pheidias?

All Cohn Churchill's reading was, in its way, sculpturesque. Of poetry, he loved Milton better than Shakespeare. Shakespeare is the painter's poet, Milton the sculptor's; and he wearied out his soul because he could never rise in clay to his own evasive mental image of the Miltonic Satan. He read Shelley, too, most Greek of Englishmen, and took more than one idea for future statues from those statuesque tragedies and poems. But best of all he loved Æschylus, whom he couldn't read in the original, to be sure, but whom he followed through half a dozen translations till he had read himself into the very inmost spirit of the Agamemnon and the Persæ and the Prometheus. The man who has fed his fancy on Æschylus, Milton, and Shelley, and his eyes on Michael Angelo, Thorwaldsen, and Flaxman, is not, after all, wholly wanting in the elements of the highest and purest culture.

Two years after Colin went to live at the little workshop in the Marylebone Road, another person came to swell the population of the great metropolis by a unit, and to correspondingly diminish the dwindling account at Wootton Mandeville. Minna Wroe was now sixteen, and for a year past she had been living out at service as kitchen-maid at the village doctor's. But Minna was an ambitious small body, and had a soul above dish-cloths. So she kept the precious nine shillings that Colin had returned to her well hoarded in her own little purse, and added to them from time to time whatever sums she could manage to save from her small wages, for wages are low in Dorsetshire, and white caps cost money both for the buying and washing, you may be certain. When her sixteenth birthday had fairly come and gone Minna gave notice to her mistress, and at the end of her month started off to London, like so many other young people of both sexes, to seek her fortune.

'Dear Colin,' she wrote to him a day or two before from the doctor's at Wootton, 'I am coming up to London to look out for a situation on Monday next, and I should be very glad if you could meet me at Paddinton Station at 6.30. I have not got a situation but I hope soon to get one there is lots to be had in London and has you are their I should like to be in London. Please dear Cohn come to meet me as I am going to Mrs. Woods of Wootton till I get a situation to lodge with love from all so no more at present from your old Friend, Minna.'

Colin took the letter from the postman, as he was working at the clay of a little bas-relief for a mural tablet, and read it over twice to himself with very mingled and uncertain feelings. On the first reading he felt only a glow of pleasure to think that little Minna, his old playmate, would now be within easy reach of him. Cohn had never considered himself exactly in love with Minna (he was only eighteen), and he had even indulged (since the sad truth must out) in a passing flirtation with the young lady at the open greengrocer's shop just round the corner; but he was very fond of Minna for all that, and in an indefinite way he had always felt as if she really belonged to him far more than anybody else did. So his first feeling was one of unmixed pleasure at the prospect of having her to live so near him. On the second reading, however, it did strike even Colin, who was only just beginning his own self-education in literary matters, that the letter might have been better spelt and worded and punctuated. He had been rising-in the social scale so gradually that, for the first time in his life, he then felt as if Minna were just one single level below him, intellectually and educationally.

He pocketed the letter with a slight sigh, and went on moulding the drapery of St. Mary Magdalene, after the design from a fresco in St. John Port Lateran. Would Minna care at all about Flaxman, he wondered to himself mutely; would she interest herself in that admirable replica by Bartolini; would she understand his torso of Theseus, or his copy in clay of the Florentine Boar, or his rough sketch for a Cephalus and Aurora? Or would she be merely a London housemaid, just like all the girls he saw of a morning cleaning the front door-steps in Harley Street, and stopping to bandy vulgar chaff with the postman, and the newspaper boy, and the young policeman? Two years had made a great deal of difference, no doubt, to both of them; and Cohn wondered vaguely in his own soul what Minna would think of him now, and what he would think of Minna.

On Monday, he was down at the station true to time, and waiting for the arrival of the 6.30 from Dorchester. As it drew up at the platform, he moved quickly along the third-class carriages, on the look-out for anybody who might answer to the memory of his little Minna. Presently he saw her jump lightly, as of old, from the carriage, a mignonne little figure, with a dark, round, merry face, and piercing black eyes as bright as diamonds. He ran up to greet her with boyish awkwardness and bashful timidity. 'Why, Minna,' he cried, 'you've grown into such a woman that I'm afraid to kiss you; but I'm very glad indeed to see you.'

Minna drew herself up so as to look as tall as possible, and answered with dignity:

'I should hope, Colin, you wouldn't want to kiss me in any case here in the station. It was very kind of you to come and meet me.'

Colin observed at once that she spoke with a good accent, and that her manner was, if anything, decidedly less embarrassed than his own. Indeed, as a rule, the young men of the working classes, no matter how much intellectual or artistic power they may possess, are far more shy, gauche, and awkward than the young women of the same class, who usually show instinctively a great deal of natural refinement of manner. He was immediately not a little reassured as to Minna's present attainments.

'I want to go to Mrs. Wood's,' Minna said, as calmly as if she had been accustomed to Paddington Station all her lifetime; 'and I've got two boxes; how ought I to get there?'

'Where is Mrs. Wood's?' Colin asked.

'At Dean Street, Marylebone.'

'Why, that's quite close to our place,' Colin cried. 'Are they big boxes? I could carry 'em, maybe.'

'No, you couldn't carry them, Colin. Why, what nonsense. It wouldn't be respectable.'

Colin laughed. 'I should have done it at Wootton, anyhow, Minna,' he answered; 'and a working stone-cutter needn't be ashamed of anything in the way of work, surely.'

'But a sculptor's got to keep up his position,' Minna put in firmly.

Colin smiled again. Already he had a nascent idea in his own head that even a sculptor could not bemean himself greatly by carrying a wooden box through the streets of London for a lady, he was getting to believe in the dignity of labour, but he didn't insist upon this point with Minna; for, young as he was, he had a notion even then that the gospel for men isn't always at the same time the gospel for women. Even a good woman would feel much less compunction against many serious crimes than against trundling a wheelbarrow full of clean clothes up Begent Street of an afternoon in the height of the season.

So Cohn was for calling a porter with a truck; but even that modified measure of conveyance did not wholly suit Minna's aristocratic fancy. 'Are they things cabs, Cohn?' she asked quietly.

'Those things are,' Cohn answered with a significant emphasis. Minna blushed a trifle.

'Oh, those things,' she repeated slowly; 'then I'll have one.' And in two minutes more, Cohn, for the first time in his life, found himself actually driving along the public streets in the inside of a hansom. Why, you imperious, extravagant little Minna, where on earth are you going to find money for such expenses as these in our toilsome, under-paid, workday London?

When they reached Mrs. Wood's door, Cohn, feeling that he must rise to the situation, pulled out his purse to pay for the hansom, but Minna waved him aside with a dignified air of authority. 'No no,' she said, 'that won't do; take my purse, Cohn. I don't know how much to pay him, and like enough he'd cheat me; but you know the ways in London.'

Colin took the purse, and opened it. The first compartment he opened contained some silver, wrapped up in a scrap of tissue paper. Colin undid the paper and took out a shilling, which he was going to hand the cabman, when Minna laid her hand upon his arm and suddenly checked him. 'No, no,' she said, 'not that, Colin. From the other side, please, will you?'

Colin looked at the contents of the little paper once more, and rapidly counted it. It was nine shillings. He caught Minna's eye at the moment, and Minna coloured crimson. Then Cohn knew at once what those nine shillings were, and why they were separately wrapped in tissue paper.

He paid the cabman, from the other half, and put the boxes inside Mrs. Wood's door way. 'And now may I kiss you, Minna?' he asked, in the dark passage.

'If you like, Colin,' Minna answered, turning up her full red lips and round face with child-like innocence, Colin Churchill kissed her: and when he had kissed her once, he waited a minute, and then he took her plump little face between his own two hands and kissed her rather harder a second time. Minna's face tingled a little, but she said nothing.

The very next morning Minna came round, by Colin's invitation, to Cicolari's workshop. Colin was busy at work moulding, and Minna cast her eye around lightly as she entered on all the busts and plaster casts that filled the room. She advanced to meet him as if she expected to be kissed, so Colin kissed her. Then, with a rapid glance round the room, her eye rested at last upon the Cephalus and Aurora, and she went straight over to look at it with wondering eyes. 'Oh, Colin,' she cried, did you do that? What a lovely image!'

Colin was pleased and flattered at once. 'You like it, Minna?' he said. 'You really like it?'

Minna glanced carefully round the room once more with her keen black eyes, and after scanning every one of the plaster casts and unfinished busts in a comprehensive survey, answered unhesitatingly: 'I like it best of everything in the room, Colin, except the image of the man with the plate over yonder.'

Colin smiled a smile of triumph. Minna was not wholly lacking in taste, certainly; for the Cephalus was the best of his compositions, and the man with the plate was a plaster copy of the Discobolus. 'You'll do, Minna,' he said, patting her little black head with his cleanest hand (to the imminent danger of the small hat with the red rose in it). 'You'll do yet, with a little coaching.'

Then Colin took her round the studio, as Cicolari ambitiously called it, and explained everything to her, and showed her plates of the Venus of Milo, and the Apollo Belvedere, and the Laocoon, and the Niobe, and several other ladies and gentlemen with very long names and no clothes to speak of, till poor Minna began at last to be quite appalled at the depth of his learning and quite frightened at her own unquestioning countrified ignorance. For as yet Minna had no idea that there was anything much to learn in the world except reading and writing, and the art of cookery, and the proper use of the English language. But when she heard Colin chattering away so glibly to her about the age of Pheidias, and the age of the Decadence, and the sculptors of the Renaissance, and the absolute necessity of going to Rome, she began to conceive that perhaps Colin in his own heart might imagine she wasn't now good enough for him; which was a point of view on the subject that had never before struck the Dorsetshire fisherman's pretty black-eyed little daughter.

By-and-by, Colin began to talk of herself and her prospects; and to ask whether she was going to put herself down at a registry office; and last of all to allude delicately to the matter of the misspelt letter. 'You know, Minna,' he said apologetically, feeling his boyish awkwardness far more than ever, 'I've tried a lot to improve myself at Exeter, and still more since I came to London. I've read a great deal, and worked very hard, and now I think I'm beginning to get on, and know something, not only about art, but about books as well. Now, I know you won't mind my telling you, but that letter wasn't all spelt right, or stopped right. You ought to be very particular, you know, about the stopping and the spelling.'

Before he could say any more, Minna looked full in his face and stopped him short immediately. 'Colin,' she said, 'don't say another 'word about it. I know what you mean, and I'm going to attend to it. I never felt it in my life till I came here this morning; but I feel it now, and I shall take care to alter it.' She was a determined little body was Minna; and as she said those words, she looked so thoroughly as if she meant them that Colin dropped the subject at once and never spoke to her again about it.

Just at that moment two customers came to speak to Colin about a statuette he was working at for them. It was an old gentleman and a grand young lady. Minna stood aside while they talked, and pretended to be looking at Cephalus and Aurora with a critical eye, but she was really listening with all her ears to the conversation between Colin and the grand young lady. She was a very grand young lady, indeed, who talked very fine, and drawled her vowels, and clipped her r's, and mangled the English language hideously, and gave other indubitable signs of the very best and highest breeding: and Minna noticed almost with dismay that she called Colin 'Mr. Churchill,' and seemed to defer to all his opinions about curves and contours and attitudes. 'You have such lovely taste, you know, Mr. Churchill,' the grand young lady said; 'and we want this copy to be as good as you can make it, because it's for a very particular friend of ours, who admired the original so much at Rome last winter.'

Minna listened in awe and trembling, and felt in her heart just a faint twinge of feminine jealousy to think that even such a grand young lady should speak so flattering like to our Colin.

'And there's the Cephalus, Papa,' the grand young lady went on. 'Isn't it beautiful? I do hope someday, Mr. Churchill, you'll get a commission for it in marble. If I were rich enough, I'd commission it myself, for I positively doat upon it. However, somebody's sure to buy it sometime or other, so it's no use people like me longing to have it.'

Minna's heart rose, choking, into her mouth, as she stood there flushed and silent.

When the grand young lady and her papa were gone, Minna said good-bye a little hastily to Colin, and shrank back, crying: 'No, no, Colin,' when he tried to kiss her. Then she ran in a hurry to Mrs. Wood's in Dean Street. But though she was in a great haste to get home (for her bright little eyes had tears swimming in them), she stopped boldly at a small bookseller's shop on the way, and invested two whole shillings of her little hoard in a valuable work bearing on its cover the title, 'The Polite Correspondent's Complete Manual of Letter Writing.' 'He shall never kiss me again,' she said to herself firmly, 'until I can feel that I've made myself in every way thoroughly fit for him.'

It wasn't a very exalted model of literary composition, that Complete Manual of Letter Writing, but at least its spelling and punctuation were immaculate; and for many months to come after she had secured her place as parlour-maid in an eminently creditable family in Regent's Park, Minna sat herself down in her own bedroom every evening, when work was over, and deliberately endeavoured to perfect herself in those two elementary accomplishments by the use of the Polite Correspondent's unconscious guide, philosopher, and friend. First of all she read a whole letter over carefully, observing every stop and every spelling; then she copied it out entire, word for word, as well as she could recollect it, entirely from memory; and finally she corrected her written copy by the printed version in the Complete Manual, until she could transcribe every letter in the entire volume with perfect accuracy. It wasn't a very great educational effort, perhaps, from the point of view of advanced culture; but to Minna Wroe it was a beginning in self-improvement, and in these matters above all others the first step is everything.

CHAPTER XI

EDUCATIONAL ADVANTAGES

And now, while Minna Wroe was waiting at table in Regent's Park, and while Colin Churchill was modelling sepulchral images for his Italian master, Cicolari, how was our other friend, Hiram Winthrop, employing his time beyond the millpond?

'Bethabara Seminary, at the time when Hiram Winthrop, the eminent American artist, was enrolled among its alumni' (writes one of his fellow-students), 'occupied a plain but substantially built brick structure, commodiously located in the very centre of a large cornfield, near the summit of a considerable eminence in Madison County, N.Y. It had been in operation close on three years when young Winthrop matriculated there. He secured quarters in a room with four fellow-students, each of whom brought his own dipper, plate, knife, fork, and other essential requisites. Mr. Winthrop was always of a solitary, retiring character, without much command of language, and not given to attending the Debating Forum or other public institutions of our academy. Nor was he fond of the society of the lady students, though one or two of them, and notably the talented Miss Aimed A. Stiles, now a prominent teacher in a lyceum at Smyrna, Mo., early detected his remarkable gifts for pictorial art, and continually importuned him to take their portraits, no doubt designing them for keepsakes to be given to the more popular male students. Young Winthrop always repelled such advances: indeed, he was generally considered in the light of a boorish rustic; and his singular aversion towards the Hopkinsite connection (in which he had nevertheless been raised by that excellent man, his father, late Deacon Zephaniah Winthrop, of Muddy Creek, N.Y.) caused him to be somewhat disliked among his college companions. His chief amusement was to retire into the surrounding country, oddly choosing for the purpose the parts remotest from the roads and houses, and there sketch the animated creation which seemed always to possess a greater interest for his mind than the persons or conversation of his fellow-citizens. He had, indeed, as facts subsequently demonstrated, the isolation of a superior individual. Winthrop remained at Bethabara, so far as my memory serves me, for two years only.'

Indeed, the Hopkinsite Seminary was not exactly the sort of place fitted to suit the peculiar tastes of Hiram Winthrop. The boys and girls from the farms around had hardly more sympathy with him than the deacon himself. Yet, on the whole, in spite of the drawbacks of his surroundings, Athens was a perfect paradise to poor Hiram. This is a universe of relativities: and compared with life on the farm at Muddy Creek, life at Bethabara Seminary was absolute freedom and pure enjoyment to the solitary little artist. Here, as soon as recitation was over, he could wander out into the woods alone (after he had shaken off the attentions of the too sequacious Almeda), whenever he liked, no man hindering. The country around was wooded in places, and the scenery, like all that in Madison

County, was beautifully undulating. Five miles along the leafy highroad brought him to the banks of Cananagua Lake, one of those immeasurable lovely sheets of water that stud the surface of Western New York for miles together; and there Hiram would sit down by the shore, and watch the great divers disappearing suddenly beneath the surface, and make little pictures of the grey squirrels and the soldier-birds on the margin of Cyrus Choke's 'Elements of the Latin Language,' which he had brought out with him, presumably for purposes of preparation against to-morrow's class-work. But best of all there was a drawing-master at Athens, and from him, by Audouin's special arrangement, the boy took lessons twice a week in perspective and the other technical matters of his art, for, as to native ability, Hiram was really far better fitted to teach the teacher. Not a very great artist, that struggling German drawing-master at Athens, with his formal little directions of how to go jig-jig for a pine-tree, and to-whee, whee, whee, for an oak; not a very great artist, to be sure; but still, a grand relief for Hiram to discover that there were people in the world who really cared about these foolish things, and didn't utterly despise them though they were so irrelevant to the truly important questions of raising corn, and pork, and potatoes.

The great joy and delight of the term, however, was Audouin's periodical visit to his little protégé. Audouin at least was determined to let Hiram's individuality have fair play. He regarded him as a brand plucked from the burning of that corn-growing civilisation which he so cordially detested; and he had made up his own mind, rightly or wrongly, that Hiram had genius, and that that genius must be allowed freely to develop itself. Hiram loved these quarterly visits better than anything else in the whole world, because Audouin was the one person he had met in his entire life (except Sam Churchill) who could really sympathise with him.

Two years after Hiram Winthrop went to Bethabara, Audouin wrote to ask whether he would come and spend a week or two at Lakeside during the winter vacation. Hiram cried when he read the letter; so much pleasure seemed almost beyond the possibilities of this world, and the deacon would surely never consent; but to his great surprise, the deacon wrote back gruffly, yes; and as soon as term was finished, Hiram gladly took the cars on the New York Central down to Nine Mile Bottom, the depot for Lakeside. Audouin was waiting to meet him at the depot, in a neat little sleigh; and they drove away gaily to the jingling music of the bells, in the direction of Audouin's cottage.

'A severe artist, winter,' Audouin said, glancing around him quickly over the frozen fields. 'No longer the canvas and the colours, but the pure white marble and the flowing chisel. How the contours of the country soften with the snow, Hiram; what a divine cloak the winter clouds spread kindly over the havoc man has wrought upon this desecrated landscape! It was beautiful, once, I believe, in its native woodland beauty; and it's beautiful even now when the white pall comes down, so, to screen and cover its artificial nakedness. The true curse of Ham (and worse) is upon us here; we have laughed at the shame of our mother earth.'

Hiram hardly understood him, he seldom quite understood his friend, but he answered, with a keen glance over the white snow, 'I love the winter, Mr. Audouin; but I apprehend I like the summer an' autumn best. You should jest have seen the crimson and gold on Cananagua Lake last fall; oh, my, the colours on the trees! nobody could ever have painted 'em. I took out my paints an' tried, but I wasn't anywhere like it, I can tell you; Mr. Mooller, he said he didn't b'lieve Claude or Turner could ever have painted a bit of Amurrican fall scenery.'

'Mr. Müller isn't a conclusive authority,' Audouin answered gravely, removing his cigar as he spoke; 'but on this occasion I surmise, Hiram, he was probably not far from a correct opinion. Still, Mr. Müller won't do for you any longer. The fact is, Hiram, sooner or later you must go to Europe. There's no teaching here good enough for you. I've made up my mind that you must go to Europe. Whether the deacon likes it or not, you've got to go, and we must manage one way or another.'

To Europe! Hiram's brain reeled round at the glorious, impossible notion. To Europe! Why, that was the wonderful romantic country where Tom Jones ran away with Amelia, where Mr. Tracy Tupman rode to Ipswich on top of the mail-coach, where Moses bought the gross of green spectacles from the plausible vagabond at the country fair. Europe! There were kings and princes in Europe; and cathedrals and castles; and bishops and soldiers; ay, he could almost believe, too, there were giants, ogres, ghosts, and fairies. In Europe, Sam Wellers waited at the wayside inns; mysterious horsemen issued darkling from arched castle gates; Jews cut pounds of flesh, Abyssinian fashion, from the living breasts of Venetian shipowners; and itinerant showmen wandered about with Earley's waxworks across a country haunted by masked highwaymen and red-coated squires, who beat you half to death for not telling them immediately which way the hare ran. As such a phantasmagoria of incongruous scenes did the mother continent of the American race present itself in some swimming panorama to Hiram's excited brain. It was almost as though Aladdin and the oneeyed calender had suddenly appeared to him in the familiar woods of Geauga County, and invited him forthwith to take the cars for Bagdad at the urgent personal request of the good Caliph Haroun al Raschid.

The boy held his breath hard, and answered in his self-restrained American manner, 'To Europe, Mr. Audouin! Well, I guess I should appreciate that, consid'able.'

'Yes, Hiram,' Audouin went on, 'I've made my mind up to that. Sooner or later you must go to Europe. But not just at once, my boy. Not till you're about nineteen, I should say; it wouldn't do you so much good till then. Meanwhile, we must put you to some other school. Bethabara has done its little best for you: you must go elsewhere, meanwhile. I mean that you shall go to some one of the eastern colleges, Yale if possible.'

'But what about father?' Hiram asked.

'Your father must be made to do as I tell him. Look here, Hiram, the fact is this. You're a boy whose individuality must be developed. The deacon mustn't be allowed to prevent it. I've taken you in hand, and I mean to see you through it. Look yonder, my boy, at the edge of the ice there on the creek; look at the musquash sitting in the sun on the brink of the open water eating a clam, and the clamshells he has left strewed along the shore and beach behind him. See him drop in again and bring up another clam, and stride sleek and shining from the water on to his little cliff of ice again. You and I know that that sight is beautiful. You and I know that it's the only thing on earth worth living for, that power of seeing the beautiful in art and nature, but how many people do you suppose there are in all America that would ever notice it? What percentage, Hiram, of our great, free, intelligent, democratic people, that sing their own praises daily with so shrill a voice in their ten thousand "Heralds," and "Tribunes," and "Courants," and "Mirrors "? How small a percentage, Hiram; how small a percentage!'

The boy coloured up crimson to the very roots of his shaggy hair. It was such a very new point of view to him. He had always known that he cared for these things towards which all other boys and men were mere dull materialistic Gallios; but it had never before occurred to him that his doing so was any mark of a mental superiority on his part. Father had he thought that it betokened some weakness or foolishness of his own nature, for he wasn't like other boys; and not to be like other boys is treated so much as a crime in junior circles that it almost seems like a crime at last even to the culprit himself in person. So Hiram coloured up with the shame of a first discovery of his own better-ness, and merely answered in the same quiet self-restrained fashion, 'I apprehend, Mr. Audouin, there ain't many folks who pay much attention to the pecooliarities of the common American musk-rat.'

All the rest of the way home, Audouin plied the boy with such subtle flattery, not meant as flattery, indeed, for Audouin was incapable of guile; if he erred, it was on the side of too outspoken truthfulness: yet, in effect, his habit of speaking always as though he and Hiram formed a class apart was really flattery of the deepest sort to the boy's nature. At last they drew up at a neat wooden cottage in a small snow-covered glen, where the circling amphitheatre of spruce pines opened out into a long sloping vista in front, and the frozen arm of the great lake spread its limitless ice sheet beyond, away over in weird perspective toward the low unseen Canadian shore. The boy uttered a little sharp cry of delight at the exquisite prospect. Audouin noticed it with pleasure. 'Well, Hiram,' he said, 'here we are at last at my lodge in the wilderness.'

'I never saw anything in all my life,' the boy answered truthfully, 'one-thousandth part so beautiful.'

Audouin was pleased at the genuine tone of the compliment. 'Yes, Hiram,' he said, looking with a complacent smile down the pine-clad glen toward the frozen lake, 'it certainly does help to wash out Broadway.'

Hiram's three weeks at Lakeside Cottage were indeed three weeks of unalloyed delight to his eager, intelligent nature. There were books there, books of the most delicious sort; Birds of America with coloured plates; Flora of New York State with endless figures; poems, novels, histories, Prescott's 'Peru,' and Macaulay's 'England.' There were works about the Indians, too; works written by men who actually took a personal interest in calumets and tomahawks. There were pictures, books full of them; pictures by great painters, well engraved; pictures, the meaning of which Audouin explained to him carefully, pointing out the peculiarities of style in each, so far as the engravings could reproduce them. Above all, there was Audouin's own conversation, morning, noon and night, as well as his friend the Professor's, who was once more staying with him on a visit. That was Hiram's first extended glimpse of what a cultivated and refined life could be made like, apart from the sordid, squalid necessities of raising pork and beans and Johnny cake.

Best of all, before Hiram left Lakeside, Audouin had driven him over to the Deacon's in his neat little sleigh, and had seriously discussed the question of his further education. And the result of that interview was that Hiram was to return no more to Bethabara, but (being now nearly sixteen) was to go instead to the Eclectic Institute at Orange. It was with great difficulty that this final step was conquered, but conquered it was at last, mainly by Audouin's masterful persistence.

"Tain't convenient for me, mister,' the deacon said snappishly, 'to go on any longer without the services of that thar boy. I want him to home to help with the farm work. He's progressing towards citizenship now, an' I've invested quite a lot of capital in his raisin', an' it's time I was beginnin' to see some return upon it.'

'Quite true and very natural,' Audouin answered with his diplomatic quickness. 'Still, you must consider the boy's future. He won't cost you much, deacon. He's a smart lad, and he can help himself a great deal in the off seasons. There's a great call for school-teachers in the winter, and college students are much sought after.'

'What might be the annual expense to an economical student?' asked the deacon dubiously.

'A hundred dollars a year,' Audouin replied boldly. He murmured to himself that whatever the difference might be between this modest estimate and the actual truth, he would pay it out of his own pocket.

The deacon gave way grudgingly at last, and to the end neither he nor Hiram ever knew that Hiram's three years at the Eclectic Institute cost his unsuspected benefactor some two hundred dollars annually.

CHAPTER XII

AN ARTISTIC ENGAGEMENT

Three years at Orange passed away quickly enough, and Hiram enjoyed his time there far better than he had done even in the solitude of Bethabara Seminary. He didn't work very hard at the classics and mathematics, it must be admitted: Professor Hazen complained that his recitations in Plato were not up to the mark, and that his Cicero was seldom prepared with sufficient diligence: but though in the dead languages his work was most too bad, the Professor allowed that in English literatoor he did well, and seemed to reach out elastically with his faculties in all directions. He spent very little time over his books to be sure, but he caught the drift, appropriated the kernel, and let the rest slide. Fact was, he created his own culture. He didn't debate in the lyceum, or mix much in social gatherings of an evening (where the female stoodents entertained the gentlemen with tea, and Johnny cake, and crullers, and improving conversation), but he walked a great deal alone in the hills, and interested himself with sketching, and the pursoot of natural history. Still, he wasn't social; so much Professor Hazen was compelled by candour to admit. When the entire strength of the Eclectic Institoot went in carriages to the annual grove-meeting at Rudolph, Hiram Winthrop was usually conspicuous by his absence. The lady stoodents fully expected that a gentleman of such marked artistic and rural proclivities would on such occasions be the life and soul of the whole party: that he would burst out occasionally into a rapturous strain at the sight of an elegant bird, or a trailing vine, or a superb giant of the primæval forest. They calculated confidently on his reciting poetry appropriate to the scene and the social occasion. But Hiram generally stopped away altogether, which operated considerable disappointment on the ladies; or if he went at all, accompanied the junior stoodents in the refreshment waggon, and scarcely contributed anything solid to the general entertainment. In short, he was a very bashful and retiring person, who didn't amalgamate spontaneously or readily with the prevalent tone of life at the Eclectic Institoot.

Nevertheless, in spite of the solitude, Hiram Winthrop liked the Institute, and often looked back afterwards upon the time he had spent there as one of the happiest portions of his life. He worked away hard in all his spare moments at drawing and painting; and some of the lady students still retain some of his works of this period, which they cherish in small gilt frames upon the parlour wall, as mementoes of their brief acquaintance with a prominent American artistic gentleman. Miss Almeda A. Stiles in particular (who followed Hiram from Betha-bara to Orange, where she graduated with him in the class of 18—) keeps even now two of his drawings in her rooms at the lyceum at Smyrna, Mo. One of them represents a large Europian bird, seated upon the bough of a tree in winter; it is obviously a copy from a drawing-master's design: the other, which is far finer and more original, is a sketch of Chattawauga Falls, before the erection of the existing sawmills and other improvements. Hiram was singularly fond of Chattawauga; but strange to say, from the very first day that the erection of the sawmills was undertaken, he refused to go near the spot, alleging no other reason for his refusal except that he regarded these useful institootions in the light of a positively wicked desecration of the work of nature. There was a general feeling at Orange that in many respects young Winthrop's sentiments and opinions were in fact painfully unAmerican.

In the holidays—no, vacation—(one mustn't apply European names to American objects), Hiram found enough to do in teaching school in remote country sections. Nay, he even managed to save a little money out of his earnings, which he put away to help him on his grand project of going to Europe, that dim, receding, but now far more historical and less romantic Europe towards which his hopes were always pointing. Audouin would gladly have sent him on his own account, Hiram knew that much well; for Audouin was comfortably rich, and he had taken a great fancy to his young protégé. But Hiram didn't want to spend his friend's money if he could possibly help it: he had the honest democratic feeling strong upon him, that he would like to go to Europe by his own earnings or not at all. So as soon as his three years at Orange were over, he determined to go to Syracuse (not the Sicilian one, but its namesake in New York State), and start in business for the time being as a draughtsman on the wood. He was drawn to this scheme by an advertisement in the 'Syracuse Daily Independent,' requiring a smart hand at drawing for a large blockengraving establishment in that city.

'My dear Hiram,' Audouin exclaimed in dismay, when his young friend told him of his project, 'you really mustn't think of it. At Syracuse, too! why, what sort of work do you conceive people would want done at Syracuse? Nothing but advertisement drawings of factories for the covers of biscuit tins, or flaring red and yellow fruits for the decoration of canned peaches.'

'Well, Mr. Audouin,' Hiram answered with a smile, 'I guess I must go in for the canned peaches, then, if nothing better offers. I've got to earn enough to take me across to Europe, one way or the other;— no, don't say that now,' for he saw Audouin trying to cut in impatiently with his ever friendly offer of assistance: 'don't say that,' and he clutched his friend's arm tightly. 'I know you would. I know you would. But I can't accept it. This thing has just got to be done in the regular way of business or not at all; and what's more, Mr. Audouin, I've just got to go and do it.'

'But, Hiram,' Audouin cried, half angrily, 'I want you to go to Europe and learn to paint splendid pictures, and make all America proud of your talent. I found you out, and I've got a sort of proprietary interest in you; and just when I expect you to begin doing something really great, you calmly propose to go to Syracuse, and draw designs for canned peaches! You ought to consider your duty to your country.'

'I'm very sorry, Mr. Audouin,' Hiram answered with his accustomed gravity, 'if I disappoint you personally; but as for the rest of America, I dare say the country'll manage to hold on a year or two longer without my pictures.'

So Hiram really went at last to Syracuse (pronounced Sirrah-kyooze), and duly applied for the place as draughtsman. The short boy who showed him in to the office went off to call one of the bosses. In a few minutes, the boss in question entered, and in a quiet American tone, with just a faint relic of some English country dialect flavouring it dimly in the background, inquired if this was the young man who had come about the drawing. 'For if so, mister,' he said with the true New Yorker ring, 'just you step right back here with me, will 'ee, a minute, and we'll settle this little bit of business right away, smart and handy.'

Hiram knew the boss in a moment, in spite of his altered voice and manner. 'Sam,' he said, taking his hand warmly (for he hadn't had so many friends in his lifetime that he had forgotten how to be grateful to any single one of them): 'Sam, don't you remember me? I'm Hiram Winthrop.'

Sam's whole voice and manner changed in a moment, from the sharp, official, Syracuse business man to something more like the old simple, easygoing, bucolic Sam Churchill, who had come out so long ago from Dorsetshire. 'Why, bless my soul, Hiram,' he exclaimed, grasping both his hands at once in an iron grip, 'so it's you, lad, is it? Well, I am glad to see you. You step right back here and let's have a look at you! Why, how you've grown, Hiram! Only don't call me Sam, too open, here;

here, I'm one of the bosses, and get called Mr. Churchill. And how's the deacon, and the missus, and old Major (you don't mind old Major? he was the off-horse at the plough, always, he was). And how are you? Been to college, I reckon, by the look of you. You come right back here and tell me all about it.'

So Hiram went right back (behind the little counter in the front office), and told Sam Churchill his whole story. And Sam in return told his. It wasn't very long, but it was all prosperous. He had left, the deacon soon after Hiram went to live at Bethabara Seminary; he had come to Syracuse in search of work; had begun trying his hand as draughtsman for a wood-engraver; had gone into partnership with another young man, on his own account; had risen as fast as people in America do rise, if they have anything in them; and was now joint boss of the biggest woodcut establishment in the whole Lake Shore section of New York State. 'See here,' he cried with infinite pride to Hiram. 'Just you look at all these labels. Hemmings' Patent Blacking, nigger woman admiring her own teeth in her master's boots, that's ours. And this: Chicago General Canning Company; Prime Fruit: I did that myself. And this: Philbrick's Certain Death to Eats: good design, rather, that one, ain't it? Here's more: Potterton's Choke-cherry Cordial; Old Dr. Hezekiah Bowdler's Elixir of Winter-green; Eselmann and Schneider's Eagle Brand Best Old Bourbon Whiskey; Smoke None but Cyrus A. Walker's Original and Only Genuine Old Dominion Honeydew. That's our line of business, you see, Hiram. That's where we've got on. We've put mind into it. We've struck out a career of our own. We've determined to revolutionise the American advertisement illustration market, When we took the thing in hand, it was all red and yellow uglinesses. We've discarded crudeness and vulgarity, we have, and gone in for artistic colouring and the best sentiments. Look at Philbrick's Certain Death, for example. That's fine, now, isn't it? We've made the fortune of the Certain Death. When we took it up, advertising I mean, there wasn't a living to be got out of Philbrick's. They had a sort of comic picture of four rats, poisoned, with labels coming out of their mouths, saying they were gone coons, and so forth. Vulgar, vulgar, very. We went in for the contract, and produced the chaste and elegant design you see before you. It has succeeded, naturally,' and Sam looked across at Hiram with the serious face of profound conviction with which he was always wont to confront the expected customer, in the interests of the joint establishment.

Poor Hiram! his heart sank within him a little when he looked at the chaste and elegant design; but he had put his hand to the plough, and he would not look back: so before the end of that day Sam Churchill had definitely engaged him as chief draughtsman to his rising establishment.

That was how Hiram came to spend two years as an advertisement draughtsman at Syracuse. He didn't deny, afterwards, that those two years were about the dreariest and most, disappointing of his whole lifetime. In his spare moments, to be sure, he still went on studying as well as he was able; and on Sundays he stole away with his easel and colours to the few bits of decently pretty scenery that lie within reach of that flat and marshy mushroom city: but for the greater part of his time he was employed in designing neat and appropriate wrappers for quack medicine bottles, small illustrations for catalogues or newspaper advertisements, and huge flaring posters for mammoth circuses or variety dramatic entertainments. It was a grinding, horrible work; and though Sam Churchill did his best to make it pleasant and bearable for him, Hiram cordially detested it with all his heart. The only thing that made it any way endurable was the image of that far-off promised European journey, on which Hiram Winthrop had fixed all his earthly hopes and ambitions.

Sam often told him of Colin, for Colin had kept up a correspondence with his thriving American brother; and it was a sort of daydream with Hiram that one day or other Colin Churchill and he should go to Rome together. For Audouin's encouragement and Colin's eagerness had inspired Hiram with a like desire: and he saved and hoarded in hopes that the time would at last come when he might get rid of advertisements, and take instead to real painting. Meanwhile he contented himself with working at his art by himself, or with such little external aid as he could get in a brand-new green-and-white American city, and hoping for the future that never came but was always coming.

CHAPTER XIII

AN EVE IN EDEN

Once a year, and once only, Hiram had a holiday. For a glorious fortnight every summer, Sam Churchill and his partner gave their head draughtsman leave to go and amuse himself wheresoever the spirit led him. And on the first of such holidays, Hiram went with Audouin to the Thousand Islands, and spent a delightful time boating, fishing, and sketching, among the endless fairy mazes of that enchanted region, where the great St. Lawrence loses itself hopelessly in innumerable petty channels, between countless tiny bosses of pine-clad rock. It was a fortnight of pure enjoyment for poor drudging advertisement-drawing Hiram, and he revelled in its wealth of beauty as he had never revelled in anything earthly before during his whole lifetime.

One morning Hiram had taken his little easel out with him from Alexandria Bay to one of the prettiest points of view upon the neighbouring mainland, a jutting spit of ice-worn rock, projecting far into the placid lake, and thickly overhung with fragrant brush of the beautiful red cedar, and was making a little water-colour sketch of a tiny islet in the foreground, just a few square yards of smooth granite covered in the centre with an inch deep of mould, and crowned by a single tall straight stem of sombre spruce fir. It was a delicate, dainty little sketch, steeped in the pale morning haze of Canadian summer; and the scarlet columbines, waving from the gnarled roots of the solitary fir tree, stood out like brilliant specks of light against the brown bark and dark green foliage that formed the background. Hiram was just holding it at arm's length, to see how it looked, and turning to ask for Audouin's friendly criticism, when he heard a clear bright woman's voice close behind him speaking so distinctly that he couldn't help overhearing the words.

'Oh, papa,' the voice said briskly, 'there's an artist working down there. I wonder if he'd mind our going down and looking at his picture. I do so love to see an artist painting.'

The very sound of the voice thrilled through Hiram's inmost marrow as he heard it, somewhat as Audouin's voice had done long ago, when first he came upon him in the Muddy Creek woodland, only more so. He had never heard a woman's voice before at all like it. It didn't in the least resemble Miss Almeda A. Stiles's, or any other one of the lady students at Bethabara or Orange, who formed the sole standard of female society that Hiram Winthrop had ever yet met with. It was a rich, liquid, rippling voice, and it spoke with the soft accent and delicate deliberate intonation of an English lady. Hiram, of course, didn't by the light of nature recognise at once this classificatory fact as to its origin and history, but he did know that it stirred him strangely, and made him look round immediately to see from what manner of person the voice itself ultimately proceeded.

A tall girl of about nineteen, with a singularly full ripe-looking face and figure for her age, was standing on the edge of the little promontory just above, and looking down inquisitively towards Hiram's easel. Her cheeks had deeper roses in them than Hiram had ever seen before, and her complexion was clearer and more really flesh-coloured than that of most pale and sallow American women. 'What a beautiful skin to paint!' thought Hiram instinctively; and then the next moment, with a flush of surprise, he began to recognise to himself that this unknown girl, whose eyes met his for an infinitesimal fraction of a second, had somehow immediately impressed him, nay, thrilled him, in a way that no other woman had ever before succeeded in doing. In one word, she seemed to him more womanly. Why, he didn't know, and couldn't have explained even to himself, for Hiram's forte certainly did not lie in introspective analysis; but he felt it instinctively, and was conscious at once of a certain bashful desire to speak with her, which he had never experienced towards a single one of the amiable young ladies at Bethabara Seminary.

'Gwen, my dear,' the father said in a dried-up Indian military tone, 'you will disturb these artists. Come away, come away; people don't like to be watched at their duties, really.'

Gwen, by way of sole reply, only bent over the edge of the little bluff that overhung the platform of rock where Hiram was sitting, and said with the same clear deliberate accent as before, 'May I look? Oh, thank you. How very, very pretty!'

'It isn't finished yet,' Audouin said, taking the words out of Hiram's mouth almost, as he held up the picture for Gwen's inspection. 'It's only a rough sketch, so far: it'll look much worthier of the original when my friend has put the last little touches to it. In art, you know, the last loving lingering touch is really everything.'

Hiram felt half vexed that Audouin should thus have assumed the place of spokesman for him towards the unknown lady; and yet at the same time he was almost grateful to him for it also, for he felt too abashed to speak himself in her overawing presence.

'Yes, the original's beautiful,' Gwen answered, taking her father's arm and leading him down, against his will, to the edge of the water: 'but the sketch is very pretty too, and the point of view so exquisitely chosen. What a thing it is, papa, to have the eye of an artist, isn't it? You and I might have passed this place a dozen times over, and never noticed what a lovely little bit it is to make a sketch of; but the painter sees it at once, and picks out by instinct the very spot to make a beautiful picture.'

'Ah, quite so,' the father echoed in a cold unconcerned voice, as if the subject rather bored him. 'Quite so, quite so. Very pretty place indeed, an excellent retired corner, I should say, for a person who has a taste that way, to sit and paint in.'

'It is beautiful,' Audouin said, addressing himself musingly to the daughter, 'and our island in particular is the prettiest of all the thousand, I do believe.'

'Your island?' Gwen cried interrogatively. 'Then you own that sweet little spot there, do you?'

'My friend and I, yes,' Audouin answered airily, to Hiram's great momentary astonishment. 'In the only really worthy sense of ownership, we own it most assuredly. I dare say some other man somewhere or other keeps locked up in his desk a dirty little piece of crabbed parchment, which he calls a title-deed, and which gives him some sort of illusory claim to the productive power of the few square yards of dirt upon its surface. But the island itself and the enjoyment of it is ours, and ours only: the gloss on the ice-grooves in the shelving granite shore, the scarlet columbines on the tall swaying stems, the glow of the sunlight on the russet boles of the spruce fir, you see my friend has fairly impounded them all upon his receptive square of cartridge paper here for our genuine title-deed of possession.'

'Ah, I see, I see,' the old gentleman said testily. 'You and your friend claim the island by prescription, but your claim is disputed by the original freeholder.'

The three others all smiled slightly. 'Oh dear, no, papa,' Gwen answered with a touch of scorn and impatience in her tone. 'Don't you understand? This gentleman—'

'My name is Audouin,' the New Englander put in with a slight inclination.

'Mr. Audouin means that the soil is somebody else's, but the sole enjoyment of the island is his friend's and his own.'

'The so-called landowner often owns nothing more than the dirt in the ditches,' Audouin explained with a wave of the hand, in his romantic mystifying fashion, 'while the observer owns all that is upon it, of any real use or beauty. For our whole lifetime, my friend and I have had that privilege and pleasure. The grass grows green for us in spring; the birds build nests for us in early summer; the fire-flies flit before our eyes on autumn evenings; the stoat and hare put on their snow-white coat for our delight in winter weather. I've seen a poet enjoy for a whole season the best part of a farm, while the crusty farmer supposed he had only had out of it a few worthless wild apples. We are the real freeholders, sir; the man with the title-deeds has merely the usufruct.'

'Oh, ah,' the military gentleman repeated, as if a light were beginning slowly to dawn upon his bewildered intelligence. 'Some reservation in favour of rights of way and royalties and so forth, in America, I suppose. Only owns the dirt in the ditches, you say, the soil presumably. Now, in England, every landowner owns the mines and minerals and springs and everything else beneath the soil, to the centre of the earth, I believe, if I've been rightly instructed.'

'It can seldom be worth his while to push his claims so far.' Audouin replied with great gravity, still smiling sardonically.

Gwen coloured slightly. Hiram noticed the delicate flush of the colour, as it mantled all her cheek for a single second, and was hardly angry with his friend for having provoked so pretty a protest. Then Gwen said with a little cough, as if to change the subject: 'These islands are certainly very lovely. They're the most beautiful thing we've seen in a six weeks' tour in America. I don't think even Niagara charmed me so much, in spite of all its grandeur.'

'You're right,' Audouin went on (a little in the Sir Oracle vein, Hiram fancied); 'at any rate, the islands are more distinctly American. There's nothing like them anywhere else in the world. They're the final word of our level American river basins. You have grand waterfalls in Europe; you have broad valleys; you have mountains finer than any of ours here east at least; but you've nothing equal in its way to this flat interwoven scenery of river and foliage, of land and water. It has no sublimity, not a particle; it's utterly wanting in everything that ordinarily makes beautiful country; but it's absolutely fairy like in its endless complexity of channels and islands, and capes and rocks and lakelets, all laid out on such an infinitesimally tiny scale, as one might imagine the sylphs and gnomes or the Lilliputians would lay out their ground plan of a projected paradise.'

'Yes, I think it's exquisite in its way,' Gwen went on. 'My father doesn't care for it because it's so flat: after Naini Tal and the Himalayas, he says, all American scenery palls and fades away into utter insignificance. Of course I haven't seen the Himalayas, and don't want to, you know, but I've been in Switzerland; and I don't see why, because Switzerland is beautiful as mountain country, this shouldn't be beautiful too in a different fashion.'

'Quite so,' Audouin answered briskly. 'We should admire all types of beauty, each after its own kind. Not to do so argues narrowness, a want of catholicity.'

The military gentleman fidgeted sadly by Gwen's side; he had caught at the word 'catholicity,' and he didn't like it. It savoured of religious discussion; and being, like most other old Indian officers, strictly evangelical, he began to suspect Audouin of High Church tendencies, or even dimly to envisage him to himself in the popular character of a Jesuit in disguise.

As for Hiram, he listened almost with envy to Audouin's glib tongue, as it ran on so lightly and so smoothly to the beautiful overawing stranger. If only, now, he himself dared talk like that, or rather if only he dared talk after his own fashion, which, indeed, to say the truth, would have been a great deal better! But he didn't dare, and so he let Audouin carry off all the conversation unopposed; while Audouin, with his easy Boston manners, never suspected for a moment that the shy, self restraining New Yorker countryman was burning all the time to put in a little word or two on his own account, or to attract some tiny share of the beautiful stranger's passing attention. And thus it came to pass that Audouin went on talking for half an hour or more uninterruptedly to Gwen, the military gentleman subsiding meanwhile into somewhat sulky silence, and Hiram listening with all his ears to hear what particulars he could glean by the way as to the sudden apparition, her home, name, and calling. They had come to America for a six weeks' tour, it seemed, 'Papa' having business in Canada, where he owned a little property, and having leave of absence for the purpose from his regiment at Chester. That was almost all that Hiram gathered as to her actual position; and that little he treasured up in his memory most religiously against the possible contingency of a future journey to England 'And you contemplate returning to Europe shortly?' Hiram ventured to ask at last of the English lady. It was the first time he had opened his lips during the entire conversation, and he was surprised even now at his own temerity in presuming to say anything.

Gwen turned towards the young artist carelessly. Though she had been evidently interested in Audouin's talk, she had not so far even noticed the painter of the little picture which had formed the first introduction to the entire party. 'Yes,' she said, as unconcernedly as if Europe were in the same State; 'we sail next Friday.'

It was the only sentence she said to him, but she said it with a bright frank smile, which Hiram could have drawn from memory a twelvemonth after. As a matter of fact, he did draw it in his own bedroom at the Alexandria Bay Hotel that very evening: and he kept it long in his little pocket-book as a memento of a gleam of light bursting suddenly upon his whole existence. For Hiram was not so inexperienced in the ways of the world that he couldn't recognise one very simple and palpable fact: he was in love at first sight with the unknown English lady.

'Really, Gwen,' the military gentleman said at this point in the conversation, 'we must go back to lunch, if we're going to catch our steamer for Montreal. Besides, you're hindering our friend here from finishing his picture. Good morning, good morning; thank you so very much for the opportunity of seeing it.'

Gwen said a little 'Good morning' to Audouin, bowed more distantly to Hiram, and taking her father's arm jumped lightly up the rocks again, and disappeared in the direction of the village. When she was fairly out of sight, Hiram sat down once more and finished his water-colour in complete silence.

'Pretty girl, Hiram,' Audouin said lightly, as they walked back to their quarters at lunch-time.

'I should think, Mr. Audouin,' Hiram answered slowly, with even more than his usual self-restraint, 'she must be a tolerably favourable specimen of European women.'

Audouin said no more; and Hiram, too, avoided the subject in future. Somehow, for the first time in his life, he felt just a little bit aggrieved and jealous of Audouin. It was he, Hiram, who had painted the picture which first caught Gwen's fancy, he called her 'Gwen' in his own mind, quite simply, having no other name by which to call her. It was he who was the artist and the selector of that particular point of view; and yet Audouin, all unconsciously as it seemed, had stepped in and appropriated to himself, by implication, the artistic honours of the situation. Audouin had talked his vague poetical nature-worship talk, it seemed to Hiram a trifle affected somehow, to-day; and had monopolised all Gwen's interest in the interview, and had left him, Hiram (the founder of the feast, so to speak), out in the cold, while he himself basked in the full sunshine of Gwen's momentary favour. And yet to Audouin what was she, after all, but a pretty passing stranger? while to him she was a revelation, a new birth, a latter-day Aphrodite, rising unbidden with her rosy cheeks from the very bosom of the smiling lake. And now she was going back again at once to Europe, that great, unknown, omnipotential Europe; and perhaps Hiram Winthrop would never again see the one woman who had struck him at first sight with the instantaneous thrill which the man who has once experienced it can never forget. Colin Churchill hadn't once yet even asked himself whether or not he was in love with Minna; but Hiram Winthrop acknowledged frankly forthwith to his own heart that he was certainly and undeniably in love with Gwen.

Who was she? that was the question. He didn't even know her surname: his sole information about her amounted exactly to this, that she was called Gwen, and that her father had been quartered at Chester. Hiram smiled to himself as he recollected the old legend of how St. Thomas à Becket's mother, a Saracen maiden, had come to England from the East, in search of her Christian lover, knowing only the two proper names, Gilbert and London. Was he, Hiram Winthrop, in this steam-ridden nineteenth century, in like manner to return to the old home of his forefathers, and make inquiry with all diligence for Gwen, Chester? The notion was of course too palpably absurd (though Audouin would have been charmed with it). Yet there can be no denying that from the moment Hiram met that beautiful English girl by the Lake of the Thousand Islands, his desire to see Europe was quickened by yet one more unacknowledged, but very powerful private attraction. If anybody had talked to him about marrying Gwen, he would have honestly laughed at the improbable notion, but in the indefinite way that young men often feel, he felt as though some vague influence drew him on towards Gwen, not as a woman to be wooed and won, but as a central object of worship and admiration.

At the hotel, they didn't know the name of the English gentleman and his daughter; the clerk said they only came for a day and expected no letters. Another guest had asked about them, too, he mentioned casually; but Hiram, accustomed to looking upon his friend as so much older than himself as to have outgrown the folly of admiring female beauty, never dreamt of supposing that that other guest was Lothrop Audouin. He searched the 'Herald,' indeed, a week later, to see if any English officer and his daughter had sailed from New York on the Friday, but there were no passengers whom he could at all identify with Gwen and her father. It didn't occur to him that they might have sailed, as they did sail, by the Canadian mail steamer from Quebec, where he couldn't have failed to discover them in the list of passengers; so he was left in the end with no other memorial of this little episode save the sketch of that sunny face, and the two names, Gwen and Chester. To those little memorials Hiram's mind turned back oftener than less solitary people could easily imagine during the next long twelve months of dreary advertisement-drawing at long, white, dusty, sun-smitten Syracuse.

CHAPTER XIV

MINNA GIVES NOTICE

Colin,' Minna Wroe said to the young workman one evening, as they walked together through the streets of London towards the Regent's Park: 'do you know what I've actually gone and done to-day? I've give notice.'

'Given notice, Minna! What for, on earth? Why, you seemed to me so happy and comfortable there. I've never seen you in any other place where you and your people seemed to pull so well together, like.'

'Ah, that's just what she said to me, Colin.' (She in this connection may be familiarly recognised as a pronoun enclosing its own antecedent.) 'She said she couldn't imagine what my reason could be for leaving; and so I just up and told her. And as it isn't any use keeping it from you any longer, I think I may as well up and tell you too, Colin. Colin, I don't mean any more to be a servant.'

Cohn looked at her, dazzled and stunned a little by the suddenness and conciseness of this resolute announcement. Half a dozen vague and unpleasant surmises ran quickly through his bewildered brain. 'Why, Minna,' he exclaimed with some apprehension, looking down hastily at her neat little figure and her pretty, dimpled gipsy face, 'you're not going, no you're not going to the drapery, are you?'

Minna's twin dimples on the rich brown cheeks grew deeper and deeper, and she laughed merrily to herself a wee musical ringing laugh. 'The drapery, indeed,' she cried, three-quarters amused and one-quarter indignant. 'The drapery, he says to me! No, Mr. Colin, if you please, sir, I'm not going to be a shop-girl, thank you. A pretty shop-girl I should make now, shouldn't I? That's just like all you men: you think nobody can go in for bettering themselves, only yourselves. If a girl doesn't want to be a parlour-maid any longer, you can't think of anything but she must want to go and be a shop-girl. I wonder you didn't say a barmaid. If you don't beg my pardon at once for your impudence, I won't tell you anything more about it.'

'I beg your pardon, I'm sure, Minna,' Colin answered submissively. 'I didn't mean to hurt your feelings.'

'And good reason, too, sir. But as you've got the grace to do it, I'll tell you all the rest. Do you know what I do with my money, Colin?'

'You save it all, I know, Minna.'

'Well, I save it all. And then, I've got grandmother's eleven pound, what she left me; and the little things I've been given now and again by visitors and such like. And I've worked all through the "Complete Manual of Letter Writing," and the "English History," and the "First School Arithmetic ": and now, Miss Woollacott, you know; her at the North London Birkbeck Girls' Schools, she says she'll take me on as a sort of a pupil-teacher, to look after the little ones and have lessons myself for what I can do, if only I'll pay her my own board and lodging.'

Colin gazed at the girl aghast. 'A pupil-teacher, Minna!' he cried in astonishment. 'A pupil-teacher! Why, my dear child, what on earth do you mean to do when you're through it all?'

Minna dropped her plump brown hand from his arm at the gate of the park, and stood looking up at him pettishly with bright eyes flashing. 'There you are again,' she said, with a little touch of bitterness in her pretty voice. 'Just like you men always. You think it's all very well for Colin Churchill to want to go and be a sculptor, and talk with fine ladies and gentlemen, and make his fortune, and become a great man by-and-by, perhaps, like that Can-over, or somebody: that's all quite right and proper; of course it is. But for Minna Wroe, whose people are every bit as good as his, to save up her money, and do her best to educate herself, and fit herself to be his equal, and become a governess, why, that of course is quite unnatural. Her proper place is to be a parlour-maid: she ought to go on all her life long cleaning silver, and waiting on the ladies and gentlemen, and changing the plates at dinner, that's just about what she's fit for. She's only a woman. You're all alike, Colin, all you men, the whole lot of you. I won't go any further. I shall just go home again this very minute.'

Colin caught her arm gently, and held her still for a minute by quiet force. 'My dear Minna,' he said, 'you don't at all understand me. If you've really got it in your mind to better yourself like that, why, of course, it's a very grand thing in you, and I admire you for your spirit and resolution. Besides, Minna,' and Colin looked into her eyes a little tenderly as he said this, 'I think I know, little woman, what you want to do it for. What I meant was just this, you know: I don't see what it'll lead to, even when you've gone and done it.'

'Why,' Minna answered, trying to disengage herself from his firm grasp, 'in the first place, let me go, Colin, or I won't speak to you; let me go this minute I say; yes, that'll do, thank you, in the first place, what I want most is to get the education. When I've got that, I can begin to look out what to do with it. Perhaps I'll be a governess, or a Board-school teacher, or suchlike. But in the second place, one never knows what may happen to one. Somebody might fall in love with me, you see, and then I should very likely get married, Colin.' And Minna said this with such a saucy little smile, that Cohn longed then and there, in the open park, to stoop down and kiss her soundly.

'Then you've really arranged it all, have you, Minna?' he asked wonderingly. You've really decided to go to Miss Woollacott's?'

Minna nodded.

'Well, Minna,' Colin said in a tone of genuine admiration, 'you may say what you like about us men being all the same (I suppose we are, if it comes to that), but I do admire you immensely for it. You've got such a wonderful lot of spirit and determination. Now, I know what you'll say; you'll go and take it wrong again; but, Minna, it's a great deal harder and more remarkable for a woman to try to raise herself than for a man to go and do it. Why, now I come to think of it, little woman, I've read of lots of men educating themselves and rising to be great people, George Stephenson, that made the steam-engines on railways, and Gibson the sculptor, and lots of painters and architects and people, but really and truly, I believe, Minna, I never read yet of a woman who'd been and done it.'

'That's because the books are all written by men, stupid, you may be certain,' Minna answered saucily. 'Anyhow, Colin, I'm going to try and do it. I'm going to leave my place at the end of the month, and go for a pupil-teacher at Miss Woollacott's. And I'm beginning the geography now, and the Second Grade English Grammar, so that I can get myself fit for it, Colin, a bit beforehand. I don't see why you should be reading all these fine books, you know, and I should be content with being no more nor a common parlourmaid.'

It was in the park, but it was getting dusky, and lovers in London are not so careful of secrecy as in the unsophisticated and less limited country. The great perennial epic of each human heart must needs work itself out somehow or other even under the Argus eyes of the big squalid ugly city. So Colin stooped down beneath the shade of the plane trees and kissed Minna twice or three times over in spite of her pretended struggling. (It is a point of etiquette with girls of Minna's class that they should pretend to struggle when one tries to kiss them.)

'Minna,' he said earnestly, 'I'm proud of you. My dear little girl, I'm really proud of you.'

'What a funny thing it is,' thought Minna to herself, 'that he never makes love to me, though! I don't know even now whether he considers himself engaged to me or not.

'Beneath the shade of the plane-trees.

How queer it is that he never makes me a proper proposal!' For Minna had diligently read her 'London Herald,' and knew well that when a young man (especially of Colin's attainments) proposes to a young lady, he ought to do it with all due formalities, in a set speech carefully imitated from the finest literary models of the eighteenth century. Instead of which, Colin only kissed her now and again quite promiscuous like, just as he used to do long since at Wootton Man-deville, and called her 'Minna' and 'little woman.' Still she did think on the whole that 'little woman' sounded after all a great deal like an irregular betrothal. (She distinctly recollected that Mabel in the 'London Herald,' and Maud de Vere in the 'Maiden's Stratagem,' always called it a betrothal and not an engagement.)

VOLUME II

CHAPTER XV

A DOOR OPENS

Another year had passed, and Colin, now of full age, had tired of working for Cicolari. It was all very well, this moulding clay and carving replicas of afflicted widows; it was all very well, this modelling busts and statuettes and little classical compositions; it was all very well, this picking up stray hints in a half-amateur fashion from the grand torsos of the British Museum and a few scattered Thorwaldsens or antiques of the great country houses; but Colin Churchill felt in his heart of hearts that all that was not sculpture. He was growing in years now, and instead of learning he was really working. Still, he had quite made up his mind that some day or other he should look with his own eyes on the glories of the Vatican and the Villa Albani. Nay, he had even begun to take lessons in Italian from Cicolari, counting his chickens before they were hatched, Minna said, so that he might not feel himself at a loss whenever the great and final day of his redemption should happen to arrive. The dream of his life was to go to Rome, and study in a real studio, and become a regular genuine sculptor. Nothing short of that would ever satisfy him, he told Minna: and Minna, though she trembled to think of Colin's going so far away from her, among all those black-eyed Italian women, too—(and Colin had often told her he admired black eyes, like hers, above all others)—poor little Minna could not but admit sorrowfully to herself that Rome was after all the proper school for Colin Churchill. 'The capital of art,' he repeated to her, over and over again; must it not be the right place for him, who she felt sure was going to be the greatest of all modern English artists?

But how was Colin ever to get there?

Going to Rome costs money; and during all these years Colin had barely been able to save enough to buy the necessary books and materials for his self-education. The more deeply he felt the desire to go, the more utterly remote did the chance of going seem to become to him. 'And yet I shall go, Minna,' he said to her almost fiercely one September evening. 'Go to Rome I will, if I have to tramp every step of the way on foot, and reach there barefoot.

Minna sighed and the tears came into her eyes; but strong in her faith and pride in Colin, strong in her eager desire that Colin should give free play to his own genius, she answered firmly with a little quiver of her lips, 'You ought to go, Colin; and if you think it'd help you, you might take all that's left of my savings, and I'd go back again willingly to the parlour-maiding.'

Colin looked at the pretty little pupil-teacher with a look of profound and unfeigned admiration. 'Minna,' he said, 'dear little woman, you're the best and kindest-hearted girl that ever breathed; but how on earth do you suppose I could possibly be wretch enough to take away your poor little savings? No, no, little woman, you must keep them for yourself, and use them for making yourself, I was going to say into a lady, but you couldn't do that, Minna, you couldn't do that, for you were born one already. Still, if you want me to be a real sculptor, I want you, little woman, just as much to be a real educated gentlewoman.' Colin said the last word with a certain lingering loving cadence, for it had a good old-fashioned ring about it that recommended it well to his simple straightforward peasant nature.

'Well, Colin,' Minna went on, blushing a bit (for that last quiet hint seemed half unintentionally to convey the impression that Colin really possessed a proprietary right in her whole future), 'we must try our best to find out some way for you to go to Rome at last in spite of everything. You know, meanwhile, you've got good employment, Colin, and that's always something.'

'Ah yes, Minna,' Colin answered with his youthful enthusiasm coming strong upon him, 'I've got employment, of course; but I don't want employment; I want opportunities, I want advice, I want instruction, I want the means of learning, I want to perfect myself. Here in London, somehow, I feel as if I was tied down by the leg, and panting to get loose again. I like Cicolari, and in my own native untaught fashion I've done my best to improve myself with him; but I feel sadly the lack of training and competition. I should like to see how other men do their work; I should like to pit myself against them and find out whether I really am or am not a sculptor. Let me but just go to Rome, and I shall mould such things and carve such statues, ah, Minna, you shall see them! And the one delight I have in life now, Minna, is to get out like this, and talk it over with you, and tell you what I mean to do when once I get at it. For you can sympathise with me more than any of them, little woman. I feel that you can realise my longing to do good work, the work I know I'm fitted for—a thousand times better than a mere decent respectable marble-hacking workman like Cicolari.'

Poor little Minna! She sighed again, and her heart beat harder than ever. It was such a privilege for her to feel that Colin Churchill, with all that great future looming large before his young imagination, still loved her best to sympathise with him in his artistic yearnings. She pressed his arm a little, in her sweet simplicity, but she said nothing.

'You see,' Colin went on, musingly, for he liked to talk it all over again and again with Minna, 'art doesn't all come by nature, Minna, as most people fancy; it wants such a lot of teaching. Of course, you've got to have the thing born in you to begin with; but you might be born a Pheidias, it's my belief, Minna, and yet, without teaching, the merest wooden blockhead at the Academy schools would beat you hollow as far as technicalities went. Look at the dissecting now! If I hadn't saved that five pounds that Sir William gave me for carving the group on the mantelpiece, I should never have known anything at all about anatomy. But just going in my spare time for those six months to the anatomy class at the University College Hospital—why, it gave me quite a different idea altogether about the human figure. It showed me how to clothe my bare skeletons, Minna.'

'I never could bear your going and doing that horrible dissection, all the same, Colin,' Minna said with a chilly little shudder. 'It's so dreadful, you know, cutting up dead bodies and all that, just as bad as if you were going to be a medical student.'

'Ah, but no sculpture worth calling sculpture's possible without it, I tell you, Minna,' Colin answered warmly. 'Why, Michael Angelo, you know, Michael Angelo was a regular downright out-and-out anatomist. It can't be wrong to do like Michael Angelo, now can it? That was a man, Michael Angelo! And Leonardo, too, he was an awful stickler for anatomy as well, Leonardo was. Why, every great sculptor and every great painter that ever I've read of, Minna, had to study anatomy. I suppose the Greeks did it, even; yes, I'm sure the Greeks did it, for just look at the legs of the Discobolus and the arms of the Theseus; how the muscles in them show the knowledge of anatomy in the old sculptors. Oh yes, Minna, I'm quite sure the Greeks did it. And the Greeks! well, the Greeks, you know, they were really even greater, I do believe, than Michael Angelo.'

'Well, Colin,' Minna answered, with the charming critical confidence of love and youth and inexperience,'I've seen all your engravings of images by Michael Angelo, and I've seen the broken-nosed Theseus, don't you call him, at the Museum, and I've seen all the things you've sent me to look at in the South Kensington; and it's my belief, Rome or no Rome, that there isn't one of them fit to hold a candle any day to your Cephalus and Aurora, that you made when you first came to London; and I should say so if the whole Royal Academy was to come up in a lump and declare your figures weren't worth anything.'

A week or two passed, and Minna, busy at staid Miss Woollacott's with her little pupils, saw no more chance than ever, though she turned it over often in her mind, of helping Colin on his way to Rome. Indeed, the North London Birkbeck Girls' School was hardly the place where one might naturally expect to find opportunities arise of such a nature. But one morning, in the teachers' room, Minna happened to pick up the 'Times,' which lay upon the table, and, looking over it, her eye fell casually upon an advertisement which at first sight would hardly have attracted her attention at all, but for the word Rome printed in it in small capitals. It was merely one of the ordinary servants' advertisements, lumped together promiscuously under the head of Wanted.

'As Valet, to go abroad (to Rome), a young man, not exceeding 30. Good wages. Some knowledge of Italian would be a recommendation. Apply to Sir Henry Wilberforce, 27 Ockenden Square, S.W.'

Minna laid down the paper with a sickening feeling at her heart: she thought she saw in it just a vague chance by which Colin could manage to get to Rome and begin his education as a sculptor. After all, it was the getting there that was the great difficulty. Colin had ten or eleven pounds put away, she knew, and though that would barely suffice to pay the railway fare on the humblest scale, yet it would be quite a little fortune to go on upon when once he got there. Minna knew from her own experience how far ten pounds will go for a careful person with due economy. Now, if only Colin would consent to take this place as valet, and Minna knew that he had long ago learnt a valet's duties at the old vicar's, he might get his passage paid to Rome for him, and whenever this Sir Henry Wilberforce got tired of him, or was coming away, or other reasonable cause occurred, Colin might leave the place and employ all his little savings in getting himself some scraps of a sculptor's education at Rome. Wild as all this would seem to most people who are accustomed to count money in terms of hundreds, it didn't sound at all wild to poor little Minna, and it wouldn't have sounded so to Colin Churchill.

But should she tell Colin anything about it? Could she bear to tell him? Let him go away from her across the sea to that dim far Italy of his own accord, if he liked; it was his fortune, his chance in life, his natural place; she knew it; but why should she, Minna Wroe, the London pupil-teacher, the

Wootton fisherman's daughter, why should she go out of her way to send him so far from her, to banish herself from his presence, to run the risk of finally losing him altogether? 'After all,' she thought, 'perhaps I oughtn't to tell him. He might be angry at it. He might think I shouldn't have looked upon such a place as at all good enough for him. He's a sculptor, not a servant; and I got to be a schoolmistress myself on purpose so as to make myself something like equal to him. It wouldn't be right of me to go proposing to him that he should take now to brushing coats and laying out shirt studs again, when he ought to be sculpturing a statue a great deal more beautiful than those great stupid, bloated, thick-legged Michael Angelos. I dare say the wisest thing for me to do would be to say nothing at all to him about it.'

'Miss Wroe,' a small red-haired pupil called out, popping her shock head through the half-open doorway, and shouting out her message in her loudest London accent, 'if yer please, ye're ten minutes late for the fourth junerer, and Miss Woollacott, she says, will yer please come at once, and not keep the third junerer waitin' any longer.'

Minna ran off hurriedly to her class, and tried to forget her troubles about Colin forthwith in the occult mysteries of the agreement of a relative with its antecedent.

But when she got back to Miss Woollacott's lodgings at Kentish Town that evening, and had had her usual supper of bread and cheese and a glass of water, Miss Woollacott took beer, but Minna as a minor was restricted to the beverage of nature, and had heard prayers read, and had gone up by herself to her small bare bedroom, she sat down on the bedside all alone, and cried a little, and thought it all out, and tried hard to come to the right decision. It would be very sad indeed to lose Colin; she could scarcely bear that; and yet she knew that it was for Colin's good; and what was for Colin's good was surely for her own good too in the long-run. Well, was it? that was the question. Of course, she would dearly love for Colin to go to Rome, and learn to be a real sculptor, and get fame and glory, and come back a greater man than the vicar himself, almost as great, indeed, as the Earl of Beaminster. But there were dangers in it, too. Out of sight, out of mind; and it was a long way to Italy. Perhaps when Colin got there he would see some pretty Italian girl or some grand fine lady, and fall in love with her, and forget at once all about his poor little Minna. Ah, no, it wasn't altogether for Minna's good, perhaps, that Colin should go to Italy.

She sat there so long, ruminating about it on her bedside without undressing, that Miss Woollacott, who always looked under the door to see if the light was out and prevent waste of the candles, called out in quite a sharp voice, 'Minna Wroe, how very long you are undressing!' And then she blew out the candle in a hurry, and undressed in the dark, and jumped into bed hastily, and covered her head up with the bedclothes, and had a good cry, very silently; and after that she felt a little better. But still she couldn't go to sleep, thinking about how very hard it would be to lose Colin. Oh, no, she couldn't bear to tell him; she wouldn't tell him; it wasn't at all likely the place would suit him; and if he wanted to go to Rome and leave her, he must just go and find a way for himself; and so that was all about it.

And then a sudden glow of shame came over Minna's cheeks, as she lay there in the dark on the little iron bedstead, to think that she should have been so untrue for a single moment to her better self and to Colin's best and highest interests. She loved Colin! yes, she loved him! from her childhood onward, he had been her one dream and romance and ideal! She knew Colin could make things lovelier than any other man on earth had ever yet imagined; and she knew she ought to do her best to put him in the way of fulfilling his own truest and purest instincts. Should she selfishly keep him here in England, when it was only at Rome that he could get the best instruction? Should she cramp his genius and clip his wings, merely in order that he mightn't fly away too far from her? Oh, it was wicked of her, downright wicked of her, to wish not to tell him. Come of it what might, she must go round and see Colin the very next day, and let him decide for himself about that dreadful upsetting advertisement. And having at last arrived at this conclusion, Minna covered her head a second time with the counterpane, had another good cry, just to relieve her conscience, and then sank off into a troubled sleep from which she only woke again at the second bell next morning.

All that day she taught with the dreadful advertisement weighing heavily on her mind, and interposing itself terribly between her and the rule of three, or the names and dates of the Anglo-Saxon sovereigns. She couldn't for the life of her remember whether Ethel-bald came before or after Ethelwulf; and she stumbled horribly over the question whether this was a personal or a demonstrative pronoun. But when the evening came, she got leave from Miss Woollacott to go round and see her cousin (a designation which was strictly correct in some remote sense, for Minna's mother and Cohn's father were in some way related), and she almost ran the whole way to the Marylebone Road to catch Colin just before he went away for the night from Cicolari's.

When Colin saw the advertisement, and heard Minna's suggestion, he turned it over a good many times in his own mind, and seemed by no means disinclined to try the chances of it. 'It's only a very small chance, of course, Minna,' he said dubitatively, 'but at any rate it's worth trying. The great thing against me is that I haven't been anything in that line for so very long, and I can't get any character, except from Cicolari. The one thing in my favour is that I know a little Italian. I don't suppose there are many young men of the sort who go to be valets who know Italian. Anyhow, I'll try it. It'll be a dreadful thing if I get it, having to leave you for so long, Minna,' and Minna's cheek brightened at that passing recognition of her prescriptive claim upon him; 'but it'll only be for a year or two; and when I come back, little woman, I shall come back very different from what I go, and then, Minna, why, then, we shall see what we shall see!' And Colin stooped to kiss the little ripe lips that pretended to evade him (Minna hadn't got over that point of etiquette yet), and held the small brown face tight between his hands, so that Minna couldn't manage to get it away, though she struggled, as in duty bound, her very hardest.

So early next day Colin put on his best Sunday clothes, and very handsome and gentlemanly he looked in them too, and walked off to Ockenden Square, S.W., in search of Sir Henry Wilberforce.

Sir Henry was a tall, spare, wizened-up old gentleman, with scanty grey hair, carefully brushed so as to cover the largest possible area with the thinnest possible layer. He was sitting in the dining-room after breakfast when Colin called; and Colin was shown in by the footman as an ordinary visitor. 'What name?' the man asked, as he ushered him from the front door.

'Colin Churchill.'

'Mr. Colin Churchill!' the man said, as Colin walked into the dining-room.

Sir Henry stared and rose to greet him with hand extended. 'Though upon my word,' he thought to himself, 'who the deuce Mr. Colin Churchill may be, I'm sure I haven't the faintest conception.'

This was decidedly awkward. Colin felt hot and uncomfortable; it began to dawn upon him that in his best Sunday clothes he looked perhaps a trifle too gentlemanly. But he managed to keep at a respectful distance, and Sir Henry, not finding his visitor respond to the warmth of his proposed reception, dropped his hand quietly and waited for Colin to introduce his business.

'I beg your pardon, sir,' Colin said a little uncomfortably, he began to feel, now, how far he had left behind the Dook's early lessons in manners—'I—I've come about your advertisement for a valet. I—I've come, in fact, to apply for the situation.'

Sir Henry glanced at him curiously. 'The deuce you have,' he said, dropping back chillily into his easy chair, and surveying Colin over from head to foot with an icy scrutiny. 'You've come to apply for the situation! Why, Wilkinson said, "Mr. Colin Churchill."' 'He mistook my business, I suppose,' Colin answered quietly, but with some hesitation. It somehow struck him already that he would find it hard to drop back once more into the long-forgotten position of a valet. 'I came to ask whether it was likely I would suit you. I can speak Italian.'

That was his trump card, in fact, and he thought it best to play it quickly.

Sir Henry looked at him again. 'Oh, you can speak Italian. Well, that's good as far as it goes; but how much Italian can you speak, that's the question?' And he added a few words in the best Tuscan he could muster up, to test the applicant's exact acquirements.

Colin answered him more quickly and idiomatically than Sir Henry had expected. In fact, Cicolari's lessons had been sound and practical. Sir Henry kept up the conversation, still in Italian, for a few minutes, and then, being quite satisfied on that score, returned with a better grace to his native English. 'Have you been out as a valet before?' he asked.

'Not for some years, sir.' Colin replied frankly. 'I went out to service at first, and was page and valet to a clergyman in Dorsetshire—Mr. Howard-Bussell, of Wootton Mandeville—'

'Knew him well,' Sir Henry repeated to himself reflectively. 'Old Howard-Russell of Wootton Mandeville! Dead these five years. Knew him well, the selfish old pig; as conceited, self-opinioned an old fool as ever lived in all England. He declared my undoubted Pinturicchio was only a Giovanni do Spagno. Whereas it's really the only quite indubitable Pinturiccliio in a private gallery anywhere at all outside Italy.'

'Except the St. Sebastian at Knowle, of course,' Colin put in, innocently.

Sir Henry turned round and stared at him again. 'Except the St. Sebastian at Knowle,' he echoed coldly. 'Except the St. Sebastian at Knowle, no doubt. But how the deuce did he come to know the St. Sebastian at Knowle was a Pinturiccliio, I wonder? Anyhow, it shows he's lived in very decent places. Well, and so you used to be with old Mr. Howard-Russell, did you? And since then, since then, what have you been doing?'

'At present, sir,' Cohn went on, 'I'm working as a marble-cutter; but circumstances make me wish to go back again to service now, and as I happen to know Italian, I thought perhaps your place might suit me.'

'No doubt, no doubt. I dare say it would. But the question is, would you suit me, don't you see? A marble-cutter, he says, a marble-cutter! How deuced singular! Have you got a character?'

'I could get one from Mr. Russell's friends, I should think, sir; and of course my present employer would speak for my honesty and so forth.'

Sir Henry asked him a few more questions, and then seemed to be turning the matter over in his own mind a little. 'The Italian,' he said, speaking to himself, for he had a habit that way, 'the Italian's the great thing. I've made up my mind I'll never go to Rome again with a valet who doesn't speak Italian. Dobbs was impossible, quite impossible. This young man has some Italian, but can he valet, I wonder? Here, you! come into my bedroom, and let me see what you can do in the way of your duties.'

Colin followed him upstairs, and, being put through his paces as a body-servant, got through the examination with decent credit. Next came the question of wages and so forth, and finally the announcement that Sir Henry meant to start for Rome early in October.

'Well, he's a very fair-spoken young man,' Sir Henry said at last, 'and he knows Italian. But it's devilish odd his being a marble-cutter. However, I'll try him. I'll write to your master, Churchill, what's his name, I'll write to him and enquire about you.'

Colin gave him Cicolari's name and address, and Sir Henry noted them deliberately in his pocket-book. 'Very good,' he said; 'I'll write and ask about your character, and if everything's all correct, I shall let you know and engage you.'

Colin found it rather hard to answer 'Thank you, sir;' but it was for Rome and art, and he managed to say it.

CHAPTER XVI

COLIN'S DEPARTURE

When Minna learnt from Colin that he had finally accepted Sir Henry Wilberforce's situation, her heart was very heavy. She wanted her old friend to do everything that would make him into a great sculptor, of course; but still, say what you will about it, it's very hard to have your one interest in life taken far away from you, and to be left utterly alone and self-contained in the great dreary world of London. Have you ever reflected, dear sir or madam, how terrible is the isolation of a girl in Minna Wroe's position, nay, for the matter of that, of your own housemaid, of cook, or parlour-maid, in that vast, unsympathetic, human ant-hill? Think, for a moment, of the warm human heart within her, suddenly cramped and turned in upon itself by the unspeakable strangeness of everything around her. She has come up from the country, doubtless, to take a 'better' place in London, and there she is thrown by pure chance into one situation or another, with two or three more miscellaneous girls from other shires, having other friends and other interests; and from day to day she toils on, practically alone, among so many unknown, or but officially known, and irresponsive faces. Is it any wonder that, under such circumstances, she looks about her anxiously for some living object round which to twine the tendrils of her better nature?—it may be only a bird, or a cat, or a lap-dog; it may be Bob the postman or policeman Jenkins. We laugh about her young man, whom we envisage to ourselves simply as a hulking fellow and a domestic nuisance; we never reflect that to her all the interest and sympathy of life is concentrated and focussed upon that one single shadowy follower. He may be as uninteresting a slip of a plough-boy, turned driver of a London railway van, as ever was seen in this realm of England; or he may be as full of artistic aspiration and beautiful imaginings as Colin Churchill; but to her it is all the same; he is her one friend and confidant and social environment; he represents in her eyes universal society; he is the solitary unit who can play upon the full gamut of that many-toned and exquisitely modulated musical instrument, her inherited social nature. Take him away, and what is there left of her?—a mere automatic human machine for making beds or grinding out arithmetic for junior classes.

Has not humanity rightly pitched, by common consent, for the main theme of all its verse and all its literature, upon this one universal passion, which, for a few short years at least, tinges with true romance and unspoken poetry even the simplest and most commonplace souls?

Colin felt the sadness of parting, too, but by no means so acutely as Minna. The door of fame was opening at last before him; Rome was looming large upon the mental horizon; dreams in marble were crystallising themselves down into future actuality; and in the near fulfilment of his life-long hopes, it was hardly to be expected that he should take the parting to heart so seriously as the little pupil-teacher herself had taken it. Besides, time, in anticipation at least, never looks nearly so long to men as to women. Don't we all know that a woman will cry her eyes out about a few months' absence, which to a man seems hardly worth making a fuss about? 'It's only for three or four years, you know, Minna,' Colin said, as lightly as though three or four years were absolutely nothing; and ah me, how long they looked to poor, lonely, heartsick little Minna! She felt almost inclined to give up this up-hill work of teaching and self-education altogether, and return once more to the old fisherman's cottage away down at Wootton Mandeville. There at least she would have some human sympathies and interests to comfort and sustain her.

But Colin had lots of work to do, getting himself ready for his great start in life; and he hardly entered to the full into little Minna's fears and troubles. He had to refurbish his entire wardrobe on a scale suited to a gentleman's servant, Minna was working hard in all her spare hours at making new shirts for him or mending old ones: he had to complete arrangements of all sorts for his eventful journey; and he had to select among his books and drawings which ones should accompany him upon his journey to Rome, and which should be consigned to the omnivorous secondhand book-stall. Milton and Shelley and Bohn's 'Æschylus' he certainly couldn't do without; they were an integral part of his stock-in-trade as a sculptor, and to have left them behind would have been an irreparable error; but the old dog-eared 'Euripides' must go, and the other English translations from the classics would have made his box quite too heavy for Sir Henry to pay excess upon at Continental rates, so Cicolari told him. Still, the Flaxman plates must be got in somewhere, even if Shelley himself had to give way to them; and so must his own designs for his unexecuted statues, those mainstays of his future artistic career. Minna helped him to choose and pack them all, and she was round so often at Cicolari's in the evening that prim Miss Woollacott said somewhat sharply at last, 'It seems to me a very good thing, Minna Wroe, that this cousin of yours is going to Rome at last, as you tell me; for even though he's your only relation in London, I don't think it's quite proper or necessary for you to be round at his lodgings every other evening.' Colin took a few lessons, too, in his future duties, from a gentleman's gentleman in Regent's Park. It wasn't a pleasant thing to do, and he sighed as he put away his books and sketches, and went out to receive his practical instruction from that very supercilious and elegant person; but it had to be done, and so he did it. Colin didn't care particularly for associating with the gentleman's gentleman; indeed, he was beginning slowly to realise now how wide a gulf separated the Colin Churchill of the Marylebone Road from the little Colin Churchill of Wootton Mande-ville. He had lived so much by himself since he came to London, he had seen so little of anybody except Minna and Cicolari, and he had been so entirely devoted to art and study, that he had never stopped to gauge his own progress before, and therefore had never fully felt in his own mind how great was the transformation that had insensibly come over him. Without knowing it himself, he had slowly developed from a gentleman's servant into an artist and a gentleman. And now he was being forced by accident or fate to take upon him once more the position of an ordinary valet.

Indeed, during the month that intervened between Colin's engagement by Sir Henry Wilberforce and his start for Rome, he wrote to his brother Sam over in America; and, shadowy memory as Sam had long since become to him, though he told him of his projected trip, and enlarged upon his hopes of attaining to the pinnacle of art in Rome, he was so ashamed of his mode of getting there that he said nothing at all upon that point, but just glided easily over the questions of means and method. He didn't want his thriving brother in America to know that he was going to Rome, with all his high ideals and beautiful dreams, in no better position than as an old man's valet.

At last the slow month wore itself away gradually for Colin, how swift and short it seemed to Minna!—and the day came when he was really to set out for Paris, on his way to Italy. He was to start with his new master from Charing Cross station, and he had taken possession of his post by anticipation a couple of days earlier. Minna mustn't be at the station to see him off, of course; that would be unofficial; and if servants indulge in such doubtful luxuries as sweethearts, they must at least take care to meet them at some seemly time or season; but at any rate she could say good-bye to him the evening before, and that was always something. Would he propose to her this time, at last, Minna wondered, or would he go away for that long, long journey, and leave her as much in doubt as ever as to whether he really did or didn't love her?

'It won't be for long, you see, little woman,' Colin said, kissing away her tears in Regent's Park, as well as he was able; 'it won't be for long, Minna; and then, when we meet again, I shall have come back a real sculptor. What a delightful meeting we shall have, Minna, and how awfully learned and clever you'll have got by that time! I shall be half afraid to talk to you. But you'll write to me every week, won't you, little woman? You'll promise me that? You must promise me to write to me every week, or at the very least every fortnight.'

It was some little crumb of comfort to Minna that he wanted her to write to him so often. That showed at any rate that he really cared for her just ever such a tiny bit. She wiped her eyes again as she answered, 'Yes, Colin; I'll take great care never to miss writing to you.'

'That's right, little woman. And look here, you mustn't mind my giving you them; there's stamps enough for Italy to last you for a whole twelvemonth, fifty-two of them, Minna, so that it won't ever be any expense to you; and when those are gone, I'll send you some others.'

'Thank you, Colin,' Minna said, taking them quite simply and naturally. 'And you'll write to me, too, won't you, Colin?'

'My dear Minna! Why, of course I will. Who else on earth have I got to write to?'

'And you won't forget me, Colin?'

'Forget you, Minna! If ever I forget you, may my right hand forget her cunning, and what more dreadful thing could a sculptor say by way of an imprecation than that, now!'

'Oh, Colin, don't! Don't say so! Suppose it was to come true, you know!'

'But I don't mean to forget you, Minna; so it won't come true. Little woman, I shall think of you always, and have your dear little gipsy face for ever before me. And now, Minna, this time we must really say good-bye. I'm out beyond my time already. Just one more; thank you, darling. Goodbye, good-bye, Minna. Good-bye, dearest. One more. God bless you!'

'Good-bye, Colin. Good-bye, good-bye. Oh, Colin, my heart is breaking.'

And when that night Minna lay awake in her own bare small room at prim Miss Woollacott's, she thought it all over once more, and argued the pros and cons of the whole question deliberately to herself with much trepidation. 'He called me "dearest," she thought in her sad little mind, 'and he said he'd never forget me; that looks very much as if he really loved me: but, then, he never asked me whether I loved him or not, and he never proposed to me, no, I'm quite sure he never proposed to me. I should have felt so much easier in my own mind if only before he went away he'd properly proposed to me!' And then she covered her head with the bed-clothes once more, and sobbed herself to sleep, to dream of Colin.

The very next evening, Colin was at Paris.

CHAPTER XVII

A LITTLE CLOUD LIKE A MAN'S HAND

At the Gare de Lyon, Colin put his master safely into his coupe-lit, and then wandered along the train looking out for a carriage into which he might install himself comfortably for the long journey. All the carriages, as on all French express trains, were first-class; and Colin soon picked one out for himself, with a vacant place next the window. He jumped in and took his seat; and in two minutes more the train was off, and he found himself, at last, beyond the possibility of a doubt, on his way to Rome.

Rome, Rome, Rome! how the very name seemed to bound and thrill through Colin Churchill's inmost nature! He looked at the little book of coupon tickets which his master had given him; yes, there it was, as clear as daylight, 'Paris, P.L.M., à Rome;' not a doubt about it. Rome, Rome, Rome! It had seemed a dream, a fancy, hitherto; and now it was just going to be converted into an actual living reality. He could hardly believe even now that he would ever get there. Would there be an accident at the summit level of the Mont Cenis tunnel, to prevent his ever reaching the goal of his ambition? It almost seemed as if there must be some hitch somewhere, for the idea of actually getting to Rome—that Rome that Cicolari had long ago told him was the capital of art—seemed too glorious and magnificent to be really true, for Colin Churchill.

For a while, the delightful exhilaration of knowing that that very carriage in which he sat was actually going straight through to Rome left him little room to notice the faces or personalities of his fellow-travellers. But as they gradually got well outside the Paris ring, and launched into the country towards Fontainebleau, Colin had leisure to look about him and take stock of the companions he was to have on his way southward. Three of them were Frenchmen only going to Lyon and Marseille, only, Colin thought to himself, naively, for he despised anybody now who was bound for anywhere on earth save the city of Michael Angelo and Canova and Thorwaldsen; but the other two were bound, by the labels on their luggage, for Rome itself. One of them was a tall military-looking gentleman, with a grizzled grey moustache, a Colonel somebody, the hat-box said, but the name was covered by a label; the other, apparently his daughter, was a handsome girl of about twenty, largely built and selfpossessed, like a woman who has lived much in the world from her childhood upward. Colin saw at once, that, unlike little Minna (who had essentially a painter's face and figure), this graceful full-formed woman was entirely and exquisitely statuesque. The very pose of her arm upon the slight ledge of the window as she leaned out to look at the country was instinct with plastic capabilities. Colin, with his professional interest always uppermost, felt a perfect longing to have up a batch of clay forthwith and model it then and there upon the spot. He watched each new movement and posture so closely, in fact (of course in his capacity as a sculptor only), that the girl herself noticed his evident admiration, and took it sedately like a woman of the world. She didn't blush and shrink away timidly, as Minna would have done under the same circumstances (though her skin was many shades lighter than Minna's rich brunette complexion, and would have shown the faintest suspicion of a blush, had one been present, far more readily); she merely observed and accepted Colin's silent tribute of admiration as her natural due. It made her just a trifle more self-conscious, perhaps, but that was all; indeed, one could hardly say whether even so the somewhat studied attitudes she seemed to be taking up were not really the ones which by long use had become the easiest for her. There are some beautiful women so accustomed to displaying their beauty to the best advantage that they can't even throw themselves down on a sofa in their own bedrooms without instinctively and automatically assuming a graceful position for all their limbs.

After a while, they fell into a conversation; and Colin, who was the most innocent and unartificial of men, was amused to find that even he, on the spur of the moment, had arrived at a very obvious, worldly-wise principle upon this subject. Wishing to get into a talk with the daughter, he felt half-unconsciously that it wouldn't do to begin by addressing her outright, but that he should first, with seeming guilelessness, attack her father. A man who is travelling with a pretty girl, in whatever relation, doesn't like you to begin an acquaintanceship of travel by speaking to her first; he resents your intrusion, and considers you have no right to talk to ladies under his escort. But when you begin by addressing himself, that is quite another matter; lured on by his quiet good sense, or his conversational powers, or his profound knowledge, or whatever else it is that he specially prides himself upon, you are soon launched upon general topics, and then the ladies of the party naturally chime in after a few minutes. To start by addressing him is a compliment to his intelligence or his social qualities; to start by addressing his companion is a distinct slight to himself, at the same time that it displays your own cards far too openly. You can convert him at once either into a valuable ally or into an enemy and a jealous guardian. Of course every other man feels this from his teens; but Colin hadn't yet mixed much in the world, and he smiled to himself at his acumen in discovering it at all on the first trial.

'Beautifully wooded country about here,' he said at the earliest opportunity the military gentleman gave him by laying down his Times (even in France your Englishman will stick to his paper). 'Not like most of France; so green and fresh-looking. This is Millet's country, you know; he always works about the outskirts of Fontainebleau.'

'Ah, indeed, does he?' the colonel responded, having only a very vague idea floating through his mind that Millet or Millais or something of the sort was the name of some painter fellow or other he had somewhere heard about. 'He works about Fontainebleau, does he, now? Dear me! How very interesting!'

Whenever people dismiss a subject from their minds by saying 'How very interesting!' you know at once they really mean that it doesn't interest them in the slightest degree, and they don't want to be bothered by hearing anything more about it; but Colin's observations upon mankind and the niceties of the English language had not yet carried him to this point of interpretative science, so he took the colonel literally at his word, and went on enthusiastically (for he was a great admirer of the peasant painter whose story was so like his own), 'Yes, he works at Fontainebleau. It was here, you know, that he painted his Angelus. Have you ever seen the Angelus?'

The colonel fidgeted about in his seat uneasily, and fumbled in a nervous way with the corner of the Times. 'The Angelus!' he repeated, meditatively. 'Ah, yes, the Angelus. Gwen, my dear, have we seen Mr. Millet's Angelus P Was it in the Academy?'

'No, papa,' Gwen answered, smiling sweetly and composedly. 'We haven't seen it, and it wasn't in the Academy. M. Millet is the French painter, you remember, the painter who wears sabots. So delightfully romantic, isn't it,' turning to Colin, 'to be a great painter and yet still to wear sabots?' This was a very cleverly delivered sentence of Miss Gwen's, for it was intended first to show that she at least, if not her father, knew who the unknown young artist was talking about (Gwen jumped readily at the conclusion that Colin was an artist), and secondly, to exonerate her papa from culpable ignorance in the artist's eyes by gently suggesting that a slight confusion of names sufficiently accounted for his obvious blunder. But it was also, quite unintentionally, delivered point-blank at Colin Churchill's tenderest susceptibilities. This grand young lady, then, so calm and selfpossessed, could sympathise with an artist who had risen, and who, even in the days of his comparative prosperity, still wore sabots. To be sure, Colin didn't exactly know what sabots were (perhaps the blue blouses which he saw all the French workmen were wearing?), for he was still innocent of all languages but his own, unless one excepts the Italian he had picked up in anticipation from Cicolari; but he guessed at least it was some kind of dress supposed to mark Millet's peasant origin, and that was quite enough for him. The grand young lady did not despise an artist who had been born in the ranks of the people.

'Yes,' he said warmly, 'it's very noble of him. Noble not merely that he has risen to paint such pictures as the Gleaners and the Angelus, but that he isn't ashamed now to own the peasant people he has originally sprung from.'

'Oh, ah, certainly,' the colonel replied in a short sharp voice, though the remark was hardly addressed to him. 'Very creditable of the young man, indeed, not to be ashamed of his humble origin. Very creditable. Very creditable. Gwen, my dear, would you like to see the paper?'

'No, thank you, papa,' Gwen answered with another charming smile (fine teeth, too, by Jingo). 'You know I never care to read in a train in motion. Yes, quite a romantic story, this of Millet's; and I believe even now he's horribly poor, isn't he? he doesn't sell his pictures.'

'The highest art,' Colin said quietly, 'seldom meets with real recognition during the lifetime of the artist.'

'You're a painter yourself?' asked Gwen, looking up at the handsome young man with close interest.

'Not a painter; a sculptor; and I'm going to Rome to perfect myself in my art.'

'A sculptor—to Rome!' Gwen repeated to herself. 'Oh, how nice! Why, we're going to Rome, too, and we shall be able to go all the way together. I'm so glad, for I'm longing to be told all about art and artists.'

Colin smiled. 'You're fond of art, then?' he asked simply.

'Fond of it is exactly the word,' Gwen answered. 'I know very little about it; much less than I should like to do; but I'm intensely interested in it. And a sculptor, too! Do you know, I've often met lots of painters, but I never before met a sculptor.'

'The loss has been theirs,' Colin put in with professional gravity. 'You would make a splendid model.'

The young man said it in the innocence of his heart, thinking only what a grand bust of a Semiramis or an Artemisia one might have moulded from Miss Gwen's full womanly face and figure; but the observation made the colonel shudder with awe and astonishment on his padded cushions. 'Gwen, my dear,' he said, feebly interposing for the second time,'hadn't you better change places with me? The draught from the window will be too much for you, I'm afraid.'

'Oh dear no, thank you, papa; not at all. I haven't been roasted, you know, for twenty years in the North-West Provinces, till every little breath of air chills me and nips me like a hothouse flower. So you think I would make a good model, do you? Well, that now I call a real compliment, because of course you regard me dispassionately from a sculpturesque point of view. I've been told that a great many faces do quite well enough to paint, but that only very few features are regular and calm enough to be worth a sculptor's notice. Is that so, now?'

'It is,' Colin answered, looking straight into her beautiful bold face. 'For example, some gipsy-looking girls, who are very pretty indeed with their brown skins and bright black eyes, and who make exceedingly taking pictures—Esthers, and Cleopatras, and so forth, you know, are quite useless from the plastic point of view: their good looks depend too much upon colour and upon passing shades of expression, while sculpture of course demands that the features should be almost faultlessly perfect and regular in absolute repose.'

The colonel looked uneasy again, and pulled up his collar nervously. 'Very fine occupation indeed, a sculptor's,' he edged in sideways. 'Delightful faculty to be able to do the living marble and all that kind of thing; very delightful, really.' The colonel was always equal to a transparent platitude upon every occasion, and contributed very little else to the general conversation at any time.

'And so delightful, too, to hear an artist talk about his art,' Gwen added with a touch of genuine enthusiasm. 'Do you know, I think I should love to be a sculptor. I should love even to go about and see the studios, and watch the beautiful things growing under your hands. I should love to have my bust taken, just so as to get to know how you do it all. It must be so lovely to see the shape forming itself slowly out of a raw block of marble.'

'Oh, you know, we don't do it all in the marble, at first,' Colin said quickly. 'It's rather dirty work, the first modelling. If you come into a sculptor's studio when he's working in the clay, you'll find him all daubed over with bits of mud, just like a common labourer.'

'How very unpleasant!' said the colonel coldly. 'Hardly seems the sort of profession fit for a gentleman—now does it?'

'Oh, papa, how can you be so dreadful! Why, it's just beautiful. I should love to see it all. I think in some ways sculpture's the very finest and noblest art of all, finer and nobler even than painting.'

'The Greeks thought so,' Colin assented with quiet assurance; 'and they say Michael Angelo thought so too. Perhaps I may be prejudiced, but I certainly think so myself. There's a purity about sculpture which you don't get about painting or any other alternative form of art. In painting you may admit what is ugly, sparingly, to be sure, but still you may admit it. In sculpture everything must be beautiful. Beauty of pure form, without the accidental aid of colour, is what we aim at. Every limb must be in perfect proportion, every feature in exquisite harmony. Any deformity, any weakness of outline, any mere ungracefulness, you see, militates against that perfection of shape to which sculpture entirely devotes itself. The coldness, hardness, and whiteness of marble make it appeal only to the highest taste; its rigorous self-abnegation in refusing the aid of colour gives it a special claim in the eyes of the purest and truest judges.'

'Then you don't like tinted statues?' the colonel put it. (He knew his ground here, for had he not seen Gibson's Venus?) 'Neither do I. I always thought Gibson made a great mistake there.'

'Gibson was a very great artist,' Colin replied, curling his lip almost disdainfully, for he felt the absurdity of the colonel's glibness in condemning the noblest of modern English sculptors off-hand in this easy, mock-critical fashion. 'Gibson was a very great artist, but I think his Venus was perhaps a step in the wrong direction for all that. Its quite true that the Greeks tinted their statues—'

'Bless my soul, you don't mean to say so! the colonel ejaculated parenthetically.

'And modern practice was doubtless founded on the mistake of supposing that, because the torsos we dig up are white now, they were white originally. But even the example of the Greeks doesn't settle every question without appeal. We've tried white marble, and found it succeed. We've tried tinting, and found it wanting. The fact is, you see, the attention of the eye can't be distracted. Either it attends to form, or else it attends to colour; rarely and imperfectly to both together. Take a vase. If it's covered with figures or flowers, our attention's distracted from the general outline to the painted objects it encloses. If its colouring's uniform, we think only of the beauty of form, because our attention isn't distracted from it by conflicting sensations. That's the long and the short of it, I think. Beauty of form's a higher taste than beauty of colour—at least, so we sculptors always fancy.'

Colin delivered these remarks as if he intended them for the colonel (though they were really meant for Miss Gwen's enlightenment), and the colonel was decidedly flattered by the cunning tribute to his tastes and interests thus delicately implied. But Gwen drank in every word the young man said with the deepest attention, and managed to make him go on with his subject till he had warmed to it thoroughly, and had launched out upon his own peculiar theories as to the purpose and function of his chosen art. All along, however, Colin pointed his remarks so cleverly at the colonel, while giving Gwen her fair share of the conversation, that the colonel quite forgot his first suspicions about the young sculptor, and grew gradually quite cordial and friendly in demeanour. So well did they get on together that, by the time they had had lunch out of the colonel's basket, Colin had given the colonel his ideas as to the heinousness of palming off as sculpture veiled ladies and crying babies (both of which freaks of art, by the way, the colonel had hitherto vastly admired); while the colonel in return had imparted to Colin his famous stories of how he was once nearly killed by a tiger in a jungle at Boolundshuhr in the North-West Provinces, and how he had assisted to burn a fox out in a hunt at Gib., and how he had shot the biggest wapiti ever seen for twenty years in the neighbourhood of Ottawa. All which surprising adventures Colin received with the same sedulous show of polite interest that the colonel had extended in turn to his own talk about pictures and statues.

At last, they reached Dijon, and there Colin got out, as in duty bound, to inquire whether his master was in want of anything. Sir Henry didn't need much, so Colin returned quickly to his own carriage.

'You have a friend in a coupé-lit, I see,' the colonel said, opening the door for the young stranger. 'An invalid, I suppose.' Colin blushed visibly, so that Miss Gwen noticed his colour, and wondered what on earth could be the meaning of it. Till that moment, to say the truth, he had been so absorbed in his talk about art, and in observing Gwen (who interested him as all beautiful women interest a sculptor), that he had almost entirely forgotten, for the time being, his anomalous position. 'No, not an invalid,' he answered evasively, 'but a very old gentleman.' 'Ah,' the colonel put in, as the train moved away from Dijon station, 'I don't wonder people travel by coupe-lit when they can afford it, in spite of the prohibitive prices set upon it by these French companies. It's most unpleasant having nothing but first-class carriages on the train. You have to travel with your own servants.'

Colin smiled feebly, but said nothing. It began to strike him that in the innocence of his heart he had made a mistake in being beguiled into conversation with these grand people. And yet it was their own fault. Miss Gwen had clearly done it all, with her seductive inquiries about art and artists.

'Or rather,' the colonel went on, 'one can always put one's own servants, of course, into another carriage; but one's never safe against having to travel with other people's. We're lucky to-day in being a pleasant party all together (these French gentlemen, though they're not companionable, are evidently very decent people); but sometimes, I know, I've had to travel on the Continent here, wedged in immovably between a fat lady's-maid and a gentleman's gentleman.'

Colin's face burned hot and crimson. 'I beg your pardon,' he said, in a faltering voice, almost relapsing in his confusion into his aboriginal Dorsetshire, 'but I ought, perhaps, to have told you sooner who you are travelling with. I am valet to Sir Henry Wilberforce: he is the gentleman in the coupé-lit, and he's my master.'

The colonel sank back on his cushions with a face as white as marble, while Colin's now flushed as red as a damask rose. 'A valet!' he cried faintly. 'Gwen, my dear, did he say a valet? What can all this mean? Didn't he tell us he was a sculptor going to Rome to practise his profession?'

'I did,' Colin answered defiantly, for he was on his mettle now. 'I did tell you so, and it's the truth. But I'm going as a valet. I couldn't afford to go in any other way, and so I took a situation, meaning to use my spare time in Rome to study sculpture.'

The colonel rocked himself up and down irresolutely for a while; then he leant back a little more calmly in his seat, and gave himself up to a placid despair. 'At the next stopping station,' he thought to himself, 'we must get out and change into another carriage.' And he took up the 'Continental Bradshaw' with a sigh, to see if there was any chance of release before they got to Ambérieu.

But if the colonel was quite unmanned by this shocking disclosure, Miss Gwen's self-possession and calmness of demeanour was still wholly unshaken. She felt a little ashamed, indeed, that the colonel should so openly let Colin see into the profound depths of his good Philistine soul; but she did her best to make up for it by seeming not in any way to notice her father's chilling reception of the charming young artist's strange intelligence. 'A valet, papa,' she cried in her sprightly way, as unconcernedly as if she had been accustomed to associating intimately with valets for the last twenty years; 'how very singular! Why, I shouldn't be at all surprised if this was that Mr. Churchill (I think the name was) that Eva told us all about, who did that beautiful bas-relief, you know, ever so long ago, for poor dear uncle Philip.' Colin bowed, his face still burning. 'That is my name,' he said, pulling out a card, on which was neatly engraved the simple legend, 'Mr. Colin Churchill, Sculptor.'

'And you used to live at Wootton Mandeville?' Gwen asked, with even more of interest in her tone than ever.

'I did.'

'Then, papa, this is the same Mr. Churchill. How very delightful! How lucky we should happen to meet you so, by accident! I call this really and truly a most remarkable and fortunate coincidence.'

'Very remarkable indeed,' the colonel moaned half inarticulately from his cushion.

Miss Gwen was a very clever woman, and she tried her best to whip up the flagging energies of the conversation for a fresh run; but it was all to no purpose. Colin was too hot and uncomfortable to continue the talk now, and the colonel was evidently by no means anxious to recommence it. His whole soul had concentrated itself upon the one idea of changing carriages at Ambérieu. So after a while Gwen gave up the attempt in despair, and the whole party was carried forward in moody silence towards the next station.

'How awfully disappointing,' Gwen thought to herself as she relapsed, vanquished, into her own corner. 'He was talking so delightfully about such beautiful things, before papa went and made that horrid, stupid, unnecessary observation. Doesn't papa see the difference between an enthusiast for art and a common footman? A valet! I can see it all now. Every bit as romantic as Millet, except for the sabots. No wonder his face glowed so when he spoke about the painter who had risen from the ranks of the people. I think I know now what it is they mean by inspiration.'

At last the train reached Amberieu. Great wits jump together; and as the carriage pulled up at the platform, both the colonel and Colin jumped out unanimously, to see whether they could find a vacant place in any other compartment. But the train was exactly like all other first-class expresses on the French railways; every place was taken through the whole long line of closely packed carriages. The colonel was the first to return. 'Gwen,' he whispered angrily to his daughter, in a fierce undertone, 'there isn't a solitary seat vacant in the whole of this confounded train: we shall have to go on with this manservant fellow, at least as far as Aix, and perhaps even all the way to Modane and Turin. Now mind, Gwen, whatever you do, don't have anything more to say to him than you can possibly help, or I shall be very severely displeased with you. How could you go on trying to talk to him again after he'd actually told you he was a gentleman's servant? I was ashamed of you, Gwen, positively ashamed of you. You've no proper pride or lady-like spirit in you. Why, the fellow himself had better feelings on the subject than you had, and was ashamed of himself for having taken us in so very disgracefully.'

'He was not,' Gwen answered stoutly. 'He was ashamed of you, papa, for not being able to recognise an artist and a gentleman even when you see him.'

The colonel's face grew black with wrath, and he was just going to make some angry rejoinder, when Colin's arrival suddenly checked his further colloquy.

The young man's cheeks were still hot and red, but he entered the carriage with composure and dignity, and took his place once more in solemn silence. After a minute he spoke in a low voice to the colonel: 'I've been looking along the train, sir,' he said, 'to see if I could find myself a seat anywhere, but I can't discover one. I think you would have felt more comfortable if I could have left you, and I don't wish to stay anywhere, even in a public conveyance, where my society is not welcome. However, there's no help for it, so I must stop here till we reach Turin, when some of the other passengers will no doubt be getting out. I shall not molest you further, and I regret exceedingly that in temporary forgetfulness of my situation I should have been tempted into seeming to thrust my acquaintance unsolicited upon you.'

The colonel, misunderstanding this proud apology, muttered half-audibly to himself: 'Very right and proper of the young man, of course. He's sorry he so far forgot his natural station as to enter into conversation with his superiors. Very right and proper of him, under the circumstances, certainly, though he ought never to have presumed to speak to us at all in the first instance.'

Gwen bit her lip hard, and tried to turn away her burning face, now as red almost as Colin's; but she said nothing.

That evening, about twelve, as they were well on the way to the Mont Cenis, and Colin was dozing as best he might in his own corner, he suddenly felt a little piece of pasteboard thrust quietly into his half-closed right hand. He looked up with a start. The colonel was snoring peacefully, and it was Miss Gwen's fingers that had pushed the card into his hollow hand. He glanced at it casually by the dim light of the lamp. It contained only a few words. The engraved part ran thus: 'Miss Gwen Howard-Russell, Denhurst.' Underneath, in pencil, was a brief note—'Excuse my father's rudeness. I shall come to see your studio at Rome. G. H. R.'

Minna was the prettiest girl Colin Churchill had ever seen; but Miss Howard-Bussell had exquisitely regular features, and when her big eyes met his for one flash that moment, they somehow seemed to thrill his nature through and through with a sort of sudden mesmeric influence.

CHAPTER XVIII

HIRAM IN WONDERLAND

Just a week after Colin Churchill reached Rome, three passengers by an American steamer stood in the big gaudy refreshment-room at Lime Street Station, Liverpool, waiting for the hour for the up express to start for London.

'We'd better have a little lunch before we get off,' St in Churchill said to his two companions, 'Don't you think so, Mr. Audouin?'

Audouin nodded. 'For my part,' he said, 'I shall have a Bath bun and a glass of ale. They remind one so delightfully of England, Will you give me a glass of bitter, please.'

Hiram drew back a little in surprise. He gazed at the gorgeous young lady who pulled the handle of the beer-engine (of course he had never seen a woman serving drink before), and then he glanced inquiringly at Sam Churchill. 'Do tell me,' he whispered in an awe-struck undertone; 'is that a barmaid?' Sam hardly took in the point of the question for the moment, it seemed so natural to him to see a girl drawing beer at an English refreshment-room, though in the land of his adoption that function is always performed by a male attendant, known as a saloon-keeper; but he answered unconcernedly: 'Well, yes, she's about that, I reckon, though I dare say she wouldn't admire at you to call her so.' Hiram looked with all his eyes agog upon the gorgeous young lady. 'Well,' he said slowly, half to himself, 'that's just charming. A barmaid! Why it's exactly the same as if it were in "Tom Jones" or "Roderick Random."'

Sam Churchill's good-humoured face expanded slowly into a broad smile. That was a picturesque point of view of barmaids which he had never before conceived as possible 'What'll you take, Hiram?' he asked. 'This is a pork-pie here; will you try it?'

'A pork-pie!' Hiram cried, enchanted.

'A pork-pie! You don't mean to say so! Will I try it? I should think I would, rather. Why, you know, Sam, one reads about pork-pies in Dickens!'

This time Audouin laughed too. 'Really, Hiram,' he said, 'if you're going on at this rate you'll find all Europe one vast storehouse of bookish allusiveness. A man who can extract a literary interest out of a pork-pie would be capable of writing poetry, as Stella said, about a broomstick. I assure you you'll find the crust sodden and the internal compound frightfully indigestible.'

'But, I say,' Hiram went on, scanning the greasy paper on the outside with the deepest attention. 'Look here, ain't this lovely, either? It says, "Patronised by his Grace the Duke of Rutland and the Gentlemen of the Melton Mowbray Hunt." I shall have some of that, anyway, though it seems rather like desecration to go and actually eat them. One can fancy the red coats and all the rest of it, can't you: and the hare running away round the corner just the same as in "Sandford and Merton"?'

"Twouldn't be a hare,' Sam replied, with just a faint British curl of the lip at the Yankee blunder (the Englishman was beginning to come uppermost in him regain now his foot was once more, metaphorically, upon his native heath). 'It'd be a fox, you know, Hiram.'

'Better and better,' Hiram cried enthusiastically, forgetting for once in his life his habitual self-restraint. 'A fox! How glorious!

Just fancy eating a Dickens's pork-pie patronised by a man they call a duke, and the red-coated squire people who hunt foxes across country with a horn and a halloo. It's every bit as good as going back to the old coaching days or the reign of Queen Elizabeth.'

'The pork-pies are quite fresh, sir,' put in the gorgeous young lady in an offended manner, evidently taking the last remark as an unjust aspersion upon the character of her saleable goods and chattels. 'We get them direct twice a week from the makers in Leicestershire.'

'There again,' Hiram exclaimed, with a glow of delight; 'why, Mr. Audouin, it's just like fairy-land. Do you hear what the lady says? she says they come from Leicestershire. Just imagine; from Leicestershire! Queen Elizabeth and the ring, and all the rest of it. Goodness gracious, I do believe this country'll be enough to turn one's head, almost, if it goes on like this much longer.'

The gorgeous young lady evidently quite agreed with him upon that important point, for she retired to a tittering conversation with three other equally gorgeous persons at the far end of the marble-covered counter. Hiram, however, was too charmed with the intense Britainicity (as Audouin called it) of everything around him to take much notice of the gorgeous young lady's personal proceedings. It was all so new and delightful, so redolent of things he had read about familiarly from his childhood upward, but never before thoroughly realised as tangible and visible actualities. Pork-pies, then, positively existed in the flesh and crust; London stout was no mere airy figment of the novelist's imagination; red-cheeked women talked before his very eyes to blue-coated policemen; and porters in mediæval uniforms bundled soldiers in still more mediæval scarlet garb into cars which they positively described as carriages, and which were seen to be divided inside into small compartments by a transverse wooden partition. Those were the third-class passengers he had read about in fiction, and yet they did not seem inclined to rise against their oppressors, but smoked and chaffed as merrily as the favoured occupants of the cushioned carriages, to say the plain truth, indeed, a great deal more merrily. All was wonderful, admirable, phantasmagoric beyond his wildest and dearest expectations. He had looked forward to a marvellous, poetical England of cathedrals and castles, but he had hardly expected that all-pervading mediæval tone which came out even in the dedication of the practical pork-pie of commerce to the cult of his Grace the Duke of Rutland and the Gentlemen of the Melton Mowbray Hunt.

To every intelligent young American, indeed, the first glimpse of England is something more than a mere introduction to a new country; it is as though the sun had gone back upon the dial of history, and had carried one bodily from the democratic modern order of tilings into the midst of an older semifeudal and vastly more heterogeneous state of society. But to Hiram Winthrop in particular, that journey by the London and North-Western Line from Liverpool to Euston was, as it were, a new spiritual birth, a first transference into the one world for which alone he was congenitally fitted. Audouin himself, with his cold Boston criticism and his cultivated indifference, was quite surprised at the young man's undisguised enthusiasm. All along the line, the panorama of England seemed but one long unfolding of half-familiar wonders—things pictured, and read about, and dreamt of, for many years, yet never before beheld or realised. First it was the carefully tilled fields, the trim hedges, the parks and gardens, the snug English farmhouses, the endless succession of cultivated land, and beautiful pleasure grounds, and well-timbered copses. Hiram cast his eye back upon

Syracuse and the deacon's farm with a feeling of awe and gratitude. Great heavens, what a contrast from the bare wheat fields and treeless roads and long unlovely snake-fences of Geauga County! Here, in fact, was tillage that even the deacon would have admired as good farming, and yet it had not succeeded in defacing the natural beauty of the undulating Cheshire country, but had rather actually improved and heightened it. Yes, this was Cheshire, and those were Cheshire cows, ultimately responsible for the historical Cheshire cheeses; while yonder was a Cheshire cat, sleeping lazily on an ivy-grown wall, though Hiram was fain to admit, without the grin for which alone the Cheshire cat is proverbially famous. Ivy, lie had never seen ivy before, ay, ivy actually clinging to an old church tower, a tower that even Hiram's unaccustomed eyes could readily date back to the Plantagenet period. That church positively had a rector; and the broken stone by the yew-tree in the churchyard (Sam Churchill being witness) was the last relic of the carved cross of Catholic antiquity. And those little white flowers scattered over the pastures, Audouin told him, were really daisies. Take it how he would, Hiram could hardly believe his own senses, that here he was, being whirled by an express train in a small oblong box of a thing they called a first-class compartment, right across the very face of that living fossil of a country, beautiful, old-fashioned, antique England.

To most of us, the journey from Liverpool to Euston lies only through a high flat country, past a number of dull, ordinary, uninteresting railway stations. It is, in fact, about as unpicturesque a bit of travelling as a man can do within the four girdling sea-walls of this beautiful isle of Britain. But to Hiram Winthrop it was the most absolutely fairylike and romantic journey he had ever undertaken in the whole course of his mundane existence. First they passed through Lancashire, and then through Cheshire, and then on over the impalpable boundary line into Staffordshire. Why, those tall towers over yonder were Lichfield Cathedral; and that little town on the left was Sam Johnson's countrified Lichfield! Here comes George Eliot's Nuneaton, and after it Tom Brown's and Arnold's Bugby. At Bletchley, you read on the notice-board: 'Change here for Oxford'; great heavens, just as if Oxford, the Oxford, were nothing more than Orange or Chattawauga! And here is Tring, where Robert Stephenson made his great cutting; and there is Harrow-on-the-Hill, where Paul Howard, the marauding buccaneer of the Caribbean Sea, received the first rudiments of faith and religion. Not a village along the line but had its resonant echo in the young man's memory; not a manor house, steeple, or farmyard but had its glamour of romance for the young man's fancy. The very men and women seemed to take the familiar shapes of well-known characters. Colonel Newcome, tall and bronzed by Indian suns, paced the platform alone at Crewe; Dick Swiveller, penniless and jaunty as ever, lounged about the refreshment-room at Blisworth Junction; even Trulliber himself, a little modernised in outer garb, but essentially the same in face and feature, dived red-cheeked after his luggage into the crowded van at Willesden. And so, by rapid stages, through a world of unspeakable delight, the engine rolled them swiftly into the midst of seething, grimy, opulent, squalid, hungry, all-embracing London.

'I do hope,' Hiram said to Sam, as they drove together through the strange labyrinth of narrow, dirty streets, to the big modern hotel of Audouin's choosing—'I do hope we shall be in time to catch your brother before he goes to Rome. Europe does look just too delicious; but you'll admit it's pretty bustling and hurrying in some places. I don't know that I'd care so much to go alone as if I had him with me.'

'Oh, he's sure to be here,' Sam answered confidently. 'Since I wired him from New York, I've made my mind easy about that. He'd wait to see me before starting; that's certain.'

'And if he isn't, Hiram,' Audouin put in, 'I'll go on with you. It's rather an undertaking to go touring alone in Europe, when you're fresh to it. We're wild men of the woods, you and I, more at home among the woodchucks and sheldrakes, I conceive, than among the hotels, and streets, and railway stations. You were born in the wilderness: I have fled to it: we're both of us out of our element in the stir and bustle here; so to fortify one another, we'll face it together.'

The fact is, their joint journey had been altogether a very hasty and unpremeditated affair. Audouin had long been urging Hiram to go to Europe, and study art in real earnest; and Hiram had been putting it off and putting it off on various pretences, but really because he didn't want to go until he was able to pay his way honestly out of his own resources. At last, however, Sam Churchill had received a letter from his brother Colin, full of Colin's completed project of going to Rome. This was a chance for Hiram, both Sam and Audouin argued, which he oughtn't lightly to throw away. Colin had been working with an Italian marble-cutter in London; he would be going to Rome with the intention of studying the highest art at the lowest possible prices; and he would probably be glad enough to meet with another young man to share expenses and to keep him company in the unknown city. So between the two, almost before he knew what he was doing, Hiram had been bustled off down to New York, put on board a White Star liner, and conveyed triumphantly over to Europe, between a double guard of Sam and Audouin. Sam had long been contemplating a visit to the old country, to see his father and mother before they died; and now the occasion thus afforded by Colin's resolution seemed propitious for taking his voyage in good company; while as to Audouin, he was so fully in earnest about redeeming Hiram from the advertising style of art, and sending him to Rome to study painting in real earnest, that he undertook to convey him in person, lest any infirmity of purpose should chance to overcome him by the way. He had at last persuaded Hiram to accept a small loan for the necessary expenses of his first year at Rome: and he had also managed to make his young friend believe that at the end of that time his art would begin to bring him in enough to live upon. For which pious fraud, Audouin earnestly trusted the powers that be would deal leniently with him, judging him only by the measure of his good intentions. For if at the end of the first year, Hiram's exchequer still showed a chronic deficit, it would be easy enough, he thought, to float another loan upon himself by way of lightening the temporary tightness of the money market.

It was late that night when they reached the hotel, so they contented themselves with dinner in the coffee-room (mark that word, a coffee-room, exactly where they used to dine in David Copperfield!) without making any attempt to see Colin the same evening. But early the next day the three sallied forth together into the streets of London, and made their way, by lanes and cross-cuts, whose very names seemed historical to Hiram, up to Cicolari's studio in the Marylebone Road. The little Italian bowed them in with great unction, three American customers by the look of them, good perhaps for a replica of the celebrated Cicolari Ariadne, and inquired politely what might be their business.

'My name is Churchill,' Sam said abruptly. 'My brother has been working with you here. Is he still in London?'

Cicolari went quickly through a short pantomime expressive of deep regret that Sam should have come to make inquiries a week too late, mingled with effusive pleasure at securing the acquaintance of Colin's most excellent and highly respected brother. 'If you had come a week ago,' he added, supplementarily, in spoken language, 'you would have been in time to see my very dear friend, your brozzer. But you are not in time; your brozzer is gone away. He is gone to Rome, to Rome' (with a spacious wave of the hand) 'to become ze greatest of living sculptors. He is a genius, and all geniuses must go to Rome. Zat is ze proper home for zem.' And Cicolari, drawing his finger rapidly round in an ever-diminishing circle, planted it at last on a spot in the very centre, supposed to symbolise the metropolis of art.

'Gone to Rome!' Sam cried disappointed. 'But why did he go so soon? Didn't he get my telegram?'

'He has had no telegram from you or he would tell me of it,' answered the Italian, with a pantomimic expression of the closest intimacy between himself and Colin. 'He went away a week ago.'

'Do you know where he's gone to in Rome?' asked Audouin.

'I do not know where he is gone to, but he has gone as valet to Sir Somebody, Sir Henry Wilberforce I sink zey call him', Cicolari answered with open hands spread before him.

Sam Churchill's democratic instincts rose at once in horror and astonishment. 'As what!' he cried. 'As valet?'

Cicolari only replied by going through the operation of brushing an imaginary coat with an aerial clothes-brush and folding it neatly on a non-existent chair by the side of the inconsolable marble widow.

After twelve years of America, Sam Churchill was certainly a little, shocked and annoyed at the idea of his own brother Colin, the future great sculptor and artist, having gone to Rome as another man's body-servant. It hurt not only his acquired republican feelings, but what lies far deeper than those, his amour propre. And he was vexed, too, that Cicolari should have blurted out the plain truth so carelessly before Hiram and Audouin. His cheeks burned hot with his discomfiture; but he only turned and said to them as coolly as he was able: 'Our bird has flown, it seems. We must fly after him.'

'How soon?' asked Audouin quickly.

'This very day,' Sam answered with decision.

'And you, Hiram?' Audouin said.

'I am as clay in the hands of the potter,' Hiram replied, smiling. 'For my own part, I should have liked to stop a week or two in London, and see some of the places one has heard and read so much about. But you've brought me over by main force between you, Mr. Audouin, and I suppose I must let you both do as you will with me. If Sam wants to follow his brother immediately, I'm ready to go with you and leave London for some future visit.'

Sam got what further particulars he could from Cicolari, hailed a passing cab impetuously, and drove straight back to the hotel. In an hour they had packed their valises again after their one night in England, and were off to Charing Cross, to catch the tidal train for Paris, on their way to Italy. Hiram watched the cliffs of Folkestone fading behind him with a somewhat heavy heart; for artist as he was, he somehow felt in the corners of his being as though England were the real unknown lady of his love, and Rome, which he had never seen, likely to prove but a cold and irresponsive sort of mistress. Still, in Audouin's care, he was just what he himself had said, clay in the hands of the potter; for Hiram Winthrop was one of those natures that no man can drive, but that any man can lead with the slightest display of genuine sympathy.

Yet he had one other cause of regret at leaving England: for Chester is in England, and Gwen was presumably at Chester. Gwen—Chester, Gwen—Chester, Gwen—Chester: absurd, romantic, utterly ridiculous; yet all the way from Folkestone to Boulogne, as the vessel lurched from side to side, it made a sort of long-drawn see-saw melody in Hiram Winthrop's brain to the reiterated names of Gwen and Chester.

CHAPTER XIX

UNWARRANTABLE INTRUSION

Sir Henry Wilberforce sat sipping his morning coffee in his most leisurely fashion by the table in his own private salon at the Hôtel de l'Allemagne in Rome. 'Capital man, this fellow Churchill,' he said to himself approvingly, as he saw Colin close the door noiselessly behind him! 'By far the best person for the place I've ever had since that fool Simpson went off so suddenly and got married, confound him. He's so quiet and unobtrusive in all his movements, and he talks so well, and has such a respectable accent and manner. Now Dobbs's accent was quite enough to drive a man wild. I always wanted to throw a boot at him, indeed I've done it more than once, he was so utterly unendurable. This fellow, on the other hand, talks really just like a gentleman; in fact, the only thing I've got to say against him, so far (there's always something or other turning up in the long run), the only thing I've got to say against him yet, is that he's positively a deuced sight too gentlemanly and nice-looking and well-mannered altogether. A servant oughtn't to be too well-mannered. Why, that old Mrs. Cregoe, with the obvious wig and the powdered face, who sits at the table d'hote nearly opposite me, actually went up and spoke to him in the passage yesterday, taking him for one of the visitors! Awkward, exceedingly awkward, when people mistake your man for your nephew, as she did! But otherwise, the fellow's really a capital servant. He, well, what the dickens do you want now, I wonder?'

'A signorina below wishes to speak with you, excellency,' the Italian servant put in, bowing.

'A signorina! What the deuce! Did she give her card, Agostino?'

'The signorina said you would not know her, signor. Shall I introduce her? Ah! here she is.'

Sir Henry rose and made a slight stiff inclination, as who should say: 'Now what the devil can you want with me, I wonder?' Gwen, nothing abashed, laid down her card upon the table, which Sir Henry then and there took up and looked at narrowly, putting on his eyeglass for the purpose.

'What an ill-mannered surly old bear,' Gwen thought to herself; 'and what an absurd thing that that delightful Mr. Churchill should have to go as the old wretch's valet. I shall take care to put a stop to that arrangement, anyhow.'

'Well,' Sir Henry said, glancing suspiciously from the card to Gwen 'May I ask, ur, to what I owe the honour of this visit?'

'Oh, certainly,' Gwen answered with perfect composure (she was never lacking in that repose that stamps the caste of Vere de Vere). 'But as it's rather a long story to tell, perhaps you'll excuse my sitting down while I tell it.' And Gwen half took a chair herself, but at the same time half compelled Sir Henry to push it towards her also, with a sort of grudging unmannerly politeness. Sir Henry, after standing himself for a second or two longer, and then discovering that Gwen was waiting for him to be seated before beginning to disclose her business, dropped in a helpless querulous fashion into the small armchair opposite, and prepared himself feebly for the tête-à-tête.

'The business I've come about,' Gwen went oft quietly, is a rather peculiar one. The fact is my father and I travelled to Rome the other day in the same railway carriage with your servant, whose name, he told us, is Colin Churchill.'

Sir Henry nodded a non-committing acquiescence. 'The deuce!' he thought to himself. 'Something or other turned up already against him., I hope, I'm sure, Miss, ur, let me see your card here once more, ur, Miss Howard-Russell, I hope, I'm sure, he didn't in any way behave impertinently, or make himself at all disagreeable to you. You see, one's obliged to put one's servants into carriages with other people on these continental lines, which of course is very unpleasant for, ur, for those other people.'

'Not at all,' Gwen answered with a charming smile, which almost melted even stony old Sir Henry. 'Not at all; quite the contrary, I assure you. His society and conversation were really quite delightful. Indeed, that's just what I've come about.'

Sir Henry wriggled uneasily in his chair, put up his eyeglass for the third time, and stared at Gwen in puzzled wonderment. His valet's society was really quite delightful! How extraordinary! Could this very handsome and quite presentable young woman, with a double-barrelled surname too, be after all nothing more than a lady's maid who had had a flirtation with his new valet? But if so, and if she had come to propose for Churchill, so to speak, what the deuce could she want to see him for? He dropped his eyeglass once more in silent dubitation, and merely muttered cautiously: 'Indeed!'

'Yes, very much so altogether,' Gwen went on boldly, in spite of Sir Henry's freezing rigidity. 'The fact is, I wanted to speak to you about him, because, you know, really and truly, he isn't a valet at all, and he oughtn't to be one.'

Sir Henry started visibly. 'Not a valet!' he cried. 'Why, if it conies to that, I've found him a very useful and capable person for the place. But I don't quite understand you. Am I to gather that you mean he's an impostor, a thief in disguise, or something of that sort? I picked him up, certainly, under rather peculiar circumstances, just because he could speak a little Italian.'

Gwen laughed a little joyous ringing laugh. 'Oh, no!' she said quickly, 'nothing of that sort, certainly. I meant quite the opposite. Mr. Churchill's a sculptor, and a very accomplished well-read artist.'

Sir Henry rose from his chair nervously.

'You don't mean to say so!' he cried in surprise. 'You quite astonish me. And yet, now you mention it, I've certainly noticed that the young man had a very gentlemanly voice and accent. And then his manners, quite unexceptionable. But what the deuce, excuse an old man's freedom of language, what the deuce, my dear madam, does he mean by playing such a scurvy trick upon me as this, passing himself off for an ordinary valet?'

'That's just what I've come about, Sir Henry. He happened to mention your name to my father and myself, and to allude to the nature of his relations with you; and I was so much interested in the young man that I looked your name up in the visitors' list in the "Italian Times," and came round to speak to you about him.'

Sir Henry raised his eyebrows slightly, but answered nothing.

'And he's not playing you any trick; that's the worst of it,' Gwen went on boldly, taking no notice of Sir Henry's indifferent politeness. 'He's poor, and he's a sculptor. He's been working for several years with a small Italian artist in the Marylebone Road.'

'Ah! yes, yes; I remember. He said he'd been engaged as a marble-cutter since he left his last situation. Why, bless my soul, his last situation was with old Mr. Philip Howard-Russell, of Wootton Mandeville. Let me see, your card, ah! quite so. He must have been some relation of yours, I should imagine.'

'My uncle,' Gwen answered, glancing up at him defiantly. To her the relationship was no introduction.

Sir Henry bowed again slightly. 'Excuse my stupidity,' he said, with more politeness than he had hitherto shown. 'I ought of course to have recognised your name at once. I knew your uncle. A most delightful man, and a brother collector. The selfish old pig,' he thought to himself with an internal sneer; 'he was the most disagreeable bumptious old fellow I ever met in the whole course of my experience. Why, he pretended to doubt the genuineness of my Pinturicchio! But at least he was a man of good family, and his niece, in spite of the interest she evidently takes in my servant Churchill, is no doubt a person whom one ought to treat civilly.' For Sir Henry was one of those ingenuous people who don't think there is any necessity at all for treating civilly that inconsiderable section of humanity which doesn't happen to be connected with men of good family.

'Yes,' Gwen went on, 'Mr. Churchill, as we learnt quite incidentally, was a long time since, when he was quite a boy, in my Uncle Philip's employment. But he has risen by his own talent since then, and now he's a sculptor: there's his card which he gave me, and he has described himself there correctly, as you see. Now, he's poor, it seems, and as he was very anxious to come to Rome, and could find no other way of coming, he decided to come here as a valet. Wasn't that splendid of him! You can see at once that such devotion to art shows what a very remarkable young man he must really be, you're a lover of art yourself, and so you can sympathise with him, to come away as a servant, so as to get to Rome and see the works of Michael Angelo, and Raphael, and—and—and—all that sort of thing, you know,' Gwen added feebly, breaking down in her strenuous effort for a completion to her imagined trio.

Sir Henry hawed a moment. 'Well,'he said slowly, 'I must confess I don't exactly agree with you that it was such a very splendid thing of him to palm himself off upon me as a servant in this abominable underhand manner. You'll excuse me, my dear madam, but it seems to me, I may be wrong, but it seems to me certainly, that a man's either a servant or a sculptor: confound it all, he can't very well be both together. If he comes to me and gets a place on the representation that he's a valet, and then goes and represents to you that he's a sculptor, why, in that case, in that case, I say, it's the very devil. You'll excuse my saying it, but hang me if I can see what there is after all so very fine or splendid about it.'

Gwen bit her lip. 'If you'd heard how beautifully he talked about art in the train,' she said persuasively, 'and how much he knew about Millet and Thorwaldsen and the old masters, and how at home he was in all the great picture-galleries in England, you wouldn't be surprised that he should wish, by hook or by crook, to come to Italy. Why, he can talk quite charmingly and delightfully about—about—about Titian and Perugino and Caravaggio, and I'm sure I don't know how many other great painters and people.'

Sir Henry bent his head again in silent acquiescence. He remembered now that mysterious remark of Colin's, on the day of their first meeting, as to the rival Pinturicchio in the Knowle gallery. The woman was evidently right: that fellow Churchill was a bit of an artist, and had been quizzing his personal peculiarities for a whole fortnight, under cover of acting as valet. Now it's all very well for an enthusiastic young sculptor to go coming to Rome as a man-servant, in order to study Michael Angelo and Thorwald-sen, so long as he comes as somebody else's man-servant; but when he comes as one's own attendant, hang it all, you know, that's quite another matter. 'Well,' Sir Henry said, looking curiously at Gwen's embarrassed face, 'and what do you wish to ask me about my man Churchill?'

Gwen flushed up angrily at the obvious insolence of his inquiry, but she took no notice of it in words for the sake of her errand. 'I only called,' she said quietly, 'though it's a little unusual for a lady to do so' (Sir Henry inclined his head gravely once more, as who should say I quite agree with you), 'because I felt so much interested in Mr. Churchill. I think it isn't right to let him remain as a servant; he ought to be allowed to continue his work as a sculptor without delay. Sir Henry, you'll release him from his engagement, I'm sure, and let him go on with his own proper studies.'

'Release him, my dear young lady,' Sir Henry answered sardonically. 'Release him! release him! By Jove, that's hardly the word I should myself apply to it. I shall certainly send him packing, you may be sure, at the earliest convenient opportunity, and he may consider himself deuced lucky if I don't get him into serious trouble for engaging himself to me under what comes perilously near being false pretences. You must excuse my frankness, Miss Howard-Russell; but I'm an old man, and I don't see why I should be left at a minute's notice here in Rome, at the mercy of these confounded foreigners, without a valet. After what you tell me, it's plain I can't have him here spying upon me all the time in every action; but it's devilish uncomfortable, I can tell you, to be left a thousand miles away from home without anybody on earth to do anything for one.'

What could Gwen say? She felt instinctively in her own mind that Sir Henry's complaint was perfectly natural and excusable. When a man engages a man-servant, he means to engage a person of a certain comparatively fixed and recognisable social status, and he certainly doesn't want to have his habits and manners of life made an open secret to a fellow-being of something like his own level of intelligence and education; But, on the other hand, she could see, too, that this nice distinction was never likely to occur to Colin's simple intelligence. Little as she had seen of him, and little as he had told her of his story, she quite understood that the old vicar's expageboy wouldn't be able, in all probability, to feel the difference to Sir Henry Wilberforce between having him for a valet and having any ordinary gentleman's servant. However, happily, it didn't much matter what Sir Henry thought about it: the important point was that that clever young Mr. Churchill was to be released forthwith from his absurd engagement and left free to follow his own natural artistic promptings. That was all, of course, that Gwen, for her part, really cared about.

'Then you'll dismiss him, I suppose?' she asked again after an awkward pause. 'You'll allow him to take to his proper work as a sculptor?'

'Why, really, my dear lady, I don't care twopence, so far as that goes, what the dickens he chooses to take to as soon as he's left me; but I'm certainly not going to keep an educated sculptor fellow spying about me any longer and collecting notes to retail by-and-by to half Rome upon my personal peculiarities. Oh dear no, certainly not. I shall pay him his month's wages and compensation for board and lodging, and I shall send him about his business this very minute.'

Gwen rose and bowed slightly in her most stately manner. 'If that's so,' she said quietly, 'the object of my visit's more than attained already. I won't keep you any longer. Good morning.'

Sir Henry rose in return and answered,

'Good morning,' with frigid courtesy.

Gwen moved towards the door, which Sir Henry was just about to open for her, when Agostino flung it wide once more from outside, and announced in a loud voice: 'Signor Churchill, Signor Vintrop.'

Gwen trembled a little. Mr. Churchill! Must she meet him, then, face to face under these very awkward circumstances? It seemed so, for there was no escape from it. She couldn't get away before they entered.

The two strangers thus announced walked into the salon together, and in a moment Gwen saw that it wasn't Colin, but somebody else, somewhat older, yet a little like him. At the very same moment Hiram Winthrop, entering that unknown room in that unknown city, felt a sudden thrill course fiercely through his inmost marrow, and looked up with a glance of instantaneous recognition to the strange lady. How wonderful! how magnificent! how unexpected! It was she; it was the glorious apparition of the Thousand Islands; it was (he knew no other name for her), it was Gwen of Chester!

Shy and retiring as he was by nature, Hiram so far forgot everything else at that moment, except his joy at this unexpected meeting, that he advanced quite naturally and held out his hand to Gwen, who took it frankly, but with a curious smile of half-inquiring welcome.

'You don't remember me, Miss Gwen,' he said in a voice of some little disappointment (he could only call her by her Christian name, which mode of address sounds far less familiar to American ears than to us more ceremonious English). 'My name is Winthrop, and I've had the pleasure of meeting you before—once—have you forgotten?... at the Thousand Islands.'

Gwen shook her head a little doubtfully. 'Well, to say the truth,' she answered with a pleasant smile, 'I don't quite recollect you. We met so many people, you see, while we were in America.'

'But I was painting a sketch of a little island near Alexandria Bay,' Hiram went on eagerly, but somewhat crestfallen (how strange that he should remember her every feature so well, while she! she had utterly forgotten him). 'Don't you recollect? you were walking with your father near the river, and you came across two of us sketching, under a little cliff at Alexandria Bay, and you came down and looked at my picture.'

'Oh, yes,' Gwen cried, a sudden flash of recognition spreading over her face. 'I remember all about it now. I remember your picture perfectly.' (Hiram's eyes brightened immediately.) 'There was a single little island in it, of course, with a solitary great dark pine towering above it, against a liquid deep blue background of cloudless sky.' (Hiram nodded in delight at her accurate description.) 'Oh yes, I remember the picture perfectly, though I've quite forgotten you yourself.

But I recollect your friend so well; such a charming person, the most delightful conversation, a Mr. Audouin, he said his name was. I remember him more distinctly than almost anybody else we met during the whole of our American visit.'

Poor Hiram! How little Gwen knew as she said those simple words she was plunging a dagger into his very heart! He almost reeled beneath that crushing, terrible disappointment. Here for all those long months he had been treasuring up the picture of Gwen upon his mental vision, thinking of her, looking at her, dreaming about her; he had come to Europe hoping and trusting somewhere or other at last to find her; he had stumbled up against her accidentally his very first day in Rome, and now that he stood there actually face to face with her, the queen of his fancy, his heart's ideal, why, she herself had positively forgotten all about him!

She remembered Audouin, that supplanter Audouin; but she had clean forgotten poor solitary yearning Hiram! What else could he expect, indeed? It was all perfectly natural. Who was he, that such a one as Gwen should ever remember him? What presumption, what folly on his part to expect he could have left the slightest image imprinted upon her memory! And yet, somehow, in spite of sober reason, he couldn't help feeling horribly and unutterably disappointed. His face fell with a sudden collapse, but he managed feebly to mutter half aloud: 'Oh, yes, a most delightful person, Mr. Audouin.'

Meanwhile, Sir Henry, fidgeting with the back of a chair in his hand, stood waiting to hear what was the meaning of this singular irruption of American barbarians. Who were they? Had they come by appointment? Why did they recognise this real or pretended niece of that old idiot, Howard-Russell? Was it all a plant to rob or intimidate him? Why the deuce did they all stand there, shaking hands and exchanging reminiscences in his own hired salon, and take no notice at all of him, Sir Henry Wilberforce, the real proprietor and sole representative authority of that sacred apartment? It was really all most extraordinary, most irregular, most mysterious.

Sam broke the momentary silence by coming forward towards the old man, and saying in his clear, half-American tone: 'I presume I'm addressing Sir Henry Wilberforce?'

Sir Henry nodded. A Yankee, clearly. And yet he gave his name as Churchill, and wanted no doubt to represent himself as the other Churchill's brother!

'Well,' Sam went on (and Gwen could not help but wait and listen), 'I've come to see you about my brother. I asked for him from the person in the white choker—'

'Agostino,' Sir Henry murmured feebly.

'But he said, as far as I could make out his lingo, that my brother was gone out. So I just thought the best thing, under the circumstances, would be to come in and speak to you.' 'And may I ask,' Sir Henry inquired, still fingering the back of the chair in a nervous manner, 'who your brother may be, and what the devil I have got to do with him?'

'Oh, his name's Churchill,' Sam answered, with some little confusion, glancing over towards Gwen, who stood listening, half-amused and half-embarrassed. 'Colin Churchill.

That's my card, you see, colonel—'

Sir Henry took it and looked at it languidly. 'I see,' he said. 'You are, ahem, my valet's brother.'

Sam flushed a little angrily. 'That's the very business I've come here about,' he said, looking as though he would like to knock down the feeble supercilious old Pantaloon who stood there quavering and shivering before him. 'My brother being determined to come to Rome to be a sculptor, and not having the means to come with of his own, you see, colonel—'

'My precise military rank, if any, must be a matter of absolute indifference to you, sir,' Sir Henry interrupted coolly.

'Well, he didn't apply to his family for the means to do so, as he might have done,' Sam went on, without noticing the interruption, 'but chose to take a place, quite beneath his natural position, as your valet, Sir Henry Wilberforce. I happened to come to England at the time from America, where I've been residing for some years, and learnt on inquiry that he had taken this very foolish step; so I followed him at once to Rome, to release him from such an unwise arrangement, if possible, and to make things pleasant all round, as between the whole lot of us. I ain't sorry that Colin's gone out, for it enables us to clear off the whole thing right away, without telling him anything about it. What I propose, Sir Henry Wilberforce,'—Sam repeated the full name each time a little viciously, with some adopted republican aversion—'is just this: I'll telegraph to London to the Couriers' Society to get you a suitable person sent out here to replace him. If you like, I'll get you a selection sent out on approval, and I'll pay their expenses; we don't want to put you to any inconvenience, you understand, Sir Henry Wilberforce. But what we stick at is only one point, my brother Colin can't stop here with you another minute; that's certain. He's got to leave right away, and go straight off to his own business.'

Sir Henry Wilberforce wrung his hands in helpless despair at this inexplicable inroad of so many aggressive strangers. 'Upon my word,' he said piteously, 'I wish to goodness I'd never seen or heard at all of this extraordinary young man Churchill. Such a deuce of a hullabaloo and corrobboree as they're kicking up about him, the whole three of them, I never heard in all my confounded lifetime. Dash their geniuses! Who the dickens wants a genius for a valet? I'll take precious good care, when once I'm out of this deuced hobble, that I never engage a fellow who's been first cousin to a marble-cutter as my servant in future. First this young lady comes down upon me and lectures me in the name of high art, what the devil do I mean by keeping this delightful young sculptor pottering about as my own body-servant. And then this pair of Yankees come down upon me, in the name of brotherly affection, and ask me what the devil do I mean by keeping this eminently respectable brother of theirs in a menial position that I never for a moment wanted him to get into. Why, what the devil do you mean yourself, sir, by invading my premises in this unceremonious manner? Who the devil cares twopence about you or your brother? If your brother's a sculptor, why the devil doesn't he stick to his own profession? What the devil does he mean by coming and passing himself off upon me as a servant? Will you have the kindness, all of you, to leave my rooms at your earliest convenience, and be dashed to you? And will you tell this interesting young sculptor, if you see him, that he may pack up his traps and clear out as soon as possible? That'll do, thank you. Good morning. Good morning.' And Sir Henry stood with the door in his hand, waiting for the three to take their departure.

That same evening, when Sir Henry came in from dinner much agitated, he found an envelope lying on his table, which he took up and opened in a surly fashion, saying to himself meanwhile: 'Some deuced impertinence of that fellow Churchill, I'll be bound, the confounded rascal.' But it contained only a couple of English bank-notes; a small memorandum of Colin's railway expenses and other disbursements made by Sir Henry on his account, as well as of the month's wages, due by a servant who voluntarily leaves his master without full notice; and finally a sheet of white note-paper, bearing the words, 'With Saml. Churchill's compliments.'

Sir Henry crumpled up the paper and memorandum angrily, with hardly a glance, and flung them into the empty grate; but he folded the notes carefully, and put them into the inner compartment of his purse. Then he sat down at his davenport and wrote out a telegram from Wilberforce, Rome, to Dobbs, 74 Albert Terrace, Dalston, London. 'Come here at once; expenses paid; wages raised five pounds; no boots thrown. Answer immediately. W.'

'And if ever I have anything to do again with these confounded marble-cutters and sculptors,' he soliloquised vehemently, 'why, my name isn't Henry Wilberforce.'

CHAPTER XX

Colin and Hiram slept that night under the same roof, at Audouin's hotel. The wheel of Fate had at last brought the two young enthusiasts together, and they fraternised at once by mere dint of the similarity of their tastes and natural circumstances. Their lives had been so like, and yet so unlike; their fortunes had been so much the same, and yet so different. It was pleasant to compare notes with one another in the smoking-room about Wootton Mande ville and Geauga County, about the deacon and the vicar, Cicolari and Audouin; all things on earth, save only Gwen and Minna. Even Hiram didn't care to speak about Gwen. Young men in America are generally far more frank with one another about their love affairs than we sober, suspicious, unromantic English; they talk among themselves enthusiastically about their sweethearts, much as girls talk together in confidence in England. But Hiram in this respect was not American. His self-contained, self-restraining nature forbade him to hint a word even of the interest he felt in the beautiful stranger he had so oddly recognised in Sir Henry's salon.

But he would meet her again, that was something! He knew her name now, and all about her. As they left Sir Henry's hotel together, Gwen had turned with one of her gracious smiles to Sam, flooding his soul with her eyes, and said in that delicious trilling voice of hers: 'I can't forbear to tell you, Mr. Churchill, that I'd been to see Sir Henry, as he hinted to you, on the very self-same errand as yourself, almost. I met your brother in the train coming here, and I learnt from him accidentally what he'd come for, and how he was coming; and I couldn't resist going to tell that horrid old man the whole story. It was so delightful, you know, so very romantic. Of course I thought he'd be only too delighted to hear it, and admire your brother's pluck and resolution so much, exactly as I did. I thought he'd say at once "A sculptor! How magnificent! Then he shan't stay here with me another minute. I'm a lover of art myself. I know what it must be to feel that divine yearning within one," or something of that sort. "I won't allow a born artist to waste another moment of his precious time upon such useless and unworthy occupations. Let him go immediately and study his noble profession; I'll use all my interest to get him the best introductions to the very first masters in all Italy." That's what a man of any heart or spirit would have said on the spur of the moment. Instead of that, the horrid old creature put up his eyeglass and stared at me so that I was frightened to death, and swore dreadfully, and said your brother oughtn't to have engaged himself under the circumstances; and used such shocking language, that I was just going to leave the room in a perfect state of terror when you came in and detained me for a minute. And then you saw yourself the dreadful rage he got into, the old wretch! I should like to see him put into prison or something. I've no patience with him.'

Hiram felt in his own soul at that moment a certain fierce demon rising up within him, and goading him on to some desperate vengeance. Was he alone the only man that Gwen didn't seem to notice or care for in any way? She was so cordial to Audouin, she was so cordial to Sam, and now she was so interested in Sam's unknown brother, whom she had only met casually in a railway carriage, that she had actually faced, alone and undaunted, this savage old curmudgeon of a British nobleman (Hiram's views as to the status of English baronets were as vague as those of the Tichborne Claimant's admirers), in order to release him from the necessary consequences of an unpleasant arrangement. But him, Hiram, she had utterly forgotten; and even when reminded of him, she only seemed to remember his personality in a very humiliating fashion as a sort of unimportant pendant or corollary to that brilliant Mr. Audouin. To him, she was all the world of woman; to her, he was evidently nothing more than an uninteresting young man, who happened to accompany that delightfully clever American whom she met at the Thousand Islands!

How little we all of us are to some people who are so very, very much to us!

But when she was leaving them at the door of her own hotel, Gwen handed Hiram a card with a smile that made amends for everything, and said so brightly: 'I hope we may see you again, Mr. Winthrop. I haven't forgotten your delightful picture. I'm so fond of everything at all artistic. And how nice it is, too, that you've got that charming Mr. Audouin still with you. You must be sure to bring him to see us here, or rather, I must send papa to call upon you. And, Mr. Churchill, as soon as your brother sets up a studio, I suppose he will now, we won't forget to drop in and see him at it. I'm so very much interested in anything like sculpture.'

Poor Hiram's heart sank again like a barometer to Very Stormy. She only wanted to see him again, then, because he'd got Audouin with him! Hiram was too profoundly loyal to feel angry, even in his own heart, with his best friend and benefactor; but he couldn't help feeling terribly grieved and saddened and downcast, as he walked along silently the rest of the way through those novel crowded streets of Rome towards the Hôtel de Russie. He felt sure he should cordially hate this horrid, interesting, interloping fellow, Sam's brother.

Sam had left a little note at the Allemagne to be given to Mr. Colin Churchill, Sir Henry's valet, as soon as ever he came back. In the note he told Colin he was to call round at once, without speaking to Sir Henry, for a very particular purpose, at the Hôtel de Russie. The letter was duly signed: 'Your affectionate brother, Sam Churchill.' Colin took it up and looked at it again and again. Yes, there was no denying it; it was Sam's handwriting, But how on earth had Sam got to Rome, and what on earth was Sam doing there? It was certainly all most mysterious. Still, the words 'without speaking to that old fool Sir Henry' were trebly underlined, and Colin felt sure there must be some sufficient reason for them, especially as the arrangement of epithets was at once so correct and so forcible. So he turned hastily to the Hôtel de Russie, filled with amazement at this singular adventure.

In Colin's mind, the Sam of his boyish memory was a Dorsetshire labourer clad in Dorsetshire country clothes, a trifle loutish (if the truth must be told), and with the easy, slouching, lounging gait of the ordinary English agricultural workman. When he called at the Russie, he was ushered up into a room where he saw three men sitting on a red velvet sofa, all alike American in face, dress, and action, and all alike, at first sight, complete strangers to him. When one of the three, a tall, handsome, middle-aged man, with a long brown moustache, and a faultless New Yorker tourist suit, rose hastily from the sofa, and came forward to greet him with a cry of 'Colin!' he could hardly make his eyes believe there was any relic of the original Sam about this flourishing and eminently respectable American citizen.

'Well, Colin,' his brother said kindly, but with such an unexpected Yankee accent, 'I surmise you ain't likely to recognise me, anyhow; that's so, ain't it? You were only such a little chap when I first went away across the millpond.'

When one sees a member of one's own family after a separation of many years, one judges of him as one judges of a stranger; and Colin was certainly pleased with the first glimpse of this resurrected and wholly transfigured Sam, he seemed such a good-humoured, easygoing, kindly-confidential sort of fellow, that Colin's heart warmed to him immediately. They fell to talking at once about old times at Wootton Mandeville, and Sam told Colin the whole story of how he came to cross the Atlantic again, and what reception he had met with that morning from Sir Henry Wilberforce. Hiram and Audouin went out while the two brothers discussed their family affairs and future prospects, ostensibly to see something of the sights of Rome, but really to let them have their talk out in peace and quietness.

'And now, Colin,' Sam said in a blunt, straightforward, friendly fashion, 'of course you mustn't see this Wilberforce man again, whatever happens. It's no use exposing yourself to a scene with him, all for nothing. You've just got to go back to the Hôtel d'Allamain on the quiet, pack up your things without saying a word to him, and walk it. I've written a note to him that'll settle everything, and I've put in two bills.'

'Two what?' Colin asked doubtfully.

'Bills,' Sam repeated with a hasty emphasis. 'Notes I think you call 'em in England; bank-notes to cover all expenses of your journey, don't you see, and baggage, and so forth. No, never you mind thanking me like that about a trifle, Colin, but just sit there quietly like a sensible fellow and listen to what I've got to say to you. It's a long time since I left the old country, you know, my boy; and I've kind o' forgotten a good deal about it. I've forgotten that you were likely to be so hard up for money as you were, Colin, or else I'd have sent you over a few hundred dollars long ago to pay your expenses. When you wrote to me that you were working with a sculptor in London, I took it for granted, anyhow, that you were making a pretty tidy thing out of it; and when you wrote that you were going to Rome to continue your studies, I thought I'd bring Hiram Winthrop along just to keep you company. But I never imagined you'd come over as I find you have done. Why, when that Sickolary man told me you'd gone as a valet, I was so ashamed I couldn't look Mr. Audouin straight in the face again for half-an-hour. And what I want to know now's just this, Who's the very best sculptor, should you say, in all Rome, this very minute?'

'There's only one really great sculptor in Rome at all, at present, that I know of,' Colin answered without a moment's hesitation.

'Nicola Maragliano.'

'Well,' Sam continued in a business-like fashion; 'I suppose he takes pupils?'

'I should doubt it very much, Sam, unless they were very specially recommended.'

'What, really? At least, we'll try, Colin. We'll see what Mr. Maragliano's terms are, any way.'

'But, my dear fellow, whatever his terms are, I can't afford them. I must work for my livelihood one way or another.'

'Nonsense,' Sam answered energetically. 'You just leave this business alone. I've got to manage it my own way, and don't you go and interfere with it. I pay, you work; do you see, Colin?'

Colin looked back at his brother with a look half incredulity, half pride. 'Oh, Sam,' he said, 'I can't let you. I really can't let you. You mustn't do it. It's too kind of you, too kind of you altogether.'

'In America,' Sam answered, taking a cigar from his pocket and lighting a vesuvian, 'we're a busy people. We haven't got time for thanks and that sort of thing, Colin; we just take what we get, and say nothing about it. I'm going out now, to have a look after one of their Vaticans, or Colosseums, or triumphal arches, or something; you'd better go and pack up your traps meanwhile at this Wilberforce creature's. You'll sleep here tonight; I'll bespeak a room for you; then you and Hiram can talk things over and arrange all comfortable. They have dinner here at the wrong end of the day, seven o'clock; mind you're back for it. Now, good-bye for the present. I'm off to hunt up some of these ancient Roman ruins.'

Sam put on his hat before Colin could thank him any further, and in half an hour more, he was meditating, with the aid of his cigar, among the big gloomy arches of the Colosseum.

So Colin took the proffered freedom, with an apologetic note to poor old Sir Henry, whom he didn't wish to treat badly; and that evening he and Hiram met to make one another's acquaintance in earnest. Hiram's spleen against the young Englishman who had had the audacity to attract Gwen's favourable attention didn't long outlast their introduction. To say the truth, both young men were too simple and too transparent not to take a sincere liking for one another almost immediately. Sam and Audouin were both delighted at the success of their scheme for bringing them together; and Sam was really very proud of his brother's drawings and designs which Colin brought down for their inspection after dinner. He had enough, of Colin's leaven in him to be able at least to recognise a true and beautiful work of art when it was set before him.

'I shall just wait a bit here in Rome so as to fix up Colin with this man Maragliano, Mr. Audouin,' Sam said, after the two younger men had retired, as they sat talking over the prospect in the billiard-room of the hotel; 'and then I shall run back to England to pay a visit to the old folk, before I return to work at Syracuse.'

'And I,' said Audouin, 'will stop the winter so as to set Hiram fairly on the right way, and let him get free play for his natural talents. He's going to be the greatest American painter ever started, Mr. Churchill; and I'm going to see that he has room and scope to work in.'

But all that night, Hiram dreamt of Chattawauga Lake, and Gwen, and the Thousand Islands, and the green fields he had seen in England. And when he woke to look out on the broad sunshine flooding the neighbourhood of the Piazza del Popolo, his heart was sad within him.

CHAPTER XXI

COLIN SETTLES HIMSELF

After breakfast next morning, Sam rose resolutely from the table, like a man who means business, and said to his brother in a tone of authority, 'Come along, Colin; I'm going to call on this Mr. Maragliano you were telling me about.'

'But, Sam,' Colin expostulated, 'he won't receive us. We haven't got any introduction or anything.'

'Not got any introduction? Yes, I guess we have, Colin. Just you bring along those drawings and designs you showed us last night, and you bet Mr. Maragliano won't want any other introduction, I promise you. In America, we'd rather see what a man can do, any day, than what all his friends put together can say to crack him up in a letter of recommendation.'

Colin ran upstairs trembling with excitement, and brought down the big portfolio, Minna's portfolio, made with cloth and cardboard by her own small fingers, and containing all his most precious sketches for statues or bas-reliefs. They turned out into the new Rome of the English quarter, and following the directions of the porter, they plunged at last into the narrow alleys down by the Tiber till they came to the entrance of a small and gloomy-looking street, the Via Colonna. It is the headquarters of the native Italian artists. Colin's heart beat fast when at length they stopped at a large house on the left-hand side and entered the studio of Nicola Maragliano.

The great sculptor was standing in the midst of a group of friends and admirers, his loose coat all covered with daubs of clay, and his shaggy hair standing like a mane around him, when Sam and Colin were ushered into his studio. Colin stood still for a moment, awestruck at the great man's leonine presence; for Maragliano was one of the very few geniuses whose outer shape corresponded in majesty to the soul within him.

But Sam, completely unabashed by the novelty of the situation, walked straight up to the famous artist, and said with a rapid jerk in his own natural, easy-going manner, 'Speak any English?'

'A leetle,' Maragliano answered, smiling at the brusqueness of the interrogation.

'Then what we want to know, sir, without wasting any time over it, is just this: Here's my brother. He wants to be made into a sculptor. Will you take him for a pupil, and if so, what'll your charge be? He's brought some of his drawings along, for you to look at them. Will you see them?'

Maragliano smiled again, this time showing all his white teeth, and looked with an air of much amusement at Colin. The poor fellow was blushing violently, and Maragliano saw that he was annoyed and hurt by Sam's brusqueness. So he took the portfolio with a friendly gesture (for he was a true gentleman), and proceeded to lay it down upon his little side-table. 'Let us see,' he said in Italian, 'what the young American has got to show me.'

'Not American,' Colin answered, in Italian too. 'I am English; but my brother has lived long in America, and has perhaps picked up American habits.'

Maragliano looked at him keenly again, nodded, and said nothing. Then he opened the portfolio and took out the first drawing. It was the design for the Cephalus and Aurora, the new and amended version. As the great sculptor's eye fell upon the group, he started and gave a little cry of suppressed astonishment. Then he looked once more at Colin, but said nothing. Colin trembled violently. Maragliano turned over the leaf, and came to the sketch for the bas-relief of the Boar of Calydon. Again he gave a little start, and murmured to himself, 'Corpo di Bacco!' but still said nothing to the tremulous aspirant. So he worked through the whole lot, examining each separate drawing carefully, and paying keener and keener attention to each as he recognised instinctively their profound merit. At last, he came to the group of Orestes and the Eumenides. It was Colin Churchill's finest drawing, and the marble group produced from it is even now one of the grandest works that ever came out of that marvellous studio. Maragliano gave a sharper and shorter little cry than ever.

'You made it?' he asked, turning to Colin.

Colin nodded in deep suspense, not unmixed with a certain glorious premonition of assured triumph.

Maragliano turned to the little group, that stood aloof around the clay of the Calabrian Peasant, and called out, 'Bazzoni!'

'Master!'

'See this design. It is the Englishman's. What think you of it?'

The scholar took it up and looked at it narrowly. 'Good;' he said shortly, in an Italian crescendo; 'excellent, admirable, surprising, extraordinary.'

Maragliano drew his finger over the curve of the Orestes' figure with a sort of free sweep, like a sculptor's fancy, and answered simply, turning to Colin, 'He says true. It is the touch of genius.'

As Maragliano said those words, Colin felt the universe reeling wildly around him, and clutched at Sam's arm for support from falling. Sam didn't understand the Italian, but he saw from Colin's face that the tremor was excess of joy, not shock of disappointment. 'Well,' he said inquiringly to Maragliano. 'You like his drawings? You'll take him for a pupil? You'll make a sculptor of him?'

'No,' Maragliano answered in English, holding up the Orestes admiringly before him; 'I cannot do zat. Ze great God has done so already.'

Sam smiled a smile of brotherly triumph. 'I thought so, Colin,' he said approvingly.

'I told him so last night, Mr. Maragliano. You see, I'm in the artistic business myself, though in another department, the advertising block trade, and I know artistic work when I look at it.'

Maragliano showed his white teeth once more, but didn't answer.

'And what'll your terms be for taking him?' Sam asked, in as business-like a fashion as if the famous sculptor had been a flourishing greengrocer, or a respectable purveyor of kippered herrings.

Maragliano glanced around him with a nervous glance. 'Zere are many people here,' he said, shrugging his shoulders. 'We cannot talk at leisure. Let us go into my private chamber.' And he led the way into a small parlour behind the studio.

Sam took a chair at once with republican promptitude, but Colin stood, his hands folded before him, still abashed by the great man's presence. Maragliano looked at him once more with his keenly interested look. 'That is well,' he said in Italian. 'Greatness always pays the highest homage to greatness. I know a true artist at sight by the way he first approaches me. Rich men condescend; pretenders fawn; ordinary men recognise no superiority save rank or money; but greatness shows its innate reverence at once, and thereby securely earns its own recognition. Be seated, I pray you. Your drawings are wonderful; but you have studied little. They are full of genuine native power, but they lack precise artistic teaching. Where have you taken your first lessons?'

'Nowhere,' Colin answered, his face glowing with pleasure at Maragliano's hearty encomium. 'I am almost entirely self-taught, and I have come to Rome to learn better.'

Maragliano listened intently. 'Wonderful!' he said; 'wonderful, truly! And yet, I could almost have guessed it. Your work is all vigour and nature, it is Greek, purely Greek, but there is not yet art in it. Tell me all about how you have learned what you know of sculpture.'

Thus invited, Cohn began, and confided to the great sculptor's sympathetic ear the whole story of his youth and boyhood. He began with the time when he moulded little clay images for Minna from the bank at Wootton Mandeville; and he went on with all the story of his acquaintance with Cicolari, down to his coming to Rome with Sir Henry Wilberforce. Maragliano nodded his interest from time to time, and when Colin had finished, he took his hand warmly in his, and cried in English, so that Sam too understood him: 'It is well. You shall be my pupil.'

'And your terms?' Sam asked with mercantile insistence. 'We're ready to agree to anything reasonable.'

'Are nossing,' Maragliano answered; 'nossing, nossing. I will teach you for ze love of art, as you will learn for it. No, no,' he went on, breaking into Italian again, as Colin tried to thank him or to expostulate with him. 'You needn't thank me. It is but the repayment of a debt. I owe it to your own Gibson, as Gibson owed it before to Canova. It is a tradition among us Roman sculptors; you will keep it up, and will repay it in due time hereafter to some future follower. Many years ago I came to Rome. I was an unknown lad from Genoa. I came as a model to Gibson's studio. I sat for an Antinous. Gibson saw me modelling little bits of clay for amusement in my off times, and said to me, "You would make a sculptor." I laughed. He gave me a little clay, and saw what I could do; I modelled a head after his Venus. Then he took me on as his pupil; and now, I am Nicola Maragliano. I am glad to repay an Englishman the debt I owe to the illustrious Gibson. You must take my lessons, as I took his, in trust for art, and not talk between brother artists about such dirt as money.'

Colin seized his hand eagerly. 'Oh, sir,' he cried in English, 'you are too noble, too generous. I shall never be able sufficiently to thank you. If you will only condescend to give me instruction, to make me your pupil, to let me model in your studio, I shall be eternally grateful to you for such unexpected kindness.'

Maragliano wrung the young man's hand with a kindly fervour. 'That is more than enough already,' he answered. 'Those who love art are all of one family. When will you come to the studio? Let me see; you have not been long in Rome?'

'We've only just come here,' put in Sam, proud of having caught the meaning of the Italian.

'Ah, well; then you will want a little time, no doubt, to look about and see the sights of Rome. What do you say to Tuesday fortnight?'

'If it's equally convenient for you, signor,' Colin answered, all aglow, 'I shall be at the studio to-morrow morning.'

Maragliano patted him gently on the head as though he were a child. 'My friend,' he said, 'you speak courageously. That is the sentiment of all true artists. You are impatient to get to work; you will not need a long apprenticeship. Let it be so then. Tomorrow morning.'

CHAPTER XXII

HIRAM GETS SETTLED

Hiram,' Audouin said, as soon as Sam and Colin had left the hotel, 'it's time for us, I surmise, to be setting about the same errand. Before we begin to look at the sights of Rome, we must arrange where you ought to locate yourself, and when you ought to commence your artistic studies.

Hiram looked blankly enough out of the window into the dusty piazza, and answered in a tone of some regret, 'Well, Mr. Audouin, if you think so, I suppose it'll be best to do it, though I can't say I'm in any particular hurry. Where do you contemplate making inquiries?'

'Why,' Audouin replied in his easy confident fashion, 'there's only one really great painter now in Rome in whose studio I should like to put you, Hiram, and that's Seguin.' Hiram's face sank. 'Seguin,' he echoed somewhat gloomily. 'Ah, Seguin! But he's a figure painter, isn't he, surely, Mr. Audouin?' Audouin smiled his pleasant smile of superior wisdom. 'Well, Hiram,' he said, 'you don't come to

Rome to paint Chattawauga Lake, do you? Yes, Seguin's a figure painter. And you'll be a figure painter, too, my dear fellow, before you've finished, yes, and a great one. Seguin's one of the finest living artists, you know, in all Europe. It's a great honour to be admitted into the studio of such a master.'

If somebody in authority had said to Hiram Winthrop, 'You must go to Seguin's and paint heroic figure pictures, or have your head cut off,' Hiram Winthrop would no doubt have promptly responded with dogged cheerfulness, 'A sainte guillotine, done,' or words to that effect, without a moment's hesitation. But when Lothrop Audouin, his guide and benefactor, said to him in a voice of friendly sympathy, 'You'll be a figure painter too, before you've finished, Hiram,' he no more dreamt of refusing or doubting (save in his own inmost soul) than a docile child dreams of resisting its parents in the matter of their choice of its school or its lessons. So he took his hat down from its peg, and followed Audouin blindly, out into that labyrinth of dirty lanes and ill-paved alleys which constitutes the genuine Rome of the native-born modern Romans.

Audouin led the way, through the modernised shops and gay bustle of the Corso, to a small side street, with squalid blotchy houses rising high against the sky on either hand, and a crowd of dirty ragged children loitering in the gutter, save when an occasional rickety carriage, drawn by a tottering skinny horse, dashed round the dark corners with a sudden swoop, and scattered them right and left with loud chattering cries into the gloomy archways. All was new and strange to Hiram, and, if the truth must be told, not particularly inviting. Past the Spaccio di Vino, the squalid temple of Dionysus, where grimy Romans in grubby coatsleeves sat drinking sour red wine from ill-washed tumblers; past the tinker's shop, where some squat Etruscan figure crouched by a charcoal stove hammering hopelessly at dilapidated pannikins; past the foul greengrocery, where straw-covered flasks of rancid oil hung up untemptingly between long strings of flabby greens and mouldering balls of country cheese; past many other sights and sounds, dimly visible to Hiram's eyes or audible to his ears in the whirl and confusion of an unknown city; till at last Audouin wheeled round the corner into the Via Colonna (where Colin had gone before), and stopped in front of a large and decently clean house, bearing on the lintel of its great oak door a little painted tin plate, 'Atelier de M. J.-B. Seguin.' Audouin turned with a smile to Hiram, poor dazzled, half-terrified Hiram, and said in a tone of some little triumph, 'There, you see, Hiram, here we are at last; in Rome, and at the great man's studio!'

And was this Rome! And was this the end of all his eager youthful aspirations! Hiram had hardly the courage to smile back in his friend's face, and assume an air of pretended cheerfulness. Already he felt in his heart that this great, squalid, sordid city was really no place for such as him. He knew he would never like it; he knew he could never succeed in it. England, beautiful, smiling England, had quite unaffectedly charmed and delighted him. There, he could find a thousand subjects ready to his hand that would exactly suit his taste and temper. It was so rich in verdure and tillage; it was so pregnant with the literary and historical interests that were nearest and dearest to him. But Rome! the very first glimpse of it was to Hiram Winthrop a hideous disillusionment. Its dirt, its mouldiness, its gloom, its very antiquity, nay, in one word, to be quite frank, its picturesqueness itself, were all to his candid American soul unendurably ugly. He hated it from top to bottom at first sight with a deadly hatred; and he felt quite sure he should hate it cordially as long as he lived in it.

Very Philistine, of course, this feeling of dissatisfaction on Hiram Winthrop's part; but then, you know, the Americans are a nation of Philistines, and after all, no man can rise wholly superior to the influence of his lifelong social environment. Indeed, it isn't easy even for an Englishman to take kindly just at first to the dirt and discomfort of southern European cities. He may put the best face upon the matter that he can; he may sedulously and successfully disguise his disgust lest he be accounted vulgar, narrowminded, insular, inartistic; he may pretend to be charmed with everything, from St. Peter's to the garlic in the cookery; yet in his heart of hearts he feels distinctly that the

Vatican barely outweighs the smells of the Ghetto, and that the Colosseum scantily atones for the filthy alleys of the Tiberside slums that cover what was once the Campus Martius. It takes some residence to get over the initial disadvantages of an Italian city. But to an American-born, an unregenerate, not yet cosmopolitanised or Italianate American, fresh from the broad clean streets and neat white houses of American cities, the squalor and griminess of Rome is a thing incredible and almost unutterable. Hiram gazed at it, appalled and awestruck, wondering how on earth he could ever manage to live for a year or two together in that all-pervading murky atmosphere of dust-laden malaria.

Besides, was he not a little sore and disappointed that Gwen had seen him, and had utterly forgotten him? Was he not just a trifle jealous, not only of Audouin, but also of Colin Churchill? All these things go to colour a man's opinion of towns and places quite as much as those recognised and potent refractive agents, the nature of his digestion or the state of the weather.

They were duly ushered up into M. Seguin's private room, and there the great painter, after a few minutes' delay, came to see them. He was a short, dry-looking, weazened-up little man, with a grizzled French moustache waxed at the ends, and an imperturbable air of being remarkably well pleased with himself, both physically and mentally. Audouin took him in hand at once, as if by agreement, and did all the talking, while Hiram stood silent and confused quite in the background. Indeed, a casual observer might easily have imagined that it was Audouin who wished to be the Frenchman's pupil, and that Hiram Winthrop was merely there as a disinterested and unconcerned bystander.

'Has Monsieur got any specimens of his work with him?' M. Seguin asked Hiram at last condescendingly. 'Anything on which one might form a provisional judgment of his probable talents?'

'I've brought a few landscapes with me from America, if you would care to see them,' Hiram answered submissively.

'To see them! Not at all, Monsieur. Do I wish to look at landscapes for my part? Far from it! Let us admit that you do not come here to me to learn landscape. The human figure, the divine human figure in all its sublime grandeur, there, Monsieur, is the goal of the highest art; there is the arena of the highest artist.' M. Seguin brought his hand carelessly down upon the fragment of ribbon on his own left breast as he finished this final sentence, as though to imply with due delicacy of feeling that he considered the highest artist and Jean Baptiste Seguin as practically convertible expressions.

Hiram inclined his head a little, partly to hide a smile. 'I'm afraid, Monsieur,' he said humbly, 'I have nothing to show you in the way of figure painting.'

'Well, well,' Seguin answered with a polite expansion of his two hands, 'give yourself the trouble to come here to-morrow morning and prepare to copy a head of mine for the Salon of last year. You have seen it?—no? then this way, Messieurs, 'I will show it to you!'

The tone of exalted condescension in which he uttered those four words, 'Je vous la montrerai,' was as though he meant to afford them a glorious treat which would render them for ever after perfectly happy.

Hiram and Audouin followed the weazened-up little man into another room, where on an easel in the light stood his great Salon painting of Sardanapalus and the Egyptian Princess. As in everything that Seguin has painted, there was undoubtedly a certain meretricious beauty and force about it.

The technique, indeed, was in its way absolutely perfect. The flesh tones had a satiny transparency; the draperies were arranged with exquisite skill and supreme knowledge; the touch was everywhere firm and solid: the art displayed was throughout consummate. Even the figures themselves, viewed as representing their historical namesakes, were not lacking in a certain theatrical grace and dignity.

Hiram felt instinctively that Sardanapalus was the masterpiece of a great artist, who had a marvellous hand and a profound knowledge of painting, but no soul in him; and even Audouin recognised at once that though the workmanship was as nearly perfect as the deepest study and the finest eye could possibly make it, yet there was a something still more profoundly artistic that was evidently wanting to the first conception of Seguin's masterpiece.

M. Seguin himself stood still for a minute or two with his hand on his hip, lips half parted and eye entranced, as though absorbed in contemplation of his own great work of art, and then glanced round sideways quite accidentally to see how its beauty affected the minds of the two strangers. Having furtively satisfied himself that Hiram was just then really appreciative of the clever light that fell obliquely upon Sardanapalus's dusky shoulder, and that Audouin was duly admiring the exquisitely painted full round arm of the Egyptian Princess, he turned to them in front once more, like one recalled from the realms of divine art to the worky-day world of actuality, and resumed the discussion of their present business.

'You will come then, to-morrow, Monsieur, and do me a study of the head of Sardanapalus. If by the time you have finished it, you display a talent worthy of being evoked, I will then accept you as one of my pupils. If not, which I do not, for the rest, anticipate, you will understand, Monsieur, in that case, that it will be with the greatest regret that I shall be compeled, ah, good; you recognise the necessity laid upon an artist. Antoine! These gentlemen, my time, the time of an artist, is very precious. Good day, Monsieur, good day to you.'

'And if he accepts you, Hiram,' Audouin said, when they got outside, 'you'd better arrange to take an apartment somewhere with young Churchill, furnished apartments suitable for art-students are cheap at Rome, they tell me, and get your meals at a trattoria. That'll make your money go farther, I estimate.'.

Hiram sighed, and almost wished in his own heart that M. Seguin would have the kindness not to recognise in him a talent worthy of being evoked by so great a master. But alas, fate willed it otherwise. M. Seguin pronounced the head, though but feebly representing the mixed virile force and feminine delicacy of his own Sardanapalus, 'sufficiently well painted, as the work of a beginner;' and Hiram was forthwith duly enrolled among the great French painter's select pupils, to start work as soon as he had had a fortnight with Audouin, 'for inspecting the sights of the city.'

CHAPTER XXIII

RECOGNITION

My dear,' said the Colonel, as Gwen and he sat at breakfast together a few mornings later, 'now, what's your programme for to-day? An off day, I hope, for, to tell you the truth, I'm beginning to get rather tired of so much sight-seeing. Yesterday, San Clemente, wasn't it? (that place with the very extraordinary frescoes!) and the Forum, and the temple of Fortuna something-or-other, where an extortionate fellow wanted to charge me a lira for showing us nothing; Wednesday, St. Peter's, which, thank goodness, we did thoroughly' and won't have to go to again in the course of our lifetimes; Tuesday, I'm sure I can't recollect what we did on Tuesday, but I know it was somewhere very tiring. I do hope today's to be an off day, Gwen. Have you made any arrangements?'

'Oh yes, papa. Don't you remember? That delightful Mr. Audouin is coming to take us round to some of the studios.'

The colonel pushed his chair away from the table somewhat testily. 'The Yankee man, you mean, I suppose?' he said, with a considerable trace of acerbity in his manner. 'That fellow who kept talking so much the other day about some German of the name of Heine (I find out from Mrs. Wilmer, by the way, that this man Heine was far from being a respectable person). So you've promised to go mooning about the studios with him, have you?'

'Yes, papa, and he'll be here at ten; so please now go at once and get ready.'

The colonel grumbled a little, it was his double privilege, as a Briton and a military man, to grumble as much as he thought necessary, on all possible occasions; but by the time Audouin arrived, he was quite ready, with his silk hat brushed up to the Bond Street pattern, and his eminently respectable kid gloves shaming Audouin's bare hands with their exquisite newness.

'How kind of you to take us, Mr. Audouin,' Gwen said, with one of her artless smiles: 'I'm really so delighted to get a chance of seeing something of the inner life of artists. And you're going to introduce us to Maragliano, too! What an honour!'

'Oh, quite so,' the colonel assented readily; 'most gratifying, certainly. A very remarkable painter, Signor Maragliano!'

'But most remarkable of all as a sculptor,' Audouin put in quickly, before Gwen had time to correct her father's well-meant blunder. 'A magnificent figure, his Psyche. This way, Miss Russell, down the Corso.'

'Our name is Howard-Russell, Mr. Audouin, if you please, two surnames, with a dash between them,' the colonel interrupted (one can hardly expect the military mind to discriminate accurately between a dash and a hyphen). 'My ancestor, the fourth earl, who was a Howard, you know, married a Lady Mary Russell, daughter of the fifth Marquis of Marsh wood, a great heiress, and took her name. That was how the Russell connection first got into the Howard family.'

'Indeed!' Audouin answered, with forced politeness. (The best bred Americans find it hard to understand our genealogical interest.) 'But the double name's a little long, isn't it, for practical purposes? In an easy-going old-world country like Europe, people can find time for so many syllables, I dare say; but I'm afraid we hurry-scurrying Americans would kick against having to give one person two surnames every time we spoke to him, colonel.'

The colonel drew himself up rather stiffly. That any man could make light of so serious a subject as the Howard-Russell name and pedigree was an idea that had hardly before even occurred to his exalted consideration.

They walked along the Corso, and through the narrow street till they arrived at the Via Colonna. Then Audouin dived down that abode of artists, with Gwen chatting away to him gaily, and the colonel stalking beside them in solemn silence, till they reached Maragliano's studio.

As they entered, the great sculptor was standing aside behind a big lump of moist clay, where Colin Churchill was trying to set up a life-size model from the Calabrian Peasant. Colin's back was turned towards the visitors, so that he did not see them enter; and the colonel, who merely observed a young man unknown kneading up some sticky material on a board, 'just the same as if he were a baker,' didn't for the moment recognise their late companion in the French railway carriage. But Gwen saw at once that it was Colin Churchill. Indeed, to say the truth, she expected to meet him there, for she had already heard all about his arrangement with Maragliano from Audouin; and she had cleverly angled to get Audouin to offer to take them both to Maragliano's, not without the ulterior object of starting a fresh acquaintance, under better auspices, with the interesting young English sculptor.

'Ah, yes,' Maragliano said to the colonel as soon as the formalities of introduction were over. 'That, signor, is my Calabrian Peasant, and that young man you see there, trying to model it, has really a most extraordinary plastic genius. He's a new pupil, and he's going to do wonders. But first, if you will wait and see, in ten minutes his Calabrian Peasant will come all to pieces.'

'Dear me!' exclaimed the colonel, with much show of polite interest. 'Come all to pieces! Really! How very extraordinary! And what is the object of that, now, signor?'

Maragliano laughed. 'He doesn't know it'll fall yet,' he answered, half whispering. 'He's quite new to this sort of work, you see, and I told him when he came the other day to begin copying the Peasant. Of course, as your knowledge of the physical laws will immediately suggest to you, signor, the arm can't possibly hold together in moist clay in that position. In fact, before long, the whole thing will collapse altogether.'

'Naturally,' the colonel answered, looking very wise, and glancing with a critical eye towards the marble original. 'That's a work, of course, that couldn't possibly be produced in clay, but only in bronze or marble.'

'But why did you set him to do it, then?' asked Gwen, a little doubtfully. 'Surely it wasn't kind to make him begin it if it can only end by getting broken.'

'Ah, signorina,' the great sculptor answered, shrugging his shoulders, 'we learn most of all by our errors. For a model like that, we always employ an iron framework, on which, as on a skeleton, we build up the clay into flesh and muscles. But this young compatriot of yours, though he has great native genius, is still quite ignorant of the technical ways of professional sculptors. He has evidently modelled hitherto only in his own self-taught fashion, with moist clay alone, letting it support its own weight the best way possible. So he has set to work trying to mould an outline of my Peasant, as he has been used to do with his own stiff upright figures. By-and-by it will tumble down; then we will send for a blacksmith; he will fix up a mechanical skeleton with iron bars and interlacing crosses of wood and wire; on that, my pupil will flesh out the figure with moist clay; and then it'll be as firm as a rock for him to work upon.'

'But it seems a great shame, all the same,' Gwen cried warmly, 'to make him do it all for nothing. It looks to me like a waste of time.'

'Not so,' Maragliano answered. 'He will get on all the faster for it in the end. He's too enthusiastic now. He must learn that art goes softly.'

The colonel turned aside with Maragliano to examine some of the other works in the studio, but Gwen and Audouin went up to watch the new pupil at his futile task. Colin turned round as they approached, and felt his face grow hot as he suddenly recognised his late beautiful fellow-traveller. But Gwen advanced to meet him so frankly, and held out her delicate hand with such an air of perfect cordiality, that he half forgot the awkwardness of the situation, and only said with a smile, 'You see my hands are not in a fit state for welcoming visitors, Miss Howard-Russell; a sculptor must be excused, you know, for having muddy fingers. But I'm so glad to see you again. I learnt from my brother how kindly you had interested yourself on my behalf with Sir Henry Wilberforce. It was very good of you, and I shall not forget the trouble you took for me.'

Gwen coloured a little. Now that she looked back upon it in a calmer moment, her interference in Colin Churchill's favour had certainly been most dreadfully unconventional.

'I'm only too glad, Mr. Churchill,' she said, 'that you've got away at last from that horrid old man. He almost frightened me out of my senses. You ought to be here working, as you're doing now, of course, and I shall watch your progress in future with so much interest. Signor Maragliano has such a high opinion of you. He says you'll do wonders.'

'Yes,' Colin answered, eagerly. 'He's a splendid man, Maragliano. It's grand to hear his generous appreciation of others, down even to the merest beginners. Whenever he talks of any other sculptor, dead or living, there's such a noble absence of any jealousy or petty reserve about his approbation. He seems as if he could never say enough in praise of anybody.' 'He looks it,' Audouin put in. 'He has a fine head and a speaking eye. I've seldom seen a grander bust and profile. Don't you think so, Miss Russell?'

'Very fine indeed,' Gwen answered. 'And so you're working at this Calabrian Peasant, Mr. Churchill. It's a beautiful piece of sculpture.'

'Oh, yes,' Colin said, standing still and regarding it for a moment with loving attention. 'It's beautiful, beautiful. When I can model a figure like that, I shall think I've done something really. But it's quite painful to me to look round and see the other men here, some of them younger than myself, to watch their power and experience, their masterly way of sketching in the figure, their admirable imitation of nature, and then to think how very little I myself have yet accomplished. It almost makes one feel despondent for one's own powers. When I watch them, I feel humbled and unhappy.'

'No, no,' Audouin said warmly. 'You needn't think so, I'm sure, Churchill. The man who distrusts his own work is always the truest workman. It's only fools or poor creatures who are satisfied with their own first tentative efforts. The true artist underrates himself, especially at first, and thereby both proves himself and makes himself the true artist.'

'Just what I felt myself,' Gwen murmured, half inaudibly (though somebody standing in the shade behind heard her quite distinctly), only I don't know how to put it nearly so cleverly.'

'And Maragliano tells me,' Audouin went on, 'that you've got some splendid designs for bas-reliefs with you, which were what really determined him to take you for his pupil. He says they're the finest things he ever yet saw done by a self-taught beginner, and that they display extraordinary promise.'

'Oh, do show them to us, Mr. Churchill,' Gwen cried, looking at him with obvious admiration (as the somebody behind again noticed). 'Have you got them here? Do show them to us!'

Colin smiled and looked a little embarrassed. Then he went off and got his portfolio, and showed the drawings one after another to Gwen and Audouin. Gwen watched them all with deep interest; Audouin praised and criticised and threw in a word or two here and there of transcendental explanation; while Colin himself now and then pointed out a motive or described his idea of the various personages. When they came to Orestes and the Eumenides, Colin held out the drawing at arm's length for a moment lovingly. 'Maradiano admired that the most,' he said with a touch of not ungraceful vanity; and Gwen, looking at it with her untutored eye, at once agreed that Maragliano had chosen wisely. 'It's beautiful,' she said, 'very beautiful. Oh, Mr. Churchill, what a splendid thing to be able to make such lovely figures! I don't think even painting can compare for a moment for nobility and purity with sculpture.'

Somebody standing beside in the shade, he was by trade a painter, felt a stab in his heart as the beautiful Englishwoman said those simple natural words of outspoken admiration.

'But, oh, Miss Russell,' Colin cried, looking up again from his own drawings to the Calabrian Peasant, in its exquisite grace of attitude, 'what's the use of looking at my poor things with such a statue as that before you?'

Gwen glanced quickly and appreciatively from one to the other. 'Why, do you know, Mr. Churchill,' she answered, with that easy boldness of criticism which distinguishes her sex, 'it may be only my ignorance of art that makes me say so, but I really prefer your Orestes even to Maragliano's Calabrian Peasant; and yet the Peasant's a magnificent statue.'

Somebody behind, putting his head a little on one side, and comparing hastily the drawing and the marble figure, confessed to his own heart, with a painful sinking sense of personal failure, that after all Gwen's judgment in the matter was not far wrong even to the more trained artistic perception.

Colin laughed. 'Ah, that's flattery, I'm afraid,' he said, turning round to her innocently; 'quite too obvious and undeserved flattery. It'd be absurd to compare my poor little drawings of course with the finished work of such an accomplished sculptor as Maragliano. You must be given to paying compliments I'm sure, Miss Russell.'

Gwen thought the conversation was taking perhaps a rather dangerous turn, so she only said, 'Oh no,' a little coldly, and then changed the subject as quickly as she was able. 'So you're going to settle down in Rome for the present?' she said. 'You've taken lodgings, I suppose, have you?'

'Oh yes, I've taken lodgings in such a funny little street, to dine at a trattoria, with a friend of Mr. Audouin's, who's come from America to study painting. You've met him before. He's here this morning. He came round with me to see the studio, and I'm sure I don't know now where he's gone to. Winthrop, Winthrop, where are you?'

Hiram Winthrop stepped out of the gloom behind with bashful eyes and cheeks burning; for he had heard all that Gwen had said to Colin, and he felt as if his own hopes and aspirations were all that moment finally crushed out of him. How much notice she took of this fluent, handsome English sculptor! how little she seemed to think of him, the poor shy, retiring, awkward, shock-headed American painter!

But Gwen didn't seem to be at all conscious of Hiram's embarrassment. She held out her hand to him just as cordially as she had held it out five minutes before to Colin; and Hiram, luckier in the matter of clay, was able to take it, and to feel its touch thrill through him inwardly with a delicious tremor. She talked to him about the ordinary polite nothings for a minute or two, had he done the Vatican yet? was he going to the Colosseum? did he like Rome as far as he had seen it?—and then Maragliano and the colonel drew a little nearer to the group, still talking to one another quite confidentially.

'Ah, yes,' Maragliano was saying, in a somewhat lower tone than before; 'a very remarkable pupil indeed, signor. If I were inclined to jealousy, I should say, a pupil who will soon outstrip his master. He will be a great sculptor, a very great sculptor. You will hear of his name one day; he will not be long in achieving celebrity.'

'Ah, indeed,' the colonel answered, in his set tone of polite indifference. 'Very interesting, really. And what might the young man's name be, signor? so that one may recognise it, you know, when it comes to be worth hearing.'

Before Maragliano could reply, there was a noise of something falling behind, and then, with a sodden sound, like dough flung down upon a board, Colin Churchill's Calabrian Peasant collapsed utterly, and sank of its own weight upon the low table where he was modelling it. There it lay in a ludicrously drunken and inglorious attitude, still present ing some outer semblance of humanity, but flattened and distorted into a grotesque caricature of the original statue. As it lay there helpless, a perfect Guy Fawkes of a Calabrian, with its pasty featureless face staring blankly upward towards the vacant ceiling, Gwen couldn't resist bursting out gaily into a genuine laugh of girlish amusement. Everybody else laughed, except two: and those two stood with burning faces beside the shattered model, glaring at one another indignantly and defiantly. Colin Churchill's cheeks were flushed with natural shame at this absurd collapse of his carefully moulded figure before the eyes of so many spectators. The colonel's were flushed with anger and horror when he saw that the promising pupil with whom his daughter had been talking so eagerly was none other than their railway acquaintance of the journey Rome ward, Sir Henry Wilber-force's valet, Colin Churchill.

'Gwen,' he cried, coming up to her with ill-concealed anger, 'I think we'd better be going. I'm afraid, I'm afraid our presence has possibly contributed to this very unfortunate catastrophe. Good morning, Mr. Churchill. I didn't know we were to have the pleasure of meeting you here this morning. Good morning.'

But Gwen wouldn't be dragged away so easily. 'Wait a minute or two, papa,' she cried in her authoritative way. 'Signor Maragliano will explain all this, and we'll go as soon as Mr. Churchill is ready to say goodbye to us. At present, you see, he's too busy with his model to pay any attention to stray visitors. I'm so sorry, Mr. Winthrop, it should have occurred while we were here, because I take so much interest in Mr. Churchill, and now I'm afraid he'll think we were all in league to raise a laugh against him. But I couldn't help it, you know; I really couldn't help it; the thing does certainly look so very comical.'

Hiram hated himself for it in his heart, but he couldn't help feeling a certain sense of internal triumph in spite of himself at this unexpected discomfiture of his supposed rival.

When they were walking home together a few minutes later, and had passed from the narrow street into an empty sleepy-looking piazza, the colonel turned and said angrily to his daughter, 'Gwen, I'm thoroughly ashamed of you, going and talking in that way to that common valet fellow. Have you no feeling for your position that you choose to lower yourself by actually paying court before my very eyes to a person in his station?'

Gwen bit her lip in silence for a minute or two, and made no reply. Then, after letting her internal indignation cool for a while, she condescended to use the one mean Philistine argument which she thought at all likely to have any effect upon the colonel's personality.

'Papa,' she said very quietly, 'it's no use telling you, of course, that he's a wonderful artist, and that he's going to make beautiful statues that everybody'll admire and talk about, for you don't understand art, and you don't care for it or see anything in it: but can't you at least understand that Mr. Churchill is a gentleman by nature, that he's rising to be a gentleman by position, that he'll come at last to be a great sculptor, and be made President of the Royal Academy, and be knighted, and entertain the Prince of Wales to dinner, and then, you know, you'd be glad enough to get an invitation anywhere to meet him.'

The colonel coughed. 'It'll be quite time to consider that question,' he said drily, 'when we see him duly gazetted. Every French soldier carries a marshal's bâton in his knapsack, I've been given to understand; but for my part, I prefer not sitting down to dinner with him, all the same, until the marshal's bâton has been properly taken out of the knapsack.'

That night, Hiram Winthrop, creeping up the dim creaking staircase to his small dark bedroom in the narrow dirty Roman lane, said to himself, with something of despair in his soul, 'She will fall in love with Churchill. I feel sure she will fall in love with Churchill. And yet he doesn't seem to notice it, or care for it. While I—'

That night, Colin Churchill, coming back, once more enthusiastic, from Maragliano's, (where the great sculptor had with his own hands rebuilt for him in outline round an iron framework the shattered Calabrian Peasant), and mounting the quaint old Roman staircase to his own funny little attic room, next door to Winthrop's, said to himself casually, in a passing idle moment, 'A beautiful girl, that Miss Howard-Bussell, certainly. More statuesque than Minna, though not perhaps so really pretty. But still, very beautiful. One of the finest profiles, I think, I have ever met with. And what an interest she seems to take in art, too! So anxious to come and see Maragliano, Mr. Audouin told me. Only, she was quite too flattering, really, about Orestes pursued by the Eumenides.'

And that night, away over yonder in lonely London, little Minna read and re-read a long letter from Colin at Rome ten times over, and pressed it tenderly to her heart, and cried to herself over it, and wondered whether Cohn would ever forget her, or would fall in love with one of those splendid dark-eyed treacherous-looking Italian women. And then, as of old, she lay awake and thought of Cohn, and the dangers of absence, with tears in her eyes, till she cried herself to sleep at last with his open letter still pressed tight against her tremulous eager little bosom.

CHAPTER XXIV

GWEN AND HIRAM

Everybody who went to Audouin's picnic at the Alban lake agreed that it was one of the most delightful entertainments given at Rome during the whole of that season.

The winter, Hiram and Cohn's first winter in Italy, had worn away quickly enough. Hiram had gone every day, as in duty bound, to paint and be chidden at M. Seguin's studio; for Seguin was one of those exalted teachers who instruct rather by example than by precept; who seem to say perpetually to their pupils, 'See how much better I have done it or would have done it than you do;' and he never for a moment succeeded in inspiring the very slightest respect or enthusiasm in Hiram's simple, quiet, unostentatious, straightforward American nature. Of course Hiram worked hard; he felt he ought to work hard. Audouin expected it of him, and he would have done anything on earth to please Audouin; but his heart was not really in it for all that, though he wouldn't for the world have acknowledged as much even to himself, and he got on far less well than many other people would have done with half his talent and half his industry. He hated the whole artifice of drapery and models, and clever arrangement of light and shade, and marvellous minuteness of technical resources, in which his French master positively revelled. He longed for the beautiful native wildness of the American woodlands, or still more, even, for the green hedgerows and parks and meadows of that enchanted England, which he had seen but in a glimpse for two days in his whole lifetime, but in whose mellow beauty, nevertheless, his heart had immediately recognised its true fatherland. It may have been narrow and sectarian and unappreciative in Hiram; no doubt it was; but he couldn't for the life of him really care for Seguin's very greatest triumphs of artistic ingenuity. He recognised their extraordinary skill, he admitted their unrivalled cleverness as tours de force of painting, he even admired their studied grace and exquisite composition as bits of harmonious form and colour; but he never could fall down before them in the least as works of art in the highest sense, or see in them anything more than the absolute perfection of cold, hard, dry, unspiritualised mechanical aptitude.

As for Colin, now that Sam had gone back to England, on his way home to America (Sam used the expression himself quite naturally now), he had thrown himself with the utmost fervour into the work of Maragliano's studio, where he soon rose to the acknowledged position of the great master's most favourite pupil. The model of the Calabrian Peasant which he built up upon the blacksmith's framework was the last copy he had to do for Maragliano. As soon as it was finished, the master scanned the clay figure with his quick critical eye, and cried almost contemptuously, 'Why, this is mere child's play for such a man as you, I see, Churchill. You must do no more copying. To-morrow you shall begin modelling from the life.' Colin was well pleased indeed to go on to this new and untried work, and he made such rapid progress in it that even Maragliano himself was quite surprised, and said confidentially to Bazzoni more than once, 'The young Englishman will go far. He has the spark of genius in him, my friend; he is a born sculptor.'

It was all so different too in Rome, from London, where Colin had been isolated, unknown, and almost friendless. There was nobody there except Cicolari, and Minna; dear little woman, he had almost omitted her, with whom he could talk on equal terms about his artistic longings and ideas and interests. But at Rome it was all so different. There was such a great society of artists! Every man's studio was open to his fellows; a lively running fire of candid criticism went on continually about every work completed or in progress. To live in such an atmosphere of art, to move amongst it and talk about it all day long, to feast his eyes upon the grand antiques and glorious Michael Angelos of the Vatican, all this was to Colin Churchill as near an approach to unmixed happiness as it is given to human beings to know in this nether world of very mixed experiences. If only he had had Minna with him! But there! Colin Churchill loved art so earnestly and singlemindedly that for its sake he could well endure even a few years' brief absence in Rome away from poor, little, loving, sorrowing Minna.

Gwen meanwhile, in spite of the colonel, had managed to see a great deal from time to time both of Colin and of Audouin. The colonel had indeed peremptorily forbidden her in so many words to hold any further communications of any sort with either of them. Colin, he said, was a person clearly beneath her both in birth and education, while Audouin was the most incomprehensible prig of a Yankee fellow he had ever had the misfortune to set eyes upon in the whole course of his lifetime. But the colonel was one of those forcible-feeble people who are very vehement always in language, but very mild in actual fact; who threaten and bluster a great deal about what they will never do, or what they will never permit, but who do or permit it all the same on the very next occasion when opportunity arises. The consequence was that Gwen, who was a vigorous young lady with a will of her own, never took much serious notice of the colonel when he was in one of his denunciatory humours, but went her own way peacefully, and did as she chose to do herself the very next minute.

Now, at the same hotel where the Howard-Russells were stopping there was a certain Mrs. Wilmer, a lady with two daughters (perfect sticks, Gwen called them), to whom Gwen, being herself alone and motherless, thought it well to attach herself for purposes of society. It's so convenient, you know, to have somebody by way of a chaperon who can take you about and get invitations for you. Happily Mrs. Wilmer, though herself as commonplace a village Lady Bountiful as ever distributed blankets and read good books to the mothers' meeting every Wednesday, was suddenly seized at Rome, under the influence of the genius loci, with a burning desire to know something about art and artists; and Gwen made use of this new-born fancy freely to go round the studios with Mrs. Wilmer, and of course to meet at times with Colin and Audouin.

At last April came, and Audouin, who had been getting very tired of so much city life (for his hermit love for the woods and solitude was only one half affected), began to long once more for the lonely delights of his own beloved solitary Lakeside. He would have been gone long before, indeed, had it not been for a curious feeling which for the first time in his life, he felt growing up within him— Audouin was falling in love with Gwen Howard-Russell. The very first day he ever met her by the Lake of the Thousand Islands, he had greatly admired her frank bold English beauty, and since he had seen a little more of her at Rome, he had found himself insensibly gliding from admiration into a less philosophical and more human attitude. Yes, he had almost made up his mind that before he left Rome, he would ask Gwen whether she would do him the supreme honour of accompanying him back to America as the mistress of Lakeside.

'Papa,' Gwen said, one bright morning in April, 'Mrs. Wilmer wants me to go with her to-day to a picnic at the Lago d'Albano.'

'A picnic!' the colonel cried severely. 'And in the Campagna, too! My dear child, as sure as fate, you'll all get the Roman fever.'

'Albano isn't in the Campagna, papa,' Gwen answered quietly. 'At least it's right up ever so high among the mountains. And Mrs. Wilmer's going to call for me at halfpast eleven.'

'Who gives the picnic?'

Gwen bit her lip. 'Mr. Audouin,' she answered shortly.

'Mr. Audouin! What, that mad Yankee man again! Then, mind, Gwen, I say you're not to go on any account.'

'But, papa, Mrs. Wilmer has accepted for me.'

'Never mind. I say, I won't allow you. Not a word more upon the subject: I won't allow you. Now, remember, I positively forbid it, and pray don't re-open the question.'

At half-past eleven, however, Gwen came down, dressed and ready. 'Papa dear,' she said, as unconcernedly as if nothing at all had been said about it, 'here's Mrs. Wilmer waiting for me outside, and I must go. I hope we shan't be back late for dinner. Good morning.'

The colonel only muttered something inarticulate as she left the room, and turned to his cigar for consolation.

'What, you here, Mr. Churchill,' Gwen cried, as they all met together a few minutes later at the Central Railway Station. 'I had no idea you were to be of the party. I thought you were so perfectly wedded to art that you never took a minute's holiday.'

'I don't often,' Colin answered, smiling; 'I have so much leeway to make up that I have to keep always at it, night and morning. But Maragliano, who's the best and most considerate of men, when he heard that Mr. Audouin had been kind enough to invite me, insisted upon it that I must give myself a day's recreation. Besides, you see,' he added after a momentary pause, looking down as if by accident into Gwen's beautiful eyes, 'there were such very special attractions.'

Gwen made a little mock curtsey. 'What a pretty speech!' she said laughingly. 'Since you've come to Rome, Mr. Churchill, you seem to have picked up the Roman habit of paying compliments.'

Colin blushed, with some inward embarrassment. The fact was, Gwen had misunderstood his simple remark: he was thinking, not of her, but only of the tomb of Pompey and the old Roman Emissary. But Gwen noticed the faint crimson rising to his cheek, and said to herself, not without a touch of pardonable vanity, 'Our young sculptor isn't quite so wholly swallowed up in his art as he wants us to believe, then. He dreams already of flying high. If he flies high enough, who knows but he may be successful.'

What a handsome young fellow he was, to be sure, and what a natural gentleman! And what a contrast, too, in his easy unselfconscious manner, to that shy, awkward, gawky slip of a Yankee painter, Mr. Hiram Winthrop! Hiram! where on earth did he get the name from? It sounded for all the world just like a fancy character out of 'Martin Chuzzlewit.'

'And you too, Mr. Winthrop! Of course we should have expected you. I don't wonder you're always about so much with Mr. Audouin. I think him, you know, the most charming talker I've ever met with.'

Hiram could have sunk into the ground with mortification at having thus always to play second fiddle to Audouin, whose grizzling hair made him seem to Gwen so much a confirmed old bachelor that she didn't think there could be any danger at all in openly speaking out her admiration for his powers as a talker.

They went by train to the station at Albano, and then drove up to the shores of the lake in carriages which Audouin had ready in waiting. Recluse and hermit as he was, when he went in for giving an entertainment, he gave it regally; and the picnic was universally pronounced to be the most splendid success of the Roman season. After lunch they dispersed a little, as people always do at picnics (or else what would be the use of that form of reunion?) and Colin somehow found himself, he didn't quite know how, strolling with Gwen down the Galleria di Sopra, that beautiful avenue of shady evergreen oaks which leads, with innumerable lovely glimpses of the lake below, from Albano towards Castel Gandolfo. Gwen, however, knew well enough how it had all happened; for she had angled most cleverly so as to avoid the pressing attentions of Audouin, and to pair off in apparent unconsciousness with the more favoured Colin. Mrs. Wilmer, walking behind with another guest to do the proprieties, had acquiesced most heartily in this arrangement, and had even managed to promote it diligently: for did it not compel Mr. Audouin to link himself for the afternoon to dear Lilian, and was it not well known that Mr. Audouin, though an American, was otherwise a most unexceptionable and eligible person, with quite sufficient means of his own to marry most comfortably upon? Whereas this young Mr. Churchill, though no doubt wonderfully clever, and a most estimable young man in his own way, was a person of no family, and with all his fortune still to make by his own exertions. And Mr. Audouin had really hardly a trace, after all, of that horrid American singsong.

'Yes,' Gwen was saying, as they reached the point of view near the Emissario: 'Signor Maragliano told me that before many months were over, he should advise you to begin modelling a real life-size figure from the life of your own invention; for he thinks you would be only wasting your time in working much longer at mere copying or academy work. He wants to see you begin carrying out some of your own beautiful original conceptions. And so do I too, you know: for we feel in a way, papa and I, as if we had discovered you, Mr. Churchill. Shall we sit down here awhile, under the oak trees? This broad shade is so very delicious.'

She gave Colin her hand, to help her down the first bit of the side path to the old Roman conduit; and as she did so, she looked into his face with her lovely eyes, and smiled her thanks to him expressively. Cohn took her hand and helped her gently down. 'You're very good to interest yourself so much in my work,' he said, with no trace of shyness or awkwardness in his manner. 'I shall be glad indeed when I'm able to begin producing something worthy in real earnest.'

Gwen was really very beautiful and very kind and very cordial. He never for a moment remembered with her the original disparity of their stations, as he did with so many other grand ladies. She seemed to put him at his ease at once, and to be so frank and complimentary and even pressing. And then, her profile was magnificent, and her eyes were really splendid!

Ah, Minna, Minna, poor little Minna, in your big noisy schoolroom away over yonder in big noisy London, well may you tremble with a cold shiver running strangely through you, you know not why, and murmur to yourself, in your quaint old-world superstition, that somebody must be walking over your grave to-day somewhere or other!

'Rome's a perfect paradise to me, you know, Mr. Churchill,' Gwen went on, musingly. 'I never fully knew, before I came here, how much I loved art. I perfectly revel in the Vatican and the Sistine Chapel, and in studios such as Signor Maragliano's. What a fortunate life yours will be, to live always among so much exquisite beauty! I should love an artist's life myself, only I suppose I should never get beyond the most amateur water-colours. But a sculptor, especially! A sculptor's career seems to me to be the grandest thing on earth a man can live for! I'd willingly give half my days, do you know, if only I could be a sculptor.'

'It's a glorious profession, certainly,' Colin answered, with kindling eyes. 'It's such a grand thing to think one belongs, however humbly, to the same great troop as Pheidias, and Michael Angelo, and Gibson, and Thorwaldsen. That, alone, of course, is something in one's life to be really proud of.'

'Poor boy! he's obtuse,' Gwen thought to herself, commiseratingly. 'He doesn't follow up the openings one gives him. But never mind. He's very young still, and doesn't know when one's leading up to him. There's plenty of time yet. By-and-by he'll grow older and wiser. What a beautiful reflection down there in the water, Mr. Churchill! No, not there: on the broader part beyond the Roman mason-work. I wish Mr. Winthrop could see it. It's just the thing he'd like so much to put on paper or canvas.'

'You're interested in Winthrop, then, are you?' Cohn asked innocently.

'Interested in him? Oh, yes, I'm interested in all art and in all artists, though not of course in all equally. I mean, I like sculpture even better than painting. But I saw a water-colour drawing of Mr. Winthrop's when I was in America, you know, where I first met him, which I thought very pretty. I can remember it yet, a sketch of blended trees and water among the channels of the Thousand Islands.'

'I've seen it,' Cohn answered: 'he's brought it with him, as well as several other American landscapes. Winthrop draws admirably, I know, and his treatment of foliage and water seems to me quite extraordinarily good. He'll make a fine artist, I'm quite confident, before he's done with it.'

Gwen pouted a little to herself. 'It's plain,' she thought, 'that Mr. Churchill isn't a person to be easily piqued by praising anybody else.' And must it not be candidly admitted that in most women's eyes such complete absence of jealousy is regarded rather as a fault in a man's nature than as a virtue? (Mind, fair and courteous reader, if I may for a moment address you personally, I say 'in most' not 'in all women's.' You yourself, like present company generally, always, of course, form one of the striking and praiseworthy exceptions to every vile masculine innuendo aimed at the real or supposed peculiarities of 'most women.' Indeed, it is on purpose to allow you that flattering loophole of escape that I always artfully employ the less exclusive or general expression.)

They sat for a while talking idly on the slope by the path that leads to the Emissary, till at last Audouin, having managed to shift off dear Lilian for a while upon another man of the party, strolled up as though by accident to join them. 'Do I intrude upon a tete-a-tete?' he asked with apparent carelessness, as he sat down upon the rocky ledge beside them. 'Is Mr. Churchill discoursing high art to you, Miss Russell, and peopling the romantic glen below with yet unhewn Egerias and Faunuses? How well this Italian scenery lends itself to those pretty half-theatrical Poussinesque embellishments! and how utterly out of place they would all look among the perfectly unkempt native savagery of our American woods and waters!'

Gwen smiled. 'We weren't discussing high art, Mr. Audouin,' she said as she drew a circle in the dust with the tip of her parasol. 'In fact we want you here to throw a little touch of fancy and idealism into the conversation. To tell you the truth, Mr. Churchill and I were only pulling to pieces the Miss Wilmers' dresses.'

'Ah, but even dress itself is in its way a liturgy, Miss Russell,' Audouin went on quickly, glancing half aside as he spoke at her own dainty bodice and little frill of coffee-coloured laces. (Gwen hadn't the least idea what he meant by a liturgy in this connection; but she thought it was something very beautiful and poetical to say, and she felt sure it was meant for a compliment; so she smiled graciously at it). 'People sometimes foolishly say that young ladies think a great deal too much about dress. For my part, it often occurs to me, when I look at other women; that they think a great deal too little of it. How rarely, after all, does one see art subservient here to nature, a beautiful woman whose dress rather expresses and accentuates than mars or clashes with her own individual type of beauty.'

'How complimentary he is,' thought Gwen; 'and at his age too! Why, I positively believe he must be very nearly forty!'

'Shall we go down and look at the Emissary?' Colin asked, interrupting Audouin's flow of pretty sentimentalities. 'It's very old, you know, Miss Russell: one of the oldest existing works of Roman engineering anywhere in Europe.'

Audouin jumped up again, and led the way down to the Emissary, where the guide was already standing, impatiently expecting so many visitors, with the little taper in his hands which he lights and sets floating down the stream in order to exhibit to the greatest advantage the full extent of the prehistoric tunnel. 'Can't I manage to shake off this fellow Churchill somehow or other,' Audouin thought to himself in inward vexation, and get half an hour's chat alone with Miss Bussell? I do believe the creature'll checkmate me now, all by his ridiculous English heavy persistency! And yet, what a scholars mate, too, to go and be shelved by such a mere hobbledehoy of a fellow as this young man Churchill!'

Half way down the steep path, they came unexpectedly upon a solitary figure, sitting with colour-box open and sheet of paper before him, just above the entrance to the old tunnel. Audouin started when he saw him. 'Why, Hiram,' he cried, 'so there you are! I've been hunting everywhere for you, my dear fellow. We couldn't, any of us, imagine where on earth you had evanished.'

Hiram didn't look up in reply, and Gwen's quick eye immediately caught the reason, though she couldn't guess at its explanation, the young American painter had certainly been crying! Sitting here alone by himself, and crying! Gwen's heart interpreted the tears at once after a true woman's fashion. He had left some little rustic sweetheart behind in America, and he didn't care to sit and chat gaily among so many other women, while she was alone without him; but had crept down here with his paint-box by himself, to make a small sketch in perfect solitude, and think about her. But who would ever have imagined that that gawky shock-headed American boy had really got so much romance in him!

'Oh, I just came down here, Mr. Audouin, to take a little view of the lake,' Hiram answered evasively, without raising his eyes. 'The bit was so pretty that, as I'd brought my things along, I couldn't resist painting it.'

'But what a shame of you,' Gwen cried, 'to run away and desert us, Mr. Winthrop. You might at least have given us the pleasure of watching you working. It's always so delightful to see a picture growing slowly into form and shape under the hands of the artist.'

Hiram's voice had a touch of gratitude in it as he answered slowly, 'I didn't know, Miss Russell, you were likely to care about it.'

'Oh, he always loves solitude,' Audouin answered lightly, in a tone that cut Hiram to the quick. 'He doesn't care for society at all. I'm afraid, in that respect, Winthrop and I are both alike, lineal descendants of the old Red Indian. There's nothing he loves so much as to get away to a corner by himself, and commune with nature, with or without his colours, just as he's been doing now, in perfect solitude. And after all, solitude's really the best society: solitude's an excellent fellow by way of a companion. Even when we're most alone, we have, not only nature with us, but such a glorious company of glorified humanity that has gone before us. We walk with Shelley down the autumn avenues of falling leaves, or we meditate with Pascal beside the great breakers of Homer's much-resounding sea. We look with Claude at the shifting lights and shades on the craggy hillside opposite there, or we gaze upon the clouds and the sunset with something of the halo that flooded the dying eyes of Turner. Somebody has well said somewhere, Miss Russell, that without solitude no great thing was ever yet accomplished. When the regenerators of the world, the Messiahs and the Buddhas, wish to begin their mission as seer and founder, they first retire for forty days' fast and meditation in the lonely wilderness. And yet, I begin to think that our solitude oughtn't to be too profound or too continuous. (Perhaps mine has been so.) It ought to be tempered, I fancy, by continual congenial intercourse with some one other like-minded spirit. After all, there's a profound truth of human nature expressed in the saying of the old Hebrew cosmogonist, "It is not good that man should be alone."'

'So I've always thought,' assented Colin Churchill gravely.

Audouin was vexed at the interruption, partly because he was just in the middle of one of his fluent, high-flown, transcendental periods, but still more because it came from that wretched interloper of a young English sculptor. He was just about to go on with a marked tone of continuity, when Gwen prevented him by taking up Hiram's unfinished picture. 'Why, this is beautiful!' she cried, with genuine enthusiasm. 'This is even better than the Alexandria Bay drawing, Mr. Winthrop: I like it immensely. What a lovely tint of purple on the crests of the little wavelets! and how beautifully you've done the steep sides of the old crater. Why, I do believe you ought to be a landscape painter, instead of going in for those dreadful historical pictures that nobody cares about. What a pity you've gone into Mr. Seguin's studio! I'm sure you'd do a thousand times better at this sort of subject.'

'We've considered very carefully the best place in which to develop my friend Winthrop's unusual powers,' Audouin answered in a cold tone; 'and we've both quite come to the conclusion that there's no teacher better for him anywhere than Seguin. Seguin's a really marvellous colourist, Miss Russell, and his mastery of all the technical resources of art is something that has never yet been approached, far less equalled, in the whole history of painting.'

Hiram looked up very shyly into Gwen's face, and said quite simply, 'I'm so glad you like it, Miss Russell. Your appreciation is worth a great deal to me.'

'More compliments!' Gwen thought to herself, smiling. 'They're all at it this afternoon. What on earth can be the meaning of it? My new poplin must be really awfully fetching.' But her smile was a kindly one, and poor Hiram, who hadn't much to treasure up in his soul, treasured it up sedulously for months to come among his dearest and most precious possessions.

In the end, as it happened, Audouin never got the chance of speaking alone with Gwen during the whole picnic. It was very annoying, certainly, for he had planned the little entertainment entirely for that very purpose; but really, as he reflected to himself at leisure in his own room that evening, it was after all only a postponement. 'In any case,' he thought, 'I wouldn't have insulted her by proposing to her to-day; for it is insulting to a woman to ask her for her hand until you can see quite clearly that she really cares for you. A human soul isn't a thing of so light value that you can beg for the gift of it into your safe keeping on a shorter acquaintance than would warrant you in asking for the slightest favour. A woman's heart, a true and beautiful woman's heart, is a dainty musical instrument to be carefully learnt before one can play upon it rightly. To take it up by force, as it were, and to say at a venture, "Let me see whether perchance I can get a tune out of this anyhow," is to treat it with far less tenderness and ceremony than one would bestow upon an unconscious Stradivarius. So perhaps it was wisely ordained by the great blind Caprice which rules this universe of ours that she and I should not speak alone and face to face together to-day at Albano.'

But Hiram lulled himself to sleep by thinking over and over again to himself that night, 'She smiled at me, and she admired my drawing.'

CHAPTER XXV

MINNA BETTERS HERSELF

Away over in London, the winter had passed far less happily for poor little Minna than it had passed at Rome for Colin Churchill. While he had been writing home enthusiastically of the blue skies and invigorating air of that delicious Italy, the fogs in London had been settling down with even more than their customary persistency over the great grey gloomy winter city. While he had been filled with the large-hearted generosity of that noble fellow Maragliano, 'May I not be proud, Minna,' he wrote, 'to have known such a man, to have heard his soft Genoese accents, to have watched his wonderful chisel at its work, to have listened to his glorious sentiments on art?'—she, poor girl, had found prim, precise, old-maidish Miss Woollacott harder to endure and more pernicketty to live with than ever. Now that Colin was gone, she had nobody to sympathise with her; nobody to whose ear she might confide those thousand petty daily personal annoyances which are to women (with all sympathetic reverence be it written) far more serious hindrances to the pursuit of happiness than the greatest misfortunes that can possibly overtake them. Worst of all, Colin, she was afraid, didn't even seem to miss her. She was so miserable in London without him; so full of grief and loneliness at his absence; while he was apparently enjoying himself in Rome quite as much without her as if she had been all the time within ten minutes' walk of his attic lodging. How perfectly happy he seemed to be in his intercourse with this Signor Maragliano that he wrote to her about! How he revelled in the nymphs, and the Apollos, and the Niobes! How his letters positively overflowed with life and enthusiasm! She was glad of it, of course, very glad of it. It was so nice to think that dear Colin should at last be mingling in the free artistic life for which she knew he was so well fitted: should be moving about among those splendid Greek and Roman things he was so very fond of. But still... well, Minna did wish that there was just a little more trace in his letters of his being sorry to be so very, very far away from her.

Besides, what dreadful note of warning was this that sounded so ominously on Sunday mornings, when she had half an hour later to lie in bed and read over all Colin's back letters, for she kept them religiously? What dreadful note of warning was this that recurred so often?—'Miss Howard-Russell, a niece of the old vicar's, and a cousin of Lord Beaminster's, who, I told you, came with me from Paris to Rome in the same carriage'... And then again, 'Miss Howard-Russell, whose name I daresay you remember'—oh, didn't she?—'came into the studio this morning and was full of praise of my figure in the clay from the living model.' And now here once more, in to-day's letter, 'Miss Howard-Russell was at the picnic, looking very pretty,' (oh, Colin, Colin, how could you!) 'and I took her round through a beautiful gallery of oaks' (Italianisai for avenue, already, but uncritical little Minna never spotted it) 'to an old Roman archway where Winthrop was painting a clever water-colour. I believe Winthrop admires her very much' (Minna fervently hoped his admiration would take a practical form:) 'but she doesn't seem at all to notice him.' Why, how closely Colin must have watched her! Minna wasn't by any means satisfied with the habits and manners of this Miss Howard-Russell. And the insolence of the woman too! to go and be a cousin to the Earl of Beaminster! Unless you happen to have lived in the western half of Dorsetshire yourself, you can have no idea how exalted a personage a cousin of the Earl of Beaminster appeared in the eyes of the Wootton Mande-ville fisherman's daughter.

'Minna Wroe,' Miss Woollacott observed in her tart voice, as the little pupil-teacher came down to breakfast on the Sunday morning after the picnic, 'you're nearly seven minutes late, six minutes and forty-nine seconds, to be precisely accurate: and I've been all that time sitting here with my hands before me waiting prayers for you. And, Minna Wroe, I've noticed that since that young man you describe as your cousin went to Rome, you've had a letter with a foreign stamp upon it every Sunday. And when those letters arrive I observe that you're almost invariably late for breakfast. Now, Minna Wroe, I should advise you to write to your cousin'—with a strong emphasis of sarcastic doubt upon the last word—'asking him to make his communications a little less frequent: or else not to lie in bed quite so late in the morning reading your cousin's weekly effusions. Family affection's an excellent thing in its way, no doubt, but it may go a little too far in the table of affinities.'

Instead of answering, to Miss Woollacott's great surprise, poor little Minna burst suddenly into an uncontrollable flood of tears.

Now Miss Woollacott wasn't really cruel or ill-natured, but merely desiccated and fossilised, after the fashion of her kind, by the long drying-up process incidental to her unfortunate condition and unhappy calling: and moreover, she shared the common and pardonable inability of all women (I say 'all' this time advisedly) to see another woman crying without immediately kneeling down beside her, and taking her hands in hers, and trying with all her heart to comfort and console her.

So in a few minutes, what with Miss Woollacott saying 'There, there, dear, I didn't mean to hurt your feelings,' and smoothing Minna's hair tenderly with her skinny old fingers (worn to the bone in the hard struggle), and muttering to herself audibly, 'I hadn't the least idea that that was what was really the matter,'—Minna was soon restored to equanimity for the present at least, and Miss Woollacott, forgetting even to read prayers in her discomposure ('Which it's the only time, mum,' said Anne the slavey to the landlady, 'as ever I know'd the ole cat to miss them since fust she come here') went on with the breakfast, beaten all along the line, and trying to pass off 'this unpleasantness' by pretending to talk as unconcernedly as possible about every distracted idea that happened to come uppermost in her poor old scantily-furnished and disconnected cranium. But when breakfast was over, and Minna had positively kissed Miss Woollacott (an unheard-of liberty), and begged her not to trouble herself any more about the matter, for she wasn't really offended, and didn't in the least mind about it she went off upstairs to her own room alone, and sat down, and had a good cry all by herself with Colin's letters, and sent down word by Anne the slavey, that if Miss Woollacott would kindly excuse her she didn't feel equal to going to church that morning. 'And the ole cat, she acshally up and says, you'd hardly believe it, mum, says she, "Well, Anne, an' if Miss Wroe doesn't feel equal to it," says she, "I think as how she'd better lie down a bit and rest herself, poor thing," says she: and when she said it, mum, you could 'a knocked me down with a feather, a'most, I was that took aback at the ole cat's acshally goin' and sayin' it. Which I do reely think she must be goin' to be took ill or somethin', or else what for should she go an' answer one back so kind and chrischun-like, mum, if she didn't feel her end was a comin'?'

And old Miss Woollacott, putting on her thin-worn thread gloves for Church upon her thin-worn skinny fingers, felt softened and saddened, and remembered with a sigh that though she had never positively had a lover herself, not a declared one, that is to say, for who knows how many hearts she may have broken in silence?—she was once young herself, and fancied she might some day have one of her own, just as well as her sister Susan, who married the collector of water-rates; and if so, she was dimly conscious in her own poor old shrivelled feminine heart, much battered though it was in its hard struggle for life till it had somewhat hardened itself on the strictest Darwinian principles in adaptation to the environment, that she too under the same circumstances would have acted very much as Minna Wroe did.

But as Minna lay on her bed alone through that Sunday morning, only for a short time disturbed by the obtrusive sympathy of Anne the slavey, she began to think to herself that it was really very dangerous after all to let Colin remain at Rome without her; and that she ought to try sooner or later to go over and join him there. And as she turned this all but impossible scheme over in her head (for if even Cohn found it hard to get over to Italy, how could she, poor girl, ever expect to find the money for such a long journey, or subsistence afterwards?), a sudden glorious and brilliant possibility flashed all unexpectedly upon her bewildered mental vision:—

Why not try to go to Rome as a governess?

It was a wild and impossible idea, too impossible to be worth discussing almost, and yet, the more she thought about it, the more feasible did it seem to become to her excited imagination. Not immediately, of course: not all at once and without due preparation. Minna Wroe had learnt the ways of the world in too hard a school of slow self-education not to know already how deep you must lay your plans, and how long you must be prepared to work them, if you hope for success in any difficult earthly speculation. But she might at least make a beginning and keep her eyes open. The first thing was to get to be a governess; the next was, to look out for openings in the direction of Italy.

It seems easy enough at first sight to be a governess; the occupation is one open to any woman who knows how to spell decently, which is far from being a rare or arduous accomplishment; and yet Minna Wroe felt at once that in her case the difficulties to be got over were practically almost insuperable. If she had only been a man, now, nobody would have asked who she was, or where she came from: they would have been satisfied with looking at her credentials and reading over the perfunctory testimonials of her pastors and masters to her deserts and merits. But as she was only a woman, they would of course want to inquire all about her; and if once they discovered that she had been in a place as a servant, it would be all up with her chances of employment for ever. The man who rises makes for himself his own position; but the woman who rises has to fight all her life long to keep down the memory of her small beginnings. That is part and parcel of our modern English Christian conception of the highest chivalry.

Little Minna Wroe, however, with her round gipsy face and pretty black eyes, was not the sort of person to be put down in what she proposed to do by any amount of initial difficulty. If the thing was possible, she would stoutly fight her way through to it. So the very next morning, during recess time, she determined to strike while the iron was hot, and went off bravely through the rain to a neighbouring Governesses' Agency. It was one of the wretched places where some lazy hulking agent fellow, assisted by his stout wife, makes a handsome living by charging poor helpless girls ten per cent, on their paltry pittance of a first year's salary, in return for an introduction to patrons too indolent to hunt up a governess for themselves by any more humane and considerate method. These are the relatively honest and respectable agencies: the dishonest and disreputable ones make a still simpler livelihood by charging an entrance-fee beforehand, and never introducing anybody anywhere.

Minna put her name down upon the agent's list, but was wise enough not to be inveigled into paying the preliminary two-and-sixpence. The consequence was that the agent, seeing his only chance of making anything out of her lay in the result of getting her a situation, sent her from time to time due notice of persons in want of a nursery governess. Minna applied to several of these in rotation, her idea being, first to get herself started in a place anyhow, and then to look out for another in a family who were going to Italy. But as she made it a matter of principle to tell inquiring employers frankly that she had once been out at service, before she went to the North London Birkbeck Girls' School, she generally found that they, one and all, made short shrift of her. Of course it's quite impossible (and in a Christian land, too,) to let one's children be brought up by a young person who has once been a domestic servant.

One day, however, before many weeks, Minna received a note from the agency, asking her whether she could call round at half-past eleven, to see two persons who were in want of nursery governesses. It was recess-hour, luckily, so she buttoned up her neat plain cloth jacket, and put on her simple straw hat, and went round to meet the inquiring employers.

The first inquiry, the agent said, was from a clergyman, Reverend Walton and wife, now waiting in the ante-room. Reverend Walton, Miss Wroe: Miss Wroe, Reverend Walton and Mrs. Walton.

Minna bowed. The Reverend Walton (as the agent described him with official brevity), without taking the slightest notice of Minna, whispered audibly to his wife: 'This one really looks as if she'd do, Amelia. Dress perfectly respectable. No ribbons and laces and fal-lal tomfoolery. Perfectly presentable, perfectly.'

Minna coloured violently; but the Reverend Walton's wife answered in the same stage aside: 'Quite a proper young woman as far as appearance goes, certainly, Cyril. And fifteen pounds a year, Mr. Coppinger said, would probably suit her.'

Minna coloured still more deeply. It couldn't be called a promising beginning. (She had sixteen pounds already, by the way, when she had been a parlour-maid. Such are the prizes of the higher education for women in the scholastic profession.)

They whispered together for a little while longer, less audibly, and then Mrs. Walton began closely to cross-question the little pupil-teacher. Minna answered all her questions satisfactorily, she had been baptised, confirmed, was a member of the Church of England, played the piano, could teach elementary French, had an excellent temper, didn't mind dining with the children, would go to early communion, could mend dresses and tuckers, wasn't particular about her food, never read books of an irreligious tendency, and would assist in the housework of the nursery whenever necessary.

'In fact,' Minna said, with as much quiet dignity as she could command, 'I'm not at all afraid of house-work, because (I think I ought to tell you) I was out at service for some years before I went to the Birkbeck Schools.' Reverend Walton lifted his eyebrows in subdued astonishment. Mrs. Walton coughed drily. Then they held another whispered confabulation for a few minutes, and at the end of it Mrs. Walton suggested blandly, in a somewhat altered tone of voice, 'Suppose in that case we were to say fourteen pounds and all found, and were to try to do altogether without the nursemaid?'

Though Minna saw that this was economy with a vengeance, cutting her down another pound, and saving the whole of the nursemaid's wages, she was so anxious to find some chance of rejoining Colin that she answered somewhat reluctantly, 'If you think that would be best, I shouldn't mind trying it.'

'Oh, if it comes to that,' Mrs. Walton said loftily, 'we don't want anybody to come to us by way of a favour. Whoever accepts our post must accept it willingly, thankfully, and in a truly religious spirit, as a door thrown open to them liberally for doing good in.'

Minna bowed faintly. 'I would accept the situation,' she said as well as she was able, though the words stuck in her throat (for was she not taking it as a horrid necessity, for Colin's sake only?) 'in just that spirit.'

Mrs. Walton nodded her triumph. 'That'll do then,' she said 'What did she say her name was, Cyril? We'll inquire about you of this Miss Jigamaree.'

Reverend Walton took out a pencil and note-book ostentatiously to put down the address.

'My name is Minna Wroe,' the poor girl said, colouring once more violently.

'Minna!' Reverend Walton said, biting the end of his pencil with a meditative frown. 'You must mean Mary. You can't have been christened Minna, you know, can you?'

'Yes, I was,' Minna answered defiantly.

'I was christened Minna, quite simply. M-I-N-N-A, Minna.'

Reverend Walton entered it in his notebook under protest. 'M-I-N-N-A,' he said, 'Minna; R-O-W-E, Rowe, I suppose.'

'No,' Minna answered, 'not R-O-W-E: W-R-O-E, Wroe.'

Reverend Walton sucked the other end of his pencil in evident hesitation. 'Never heard of such a name in all my life,' he said, dubitatively. 'Must be some mistake somewhere.

All the Rowes I ever heard of were R-O-W-E's.'

Minna didn't tell him that the names Rowe and Wroe are perfectly distinct in origin and meaning, because she wasn't aware of that interesting fact in the history and etymology of English nomenclature: but she did answer stoutly, with some vehemence, 'My family have always spelt the name as I spell it.'

Reverend Walton sneered visibly. 'Probably,' he said, 'your family didn't know any better. Nothing's more common in country parishes than to find that people don't know even how to spell their own names. At any rate, while you remain a member of our household, you'd better arrange to call yourself Mary Bowe, R-O-W-E, spelt in the ordinary proper civilised manner.'

Poor Minna's smothered indignation could restrain itself no longer. 'No,' she said firmly, with flashing eyes (in spite of her guaranteed good temper),'I'll call myself nothing of the sort. I'm not ashamed of my name, and I won't change it.' (A rash promise that, on the part of a young lady.) 'And you needn't take the trouble to apply to Miss Woollacott, thank you, for on further consideration I've come to the conclusion that your place won't suit me. And so good morning to you.'

Reverend Walton and wife conferred together in a loud whisper with one another for a few minutes more, and then with a profound salutation walked with dignity in perfect silence out of the ante-room. 'And I think, Cyril,' Mrs. Walton observed in a stage aside as they held the door ajar behind them, 'we're very lucky indeed to have seen the young woman in one of her exhibitions of temper, for besides her unfortunate antecedents, dear, I'm quite convinced, in my own mind, that she isn't a really Christian person.'

'Won't do, that lot?' the agent said, popping his head in at the door to where Minna stood alone and crimson; 'ah, I thought not. Too much in this line, aren't they?'—and the agent cleverly drove in an imaginary screw into the back of his left hand with a non-existent screw-driver in his right. 'Well, well, one down, t'other come on. You'll see Reverend O'Donovan, now, miss, won't you?' 'What, another clergyman?' Minna cried a little piteously. 'Oh, no, not now, if you please, Mr. Coppinger. I feel so flurried and frightened and agitated.'

'Bless your heart, miss,' the agent said, not unkindly, 'you needn't be a bit afraid, you know, of Reverend O'Donovan. He's a widower, he is, four children, nice old fatherly person, you needn't be a bit afraid of seeing him. Besides, he's waiting for you.' Thus reassured, Minna consented with some misgivings to go through the ordeal of a further interview with the Reverend O'Donovan.

In a minute the agent returned, ushering into the room a very brutal-looking old gentleman, the most surprising that Minna remembered ever to have seen in the whole course of her experience. In spite of his old-fashioned clerical dress, she could hardly believe that he could really be a clergyman. He seemed to her at first sight the exact model of the Irish villain of Mr. Tenniel's most distorted fancy in the 'Punch' cartoons. She couldn't make out all his features at once, she was so much afraid of him; but she saw immediately that what made his face so especially ugly was the fact that he had a broken nose, just like a prizefighter. Minna quite shrank from him as he came in, and felt she should hardly have courage to get through the interview.

But the old clergyman put a chair for her with old-fashioned politeness, and then said in a gentle musical voice which quite astonished her coming from such a person, 'Pray be seated, Miss Wroe; I learned your name from Mr. Coppinger. We may have to talk over matters at a little length, I'm an old man and prosy, so we may as well make ourselves comfortable together beforehand. That's my name, you see, Cornelius O'Donovan; a very Irish one, isn't it? but we don't live in Ireland; in fact I've never been there. We live at a very quiet little country village in the weald of Surrey. Do you like the country?'

There was something so sweet and winning in the old clergyman's cultivated voice, in spite of his repulsive appearance, that Minna plucked up heart a little, and answered timidly, 'Oh, yes, I'm a country girl myself, and I'm awfully fond of the country, though I've had to live for some years in London. I come from Dorsetshire.'

'From Dorsetshire!' Mr. O'Donovan answered in the same charming gentle accent.

'Why, that's quite delightful, indeed, almost providential. I was born in Dorsetshire myself, Miss Wroe; my father had a parish there, a sweet little fisher village parish, Moreton Freshwater: do you happen to know it?'

'Moreton!' Minna repeated warmly. 'Moreton! oh yes, of course I do. Why, it's just close to our home. My folks live at Wootton Mandeville.'

'God bless my soul!' exclaimed the old clergyman with a little start. 'This is really providential, quite providential. I knew Wootton Mandeville when I was a boy, every stone in it. Dear me! and so you come from Wootton Mandeville, do you? Ah, well, I'm afraid all the people I knew at Wootton must be dead long ago. There was old Susan who sold apples at the corner by the Buddie, where the coach used to stop to set down passengers; she must have been dead, well, before you were born, I should say, certainly. And old Jack Legge that drove the coach; a fine old fellow, he was, with a green patch on the eye that Job Puddicombe blinded; I can remember his giving me a lift, as what we used to call a super, defrauding his employers, I'm sorry to say; but in the West Country, you know, in the old days, people did those things and thought no harm of them. And Ginger Radford, the smuggler; I'm afraid he was a bad lot, poor man, but by Jove, what a fine, hearty, open, manly fellow. Ah yes, capital people, even the worst of them, those good old-fashioned West Country folks.'

The old clergyman paused a moment to wipe his glasses, and looked at Minna pensively. Minna began to notice now that, though his face was so very dreadful to look at, his eyes were tender and bright and fatherly. Perhaps after all he wasn't really quite so terrible as she at first imagined him.

'Ah,' Mr. O'Donovan went on, replacing his spectacles, 'and there was Dick Churchill and his son Fiddler Sam, too, who used to draw pictures. You might have known Fiddler Sam; though, bless my heart, even Sam must be an old man nowadays, for he was older than I was. And then there was Fisherman Wroe, and his son Geargey; fine young fellow, Geargey, with a powerful deal of life and spirit in him—why.... God bless my soul, they said your name was Miss Wroe, didn't they? If I may venture to ask you, now, excuse me if I'm wrong, you don't happen to be a daughter of George Wroe's of Wootton, do you?'

'Yes,' Minna answered, warming a little towards the old gentleman, in spite of his repulsive countenance (it didn't look half so bad already, either, and she noticed that when once you got accustomed to the broken nose, it began to beam with courtesy and benevolence.) 'I'm George Wroe's daughter.'

Mr. O'Donovan's face lighted up at once with a genial smile of friendly recognition. 'George Wroe's daughter!' he cried, with much animation. 'George Wroe's daughter! Why, this is really most providential, my dear. God bless my soul, we don't need any introduction to one another. I knew your father well: many's the time we've been out fishing for whiting pollock on the Swale Daze together; a fine young fellow as ever lived, my dear, your father. When you see him again, he's living, I trust, that's well; I'm glad to hear it, whenever you see him again, my child, just you ask him whether he remembers Con O'Donovan (that's my name, you see, Cornelius; fifty years ago they used to call me Con O'Donovan). And just you ask him, too, whether he remembers how we got chased by the revenue cutter from Portland Roads mistaking us for the gig of the French smack, that brought over brandy (smuggled, I'm sorry to say, ah, dear me, dear me!) to tranship into old Gingery Radford's "Lively Sally "; and how we ran, and the cutter chased us, and we put on all sail, and made for Golden Cap, and the cutter went fifteen miles out of her way bearing down upon us, and caught us at last, and overhauled us, and found after all we'd nothing aboard but a small cargo of lob-worms and launces! Ah, bless my soul, that was a splendid run, that was! Oh, ho, ho! a splendid run, that one!' and Mr. O'Donovan laughed to himself a big, gentle, good-humoured laugh at the recollection of the boisterous jokes of fifty years ago, and of the captain of the cutter, who swore at them most terribly, in a varied and extensive assortment of English profanity, after the fashion of the United Service at the beginning of the present century.

'And now, my dear,' he went on, after another short pause, 'I won't call you Miss Wroe any longer, if you're my old friend Geargey's daughter, excuse our plain old Dorsetshire dialect. So you want to be a governess? Well, well, tell me all about it, now. How did it all happen?'

By this time Minna had got so far accustomed to the old gentleman, that she began her whole story from the very beginning, and told it without shame or foolish hesitation. When Mr. O'Donovan had heard it through with profound attention, he looked at the little gipsy face with a look of genuine admiration, and then murmured to himself quite softly, 'God bless my soul, what a very remarkable plucky young lady! Quite a worthy daughter of my dear brave old friend Geargey! Went out to service to begin with; perfectly honourable of her; the Wroes were always a fine, manly, honest, courageous, self-respecting lot, but never above doing a turn of decent work either, whenever it was offered to them. And then turned schoolmistress; and now wants to better herself by being a governess. Most natural, most natural; and very praiseworthy. A most excellent thing, honest domestic service, too many of our girls nowadays turn up their noses at it, but not of course at all suitable for a young lady of your attainments and natural refinement, my dear; oh no, no, far from it, far from it.' 'Well, my dear,' he continued, looking at her gently once more, 'this is just what the matter is. We want a nursery governess for four little ones, girls, the eldest nine; motherless, motherless.'

As Mr. O'Donovan repeated that word pathetically, as if to himself, Minna saw that his face would have been quite handsome but for the broken nose which disfigured it for the first twenty minutes of an acquaintance only. 'Are they your daughters, sir?' she ventured to ask, with a sympathetic tinge of feeling in her voice.

'No, my dear, no,' Mr. O'Donovan answered, with the tears standing in the corners of his bright eyes. 'Granddaughters, granddaughters. I never had but one child, their mother; and she, my dear—' he pointed above, and then, turning his hand vaguely eastward, muttered softly, 'India.'

There was a moment's silence, before Minna went on to ask further particulars; and as soon as the old clergyman had answered all her questions to her perfect satisfaction, he asked in a quiet, assured sort of tone, 'Then I may take it for granted, may I, that you'll come to us?'

'Why, certainly,' Minna answered, her heart throbbing a little,'if you'll take me, sir.' 'Take you!' Mr. O'Donovan echoed. 'Take you! God bless my soul, my dear, why, of course we'll be only too glad to get my old friend Geargey's daughter. And when you're writing to your father, my child, just you mention to him that you're going to Con O'Donovan's, and ask him if he remembers—'

But the remainder of Mr. O'Donovan's reminiscence about how that astonishingly big conger-eel bit the late vicar in the hand ('I never laughed so much in my life, my dear, as to see the astonishment and indignation of that pompous self-satisfied old fellow, a most exemplary man in every respect, of course, but still, we must admit, an absurdly pompous old fellow ') has no immediate connection with the general course of this history.

However, before Minna finally closed with the old rector's offer, she felt it incumbent upon her to tell him the possibility of her leaving her situation in the course of time, in order to go to Rome; and the rector's face had now grown so peculiarly mild in her eyes, that Minna even ventured to hint indirectly that the proposed visit was not wholly unconnected with the story of her cousin Colin, which story she was thereupon compelled to repeat forthwith to the patient old man with equal minuteness. Mr. O'Donovan smiled at her that placid gentle smile, devoid of all vulgar innuendo or nonsense, with which an old gentleman can sometimes show that he reads the secret of a young girl's bosom.

'And are you engaged to your cousin Colin, my dear?' he asked at last, quite innocently and simply.

'Not exactly engaged, you know,' Minna answered, blushing, 'but—'

'Ah, yes, quite so, quite so; I know all about it,' Mr. O'Donovan replied with a kindly gesture. 'Well, my dear, I don't see why you shouldn't come and live with us for the present, at least as a stop-gap; and meanwhile, I'll try my best to look out for some family who are going to Rome for you. We might advertise in the Guardian; capital paper for advertisements of that sort, the Guardian. Anyhow, meanwhile, you'll come and take us as we are; and very providential, too, very providential. To think I should have been lucky enough, quite by accident (as the world says), to hit upon a daughter of my old friend Geargey! And I'm so glad you're not afraid of me, either, because of my misfortune. A great many people are, just at first, especially. But it wears off, it wears off with habituation. A cricket-ball, my dear, that's all—when I was under twenty; off Sam Churchill's bat, too; but no fault of his, of course, I was always absurdly short-sighted. You'll get accustomed to it in time, my child, as I myself have.'

But Minna didn't need time to get accustomed to it, for she could now see already that old Mr. O'Donovan's face was really a very handsome, gentle, and cultivated one; and that even in spite of the broken nose, you felt at once how handsome it was, as soon as it was lighted up by his genial smile and the pleasant flash of his bright old eyes. And in one month from that morning, she was comfortably installed, under Mr. O'Donovan's guidance, in the delightful ivy-covered parsonage of a remote and beautiful little Surrey village.

CHAPTER XXVI

And in a few weeks, Miss Russell, we shall all be scattered to the four winds of heaven! You'll be gone to England, the Wilmers to Aix, I to America, and except Winthrop and Churchill, our whole little Anglo-American colony will have deserted Rome altogether for summer quarters! I'm sorry for it, in some ways, for our winter has really been a most enjoyable one.'

'And so am I, Mr. Audouin, very sorry. But we must all meet here again some day or other. Papa's promised that in four years he'll bring me back for another trip. His next three winters will be taken up with his new duties at York, of course; but as soon as he's free again, he's going to bring me to Rome for a second visit. Perhaps by that time you'll be over once more, on a journey of inspection to look up your clever young protégé, Mr. Winthrop.'

Audouin hesitated. Should he propose to her then and there, or should he wait for four more long solitary American winters? he would lead up to it tentatively, first of all, and see whether fortune favoured his present adventure. 'Well,' he answered, dubiously, 'I hardly know whether to say yes or no to that invitation, Miss Russell. I'm not fond of cities, and I've longed many, many times this winter for the expansive breadth of our American woodlands. I wasn't born to be in populous city pent; I pine for the resinous smell of the primæval forest. Only one thing, indeed, has kept me here so long this journey; your presence at Rome, Miss Russell.'

He looked at her as he spoke those words to see whether there was any response in her eyes or not; but Gwen only answered carelessly, 'What pretty things you always say to one, Mr. Audouin! Our English young men have quite lost the fine old-fashioned art of paying compliments, I imagine; but you and Mr. Winthrop seem to have kept it up beyond the Atlantic in a state of the highest original perfection. You almost remind one of Sir Charles Grandison.'

Audouin's eyes dropped. Clearly there was no chance of pressing the question with the beautiful Englishwoman just at present. Well, well, she was very young yet; better wait a year or two for her ideas to expand and ripen. Very young people always think anyone above thirty so extremely ancient; as they grow older themselves, their seniors by a decade or so seem to grow progressively younger, as if to meet them. 'Well, I'll close with your suggestion and make it an engagement, Miss Russell,' he said, half sighing.

'If you'll come back to Rome in four years' time, I'll come back the same winter to see how friend Hiram progresses with his artistic studies. Four years is a short space of time in a human life, after all; and if you contemplate being here at the end of that space, why, Rome will at least have one more attraction for me then than ever.'

Gwen laughed, and turned off the conversation to the latest nothing of Roman society.

A week later, Audouin went away to sail for America. But he carried back with him a little memento which strangely surprised the servants at Lakeside, when he set it up in a velvet-covered frame, among the Greek vases and tiny Egyptian sardonyx mummies, on his study mantelpiece. It was the photograph of a young lady in an English riding costume, by Montabone of the Piazza di Spagna; and when the housemaid slipped it out, 'jest to see who on airth could hev give it to him,' she found on the back the little inscription, 'For Mr. Audouin, with Gwen Howard-Russells best remembrances.'

Gwen herself, too, went before long; but before she went, she mentioned casually to Colin Churchill that she expected to be back at Rome in about four winters.

'We shall all be delighted to see you in Italy again, Miss Howard-Russell,' Colin answered, with hardly more than mere formal politeness. 'Won't we, Winthrop? Miss Russell is such a sincere admirer of painting and sculpture.'

Was that man's heart as cold and hard as the marble from which he cut his weeping nymphs and Calabrian peasants? Did he want a woman to go down upon her knees before him, or didn't he see when she was making as easy running for him as any man can expect from civilised society? He was really too provoking.

The night before Gwen left Rome, however, a little oblong parcel arrived at the hotel for her, containing a picture or something of the sort, left at the door by an English signor, the porter said. Was it one of Colin Churchill's designs for his unexecuted statues, Gwen wondered? She cut the string hastily, and opened the packet with a little internal flutter. No, wrong, evidently not from Mr. Churchill. It was a watercolour sketch of the Emissario at the Lago d'Albano, carefully finished in the minutest detail; and at the back was written in pencil, somewhat shakily, 'With Hiram Winthrop's compliments.'

'How very polite of Mr. Winthrop,' Gwen said in a careless voice that hardly hid her disappointment. 'He saw I was taken with the picture, and he's finished it off beautifully, and sent it to me for a parting present. It's a beautiful sketch, papa, isn't it? Come and see what Mr. Winthrop has sent me, Mrs. Wilmer.'

'A very well-behaved young man indeed,' the colonel put in, looking at the sketch casually, as if it were an object unworthy of a British field-officer's serious attention. 'A very well-behaved young man, although an American, and much less forward than that sculptor fellow, who's always thrusting himself upon us on every conceivable occasion.'

Hiram Winthrop had no photographs, but he had a great many little pencil sketches of a certain beautiful, proud-faced Englishwoman, which he didn't display upon the mantelpiece of his attic bedroom down the narrow Roman alley, because he preferred to keep them securely locked up in a small box, whence he took them out religiously every night and morning during the four years he spent in exile in that terrible, grimy, unnatural city. It was a very clear-cut, sculpturesque face indeed, but in spite of all Hiram's efforts at softening, it somehow managed to look most terribly inexorable. If Gwen found Colin Churchill blind, Hiram Winthrop found Gwen herself absolutely adamantine.

CHAPTER XXVII

THE DEACON MAKES A GOOD END

In his bright little study at Lakeside, Lothrop Audouin had just laid down a parchment-bound volume of Carlyle's 'French Revolution' and turned to look out of the pretty bay-window, embowered in clematis and Virginia creeper, that opened on to the placid tawny creek and the blue expanse of more distant Ontario. 'How unawares the summer has crept upon us,' he murmured to himself, half-audibly, as was his fashion. 'When I first got back from Rome in early May, the trees were all but leafless; and now July is far gone, and before many weeks we shall be beginning to think of the melting tints of our golden autumn. That's the difference, really, between revolution and evolution. The most truly important events make no stir on their first taking place; they grow, surely but silently. The changes to which all things conspire, and for which they have prepared the way beforehand, produce no explosion, because they are gradual, and the universe consents to them. A birth takes place in silence, and sums up the result of endless generations; but a murder, which is at war with the constitution of things, creates a tumult immediately. What a fracas over Camille at the Café Foy! and yet, with a whiff of grapeshot, the whole fabric of liberty disappears bodily. What a slow growth the democratic constitution of Massachusetts! and yet, when a convulsion seizes on the entire continent, and north and south tear one another to pieces for a grand idea, the democratic constitutions float unhurt upon the sea of commotion, and come out intact in the fulness of time with redoubled splendour! A good idea! I'll enter it in my diary, elaborated a little into better English.' For Audouin was a writer by instinct, and though he had never yet perpetrated a printed book, he kept a dainty little journal in his desk, in which he jotted down side by side his pretty thoughts, as they occurred to him, and his observations, half-scientific, half-fanciful, on the progress of nature all around him. This diary he regarded as his chief literary testament; and he meant to leave it in his will to Hiram Winthrop, with strict injunctions that it should be published after his death, for private circulation only, among the select few who were competent to understand it. Surely a good man and true may be permitted, in the byways and background of his inner nature, to indulge in his harmless little foibles and affectations.

He had risen to take out the diary, full of his little poetical conceit, when the maid (Audouin wasn't such a recluse that he didn't like to keep his hermitage well-appointed) brought in a note for him on a quaintly chased Japanese salver. He took the note and glanced at it casually. It hadn't come by post, but by hand, a rare event in the isolation of Lakeside, where neighbours were none, and visitors few and distant. He broke open the envelope, and read the few pencilled lines within hastily:—

'Deacon Winthrop would be obliged if you would come over at once to see him, as I am seriously ill, and the Lord is calling me. For Deacon Winthrop, faithfully, Keziah H. Hoptree.'

Audouin put on his hat at once, and went to the porch, with its clambering roses, to see the bearer, who sat in a high buggy, flipping the flies off his horse's ear with his long whipcord.

'Wal,' the man said, 'I guess, Mr. Audouin, you'd better look alive if you want to see the deacon comfortably afore the Lord's taken him.'

'All right,' Audouin answered, with Yankee irreverence, jumping up hastily into the tall buggy. 'Drive right away, sir, and we'll run a race to see which gets there first, ourselves, or Death, the Great Deliverer.'

The man drove along the rough unmade roads as only an American farmer can drive in a life-and-death hurry.

Geauga County hadn't altered greatly to the naked eye since the days long, long ago, when Hiram Winthrop used to sulk and hide in the blackberry bottom. The long straight road still stretched as of yore evenly between its two limits, in a manner calculated to satisfy all the strictest requirements of a definition in Euclid; and the parallel lines of snake fence on either hand still ran along at equal distances till they seemed to meet on the vanishing point of the horizon, somewhere a good deal on the hither side of mathematical infinity. The farms were still all bare, gaunt, dusty, and unlovable; the trees were somewhat fewer even than of old (for this was now acknowledged to be an unusually fine agricultural section), and the charred and blackened stumps that once diversified the weedy meadows had long for the most part been pulled up and demolished by the strenuous labours of men and horses. But otherwise Audouin could notice little difference between the Muddy Creek of fifteen years ago, and the Muddy Creek of that present moment. Fifteen more crops of fall and spring wheat had been reaped and garnered off the flat expanses; fifteen more generations of pigs (no, hogs) had been duly converted into prime American pork, and thence by proper rotation into human fat, bone, and muscle; fifteen winters had buried with their innocent sheet of white the blank desolation of fifteen ugly and utilitarian summers; but the farmers and farmhouses, though richer and easier than before, had not yet wakened one whit the more than of old to a rudimentary perception of the fact that the life of man may possibly consist of some other elements than corn, and pork, and the rigorous Calvinistic theology of Franklin P. Hopkins. Beauty was still crying in the streets of Muddy Creek, and no man regarded her.

At last the long dreary drive was over, a drive, Audouin thought to himself with a sigh, which couldn't be equalled anywhere in the world for naked ugliness, outside this great, free, enlightened, and absolutely materialised republic, and the buggy drew up at the gate of Deacon Zephaniah Winthrop's homestead, in the exact central spot of that wide and barren desert of utter fruitfulness. Audouin leaped from the buggy hastily, and went on through the weedy front yard to the door of the bare white farmhouse.

'Wal, I'm glad you've kem, anyhow,' the hired help (presumably Keziah H. Hoptree) exclaimed in her shrill loud voice as she opened the door to him; 'for deacon's jest tearin' mad tew see you afore the Lord takes him; he says he wants tew give you a message fur Hiram, an' he can't die in peace until he's given it.'

'Is he very ill?' Audouin asked.

'Not so sick tew talk to,' the girl answered, harshly; 'but Dr. Eselman, he says he ain't goin' to live a week longer. He's bin doctoring himself, that's whar it is, with Chief Tecumseh's Paregoric Elixir; an' now he's gone so fur that Dr. Eselman reckons he can't never git that thar Elixir out of his con- stitooshun nohow. Jest you step right in here, judge, an' see him.'

Audouin followed her into the sick room, where the old deacon, thinner, bonier, and more sallow than ever, lay vacantly on his propped-up pillows.

'You set you down thar, mister,' he began feebly, as soon as he was aware of Audouin's presence, 'an' make yourself right comfortable. I wanted to see you, you may calkilate, to give you a message for Hiram.' He paused a little between each sentence, as if he spoke with difficulty; and Audouin waited patiently to hear what it might be, with some misgiving.

'You tell him,' the deacon went on in his slow jerky manner, 'when you see him or correspond to him, that I forgive him.'

It was with some effort that Audouin managed to answer seriously, 'I will, Mr. Winthrop, you may rely upon it.'

'Yes,' the deacon continued with as much Christian magnanimity as his enfeebled condition would permit him to express; 'I forgive him. Freely and on-reservedly, I forgive him. Hiram ain't bin a son to me as I might hev anticipated. Thar was too much of his mother's family in him altogether, I reckon. The Winthrops was never a wild lot, an' wouldn't hev gone off paintin' pictures and goin' to Italy as that thar boy's done, anyhow. I might hev expected that Hiram would hev stopped to home to help me with the farm, and git things comfortable some; but thar, he was allus one o' the idlest, sulkiest, onaccountablest boys I ever met with, nowhar. He's gone off, foolin' around with them thar pictures, an' I don't suppose he'll never come to any good, nohow. But I forgive him, mister; I freely forgive him.'Tain't what one might hev looked fur from a young man who was raised in the Hopkinsite confession, an' whose parents were both of 'em believers; but these things do come out most onaccountably, that they might all be damned who believed not the truth but had pleasure in on-righteousness.'

Audouin merely bowed his head in solemn silence. The picture of the gaunt, hard-faced old man, sitting up in bed upon his pillows in his loneliness, and speaking thus, after his kind, of the son whom he had alienated from him by his unsympathetic harshness, was one too dreary for him to look at without an almost visible shudder.

'It's a mercy,' the deacon meandered on, after a short pause, gasping for breath, 'that his poor mother didn't never live to see the worst of it. Hiram might hev kem home, and helped me look after the farm and the cattle; instead of which, I've had to git in hired helps, since Mis' Winthrop died, while he was off somewhere or other painting pictures. He's in Italy now, learnin' still, he says, when he wrote to me last; I should hev expected he'd hev learnt the trade completely afore this, an' be practisin' it for a livin', as anybody might expect at his age, nat'rally. But he'll hev to come home, now, anyhow, and take to the farm; fur of course it goes to him, mister, an' I hope now he'll give up them thar racketty ways he's got into, and begin to settle down a bit at last, into a decent farmer. He's no boy now, Hiram ain't, an' he ought to be gettin' steady. I don't say I hev any complaint against you personally, mister, on that score,' the deacon went on, shaking his head magnanimously. 'You've led him into it, I know; but I understand you meant it for the best, though it's turned out oncommon bad; an' I'm a Christian man, I hope, an' I bear you no grudge for it. But what I want you to write an' tell him's jest this. You write an' say that his father, afore he died, freely forgave him, an' left him the farm and fixins. In time to come, mister, I dessay that thar boy'll often regret an' think to himself, "While my father was here, I might have made more of him." But it'll be a comfort to him anyhow to know that I forgave him; an' you jest take an' write it to him, an' I'll be obliged to you.' Audouin sat a long time by the old man's bed, wondering whether any word of regret or penitence would come from him for his own grievous error in making his son's young life a burden and a misery to him (for Hiram, with all his reticence, had let his friend see by stray side hints how sad his days had been in Geauga County); but no word came, nor was the possibility of it within the deacon's narrow self-righteous self-satisfied soul. The hours wore away, and Audouin watched and waited, but still the deacon went on at intervals, all about his own goodness to Hiram, and Hiram's natural unregenerate liking for painting pictures. At last, Keziah came in, and warned Audouin that the deacon mustn't be allowed any longer to excite himself. So Audouin went away, sad and disheartened. 'Great heavens!' he said to himself, as he jumped up again into the buggy, which was waiting to take him back to Lakeside; 'in spite of our common schools, and our ten thousand newspapers, and all our glib American buncombe about enlightenment, and education, and our noble privileges, is there any country in the world, I wonder, where the gap between those who think and feel and know, and those who wallow in their own conceited ignorance and narrowness and brutality, yawns wider and deeper than in these United States of ours, at the latter end of this emancipated nineteenth century? Look at the great gulf fixed between Boston, or even Chicago, and Geauga County! Why, the Florentines of the middle ages, the old Etruscans, the naked Egyptian, the Chinaman, the Hindoo coolie, are all of them a whole spiritual world ahead of Deacon Winthrop! They at least know, or knew, that the human heart has in it some higher need than corn, or pork, or rice, or millet; that man shall not live by bread alone; that of all the gifts God gave to man, He gave none better than the knowledge of beauty! Ay, even the monkey that plays among the mango trees considers the feathers in the parrot's tail as worthy of his passing attention as the biggest cocoanut.

'And yet, not higher, after all, those Chinamen, when one comes to think of it; for is there not mysteriously inherent somehow, in the loins of that utterly sensual materialised clod, the potentiality of begetting Hiram Winthrop?

'I wonder what sort of people my own eight great-grandparents would be, if I could only get them into the little sitting-room at Lakeside, and compare notes with them about heaven and earth, and Herbert Spencer, and the Apollo Belvedere!'

A week later, Audouin had to write to Hiram, and tell him that the deacon had passed away, and had forgiven him. 'How, my dear Hiram,' Audouin wrote, towards the end of his letter, 'your father leaves the farm at Muddy Creek to you; and if you take my advice, you will sell it at once, for what it'll fetch (not much, I doubt me) and apply the principal to paying your expenses for a year or two more at Seguin's studio. You hold your pictorial talents in trust for the American nation, which even now sadly needs them; and you mustn't throw away your chances of the highest self-improvement for the sake of a little filthy lucre, which, even if invested, would really bring you in next to nothing. Nay, rather, to use it in studying at Rome is really to invest it in the best possible manner; for, merely judging the result as a Wall Street speculator would judge it, by the actual return in dollars and cents, United States currency, your pictures will bring you in tenfold in the end of what you spend in preparing to paint them. Though not for money, I hope, Hiram, not for money, but for art's sake, and for the highest final development of this our poor groping humanity, which is still so base, take it for all in all, that I sometimes almost wonder whether it can be really worth our while to try to do anything to improve it.'

Yet so strangely compounded is this human nature of ours for all that, that when Hiram Winthrop read that letter to himself in his own small room beneath the roof of the Roman attic, he lay down upon his bed, and cried passionately in the dusk for the poor narrow-minded old deacon; and thought with a sort of regretful tenderness of the dim old days in the blackberry bottom; and murmured to himself that when he was a boy he was no doubt terribly obstinate and perverse and provoking. And now that he was a man, must he not strive to do as Audouin told him? the one true friend he had yet met with. And then he undressed and lay awake a long time, with the sense of utter loneliness pressing upon his poor solitary head more drearily than ever.

CHAPTER XXVIII

AN ART PATRON

The four years that passed before Gwen Howard-Russell and Lothrop Audouin returned to Rome, were years of bright promise and quick performance for Cohn Churchill. He hadn't been eighteen months with Maradiano, when the master took him aside one day and said to him kindly, 'My friend, you will only waste your time by studying with me any longer. You must take a studio on your own account, and begin earning a little money.'

'But where can I get one?' Colin asked.

'There is one vacant five doors off,' Maragliano answered. 'I have been to see it, and you can have it for very little. It's so near, that I can drop in from time to time and assist you with my advice and experience. But indeed, Churchill, you need either very little; for I fear the time is soon coming when the pupil is to excel the master.'

'If I thought that, master,' Cohn replied smilingly, 'I should stop here for ever. But as I know I can never hope to rival you, I shall take the studio, and tempt fortune.'

It was one morning during the next winter that Cohn was hard at work upon his clay group of Autumn borne by the Breezes, then nearly completed, when the door of the new studio opened suddenly, and a plain, farmer-looking old man in a tweed suit, entered unannounced.

'Good morning, Mr. Churchill,' he said, in a voice of infinite condescension. 'My niece sent me here to look at your statues, you know. You've got some very pretty things here, really. Some very pretty things indeed, as Gwen told me.'

'Oh, I see,' Colin answered, with a smile of recognition. 'It was Miss Howard-Russell, then, who told you where to find me.'

'Well, not exactly,' the visitor went on, peering at the Autumn with a look of the intensest critical interest; 'she told me I should find you at the studio of a man of the name of Miaragliano, or something, I think she called him. Well, I went there, ferreted out the place, and found a fuzzy-headed foreigner Italian fellow, all plastered over with mud and rubbish, who spoke the most ridiculous broken English; and he told me you'd moved to these new quarters. So I came on here to look you up and give you a commission, you know, I think you call it. My niece, she's really a first cousin once removed, or something equally abstruse, I fancy, but I always speak of her as my niece for short, because she's a good deal younger than I am, and I stand to her in loco avunculi; in loco avunculi, Mr. Churchill. Well, she positively insisted upon it that I must come and give you a commission.'

'It was very good of her, I'm sure,' Colin answered, his heart fluttering somewhat; for this was positively his first nibble. 'May I ask if you are also a Mr. Howard-Russell?'

The visitor drew himself up to his utmost height with much dignity, as though he felt surprised to think that Colin could for a single moment have imagined him to be nothing more on earth than a plain Mister. 'No,' he said, in a chilly voice; 'I fancied my niece had mentioned my name to you. I am Lord Beaminster.'

Colin bowed his head slightly. He wasn't much used to earls and viscounts in those days, though he grew afterwards to understand the habits and manners of the species with great accuracy; but he felt that after all the Earl of Beaminster, mighty magnate and land-owner as he was, didn't really differ very conspicuously in outer appearance from any other respectable fox-hunting country gentleman. Except that, perhaps, he looked, if anything, a trifle stupider than the average.

The earl considerately left Colin a minute or so to accustom himself to the shock of suddenly mixing in such exalted society, and then he said again, narrowly observing the Autumn, 'Some very pretty things, indeed, I must admit. Now, what do you call this one? A capital group. I've half a mind to commission it.'

'That's Autumn borne by the Breezes,' Colin answered, gazing up at it for the thousandth time with a loving attention. 'My idea was to represent Autumn as a beautiful youth, scattering leaves with his two hands, and upheld by the wild west wind, "the breath of autumn's being," as Shelley calls it.'

'Quite so,' the earl said, assuming once more a studied critical attitude; 'but I don't see the leaves, you know, I don't see the leaves, Mr. Churchill.'

'It would be impossible, of course,' Colin replied, 'to represent any of the leaves as falling through the air unsupported; and so I didn't care to put any in Autumn's hands, even, preferring to trust so much to the imagination of the spectator. In art it's a well-known canon that one ought, in fact, always to leave something to the imagination.'

'But might I suggest,' Lord Beaminster said, putting his head a little on one side, and surveying the figure with profound gravity, 'that you might easily support the falling leaves by an imperceptible wire passing neatly through a small drilled eye into the legs of the Breezes.'

Colin smiled. 'I don't think,' he said, 'that that would be a very artistic mode of treatment.'

'Indeed,' the earl answered with some hesitation 'Well, I'm surprised to hear you say that, now; for my father, who was always considered a man of very remarkable taste, and a great patron of art and artists, had a Triton constructed for our carp-pond at Netherton, blowing a spout of water, in marble, from his trumpet, and the falling drops, where the spout broke into spray, were all secured by wires in the way I mention. Still, of course,' this with a deferential air of mock-modesty, 'I couldn't dream of pitting my opinion, a mere outsider's opinion, against yours in such a matter. But couldn't you at least make the leaves tumble in a sort of spire, you know, reaching to the ground; touching one another, of course, so as to form a connected column, which would give support to the right arm, now so very extended and aerial-looking.'

'Why,' Colin answered, beginning to fancy that perhaps even admission to the British peerage didn't naturally constitute a man a great art-critic, 'I don't think marble's a good medium in any case for representing anything so thin and delicate as falling leaves; and though of course a clever sculptor might choose to make the attempt, by way of showing his skill in overcoming a technical difficulty, for my part I look upon such mere mechanical tours de force as really unworthy of a true artist. Obedience to one's material rather than defiance of it is the thing to be aimed at. And, to tell you the truth, the pose of that right arm that you so much object to is the very point in the whole group that I most pride myself upon. Maragliano says it's a very fine and original conception.'

The earl stared at him intently for two seconds, in blank astonishment. What a very-extraordinary and conceited young fellow, really! The idea of his thus contradicting him, the Earl of Beaminster, in every particular! Still, Gwen had specially desired him to buy something from this man Churchill, and had said that he was going to become a very great and distinguished sculptor. For Gwen's sake, he would try to befriend the young man, and take no notice of his extraordinary rudeness.

'Well,' he said slowly, after a long pause,

'I won't quarrel with you over the details. I should like to have that group in marble, and if you'll allow me, I'll commission it. Only, as we don't agree about the pose of the Autumn, I'll tell you what we'll do, Mr. Churchill; we'll compromise the matter. Suppose you remove the figure altogether, and put a clock-dial in its place. Then it'd do splendidly, you see, for the top of the marble mantelpiece at Netherton Priory.'

Colin leant back against the parapet of the wainscot in blank dismay. What on earth was he to say to this terrible Goth of a Lord Beaminster? He wanted a first commission, badly enough, in all conscience, but how could he possibly consent to throw away the labour of so many days, and to destroy the beauty of that exquisite group by putting a dial in the place of Autumn. The idea was plainly too ridiculous. It was sacrilege, it was crime, it was sheer blasphemy against the divinity of beauty. 'I'm very sorry, Lord Beaminster,' he said, at last, regretfully. 'I should much have liked to execute the group for you in marble; but I really can't consent to sacrifice the Autumn. It's the central figure and inspiring idea of the entire composition. If you take it at all, I think you ought to take it exactly as the sculptor himself has first designed it. An artist, you know, gives much time and thought to what he is working upon. Be it merely the particular turn or twist of the bit of drapery he is just then modelling, his whole soul for that one day is all fixed and centred upon that single feature. The purchaser ought to remember that, and oughtn't to alter on a moment's hasty consideration what has cost the artist whole weeks and months of patient thought and arduous labour. And yet, I'm sorry not to perform my first work in marble for you; for I'm a West Dorset man myself by birth and training, and I should have liked well to see my "Autumn and the Breezes" standing, where it ought to stand, in one of the big oriel windows of Nether ton Priory.' That last touch of unconscious and unintentional flattery just succeeded in turning the sharp edge of Lord Beaminster's anger. When Colin at first positively refused to let him have the group with the dial in the centre, the earl could hardly conceal in his face his smouldering indignation. Such conceit, indeed, and such self-will he could never have believed in if he hadn't himself actually met with them. It positively took his breath away. But when Colin so far relented as to touch his territorial pride upon the quick (for the earl regarded himself as the personal embodiment of all West Dorset), Lord Beaminster relented too, and answered with something like geniality, 'Well, well! I'm always pleased when one of my own people rises to artistic or literary eminence, Mr. Churchill. We won't quarrel about trifles. You come from Wootton Mande ville, don't you? Ah, yes! Well, I'm the lord of the manor of Wootton, as you know, of course, and I'm pleased to think you should have come from one of my own places. We'll take the figures as they stand; we'll take them as they stand, and I'll find a place for them somewhere at Netherton, I can promise you. Now how much will you charge me for this group, Autumn and all, in marble?'

Colin stood for a moment perfectly irresolute. That was a question about which, in his abstract devotion to the goodness of his artistic work, he had never yet given the slightest consideration. 'Well, I should think,' he said hesitatingly, 'I don't know if I'm asking too much, it's a big composition, and there are a good many figures in it. Suppose we were to say five hundred guineas?'

The earl nodded a gracious acquiescence.

'But perhaps,' Colin went on timidly, 'I may have asked too much in my inexperience.' 'Oh, no; not at all too much,' the earl answered, with a munificent and expansive wave of his five big farmer fingers. 'I like to encourage art, and above all art in a West Dorset man.'

'You're very kind,' Colin murmured, rather humbly, feeling as though he had much to be grateful for. 'I shall do my best to execute the group in marble to your satisfaction, so that it may be worthy of its place in the oriels at Netherton.'

'I've no doubt you will,' the earl put in with noble condescension: 'no doubt at all in the world about it. I'm glad to have the opportunity of extending my patronage to a Wootton sculptor. I'm devoted to art, Mr. Churchill, quite devoted to it.'

Colin smiled, but answered nothing.

The earl stopped a little longer, inspecting the drawings and models, and then took his departure with much stately graciousness, to Colin's intense relief and satisfaction. As he went out, the door happened to open again, and in walked Hiram Winthrop.

'My dear Winthrop!' Colin cried out in exultation, 'congratulate me! I've just got a commission for Autumn and the Breezes!'

'What, in marble?' Hiram said, grasping his hand warmly.

'Yes, in marble.'

'My dear fellow, I'm delighted. And you deserve it, too, so well. But who from? Not that fat old gentleman with the vacant face that I met just now out there upon the doorstep!'

'The same, I assure you. Our great Dorsetshire magnate, the Earl of Beaminster!' Hiram's face fell a little. 'The Earl of Beaminster!' he echoed with a voice of considerable disappointment. 'You don't mean to say an earl only looks like that! and dresses like that, too! Why, one would hardly know him from a successful dry-goods man! Besides,' he thought to himself silently, 'she must have sent him. He's her cousin.'

Colin had no idea what manner of thing a dry-goods man might be, but he recognised that it probably stood for some very prosaic and everyday employment. 'Yes,' he said, half laughing, 'that's an earl; and as you say, my dear fellow, he hardly differs visibly to the naked eye from you and me poor common mortals.'

'But, I say, Churchill,' Hiram put in with American practicality, 'what are you going to let this Beaminster person have the group for?'

'Well, I didn't know exactly what to charge him for it, never having sold a work on my own account before; but I said at a venture, five hundred guineas. I should think that wasn't bad, you know, for a first commission.'

Hiram raised his eyebrows ominously. 'Five hundred guineas, Churchill,' he muttered with obvious mistrust; 'five hundred guineas! Why, my dear fellow, have you asked yet what would be the cost even of the block of marble?'

'The block of marble!' Colin repeated, blankly. 'The cost of the marble! Why, upon my soul, Winthrop, I never took that at all into consideration.'

'Let's go round to Maragliano's at once,' Hiram suggested, in some alarm, 'and ask him what he thinks of your bargain. I'm awfully afraid, do you know, Churchill, that you've put your foot in it.'

When the great sculptor heard that Colin had really got a commission for his beautiful group, he was at first extremely jubilant, clapping his hands, laughing, and crying out eagerly many times over, 'Am I a prophet, then?' with Italian demonstrativeness. But as soon as Colin went on to say that he had promised to execute the thing in marble for 12,500 lire, Maragliano ceased from his capering immediately, and assumed an expression of the most profound and serious astonishment. 'Twelve thousand lire!' he cried in horror, lifting up both his hands with a deprecatory gesture; 'twelve thousand lire! Why, my dear friend, the marble alone will cost you nearly that, without counting anything for your own time and trouble, or the workmen's wages. A splendid stroke of business, indeed! If I were you, I'd go and ask the Count of Beaminster at once to let me off the bargain.'

Colin's disappointment was, indeed, a bitter one; but he had too keen a sense both of commercial honour and of personal dignity to think of begging off a bargain once completed. 'Oh, no,' he said, 'that would never do, master. I shall execute the commission at the price I named, even if I'm actually out of pocket by it. At any rate, it'll be a good advertisement for me. But, after all, I'm really sorry I ever said I'd let him have it! Just think, Winthrop, of my spending so much loving, patient care upon every twist and fold of the robes of those delightful Breezes, and then having to sell them in the end to a monster of a creature who wanted me to replace the Autumn by a bronze dial. It's really too distressing!'

'Ah, my friend,' Maragliano said sympathetically, 'that is the Nemesis of art, and you'll have to get accustomed to it from the beginning. It is the price we pay for the nature of our clientele. We get well paid, because we have to work chiefly for the very wealthy. But after we have worked up some statue or picture till every line and curve of it exactly satisfies our own critical taste, we have to sell it perhaps to some vulgar rich man, who buries it in his own drawing-room in New York or Manchester. The man of letters gets comparatively little, because no rich man can buy his work outright, and keep it for his own personal glorification; but in return, he feels pretty sure that those whose opinion he most wishes to conciliate, those for whose appreciative taste he has polished and repolished his rough diamond, will in the end see and admire the work he has so carefully and lovingly performed for them. We are less lucky in that respect; we have to cast our pearls before swine too often, and all for the sake of filthy lucre.'

As it turned out, however, the group of Autumn and the Breezes, in spite of this unpromising beginning, really formed the foundation of all Colin Churchill's future fortunes. Colin worked away at it with a will, nothing daunted by the discovery that it would probably cost him something more than he got for it; and in due time he despatched it to the earl in England, at a loss to himself of a little over twenty guineas. Still, the earl, being a fussy, consequential man, sent more than one friend during the progress of the work to see the group that Churchill was making for him. 'One of my own people, you know, a poor boy off my Dorsetshire estate, conceited I'm afraid, but not without talent; and I've taken it into my head to patronise him, just for the sake of the old feudal connection and all that sort of thing.' Some of the friends were better judges of sculpture than the earl himself, and when the Autumn was nearly finished, Colin was pleased to find that that distinguished connoisseur, Sir Leonard Hawkins, was much delighted with its execution. Next time Sir Leonard came he looked over Colin's designs carefully, and was greatly struck with the sketch for the Clytemnestra. He asked the price, and Cohn, wise by experience, stipulated for time to consult Maragliano. When he had done so, he said 700L.; and this time he made for himself a clear 250L. That was a big sum for a man in Colin Churchill's position; but it was only the beginning of a great artist's successful career. Commissions began to pour in upon him freely; and before Gwen Howard-Russell returned to Rome, Colin was already making far more money than in his wildest anticipation he had ever dreamt of. He must save up, now, to repay Sam; and when Sam's debt was fairly cancelled, then he must save up again for little Minna.

VOLUME III

CHAPTER XXIX

A VIEW OF ROME, BY HIRAM WINTHROP

In the midst of an undulating sunlit plain, fresh with flowers in spring, burnt and yellow in summer and autumn, a great sordid shrivelled city blinks and festers visibly among the rags and tatters in the eye of day. Within its huge imperial walls the shrunken modern town has left a broad skirt of unoccupied hillocks; low mounds covered by stunted straggling vineyards, or broken here and there by shabby unpicturesque monasteries, with long straight pollard-lined roads stretching interminably in dreary lines between the distant boundaries. In the very centre, along some low flats that bound a dull, muddy, silent river, the actual inhabited city itself crouches humbly beneath the mouldering ruins of a nobler age. A shapeless mass of dingy, weather-stained, discoloured, tile-roofed buildings, with all its stucco peeling in the sun, it lies crowded and jammed into a narrow labyrinth of tortuous alleys, reeking with dirt, and rich in ragged filthy beggars. One huge lazaretto of sin and pestilence, choked with the accumulated rubbish and kitchen-middens of forty centuries, that was Hiram Winthrop's Rome, the Rome which fate and duty compelled him to exchange for the wild woods and the free life of untrammelled nature.

Step into one of the tortuous alleys, and you see this abomination of desolation even more distinctly, under the pitiless all-exposing glare of an Italian sky. The blotchy walls rise so high into the air to right and left, that they make the narrow lane gloomy even at midday; and yet, the light pours down obliquely upon the decaying plaster with so fierce a power that every rent and gap and dirt-stain stands out distinctly, crying in vain to the squalid tenants in the dens within to repair its unutterable dilapidation. Beneath, the little slippery pavement consists of herringbone courses of sharp stones; overhead, from ropes fastened across the street, lines of rags and tatters flutter idly in the wind, proving (what Hiram was otherwise inclined to doubt) that people at Rome do sometimes ostensibly wash their garments, or at least damp them. Dark gloomy shops line either side; shops windowless and doorless, entered and closed by shutters, and just rendered visible by the feeble lamp that serves a double duty as lightener of the general darkness, and taper to the tiny painted shrine of the wooden Madonna. A world of hungry ragged men, hungry dirty slatternly women, hungry children playing in the gutter, hungry priests pervading the very atmosphere, that on a closer view was Rome as it appeared to Hiram Winthrop.

To be sure, there was a little more of it. Up towards the Corso and Piazza del Popolo, there was a gaunt, modern Haussmannised quarter, the Rome of the strangers, cleaner by a fraction, whiter by a great deal, less odorous by a trifle, but still to Hiram Winthrop utterly flat, stale, and unprofitable. The one Rome was ugly, if picturesque; the other Rome was modern, and not even ugly.

Work at Seguin's studio was also to Hiram a wretched mockery of an artistic training. The more he saw of the French painter, the more he disliked him: and what was worse, the dislike was plainly mutual. For Audouin's sake, because Audouin had wished it, Hiram went on working feebly at historical pictures which he hated and could never possibly care for; but he panted to be free from the wretched bondage at once and for ever. Two years after his arrival in Rome, where he was now living upon the little capital he had derived from the sale of the deacon's farm, Hiram determined, on Audouin's strenuous advice, by letter delivered, to send a tentative painting to Paris for the Salon. Seguin watched it once or twice in the course of its completion, but he only shrugged his lean shoulders ominously, and muttered incomprehensible military oaths to himself, which he had picked up half a century before from his father, the ex-corporal. (On the strength of that early connection with the army, Seguin, in spite of his shrivelled frame, still affected a certain swaggering military air and bearing upon many occasions.) When it was finished, he looked at it a trifle contemptuously, and then murmured: 'Good. That will finish him. After that—' An ugly grimace did duty for the rest of the sentence.

Still, Hiram sent it in, as Audouin had desired of him; and in due time received the formal intimation from the constituted authorities of the Salon that his picture had been rejected. He knew it would be, and yet he felt the disappointment bitterly. Sitting alone in his room that evening (for he would not let even Colin share his sorrow) he brooded gloomily by himself, and began to reflect seriously that after all his whole life had been one long and wretched failure. There was no denying it, he had made a common but a fatal error; he had mistaken the desire to paint for the power of painting. He saw it all quite clearly now, and from that moment his whole career seemed in his eyes to be utterly dwarfed and spoiled and blighted.

There was only one part of each of those four years of misery at Rome that Hiram could ever afterwards look back upon with real pleasure. Once every summer, he and Colin started off together for a month's relaxation in the Tyrol or Switzerland. On those trips, Hiram forgot all the rest of his life altogether, and lived for thirty clear days in a primitive paradise. His sketch-book went always with him, and he even ventured to try his hand upon a landscape or two in oils, now that he was well out of the way of Seguin's chilly magisterial interference. Colin Churchill always praised them warmly: 'But then Colin, you know' (Hiram said to himself). 'is always such a generous enthusiastic fellow. He has such a keen artistic eye himself, of course, that he positively reads beauty into the weakest efforts of any other beginner. Still, I do feel that I can put my soul into drawing these rocks and mountains, which I never can do in painting a dressed-up model in an artificial posture, and pretending that I think she's really Cleopatra. If one had the genuine Cleopatra to paint, now, exactly as she threw herself naturally down upon her own Egyptian sofa, why that might possibly be quite another matter. But, even so, Cleopatra could never have moved me half so much as the gloss on the chestnuts and the shimmer of the cloud-light on the beautiful purple water down below there.'

Sometimes, too, Hiram took Colin with him out into the Campagna; not that he loved the Campagna, there was an odour of Rome about it; but still at least it was a sort of country, and to Hiram Winthrop that was everything. One day, in his fourth year in Italy, he was sitting on a spring afternoon with Colin beside the arches of a broken aqueduct in that great moorland, which he had been using as the foreground for a little water-colour. He had finished his sketch, and was holding it at different angles before him, when Colin suddenly broke the silence by saying warmly: 'Some day, Winthrop, I'm sure you must sell them.'

Hiram shook his head despondently. 'No, no, Churchill,' he answered with a half-angry wave of his disengaged hand. 'Even while I was at Seguin's, I knew I could never do anything worth looking at, and since I took this little studio myself, I feel sure of it. It's only your kindness that makes you think otherwise.'

Colin took the sketch from him for a moment and eyed it carefully. 'My dear fellow,' he said at last, 'believe me, you're mistaken. Just look at that! Why, Winthrop, I tell you candidly, I'm certain there's genius in it.'

Hiram smiled bitterly. 'No, no, not genius, I assure you,' he answered with a sigh, 'but only the longing for it. You have genius, I have nothing more than aspiration.'

Yet in his own heart, when Colin once more declared he was mistaken, Hiram Winthrop, looking at that delicate sketch, did almost for the moment pluck up courage again, and agree with his friend that if only the public would but smile upon him, he, too, might really do something worth the looking at.

He went home, indeed, almost elated, after so many months of silent dejection, by that new-born hope. When he reached their rooms in the alley (for Colin, in his desire to save, still stood by him, in spite of altered fortunes) he found a large official envelope of French pattern lying casually upon the table. He knew it at once; it bore the official seal of the Académie Française. He tore open the letter hastily. Was it possible that this time they might really have hung him? What did it say? Let him see... A stereotyped form.... 'Regret to announce to you.... great claims upon their attention.... compelled to refuse admission to the painting submitted to their consideration by M. Winthrop.'

Hiram let the letter drop out of his hands without a word. For the third time, then, his picture had been rejected for the Paris Salon!

A day or iwo later, the agent to whom he always confided his works for the necessary arrangements, wrote to him with florid French politeness on the subject of its final disposal. Last year he had been able to give Monsieur but forty francs for his picture, while the year before he had felt himself justified in paying sixty. Unfortunately, neither of these pictures had yet been sold; Monsieur's touch evidently did not satisfy the exacting Parisian public. This year, he regretted to tell Monsieur, he would be unable to offer him anything for the picture itself; but he would take back the frame at an inestimable depreciation on the original figure. He trusted to merit Monsieur's honoured commands upon future occasions.

Those four pounds were all the money Hiram had yet earned, in four years, by the practice of his profession; and the remains of the deacon's patrimony would hardly now suffice to carry him through another winter.

But then, that winter, Gwen was coming.

If it had not been for the remote hope of still seeing Gwen before he left Rome for ever, Hiram was inclined to think the only bed he would have slept in, that dreary, weary, disappointing night, was the bed of the Tiber.

CHAPTER XXX

MINNA'S RESOLUTION

As Minna Wroe opened her eyes that morning in the furnished house in the Via Clementina, she could hardly realise even now that she was actually at Rome, and within half-an-hour's walk of dear Colin.

Yes, that was mainly how the Eternal City, the capital of art, the centre of Christendom, the great museum of all the ages, envisaged itself as of course to the frank barbarism of poor wee Minna's simple little bosom. Some of us, when we go to Rome, see in it chiefly a vast historical memory, the Forum, the Colosseum, the arch of Titus, the ruined Thermæ, the Palace of the Caesars. Some of us see in it rather a magnificent panorama of ancient and modern art, the Vatican, St. Peter's, the Apollo, the Aphrodite, the great works of Michael Angelo, and Raphael, and the spacious broad-souled Renaissance painters. Some see in it a modern gimcrack Italian metropolis; some, a fashionable English winter residence; some, a picturesque, quaint old-world mediæval city; some, a Babylon doomed before long to a terrible fiery destruction; and some, a spiritual centre of marvellous activity, with branches that ramify out in a thousand directions over the entire civilised and barbarous world. But Minna Wroe thought of that wonderful composite heterogeneous Rome for the most part merely as the present home and actual arena of Colin Churchill, sculptor, at Number 84 in the Via Colonna.

It had been a grand piece of luck for Minna, the chance that brought her the opportunity of taking that long-looked-for, and much desired journey. To be sure, she had been very happy in her own way down in the pretty little rural Surrey village. Mr. O'Donovan was the kindest and most fatherly old clergyman that ever lived; and though he did bother her just a little now and then with teaching in the Sunday school and conducting the Dorcas society, and taking charge of the Mothers' meeting, still he was so good and gentle and sympathetic to her at all times, that Minna could easily have forgiven him for twice as much professional zeal as he ever himself displayed in actual reality. Yet for all that, though the place was so pretty, and the work so light, and the four little girls on the whole such nice pleasant well-behaved little mortals, Minna certainly did miss Colin very terribly. Some employers would doubtless have said to themselves when they saw the governess moping and melancholy in spite of all the comfort that was provided for her: 'Well, what more on earth that girl can possibly be wanting really passes my poor finite comprehension.' But Mr. O'Donovan knew better. He was one of those people who habitually and instinctively put themselves in the place of others; and when on Sunday mornings after the letter with the twenty-five centesimi stamp had arrived at the rectory, he saw poor Minna moving about the house before church, looking just a trifle tearful, he said to himself with a shake of his dear kindly old broken-nosed head: 'Ah well, ah well; young people will be young people; and I've often noticed that however comfortable a girl of twenty-two may be in all externals, why, God bless my soul, if she's got a lover five hundred miles away, she can't help crying a bit about him every now and then, and very natural!' Minna gratefully observed too, that on all such occasions Mr. O'Donovan treated her with more than his usual consideration, and seemed to understand exactly what it was that made her rather sharper than her wont with the small feelings of the four little ones.

And Mr. O'Donovan never forgot his promise to Minna to look out for a family who were going to Rome and who wanted an English governess. 'But, bless my soul,' he thought to himself, 'who on earth would ever have believed beforehand what a precious difficult thing it is to find a person who fulfils at once both the conditions? People going to Rome, dozens of 'em; people wanting a governess, dozens of 'em also; but people going to Rome and wanting a governess, I regret to say, not a soul to be heard of. Sounds just like a Senate House problem, when I was a young fellow at Cambridge: If out of x A's there are y B's and z C's, what are the chances that any B is also a C?

Answer, precious little.' Indeed, the good old parson even went the length of putting an advertisement into the Guardian twice a year, without saying a word about it to Minna: 'A Clergyman (beneficed) wishes to recommend highly qualified Young Lady as English nursery Governess to a Family wintering at Rome.' But he never got a single answer. 'Dear, dear,' the kind old gentleman muttered to himself, on each such occasion when the post passed by day after day without bringing him a single one of the expected applications, 'that's always the way, unfortunately. Advertise that you want a governess, and you have fifty poor young girls answering at once, wasting a penny stamp a-piece, and waiting eagerly to know whether you'll be kindly pleased to engage 'em. Advertise that you want a place as governess, and never a soul will take a moment's notice of you. Supply and demand, I believe they call it in the newspapers; supply and demand; but in a Christian country one might have imagined they'd have got something more charitable to give us by this time than the bare gospel of Political Economy. When I was young, we didn't understand Political Economy; and Mr. Malthus, who wrote about it, used to be considered little better than a heathen. Still, I've done my duty, as far as I've been able; that's one comfort. And if I can't succeed in getting a place for George Wroe's daughter to go and join this wonderful clever lover of hers at Rome (confound the fellow, he's making a pot of money I see by the papers; why the dickens doesn't he send over and fetch her?)—well anyhow, dear Lucy's children are getting the benefit of her attention, meanwhile, and what on earth I should do without her now, I'm sure I haven't the slightest conception.'

At last, however, after one of these regular six-monthly notices the rector happened to come down to breakfast one morning, and found a letter in a strange foreign-looking hand lying beside his porridge on the dining-room table. He turned it over and looked anxiously at the back:—yes, it was just as he hoped and feared; it bore a London post-mark, and had a Byzantine-look-ing coronet embossed upon it in profuse gilding and brilliantly blazoned heraldic colours. The old man's heart sank within him. 'Confound it,' he said to himself, half-angrily, 'I do believe I've gone and done my duty this time with a regular vengeance. This is an answer to the advertisement at last, and it's an application from somebody or other to carry off dear little Miss Wroe to Rome as somebody's governess. Hang it all, how shall I ever manage, at my age too, to accommodate myself to another young woman! I won't open it now. I can't open it now. If I open it before prayers and breakfast, and it really turns out to be quite satisfactory, I shall break down over it, I know I shall; and then little Miss Wroe will see I've been crying about it, and refuse to leave us, she's a good girl, and if she knew how much I valued her, she'd refuse to leave us; and so after all she'd never get to join this sculptor son of young Sam Churchill's that she's for ever thinking of. I'll put it away till after breakfast. Perhaps indeed it mayn't be at all the thing for her, which would be very lucky, no, I mean unlucky;— well, there, there, what a set of miserable selfish wretched creatures we are really, whenever it comes to making even a small sacrifice for one another. Con O'Donovan, my boy, you know perfectly well in your heart of hearts you were half-wishing that that poor girl wasn't going at last to join her lover that she's so distracted about; and yet after that, you have the impudence to get up in the pulpit every Sunday morning, and preach a sermon about our duty to others to your poor parishioners, perhaps, even out of the fifth chapter of Matthew, you confounded hypocrite! It seems to me there's a good deal of truth in that line of Tennyson's, though it sounds so cynical:

However we brave it out, we men are a little breed!

Upon my soul, when I come to think of it, I'm really and truly quite ashamed of myself.'

Do you ever happen to have noticed that the very men who have the smallest possible leaven of littleness, or meanness, or selfishness, in their own natures are usually the exact ones who most often bitterly reproach themselves for their moral shortcomings in this matter?

When the rector came to open the envelope by-and-by in his own study, he found it contained a letter in French from a Russian countess, then in London, who proposed spending the winter in Italy. 'Madame had seen M. O'Donovan's Advertisement in a journal of his country, and would be glad to learn from Monsieur some particulars about the young lady whom he desired to recommend to families. Madame required a governess for one little girl, and proposed a salary of 2,500 francs.' The old man's eyes brightened at the idea of so large an offer, one hundred pounds sterling, and then he laid down the letter again, and cried gently to himself, as old people sometimes do, for a few minutes. After that, he reflected that Georgey Wroe's daughter was a very good girl, and deserved any advancement that he could get for her; and Georgey was a fine young fellow himself, and as clever a hand at managing a small smack in a squall off the Chesil as any fisherman, bar none, in all England. God bless his soul, what a run that was they had together, the night the 'Sunderbund' East Indiaman went to pieces off Deadman's Bay, from Seaton Bar right round the Bill to Lulworth! He could mind even now the way the water broke over the gunwale into Georgey's face, and how Georgey laughed at the wind, and swore it was a mere breeze, and positively whistled to it. Well, well, he would do what he could for Georgey's daughter, and he must look out (with a stifled sigh) for some other good girl to take care of Lucy's precious little ones.

So he sat down and wrote off such a glowing account of Minna's many virtues to the Russian countess in London, an account mainly derived from his own calm inner belief as to what a perfect woman's character ought to be made up of—that the Russian countess wrote back to say she would engage Mdlle. Wroe immediately, without even waiting to see her. Till he got that answer, Mr. O'Donovan never said a word about the matter to Minna, for fear she might be disappointed; but as soon as it arrived, and he had furtively dried his eyes behind his handkerchief, lest she should see how sorry he was to lose her, he laid the two letters triumphantly down before her, and said, in a voice which seemed as though he were quite as much interested in the event as she was: 'There you see, my dear, I've found somebody at last for you to go to Rome with.' Minna's head reeled and her eyes swam as she read the two letters to herself with some difficulty (for her French was of the strictly school-taught variety); but as soon as she had spelt out the meaning to her own intense satisfaction, she flung her arms round old Mr. O'Donovan's neck, and kissed him twice fervently. Mr. O'Donovan's eyes glistened, and he kissed her in return gently on her forehead. She had grown to be to him almost like a daughter, and he loved her so dearly that it was a hard wrench to part from her. 'And you know, my dear,' he said to her with fatherly tenderness, 'you won't mind my mentioning it to you, I'm sure, because I need hardly tell you how much interest I take in my old friend Georgey's daughter; but I think it's just as well the lady's a foreigner, and especially a Russian, because they're not so particular, I believe, about the conventionalities of society as our English mothers are apt to be; and you'll probably get more opportunities of seeing young Churchill when occasion offers than you would have done if you'd happened to have gone abroad with an English family.'

When Minna went away from the country rectory, at very short notice, some three weeks later, Mary the housemaid observed, with a little ill-natured smile to the other village gossips, that it wasn't before it was time, neither; for the way that that there Miss Wroe, as she called herself, had been carrying on last month or two along of poor old master, and him a clergyman, too, and old enough to know better, but there, what can you expect, for everybody knows what an old gentleman is when a governess or anybody can twist him round her little finger, was that dreadful that really she often wondered whether a respectable girl as was always brought up quite decent and her only a fisherman's daughter, too, as master hisself admitted, but them governesses, when they got theirselves a little eddication and took a sitooation, was that stuck-up and ridiculous, not but what she made her always keep her place, for that matter, for she wasn't going to be put down by none of your governesses, setting themselves up to be ladies when they wasn't no better nor she was, but at any rate it was a precious good thing she was gone now before things hadn't gone no further, for if she'd stayed, why, of course, there wouldn't have been nothing left for her to do, as had always lived in proper families, but to go and give notice herself afore she'd stop in such a sitooation.

And Mrs. Upjohn, the doctor's wife, smiled blandly when Mary spoke to her about it, and said in a grave tone of severe moral censure: 'Well, there, Mary, you oughtn't to want to meddle with your master's business, whatever you may happen to fancy. Not but what Miss Wroe herself certainly did behave in a most imprudent and unladylike manner; and I can't deny, of course, that she's laid herself open to every word of what you say about her. But then, you know, Mary, she isn't a lady; and, after all, what can you expect from such a person?' To which Mary, having that profound instinctive contempt for her own class which is sometimes begotten among the essentially vulgar by close unconscious introspection, immediately answered: 'Ah, what indeed!' and went on unrebuked with her ill-natured gossip. So high and watchful is social morality amid the charming Arcadian simplicity of our outlying English country villages.

But poor little Minna, waking up that very morning in the Via Clementina, never heeded their venomous backbiting one bit, and thought only of going to see her dear Colin. What a surprise it would be to him to see her, to be sure; for Minna, fearful that the scheme might fall through before it was really settled, had written not a word to him about it beforehand, and meant to surprise him by dropping in upon him quite unexpectedly at his studio without a single note of warning.

'Ah, my dear,' the countess said to her, when Minna, trembling, asked leave to go out and visit her cousin, that dim relationship, so inevitable among country folk from the same district, had certainly more than once done her good service, 'you have then a parent at Rome, a sculptor? Yes, yes, I recall it; that good Mr. O'Donovan made mention to me of this parent. He prayed me to let you have the opportunity from time to time of visiting him. These are our first days at Rome. For the moment, Olga will demand her vacations: she will wish to distract herself a little with the town, before she applies herself seriously to her studies of English. Let us say to-day, then: let us say this very morning. You can go, my child: you can visit your parent: and if his studio encloses anything of artistic, you pass me the word, I go to see it. But if they have the instinct of the family strong, these English! I find that charming; it is delicious: it is all that there is of most pure and poetical. She wishes to visit her cousin, who is a sculptor and whom she has not seen, it is now a long time; and she blushes and trembles like a French demoiselle who comes from departing the day itself from the gates of the convent. One would say, a lover. I find it most admirable, this affection of the family, this lasting reminiscence of the distant relations. We others in Russia, we have it too: we love the parent: but not with so much empressement. I find that trait there altogether essentially English.'

Mrs. Upjohn would have considered the countess 'scarcely respectable,' and would have avoided her acquaintance carefully, unless indeed she happened to be introduced to her by the squire's lady, in which case, of course, her perfect propriety would have been sufficiently guaranteed: but, after all, which of them had the heart the most untainted? To the pure all things are pure: and contrariwise.

So Minna hastened out into those unknown streets of Rome, and by the aid of her self-taught Italian (which was a good deal better than her French, so potent a tutor is love) she soon found her way down the Corso, and off the side alley into the narrow sunless Via Colonna. She followed the numbers down to the familiar eighty-four of Colin's letters, and there she saw upon the door a little painted tin-plate, bearing in English the simple inscription: 'Mr. C. Churchill's Studio.' Minna's heart beat fast for a moment as she mounted the stairs unannounced, and stood within the open door of Colin's modelling room.

A few casts and other sculptor's properties filled up the space between the door and the middle of the studio. Minna paused a second, and looked timidly from behind them at the room beyond. She hardly liked to come forward at once and claim acquaintance: it seemed so strange and unwomanly so to announce herself, now that she had actually got to face it. A certain unwonted bashfulness appeared somehow or other to hold her back; and Minna, who had her little superstitions still, noted it in passing as something ominous. There were two people visible in the studio, both men; and they were talking together quite earnestly, Minna could see, about somebody else who was obviously hidden from her by the Apollo in the foreground. One of them was a very handsome young man in a brown velvet coat, with a loose Rembrandtesque hat of the same stuff stuck with artistic carelessness on one side of his profuse curls: her heart leaped up at once as she recognised with a sudden thrill that that was Colin, transfigured and glorified a little by success, but still the same dear old Colin as ever, looking the very image of a sculptor, as he stood there, one arm poised lightly on his hip, and turning towards his companion with some wonderful grace that no other race of men save only artists can ever compass. Stop, he was speaking again now; and Minna, all unconscious of listening or prying, bent forward to catch the sound of those precious words as Colin uttered them.

'She's splendid, you know, Winthrop,' Colin was saying enthusiastically, in a voice that had caught a slight Italian trill from Maragliano, unusual on our sterner English lips: 'she's grand, she's beautiful, she's terrible, she's magnificent. Upon my word, in all my life I never yet saw any woman one-half so glorious or so Greek as Cecca. I'm proud of having discovered her; immensely proud. I claim her as my own property, by right of discovery. A lot of other fellows would like to inveigle her away from me; but they won't get her: Cecca's true metal, and she sticks to her original inventor. What a woman she is, really! Now did you ever see such a perfectly glorious arm as that one?'

Minna reeled, almost, as she stood there among the casts and properties, and felt half inclined on the spur of the moment to flee away unseen, and never again speak or write a single word to that perfidious Colin. Cecca, indeed! Cecca! Cecca! Who on earth was this woman Cecca, she would like to know; and what on earth did the faithless Colin ever want with her? Splendid, grand, beautiful, glorious, terrible, magnificent! Oh, Colin, Colin, how could you break her poor little heart so? Should she go back at once to the countess, and not even let Colin know she had ever come to Rome at all to see him? It was too horrible, too sudden, too crushing, too unexpected!

The other man looked towards the unseen Cecca, Minna somehow felt in her heart that Cecca was there, though she couldn't see her, and answered with an almost imperceptible American accent, 'She's certainly very beautiful, Churchill, very beautiful. My dear fellow, I sincerely congratulate you.'

Congratulate you! What! had it come to that? Oh horror! oh shame! had Colin been grossly deceiving her? Had he not only made love in her absence to that black-eyed Italian woman of whom she had always been so much afraid, but had he even made her an offer of marriage, without ever mentioning a word about it to her, Minna? The baseness, the deceit, the wickedness of it! And yet, this Minna thought with a sickening start, was it really base, was it really deceitful, was it really wicked? Colin had never said he would marry her; he had never been engaged to her, oh no, during all those long weary years of doubt and hesitation she had always known he wasn't engaged to her, she had known it, and trembled. Yes, he was free; he was his own master; he could do as he liked: she was only his little cousin Minna: what claim, after all, had she upon him?

At that moment Colin turned, and looked almost towards her, without seeing her. She could have cried out 'Colin!' as she saw his beautiful face and his kindly eyes, too kindly to be untrue, surely, turned nearly upon her; but Cecca, Cecca, the terrible unseen Cecca, somehow restrained her. And Cecca, too, had actually accepted him. Didn't the Yankee man call Winthrop say, 'I congratulate you'? There was only one meaning possible to put upon such a sentence. Accept him! Why, how could any woman conceivably refuse him? as he moved forward there with his delicate clear-cut face, a face in which the aesthetic temperament stood confessed so unmistakably, Minna could hardly blame this unknown Cecca if she fell in love with him. But for herself, oh, Colin, Cohn, Colin, it was too cruel.

She would at least see Cecca before she stole away unperceived for ever; she would see what manner of woman this was that had enticed away Colin Churchill's love from herself, if indeed he had ever loved her, which was now at least far more than doubtful. So she moved aside gently behind the clay figures, and came in sight of the third person.

It was the exact Italian beauty of her long-nursed girlish terrors! A queenly dark woman, with supple statuesque figure and splendidly set head, was standing before the two young artists in an attitude half studied pose, half natural Calabrian peasant gracefulness. Her brown neck and arms were quite bare; her large limbs were scarcely concealed below by a short and clinging sculpturesque kirtle. She was looking towards Colin with big languishing eyes, and her smile, for she was smiling, had something in it of that sinister air that northerners often notice among even the most beautiful women of the Mediterranean races. It was plain that she couldn't understand what her two admirers were saying in their foreign language; but it was plain also that she knew they were praising her extraordinary beauty, and her eyes flashed forth accordingly with evident pride and overflowing self-satisfaction. Cecca was beautiful, clearly beautiful, both in face and figure, with a rich, mature southern beauty (though in years perhaps she was scarcely twenty), and Minna was forced in spite of herself to admire her form; but she felt instinctively there was something about the girl that she would have feared and dreaded, even if she hadn't heard Colin Churchill speaking of her with such unstinted and unhesitating admiration. So this was Cecca! So this was Cecca! And so this was the end, too, of all her long romantic day-dream!

As she stood there, partly doubting whether to run away or not, Cecca caught sight of her half hidden behind the Apollo, and turning to Colin, cried out sharply in a cold, ringing, musical voice as clear and as cold as crystal, 'See, see; a signorina! She waits to speak with you.'

Colin looked round carelessly, and before Minna could withdraw his eyes met hers in a sudden wonder.

'Minna!' he cried, rushing forward eagerly to meet her, 'Minna! Minna! Why, it must be Minna! How on earth did you manage to get to Rome, little woman? and why on earth didn't you let me know beforehand you were really coming?'

He tried to kiss her as he spoke, but Minna, half doubtful what she ought to do, with swimming brain and tearful eyes, held him off mechanically by withdrawing herself timidly a little, and gave him her hand instead with strange coldness, much to his evident surprise and disappointment.

'She's too modest to kiss me before Winthrop and Cecca,' Colin thought to himself a little nervously; 'but no matter, Winthrop, this is my cousin from England, Miss Wroe, that I've so often spoken to you about.'

His cousin from England! His cousin!! His cousin!!! Ah, yes, that was all he meant by it nowadays clearly. He wanted to kiss her, but merely as a cousin; all his heart, it seemed, was only for this creature he called Cecca, who stood there scowling at her so savagely from under her great heavy eyebrows. He had gone to Rome, as she feared so long ago, and had fallen into the clutches of that dreaded terrible Italian woman.

'Well, Minna,' Colin said, looking at her so tenderly that even Minna herself half believed he must be still in earnest, 'and so you've come to Italy, have you? My dear little girl, why didn't you write and tell me all about it? You've broken in upon me so unexpectedly.' ('So I see,' thought Minna.) 'Why didn't you write and let me know beforehand you were coming to see me?

Minna's heart prompted her inwardly to answer with truth, 'Because I wanted to surprise you, Colin;' but she resisted the natural impulse, much against the grain, and answered instead with marked chilliness, 'Because I didn't know my movements were at all likely to interest you.'

As they two spoke, Hiram Winthrop noticed half unconsciously that Cecca's eyes were steadily riveted upon the newcomer, and that the light within them had changed instantaneously from the quiet gleam of placid self-satisfaction to the fierce glare of rising anger and jealous suspicion.

Colin still held Minna's hand half doubtfully in his, and looked with his open face all troubled into her pretty brown eyes, wondering vaguely what on earth could be the meaning of this unexpected coldness of demeanour.

'Tell me at least how you got here, little woman,' he began again in his soft, gentle voice, with quiet persuasiveness. 'Whatever brought you here, Minna, I'm so glad, so very glad to see you. Tell me how you came, and how long you're going to stop with me.'

Minna sat down blankly on the one chair that stood in the central area of the little studio, not because she wanted to stay there any longer, but because she felt as if her trembling knees were positively giving way beneath her. 'I've taken a place as governess to a Russian girl, Colin,' she answered shortly; 'and I've come to Rome with my pupil's mother.'

Colin felt sure by the faintness of her voice that there was something very serious the matter. 'Minna dearest,' he whispered to her half beneath his breath, 'you aren't well, I'm certain. I'll send away my friend and my model, and then you must tell me all about it, like a dear good little woman.'

Minna started, and her face flushed suddenly again with mounting colour. 'Your model,' she cried, pointing half contemptuously towards the scowling Cecca. 'Your model! Is that woman over there a model, then?'

'Yes, certainly,' Colin answered lightly.

'This lady's a model, Minna. We call her Cecca, that's short for Francesca, you know, and she's my model for a statue of a Spartan maiden I'm now working upon.'

But Cecca, though she couldn't follow the words, had noticed the contemptuous tone and gesture with which Minna had scornfully spoken of 'that woman,' and she knew at once in her hot Italian heart that she stood face to face with a natural enemy. An enemy and a rival. For Cecca, too, had in her own way her small fancies and her bold ambitions.

'She's very beautiful, isn't she?' Hiram Winthrop put in timidly, for he saw with his keen glance that Cecca's handsome face was growing every moment blacker and blacker, and he wanted to avert the coming explosion.

'Well, not so very beautiful to my mind,' Minna answered, with studied coolness, putting her head critically a little on one side, and staring at the model as if she had been made of plaster of Paris; 'though I must say you gentlemen seemed to be admiring her immensely when I came into the room a minute or two ago. I confess she doesn't exactly take my own personal fancy.'

'What is the signorina saying?' Cecca broke in haughtily, in Italian. She felt sure from the scornful tone of Minna's voice that it must at least be something disparaging.

'She says you are beautiful, Signora Cecca,' Colin answered hurriedly, with a sidelong deprecatory glance at Minna. 'Bella bella, bella, bellissima.'

'Bellissima, si, bellissima,' Minna echoed, half frightened, she knew not why; for she felt dimly conscious in her own little mind that they were all three thoroughly afraid in their hearts of the beautiful, imperious Italian woman.

'It is a lie,' Cecca murmured to herself quietly. 4 But it doesn't matter. She was saying that she didn't admire me, and the Englishman and the American tried to stop her. The sorceress! I hate her!'

CHAPTER XXXI

COUSINS

They stood all four looking at one another mutely for a few minutes longer, and then Colin broke the ominous silence by saying as politely as he was able, 'Signora Cecca, this lady has come to see me from England, and we are relations. We have not met for many years. Will you excuse my dismissing you for this morning?'

Cecca made a queenly obeisance to Colin, dropped a sort of saucy Italian curtsey to Minna, nodded familiarly to Hiram, and swept out of the studio into the dressing-room without uttering another word.

'She'll go off to Bazzoni's, I'm afraid,' Hiram said, with a sigh of relief, as she shut the door noiselessly and cautiously behind her. 'He's downright anxious to get her, and she's a touchy young woman, that's certain.'

'I'm not at all afraid of that,' Colin answered, smiling; 'she's a great deal too true to me for any such tricks as those, I'm sure, Winthrop. She really likes me, I know, and she won't desert me even for a pique, though I can easily see she's awfully offended.'

'Well, I hope so,' Hiram replied gravely. 'She's far too good a model to be lost. Goodbye, Churchill. Good morning, Miss Wroe. I hope you'll do me the same honour as you've done your cousin, by coming to take a look some day around my studio.'

'Well, Minna,' Colin said as soon as they were alone, coming up to her and offering once more to kiss her, 'why, little woman, what's the matter? Aren't you going to let me kiss you any longer? We always used to kiss one another in the old days, you know, in England.'

'But now we're both of us quite grown up, Colin,' Minna answered, somewhat pettishly, 'so of course that makes all the difference.'

Cohn couldn't understand the meaning of this chilliness; for Minna's late letters, written in the tremor of delight at the surprise she was preparing for him, had been more than usually affectionate; and it would never have entered into his head for a moment to suppose that she could have misinterpreted his remarks about Cecca, even if he had known that she had overheard them. To a sculptor, such criticism of a model, such enthusiasm for the mere form of the shapely human figure, seem so natural and disinterested, so much a necessary corollary of his art, that he never even dreams of guarding against any possible misapprehension. So Colin only bowed his head in silent wonder, and answered slowly, 'But then you know, Minna, we're cousins. Surely there can be no reason why cousins when they meet shouldn't kiss one another.' He couldn't have chosen a worse plea at that particular moment; for as he said it, the blood rushed from Minna's cheeks, and she trembled with excitement at that seeming knell to all her dearest expectations. 'Oh, well, if you put it upon that ground, Colin,' she faltered out half tearfully, 'of course we may kiss one another, as cousins.'

Colin seized her in his arms at the word, and covered her pretty little gipsy face with a string of warm, eager kisses. Even little Minna, in her fright and anxiety, could not help imagining to herself that those were hardly what one could call in fairness mere everyday cousinly embraces. But her evil genius made her struggle to release herself, according to the code of etiquette which she had learnt as becoming from her friends and early companions; and she pushed Colin away after a moment's doubtful acquiescence, with a little petulant gesture of half-affected anger. The philosophic observer may indeed note that among the English people only women of the very highest breeding know how to let themselves be kissed by their lovers with becoming and unresisting dignity. Tennyson's Maud, when her cynic admirer kissed her for the first time, 'took the kiss sedately.' I fear it must be admitted that under the same circumstances Minna Wroe, dear little native-born lady though she was, would have felt it incumbent upon her as a woman and a maiden to resist and struggle to the utmost of her power.

As for Colin, having got rid of that first resistance easily enough, he soon settled in his own mind to his own entire satisfaction that Minna had been only a little shy of him after so long an absence, and had perhaps been playing off a sort of mock-modest coyness upon him, in order to rouse him to an effective aggression. So he said no more to her about the matter, but asked her full particulars as to her new position and her journey; and even Minna herself, disappointed as she was, could not help opening out her full heart to dear old Colin, and telling him all about everything that had happened to her in the last six weeks, except her inner hopes and fears and lamentations. Yes, she had come to Rome to live, she didn't say 'on purpose to be near you, Colin', and they would have abundant opportunities of seeing one another frequently; and Madame was very kind, for an employer, you know, as employers go, you can't expect much, of course, from an employer. And Colin showed her all his busts and statues; and Minna admired them profoundly with a genuine admiration. And then, what prices he got for them! Why, Colin, really nowadays you're become quite a gentleman! And Colin, to whom that social metamorphosis had long grown perfectly familiar, laughed heartily at the naïve remark and then looked round with a touch of professional suspicion, for fear some accidental patron might have happened to come in and overhear the simple little confession. Altogether, their conversation got very close and affectionate and cousinly.

At last, after they had talked about everything that most concerned them both, save only the one thing that concerned them both more than anything, Minna asked in as unconcerned a tone as she could muster up, 'And this model, Colin, Cecca, I think you called her, what of her?'

Colin's eye lighted up with artistic enthusiasm as he answered warmly, 'Oh, she's the most beautiful girl in all Rome, little woman. I found her out by accident last year, at a village in Calabria where Winthrop and I had gone for a Christmas holiday; and I induced her to come to Rome and go in for a model's life as a profession. Isn't she just magnificent, Minna?'

'Very magnificent indeed, I dare say,' Minna answered coldly; 'but not to my mind by any means pleasing.'

'I wonder you think that,' Colin said in frank astonishment: for he was too much a sculptor even to suspect that Minna could take any other view of his model except the purely artistic one. 'She was the original of that Nymph Bathing of mine that you see over yonder.'

Minna looked critically at the Nymph Bathing, a shameless hussy, truly, if ever there was one, and answered in a chilly voice, 'I like it the least of all your statues, if you care to have my opinion, Colin.'

'Well, now, I'm awfully sorry for that, Minna,' Colin went on seriously, regarding the work with that despondent eye with which one always views one's own performances after hearing by any chance an adverse criticism; 'for I rather liked the nymph myself, you know, and I can generally rely upon your judgment as being about the very best to be had anywhere in the open market. There's no denying, little woman, that you've got a born taste somehow or other for the art of sculpture.'

If only women would say what they mean to us! but they won't, so what's the use of bothering one's head about it? They'll make themselves and us unhappy for a twelvemonth together, lucky indeed if not for ever, by petting and fretting over some jealous fancy or other, some vague foolish suspicion, which, if they would but speak out frankly for a moment, might be dispelled and settled with a good hearty kiss in half a second. Our very unsuspiciousness, our masculine downrightness and definiteness, make us slow to perceive their endless small tiffs and crooked questions; slow to detect the real meaning that underlies their unaccountable praise and blame of other people, given entirely from the point of' view of their own marvellous subjective universe. The question whether Cecca was handsome or otherwise was to Colin Churchill a simple question of external aesthetics; he was as unprejudiced about it as he would have been in judging a Greek torso or a modern Italian statue. But to Minna it was mainly a question between her own heart and Colin's. If she had only told him then and there her whole doubt and trouble, confessed it, as a man would have confessed it, openly and simply, and asked at once for a straightforward explanation, she would have saved herself long weeks of misery and self-torture and internal questionings. But she did not; and Colin, never doubting her misapprehension, dropped the matter lightly as one of no practical importance whatsoever.

So it came to pass that Minna let that first day at Rome slip by without having come to any understanding at all with Colin; and went home to Madame's still in doubt in her own troubled little mind whether or not she was really and truly quite engaged to him. Did he love her, or did he merely like her? Was she his sweetheart, or merely an old friend whom he had known and confided in ever since those dim old days at Wootton Mandeville? Minna could have cried her eyes out over that abstruse and difficult personal question. And Colin never even knew that the question had for one moment so much as once occurred to her.

'I may have one more kiss before you go, little woman,' Colin said to her tenderly, as she was on the point of leaving. Minna's eyes glistened brightly. 'One more kiss, you know, dear, for old times' sake, Minna.' Minna's eyes filled with tears, and she could hardly brush them away without his perceiving it. It was only for old times' sake, then, for old times' sake, not for love and the future. Oh, Colin, Colin, how bitter! how bitter!

'As a cousin, Colin?' she murmured interrogatively.

Cohn laughed a gay little laugh. 'Strictly as a cousin,' he answered merrily, lingering far longer on her lips, however, than the most orthodox cousinly affection could ever possibly have sufficed to justify.

Minna sighed and jumped away hastily. That night, in her own room, looking at Colin's photograph, and thinking of the dreadful Italian woman, and all the dangers that beset her round about, she muttered to herself ever so often, 'Strictly as a cousin, he said strictly as a cousin, for old times' sake, strictly as a cousin.'

There was only one real comfort left for her in all the dreary, gloomy, disappointing outlook. At least that horrid high-born Miss Gwen Howard-Russell (ugh, what a name!) had disappeared bodily altogether from off the circle of Cohn's horizon.

CHAPTER XXXII

RE-ENTER GWEN

Lothrop Audouin and Hiram Winthrop were strolling arm in arm together down the Corso.

Audouin had just arrived from Paris, having crossed from America only a week earlier.

Four years had made some difference in his personal appearance; his beard and hair were getting decidedly grizzled, and for the first time in his life Hiram noticed that his friend seemed to have aged a great deal faster and more suddenly than he himself had. But Audouin's carriage was still erect and very elastic; there was plenty of life and youth about him yet, plenty even of juvenile fire and originality.

'It's very disappointing certainly, Hiram,' he said, as they turned into the great thoroughfare of the city together, 'this delay in getting your talents recognised: but I have faith in you still; and to faith, you know, as the Hebrew preacher said, all things are possible. The great tardigrade world is hard to move; you need the pou sto of a sensation to get in the thin edge of your Archimedean lever. But the recognition will come, as sure as the next eclipse; meanwhile, my dear fellow, you must go on working in faith, and I surmise that in the end you will move mountains. If not Soracte just at once, my friend, well at any rate to begin upon the Monte Testaccio.'

Hiram smiled half sadly. 'But I haven't faith, you know, Mr. Audouin,' he answered, in as easy a tone as he could well muster. 'I begin to regard myself in the dismal light of a portentous failure. Like Peter, I feel myself sinking in the water, and have no one to take me by the hand and lift me out of it.'

Audouin answered only by an airy wave of his five delicate outspread fingers. 'And Miss Russell?' he asked after half a second's pause. 'Has she come to Rome yet? You know she said she would be here this winter.'

As he spoke, he looked deep into Hiram's eyes with so much meaning that Hiram felt his face grow hot, and thought to himself,'What a wonderful man Mr. Audouin is, really! In spite of all my silence and reserve he has somehow managed to read my innermost secret. How could he ever have known that Miss Russell's was the hand I needed to lift me out of the Sea of Gennesaret!'

But how self-contained and self-centred even the best of us are at bottom! for Audouin only meant to change the subject, and the deep look in his eyes when he spoke about Gwen to Hiram had reference entirely to his own heart and not to his companion's.

'I haven't seen or heard anything of her yet,' Hiram answered shyly, 'but the season has hardly begun so far, and I calculate we may very probably find her at Rome in the course of the next fortnight.'

'How he looks down and hesitates!' Audouin thought to himself in turn as Hiram answered him. 'How on earth can he have succeeded in discovering and recognising my unspoken secret?'

So we walk this world together, cheek by jowl, yet all at cross purposes, each one thinking mainly of himself, and at the same time illogically fancying that his neighbour is not all equally engrossed on his own similarly important personality. We imagine he is always thinking about us, but he is really doing quite otherwise—thinking about himself exactly as we are.

They walked on a few steps further in silence, each engaged in musing on his own thoughts, and then suddenly a voice came from a jeweller's shop by the corner, 'Oh, papa, just look! Mr. Audouin and his friend the painter.'

As Gwen Howard-Russell uttered those simple words, two hearts went beating suddenly faster on the pavement outside, each after its own fashion. Audouin heard chiefly his own name, and thought to himself gladly, 'Then she has not forgotten me.' Hiram heard chiefly the end of the sentence, and thought to himself bitterly, 'And shall I never be more to her then than merely that—"his friend the painter"?'

'Delighted to see you, Mr. Audouin,' the colonel said stiffly, in a voice which at once belied its own spoken welcome. 'And you too, Mr.—ur—Mr. —'

'Winthrop, papa,' Gwen suggested blandly; and Hiram was grateful to her even for remembering it.

'Winthrop, of course,' the colonel accepted with a decorous smile, as who should gracefully concede that Hiram had no doubt a sort of right in his own small way to some kind of cognomen or other. 'And are you still painting, Mr. Winthrop?'

'I am,' Hiram answered shortly. [The subject was one that did not interest him.] 'And you, Miss Russell? Have you come here to spend the winter?'

'Oh yes,' Gwen replied, addressing herself, however, rather to Audouin than to Hiram. 'You see we haven't forgotten our promise. But we're not stopping at the hotel this time, we're at the Villa Panormi, just outside the town, you know, on the road to the Ponte Molle.

A cousin of ours, a dear stupid old fellow—'

'Gwen, my dear! now really you know, the Earl of Beaminster, Mr. Audouin.'

'Yes, that's his name; Lord Beaminster, and a dear old stupid as ever was born, too, I can tell you. Well, he's taken the Villa Panormi for the season; it belongs to some poor wretched creature of a Roman prince, I believe (his grandfather was lackey to a cardinal), who's in want of money dreadfully, and he lets it to my cousin to go and gamble away the proceeds at Monte Carlo. It's just outside the Porta del Popolo, about a mile off; and the gardens are really quite delightful. You must both of you come there very often to see us.'

'But really, Gwen, we must ask Beaminster first, you know, before we begin introducing our friends to him,' the colonel interjected apologetically, casting down a furtive and uneasy glance at Hiram's costume, which certainly displayed a most admired artistic disorder. 'We ought to send him to call first at Mr., ur, Winthrop's studio.'

'Of course,' Gwen answered. 'And so he shall go this very afternoon, if I tell him to. The dear old stupid always does whatever I order him.'

'If we continue to take up the pavement in this way,' Audouin put in gravely, 'we shall get taken up ourselves by the active and intelligent police officers of a redeemed Italy. Which way are you going now, Miss Russell? towards the Piazza? Then we'll go with you if you will allow us. Hiram, my dear fellow, if you'll permit me to suggest it, it's very awkward walking four abreast on these narrow Roman side-walks, pavements, I mean; forgive the Americanism, Miss Russell. Yes, that's better so. And when did you and the colonel come to Rome. Now tell me?'

In a moment, much to Hiram's chagrin, and the colonel's too, Audouin had managed to lead the way, tête-à-tête with Gwen, shuffling off the two others to follow behind, and get along as best they might in the background together. Now the colonel was not a distinguished conversationalist, and Hiram was hardly in a humour for talking, so after they had interchanged a few harmless conventionalities and a mild platitude or two about the weather, they both relapsed into moody silence, and occupied themselves by catching a scrap every now and then of what Gwen and Audouin were saying in front of them.

'And that very clever Mr. Churchill, too, Mr. Audouin! I hear he's getting on quite wonderfully. Lord Beaminster bought one of his groups, you know, and brought him into fashion, partly by my pushing, I must confess, to be quite candid, and now, I'm told, he's commanding almost any price he chooses to ask in the way of sculpture. We haven't seen him yet, of course, but I mean papa and my cousin to look him up in his own quarters at the very earliest opportunity.'

'Oh, a clever enough young artist, certainly, but not really, Miss Russell, half so genuine an artist in feeling as my friend Win-throp.'

Hiram could have fallen on his neck that moment for that half-unconscious piece of kindly recommendation.

A few steps further they reached the corner of the Via de' Condotti, and Gwen paused for a second as she looked across the street, with a little sudden cry of recognition. A handsome young man was coming round the corner from the Piazza di Spagna, with a gipsy-looking girl leaning lightly on his arm, and talking to him with much evident animation. It was Colin and Minna, going out together on Minna's second holiday, to see the wonders of the Vatican and St. Peter's.

'Mr. Churchill!' Gwen cried, coming forward cordially to meet him. 'What a delightful rencontre! We were just talking of you.

And here are other friends, you see, besides, Mr. Winthrop, my father, and Mr. Audouin.' Minna stood half aside in a little embarrassment, wondering who on earth the grand lady could be (she had penetration enough to recognise at once that she was a grand lady) talking so familiarly with our Colin.

'Miss Howard-Russell!' Colin cried on his side, taking her hand warmly. 'Then you've come back again! I'm so glad to see you! And you too, Mr. Audouin; this is really a great pleasure. Miss Russell, I owe you so many thanks. It was you, I believe, who sent my first patron, Lord Beaminster, to visit my studio.'

'Oh, don't speak of it, please, Mr. Churchill. It's we who owe you thanks rather, for the pleasure your beautiful group of Autumn has given us. And dear stupid old Lord Beaminster used to amuse everybody so much by telling them how he wanted you to put a clock-dial in the place of the principal figure, until I managed at last to laugh him out of it. I made his life a burden to him, I assure you, by getting him to see how very ridiculous it was of him to try to spoil your lovely composition.'

They talked for a minute or two longer at the street corner, Gwen explaining once more to Colin how she and the colonel had come as Lord Beaminster's guests to the Villa Panormi; and meanwhile poor little Minna stood there out in the cold, growing redder every second, and boiling over with indignation to think that that horrid Miss Howard-Russell should have dropped down upon them from the clouds at the very wrong moment, just on purpose to make barefaced love so openly to her Colin.

It was Gwen herself, however, who first took notice of Minna, whom she saw standing a little apart, and looking very much out of it indeed among so many greetings of old acquaintances. 'And your friend?' she said to Colin kindly. 'You haven't introduced her to us yet. May we have the pleasure?' And she took a step forward with womanly gentleness to relieve the poor girl from her obvious embarrassment.

'Excuse me, Minna dear,' Colin said, taking her hand and leading her forward quietly.

'My cousin, Miss Wroe: Miss Howard-Bussell, Colonel Howard-Russell, Mr. Audouin, Mr. Winthrop.'

Minna bowed to them all stiffly with cheeks burning, and then fell back again at once angrily into her former position.

'And have you come to Rome lately, Miss Wroe?' Gwen asked of her with genuine kindness. 'Are you here on a visit to your cousin, whose work we all admire so greatly?'

'I came a week ago,' Minna answered defiantly, blurting out the whole truth (lest she should seem to be keeping back anything) and pitting her whole social nonentity, as it were, against the grand lady's assured position.

'I came a week ago; and I'm a governess to a little Russian girl here; and I'm going to stop all the winter.'

'That'll be very nice for all of us,' Gwen put in softly, with a look that might almost have disarmed Minna's hasty suspicions. 'And how exceedingly pleasant for you to have your cousin here, too! I suppose it was partly on that account, now, that you decided upon coming here?'

'It was,' Minna answered shortly, without vouchsafing any further explanation.

'And where are you going now, Mr. Churchill?' Gwen asked, seeing that Minna was clearly not in a humour for conversation. 'Are you showing your cousin the sights of Rome, I wonder?'

'Exactly what I am doing, Miss Russell. We're going now to see the Vatican.'

'Oh, then, do let us come with you! I should like to go too. I do love going through the galleries with an artist who can tell one all about them!'

'But, Gwen, my dear, Beaminster's lunch hour—

'Oh, bother Lord Beaminster's lunch hour, papa! Hire somebody to go and tell him we've been detained and can't possibly be back by lunch-time. I want to go and see the Vatican, and improve the opportunity of making Miss Wroe's better acquaintance.' Minna bowed again with bitter mock solemnity.

So they all went to the Vatican, spoiling poor little Minna's holiday that had begun so delightfully (for she and Colin had talked quite like old times on their way from the Via Clementina), and tiring themselves out with strolling up and down those eye-distracting corridors and galleries. It was a queer game of cross questions and crooked answers all round between them. Audouin, flashing gaily as of old, and scintillating every now and then with little bits of crisp criticism over pictures or statues, was trying all the time to get a good talk with Gwen Howard-Russell, and to oust from her side the unconscious Colin. Gwen, smiling benignly at Audouin's quaintly worded sallies, was doing her best to call out Colin's opinions upon all the works in the Vatican off-hand. Hiram, only anxious to avoid being bored by the Colonel's vapid remarks upon the things he saw (he called Raphaels and Guidos and Titians alike 'pretty, very pretty'), was chiefly engaged in overhearing the conversation of the others. And Minna, poor little Minna, to whom Colin paid as much assiduous attention as the circumstances permitted, was longing all the time to steal away and have a good cry about the horrid goings on of that abominable Miss Howard-Russell.

From the minute Minna had seen Gwen, and heard what manner of things Gwen had to say to Colin, she forgot straightway all her fears about the Italian Cecca creature, and recognised at once with a woman's instinct that her real danger lay in Gwen, and in Gwen only. It was with Gwen that Colin was likely to fall in love; Gwen, with her grand manners and her high-born face and her fine relations, and her insinuating, intoxicating adulation. How she made up to him and praised him! How she talked to him about his genius and his love of beauty! How she tried to flatter him up before her own very face! Miss Gwen was beautiful; that much Minna couldn't help grudgingly admitting. Miss Gwen had a delightful self-possession and calmness about her that Minna would have given the world to have rivalled. Miss Gwen had everything in her favour. No wonder Colin was so polite and courteous to her; no wonder poor little trembling Minna was really nowhere at all beside her. And then she had done Colin a great service; she had recommended Lord Beaminster and many other patrons to go and see his studio. Ah me! how sad little Minna felt that evening when she tried to compare her own small chances with those of great, grand, self-possessed Miss Howard-Russell! If only Cohn loved her! But he had as good as said himself that he didn't love her, not worth speaking of: he had said he kissed her 'strictly as a cousin.'

As Gwen and the colonel drove back in a hired botto to the Villa Panormi in the cool of the evening, Gwen said to her papa quite innocently, 'What a charming young man that delightful Mr. Churchill is really! Did. you notice how kind and attentive he was to that funny little cousin of his in the brown bonnet? Only a governess, you know, come to Rome with a Russian family; and yet he made as much of her, almost, as he did of you and me and Mr. Audouin! So thoughtful and good of him, I call it; but there, he's always such a perfect gentleman. I dare say that's the daughter of some washerwoman or somebody down at Wootton Mandeville, and he pays her quite as much attention as if she were actually a countess or a duchess.'

'You don't seem to remember, Gwen,' the colonel answered grimly, 'that his own father was only a kitchen gardener, and that he himself began life, I understand, as a common stonecutter.'

'Nonsense!' Gwen replied energetically.

'You seem to forget on the other hand, papa, that he was born a great sculptor, and that genius is after all the only true nobility.'

'It wasn't so when I was a boy,' the colonel continued, with a grim smile; 'and I fancy it isn't so yet, Gwen, in our own country, whatever these precious Yankee friends of yours may choose to tell you.'

CHAPTER XXXIII

CECCA

A fortnight later, Signora Cecca walked sulkily down the narrow staircase of the handsome Englishman's little studio. Signora Cecca was evidently indulging herself in the cheap luxury of a very bad humour. To an Italian woman of Cecca's peculiarly imperious temperament, indulgence in that congenial exercise of the spleen may be looked upon as a real and genuine luxury. Cecca brooded over her love and her wrath and her jealousy as thwarted children brood over their wrongs in the solitude of the bedroom where they have been sent to expiate some small everyday domestic offence in silence and loneliness. The handsome Englishman had then a sweetheart, an innamorata, in his own country, clearly; and now she had come to Rome, the perfidious creature, on purpose to visit him. That was a contingency that Cecca had never for one moment counted upon when she left her native village in Calabria and followed the unknown sculptor obediently to Rome, where she rose at once to be the acknowledged queen of the artists' models.

Not that Cecca had ever seriously thought, on her own part, of marrying Colin. Mother of heaven, no! for the handsome Englishman was a heretic and a foreigner; and to marry him would have been utterly shocking to all Cecca's deepest and most ingrained moral and religious feelings. For Cecca was certainly by no means devoid of principle. She would have stuck a knife into you in a quarrel as soon as look at you: she would have poisoned a rival remorselessly in cold blood under the impelling influence of treacherous Italian jealousy without a moment's hesitation, but she would have decidedly drawn a sharp line at positively marrying a foreigner and a heretic. No, she didn't want to marry Colin. But she wanted to keep him to herself as her own private and particular possession: she wanted to have him for her own without external interference: she wanted to prevent all other women from having anything to say or to do with her own magnificent handsome Englishman. He needn't marry her, of course, but he certainly mustn't be allowed to go and marry any other woman.

'If I were a jealous fool,' Cecca thought to herself in her own vigorous Calabrian patois, 'I should run away and leave him outright, and make Bazzoni's fortune all at once by letting him model from me. But I'm not a jealous fool, and I don't want, as the proverb says, to cut off my own right hand merely in order to fling it in the face of my rival. The English signorina loves the handsome Englishman, that's certain. Then, mother of God, the English signorina will have to pay for it. Dear little Madonna della Guardia, help me to cook her stew for her, and you shall have tapers, ever so many tapers, and a couple of masses too in your own little chapel on the headland at Monteleone. There is no Madonna so helpful at a pinch as our own Madonna della Guardia at Monteleone. Besides, she isn't too particular. She will give you her aid on an emergency, and not be so very angry with you after all, because you've had to go a little bit out of your way, perhaps, to effect your purpose. Blood of St. Elmo, no: she took candles from the good uncle when he shot the carabiniere who came to take him up over the affair of the ransom of the American traveller; and she protected him well for the candles too, and he has never been arrested for it even to this very minute.

The English signorina had better look out, by Bacchus, if she wants to meddle with Cecca Bianchelli and Madonna della Guardia at Monteleone. Besides, she's nothing but a heretic herself, if it comes to that, so what on earth, I should like to know, do the blessed saints in heaven care for her?'

Signora Cecca stood still for a moment in the middle of the Via Colonna, and asked herself this question passionately, with a series of gesticulations which in England might possibly have excited unfavourable attention. For example, she set her teeth hard together, and drew an imaginary knife deliberately across the throat of an equally imaginary aerial rival. But in Rome, where people are used to gesticulations, nobody took the slightest notice of them.

'She has been four times to the studio already,' Signora Cecca went on to herself, resuming her homeward walk as quietly as if nothing at all had intervened to diversify it: 'and every time she comes the handsome Englishman talks to her, makes love to her, fondles her almost before my very eyes. And she, the basilisk, she loves him too, though she pretends to be so very coy and particular: she loves him: she cannot deceive me: I saw it at once, and I see it still through all her silly transparent pretences. She cannot take in Cecca Bianchelli and Madonna della Guardia at Monteleone. She loves him, the Saracen, and she shall answer for it. No other woman but me shall ever dare to love the handsome Englishman.

'The other English signorina, to be sure, she loves him too: but then, pooh, I don't care for her, I don't mind her, I'm not afraid of her. The Englishman doesn't love her, that's certain. She's too cold and white-faced. He loves the little one. The little one is prettier; she has life in her features; she might almost be an Italian girl, only she's too insipid. She shall answer for his loving her. I hate her; and the dear little Madonna shall have her candles.'

As she walked along, a young man in a Roman workman's dress came up to her wistfully, and looked in her face with a doubtful expression of bashful timidity. 'Good morning, Signora Cecca,' he said, with curiously marked politeness. 'You come from the Englishman's studio, I suppose? You have had a sitting?'

Cecca looked up at him haughtily and coldly. 'You again, Giuseppe,' she said, with a toss of her beautiful head and a curl of her lip like a tragedy Cleopatra. 'And what do you want with me? You're always bothering me now about something or other, on the strength of some slight previous boyish acquaintance.'

The young man smiled her back an angry smile, Italian fashion. 'It's Giuseppe now, I suppose,' he said, with a sniff: 'it used to be Beppo down there yonder at Monteleone. I shall have to take to calling you in your turn "Signora Francesca," I'm thinking: you've grown too fine for me since you came to Rome and got among your rich sculptor acquaintances. A grand trade indeed, to sit half the day, half uncovered, in a studio for a pack of Englishmen to take your figure and make statues of you! I liked you far better, myself, when you poured the wine out long ago at the osteria by the harbour at Monteleone.'

Cecca looked up at him once more haughtily. 'You did?' she said. 'You did, did you? Well, that was all very well for a fellow like you, only fit to tend a horse or chop up rotten olive roots for firewood. But for me that sort of life didn't answer. I prefer Rome, and fame, and art, and plenty.' And as she said the last words she clinked the cheap silver bracelets that she wore upon her arm, and touched the thin gold brooch that fastened up the light shawl thrown coquettishly across her shapely shoulders.

'You don't,' Giuseppe answered boldly.

'You are not happy here, Cecca mia, as you were at Monteleone. You worry your heart out about your Englishman, and he does not love you. What does he think of you or care for you? You are to him merely a model, a thing to mould clay from; no more than the draperies and the casts that he works with so carelessly in his studio. And it is for that that you throw me over—me, Beppo, who loved you always so dearly at Monteleone.'

Cecca looked at him and laughed lightly. 'You, Beppo!' she cried, as if amused and surprised. 'You, my friend! You thought to marry Cecca Bianchelli! Oh no, little brother; that would be altogether too ridiculous. There is no model in Rome, do you know, who has such a figure or earns so much money as I do.'

'But you loved me once, or at least you said so, Signora Francesca.'

'And you should hear how the excellencies admire me, and call me beautiful, Signor Giuseppe.'

'Cecca, Cecca, you know I have come to Rome for your sake only. I don't want you to love me, I only want to see you and be near you. Won't you let me come and see you this evening?'

'Very sorry, Signor Giuseppe. It would have given me the deepest satisfaction, but I have a prior engagement. A painter of my acquaintance takes me to the Circo Beale.'

'But, Cecca, Cecca!'

'Well, Beppo?'

'Ah, that is good, "Beppo." You relent then, Signora?'

'As between old friends, Signor Giuseppe, one may use the diminutive.'

'And you will let me come then tomorrow night and see you for half an hour—for half an hour only, Cecca?'

'Well, you were a good friend of mine once, and I have need of you for a project of my own, at the moment. Yes, you may come if you like, Beppo.'

'Ten thousand thanks, Signora. You are busy, I will not keep you. Good evening, Cecca.'

'Good evening, my friend. You are a good fellow after all, Beppo. Good evening.'

CHAPTER XXXIV

HIRAM SEES LAND

Upon my word,' Gwen Howard-Russell thought to herself in the gardens of the Villa Panormi, 'I really can't understand that young Mr. Churchill. He's four years older, and he ought to be four years wiser now, than when we were last at Rome, but he's actually just as stupid and as dull of comprehension as ever; he positively doesn't see when a girl's in love with him. He must be utterly bound up in his sculpture and his artistic notions, that's what it is, or else he'd surely discover what one was driving at when one gives him every possible sort of opportunity. One would have thought he'd have seen lots of society during these four winters that he's been comparatively famous, and that he would have found out what people mean when they say such things to him. But he hasn't, and I declare he's really more polite and attentive even now to that little governess cousin of his, with the old-fashioned bonnet, than he is to me myself, in spite of everything.'

For it had never entered into Gwen's heart to think that Colin might possibly be in love himself with the little gipsy-faced governess cousin.

'Cousin Dick,' Gwen said a few minutes later to Lord Beaminster, 'I've asked Mr. Churchill and my two Americans to come up and have a cup of tea with us this afternoon out here in the garden.'

'Certainly, my dear,' the earl answered, smiling with all his false teeth most amiably; 'the house is your own, you know. (And, by George, she makes it so, certainly without asking me. But who on earth could ever be angry with such a splendid high-spirited creature?) Bring your Americans here by all means, and give that man with the outlandish name plenty of tea, please, to keep him quiet. By Jove, Gwen, I never can understand for the life of me what the dickens the fellow's talking about.'

In due time the guests arrived, and Gwen, who had determined by this time to play a woman's last card, took great care during the whole afternoon to talk as much as possible to Hiram and as little as possible to Colin Churchill. She was determined to let him think he had a rival; that is the surest way of making a man discover whether he really cares for a woman or otherwise.

'Oh yes, I've been to Mr. Winthrop's studio,' she said in answer to Audouin's inquiry, 'and we admired so much a picture of a lake with such a funny name to it, didn't we, papa? It was really beautiful, Mr. Winthrop. I've never seen anything of yours that I've been pleased with so much. Don't you think it splendid, Mr. Audouin?'

'A fine picture in its way, yes, certainly, Miss Russell; but not nearly so good, to my thinking, as the Capture of Babylon he's now working on.'

'You think so, really? Well, now, for my part I like the landscape better. There's so much more originality and personality in it, I fancy. Mr. Winthrop, which do you yourself like the best of your performances?'

Hiram blushed with pleasure. Gwen had never before taken so much notice of him. 'I'm hardly a good judge myself,' he faltered out timidly. 'I wouldn't for worlds pit my own small opinion, of course, against Mr. Audouin's. I'm trying my best at the Capture of Babylon, naturally, but I don't seem to satisfy my own imaginary standard in historical painting, somehow, nearly as well as in external nature. For my own part, I like the landscapes best. I quite agree with you, Miss Russell, that Lake Chattawauga is about my high-water mark.'

('Lake Chattawauga!' the earl interjected pensively, but nobody took the slightest notice of him. 'Lake Chattawauga! Do you really mean to say you've painted the picture of a place with such a name as Lake Chattawauga? I should suppose it must be somewhere or other over in America.')

'I'm so glad to hear you say so,' Gwen answered cordially, 'because one's always wrong, you know, in matters of art criticism; and it's such a comfort to hear that one may be right now and again if only by accident. I liked Lake Chattawauga quite immensely; I don't know when I've seen a picture that pleased me so much, Mr. Winthrop. What do you say, Mr. Churchill?'

'I think you and Winthrop are quite right, Miss Russell. His landscapes are very, very pretty, and I wish he'd devote himself to them entirely, and give up historical painting and figure subjects altogether.'

('The first time I ever noticed a trace of professional jealousy in young Churchill,' thought Audouin to himself sapiently. 'He doesn't want Hiram, apparently, to go on with the one thing which is certain to lead him in the end to fame and fortune.')

'And there was a lovely little sketch of a Tyrolese waterfall,' Gwen began again enthusiastically. 'Wasn't it exquisite, papa? You know you said you'd so much like to buy it for the dining-room.'

Hiram flushed again. 'I'm so glad you liked my little things,' he said, trembling with delight. 'I didn't think you cared in the least for any of my work, Miss Russell. I was afraid you weren't at all interested in the big canvases.'

'Not like your work, Mr. Winthrop!' Gwen cried, with half a glance aside at Colin. 'Oh yes, I've always admired it most sincerely! Why, don't you remember, our friendship with you and Mr. Audouin began just with my admiring a little water-colour you were making the very first day I ever saw you, by the Lake of the Thousand Islands?' (Hiram nodded a joyful assent. Why, how could he ever possibly forget it?) 'And then you know there was that beautiful little sketch of the Lago Albano, that you gave me the day I was leaving Italy last. I have it hung up in our drawing-room at home in England, and I think it's one of the very prettiest pictures I ever looked at.'

Hiram could have cried like a child that moment with the joy and excitement of a long pent-up nature.

And so, through all that delightful afternoon, Gwen kept leading up, without intermission, to Hiram Winthrop. Hiram himself hardly knew what on earth to make of it. Gwen was very kind and polite to him to-day, that much was certain; and that, at least, was quite enough to secure Hiram an unwonted amount of genuine happiness. How he hugged himself over her kindly smiles and appreciative criticisms! How he fancied in his heart, with tremulous hesitation, that she really was beginning to care just a little bit for him, were it ever so little! In short, for the moment, he was in the seventh heaven, and he felt happier than he had ever felt before in his whole poor, wearisome, disappointed lifetime.

When they were going away, Gwen said once to Hiram (holding his hand in hers just a second longer than was necessary too, he fancied), 'Now, remember, you must come again and see us very soon, Mr. Winthrop, and you too, Mr. Audouin. We want you both to come as often as you're able, for we're quite dull out here in the country, so far away from the town and the Corso.' But she never said a single word of that sort to Cohn Churchill, who was standing close beside them, and heard it all, and thought to himself, 'I wonder whether Miss Russell has begun to take a fancy at last to our friend Winthrop? He's a good fellow, and after all she couldn't do better if she were to search diligently through the entire British peerage.' So utterly had Gwen's wicked little ruse failed of its deceitful, jealous intention.

But as they walked Rome-ward together, to the Porta del Popolo, Audouin said at last musingly to Hiram, 'Miss Russell was in a very gracious mood this afternoon, wasn't she, my dear fellow?'

He looked at Hiram so steadfastly while he said it that Hiram almost blushed again, for he didn't like to hear the subject mentioned, however guardedly, before a third person like Colin Churchill. 'Yes,' he answered shyly, 'she spoke very kindly indeed about my little landscapes. I had no idea before that she really thought anything about them. And how good of her, too, to keep my water-colour of the Lago Albano in her own drawing-room!'

Audouin smiled a gently cynical little Bostonian smile, and answered nothing.

'How strangely one-sided and egotistic we are, after all!' he thought to himself quietly as he walked along. 'We think each of ourselves, and never a bit of other people. Hiram evidently fancied that Miss Russell, Gwen, why not call her so?—wanted him to come again to the Villa Panormi. A moment's reflection might have shown him that she couldn't possibly have asked me, without at the same time asking him also! And it was very clever of her, too, to invite him first, so as not to make the invitation look quite too pointed. She was noticeably kind to Hiram to-day, because he's my protégé. But Hiram, with all his strong, good qualities, is not keen-sighted, not deep enough to fathom the profound abysses of a woman's diplomacy! I don't believe even now he sees what she was driving at. But I know: I feel certain I know; I can't be mistaken. It was a very good sign, too, a very good sign, that though she asked me (and of course Hiram with me) to come often to the villa, she didn't think in the least of asking that young fellow Churchill. It's a terribly presumptuous thing to fancy you have won such a woman's heart as Gwen Howard-Russell's; but I imagine I must be right this time. I don't believe I can possibly be mistaken any longer. The convergence of the evidences is really quite too overwhelming.'

CHAPTER XXXV

MAN PROPOSES

Ten days had passed, and during those ten days Gwen had met both Hiram and Colin on two or three occasions. Each time she saw them together she was careful to talk a great deal more with the young American than with his English companion. At last, one Sunday afternoon, both the young men 'had gone out to the Villa Panormi with Audouin, for a cup of afternoon tea in the garden; and after tea was over, they had stolen away in pairs down the long alleys of oranges, and among the broken statues and tazzas filled with flowers upon the mouldering balustraded Italian terraces. 'Come with me, Mr. Winthrop,' Gwen cried gaily to Hiram (with a side glance at Colin once more to see how he took it). 'I want to show you such a lovely spot for one of your pretty little watercolour sketches, a bower of clematis, with such great prickly pears and aloes for the foreground, that I'm sure you'll fall in love with the whole picture the moment you see it.'

Hiram followed her gladly down to the arbour, a little corner at the bottom of the garden, rather English than Italian in its first conception, but thickly overgrown with tangled masses of sub-tropical vegetation. It's very pretty,' he said, 'certainly very pretty. Just the sort of thing that Mr. Audouin would absolutely revel in.'

'Shall I call him?' Gwen asked, going to the door of the arbour and looking about her carelessly. 'He must be somewhere or other hereabout.'

'Oh no, don't, Miss Russell,' Hiram answered hastily. 'He's having a long talk with Churchill about art, from what I overheard. Don't disturb them. Mr. Audouin has a wonderful taste in art, you know: I love to hear him talk about it in his own original pellucid fashion.'

'You're very fond of him, aren't you?' Gwen asked, looking at him with her big beautiful eyes. 'Is he any relation of yours?' 'Relation!' Hiram cried, 'oh dear no, Miss Bussell. But he's been so kind to me, so very kind to me! You can't imagine how much I owe to Mr. Audouin.'

He said it so earnestly, and seemed to want so much to talk about him, that Gwen sat down upon the stone seat in the little arbour and answered with womanly interest, 'Tell me all about it, then, Mr. Winthrop. I should like to hear how you came to pick up with him.'

Thus encouraged, Hiram, to his own immense astonishment, let loose the floodgates of his pent-up speech, and began to narrate the whole story of his lonely childhood, and of his first meeting with Audouin in the primeval woods of Geauga County. He was flattered that Gwen should have asked him indirectly for his history: more flattered still to find that she listened to his hasty reminiscences with evident attention. He told her briefly about his early attempts at drawing in the blackberry bottom; how the deacon had regarded his artistic impulses as so many proofs of original sin; how he had followed the trappers out into the frozen woodland; how he had met Audouin there by accident; and how Audouin had praised his drawings and encouraged him in his fancies, being the first human being he had ever known who cared at all for any of these things. 'And when you spoke so kindly about my poor little landscape the other day, Miss Russell,' he added, looking down and hesitating, 'I felt more happy than I had ever felt before since that day so long ago, in the woods away over yonder in America.'

But Gwen only smiled back a frank smile of unaffected sympathy, and answered warmly, 'I'm so glad you think so much of my criticism, I'm sure, Mr. Winthrop.'

Then Hiram went on and told her how he had worked and struggled at school and college, and at the block-cutting establishment; and how he had longed to go to England and be an artist; and how he had never got the opportunity. And then he spoke of the first day he had ever seen Gwen herself by the Lake of the Thousand Islands.

Till that moment it hadn't struck Gwen how very earnest Hiram's voice was gradually growing; but as he came to that first chance meeting at Alexandria Bay, she couldn't help observing that his lips began to tremble a little, and that his words were thick with emotion. For a second she thought she ought to rise up and suggest that they should join the others over yonder in the garden: but then she changed her mind again, and felt sure she must be mistaken. The young American artist could never mean to have the boldness to propose to her on the strength of so little encouragement. And besides, his story was really so interesting, and she was so very anxious to hear out the rest of it to the very end.

'And so you liked England immensely?' she asked him, when he reached in due course that part of his simple straightforward confidences. 'I wonder you didn't stop there and take regularly to landscape painting.'

'I was sorely tempted to stop,' Hiram answered, daring to look her straight in the eyes now; for he almost flattered himself she knew what he was going to say to her next.

'I came away from England most reluctantly, at Mr. Audouin's particular request: but I longed at the time to remain, for I had borne two words ringing in my ears from America to England, and those two words were just two names—Gwen and Chester.'

Gwen started away suddenly with a half-frightened expression, and said to him in a colder tone, 'Why, what do you mean? Explain yourself, please, Mr. Winthrop. My name you know is Gwen, and papa and I used once to live in Chester.'

Hiram took her hand timidly in his with an air of gentle command, and made her sit down again once more for a minute upon the seat in the arbour. 'You must hear me out to the end now, Miss Bussell,' he said in a very soft, firm voice, 'whatever comes of it. You mustn't go away yet. I didn't mean to speak so soon, but I have been hurried into it. I've staked my whole existence on a single throw, and you mustn't run away and leave me in the midst of it undecided.'

Gwen turned pale with nervousness, and withdrew her hand, but sat quite still, and listened to him attentively.

'From the first moment I ever saw you, Miss Russell,' he went on passionately, 'I felt you were the only woman I had ever loved or ever could love. I didn't know your full name, or who you were, or where you lived; but I heard your father call you Gwen, and I heard you say you had been at Chester. Those were the only two things I knew at all about you. And from the day when I saw you there looking over my sketch beside the Thousand Islands, I kept those two names of Gwen and Chester engraved upon my heart until I came to Europe. I keep one of them engraved there still until this very minute. And whatever you say to me, I shall keep it there unaltered until I die.... Oh, Miss Russell, I don't want you to give me an answer at once, I hope you won't give me an answer at once, because I can see from your face what that answer would most likely be: but I love you, I love you, I love you; and as long as I live I shall always, always love you.'

'I think, Mr. Winthrop,' Gwen said, slowly rising and hesitating, 'we ought to go back now and join the others.'

Hiram looked at her with a concentrated look of terror and despair that fairly frightened her. 'Not for one moment yet,' he whispered quite softly, 'not for one moment yet, I beg and pray of you. I have something else still to say to you.'

Gwen faltered for another second, and then stood still and listened passively.

'Miss Russell,' he began again, with white lips and straining eyeballs, 'I don't want you to give me an answer yet; but I do want you to wait a little and consider with yourself before you give me it. If you say no to me all at once, you will kill me, you will kill me. I have lived for so many weary years in this hope, so long deferred, that it has become a part, as it were, of my very being, and you can't tear it out of me now without lacerating and rending me. But I thought, I fancied, it was wildly presumptuous of me, but still I fancied, that this last week or two you had been more kind to me, more interested in me, more tolerant of me at least, than you used to be formerly.'

Gwen's heart smote her with genuine remorse when she heard that true accusation. Poor young fellow! She had undoubtedly led him into it, and she felt thoroughly ashamed of herself for the cruel ruse she had unwittingly practised upon him. Who would ever have thought, though, that the Yankee painter was really and truly so much in love with her?

She sighed slightly; for no woman can hear a man declare his heartfelt admiration for herself without emotion; and then she answered feebly, 'I... I... I only said I admired your pictures immensely, Mr. Winthrop.' Hiram could hardly gasp out a few words more. 'Oh, Miss Russell, don't give me an answer yet, don't give me an answer yet, I implore you. Wait and think it over a little while, and then answer me. You have never thought of me before in this way, I can see; you haven't any idea about me: wait and think it over, and remember that my whole life and happiness hangs upon it. Wait, oh! please wait and think it over.'

He pleaded with so much earnestness in his tone, and he looked so eagerly into her swimming eyes, that Gwen forgot for the moment his Yankee accent and his plain face and his unpolished manners, and saw him only as he was, an eager lover, begging her for mercy with all the restrained energy of a deep and self-contained but innately passionate nature. She could not help but pity him, he was so thoroughly and profoundly in earnest. For a moment her heart was really touched, not with love, but with infinite compassion, and she answered, half remorsefully, 'I'm afraid I can't hold you out much hope, Mr. Winthrop; but it shall be as you say; I will think it over, and let you have my full answer hereafter.' Hiram seized her hand eagerly. She tried to withdraw it, but he would not let her. 'Thank you,' he cried almost joyously; 'thank you, thank you! Then you don't refuse me utterly; you don't reject me without appeal; you will take my plea into consideration? I will not ask you again. I will not obtrude myself upon your notice unwillingly; but let me know in a fortnight. Do take a fortnight; my whole life is staked upon it; let it have a fortnight.'

Gwen's eyes were brimmed with two rising tears as she answered, trembling, 'Very well, it shall be a fortnight. Now we must go, Mr. Winthrop. We've stopped here too long. The others will be waiting for us.' And she drew her hand away from his as quietly as she was able, but not without a certain small inobtrusive sympathetic pressure. In her heart she pitied him.

As she passed out and joined the party at the far end of the garden, Hiram noticed that she didn't go up to speak at once to Colin Churchill. She let Audouin, nothing loth, lead her off down the alley of orange trees, and there she began speaking to him as if quite casually about Hiram.

'Your friend Mr. Winthrop has been telling me how kind you've been to him, and how much he owes to you,' she said, twirling a flower nervously between her fingers. 'How good of you to do all that you have done for him! Do you know, I quite envy you your opportunities for discovering such a genius in neglected places. I didn't know before, Mr. Audouin, that among all your other good qualities you were also a philanthropist. But your protégé there is quite warm and enthusiastic about all your goodness and kindness to him both here and in America.'

She looked straight at him all unconsciously as she spoke, and her eyes, though of course she had hastily wiped them on leaving the arbour, glistened a little still with the two tears that had risen unbidden to their lids when she was talking a minute before with Hiram. Audouin noticed the glistening with a quiet delight, and naturally coupled that and her words together into a mistaken meaning. 'If only we were quite alone now,' he thought to himself regretfully, 'this would be the exact moment to say what I wish to her. But no matter; another opportunity will crop up before long, I don't doubt, and then I can speak to her quite at my leisure.'

As for Gwen, when she found herself alone in her room that evening, she sat down in the easy-chair by the bedside, and took a most unconscionable time in unfastening her necklet and earrings, and putting them away one by one in the little jewel-case. 'He's very much in love with me, that's certain,' she said to herself meditatively. 'Who could ever have imagined it? I never should have talked to him so much if I had fancied he could possibly have misunderstood me. Poor fellow, I'm awfully sorry for him. And how dreadfully distressed he looked when I didn't answer him! It quite made me take a sort of fancy to him for the moment.... What a romantic history, too! Fell in love with me at first sight, that day by the Thousand Islands! And I never even so much as looked at him..... This necklet doesn't at all become me. I shall get another one next time I go down the Corso.... But he paints beautifully, and no doubt about it; and that charming Mr. Audouin says he's really quite an artistic genius. I'm positively grieved with myself that I shall have to refuse him. He'll break his heart over it, poor young man; I'm sure he'll break his heart over it. Of course one doesn't mind breaking most men's hearts one bit, because, you see, in the long run they're none the worse for it. But this young Mr. Winthrop's another sort of person; if you break his heart, just this one time only, that'll be the end of him at once and for ever.... And what an unhappy life he seems to have had of it, too! One would be quite sorry to add to it by making him miserable with a refusal..... Ah, well, he's really a very good sort of young man in his way. What a pity he should be an American!... And yet why should Americans differ so much from other people, I wonder? What a wistful look he gave me when he asked me not to answer him now immediately. Upon my word, in a sort of way I really do like him just a little bit, the poor young fellow.'

CHAPTER XXXVI

CECCA SHOWS HER HAND

Have you brought me the medicine, Beppo?'

'The what, Signora Cecca? Oh, the medicine? I don't call it medicine: I call it—'

Cecca clapped her hand angrily upon his lips. 'Fool,' she said, 'what are you babbling about? Give me the bottle and say no more about it. That's a good friend indeed. I owe you a thank-you for this, truly.'

'But, Cecca, what do you want it for? You must swear to me solemnly what you want it for. The police, you know—'

Cecca laughed merrily, a joyous laugh, with no sorcery in it. One would have said, the guileless merriment of a little simple country maiden. 'The police, indeed,' she cried, softly but gaily. 'What have the police got to do with it, I wonder? I want to poison a cat, a monster of a cat, that wails and screams every night outside my window; and you must go and wrap the thing up in as much mystery as if—Well, there! it's lucky nobody at Rome can understand good sound Calabrian even if they overhear it, or you'd go and make the folks suspicious with your silly talking, and so loud, too.'

Giuseppe looked at her, and muttered slowly something inarticulate. Then he looked again in a stealthy, frightened fashion; and at last he made up his mind to speak out boldly.

'Cecca! stop! I know what you want that little phial for.'

Cecca turned and smiled at him saucily. 'Oh, you know!' she said in a light ironical tone. 'You know, do you? Then, body of God, it's no use my telling you, so that's all about it.'

'Cecca,' the young man said again, snatching at the tiny bottle, which she still held gingerly between her finger and thumb, as if toying with it and fondling it, 'I've been watching you round at the Englishman's studio, and I've found out what you want the, the medicine for.'

Cecca's forehead puckered up quickly into a scowling frown (as when she sat for Clytemnestra), and she answered angrily, 'You've been playing the spy, then, have you really? I thank you, Signor Giuseppe, I thank you.'

'Listen, Cecca. I have been watching the Englishman's studio. There comes an English lady there, a beautiful tall lady, with a military father, a lady like this:' and Giuseppe put on in a moment a ludicrous caricature of Gwen's gait and carriage and manner. 'You have seen her, and you are jealous of her.'

Quick as lightning, Cecca saw her opportunity, and caught at it instinctively with Italian cunning. Giuseppe was right in principle, there was no denying it; but he had mistaken between Gwen and Minna. He had got upon the wrong tack, and she would not undeceive him. Keeping her forehead still dexterously bent to the same terrible scowl as before, and never for a second betraying her malicious internal smile of triumph, she answered, as if angry at being detected, 'Jealous! and of her! Signor Giuseppe, you are joking.'

'I am not joking, Cecca. I can see you are jealous this very moment. You love the Englishman. What is the good of loving him? He will not marry you, and you will not marry him: you would do much better to take, after all, to poor old Beppo. But you're jealous of the tall lady, because you think the Englishman's in love with her. What does it matter to you or me whether he is or whether he isn't? And it is for her that you want the medicine.'

Cecca drew a long breath and pretended to be completely baffled. 'Give me the bottle,' she cried; 'give me the bottle, Beppo.'

Giuseppe held it triumphantly at arm's length above his head.

'Not till you swear to me, Cecca, that you don't want to use it against the tall lady.' Cecca wrung her hands in mock despair. 'You won't give it to me, Beppo? You won't give it to me? What do you want me to swear it by? The holy water, the rosary, the medal of the holy father?'

Giuseppe smiled a smile of contemptuous superciliousness.

'Holy water!—rosary!—Pope!' he cried, 'Much you care for them indeed, Signora. No, no; you must swear by something that will bind you firmly. You must swear on your own little pocket image of Madonna della Guardia of Monteleone.'

Cecca pouted. (To the daughter of ten generations of Calabrian brigands a detail like a little poisoning case was merely a matter for careless pouting and feminine vagaries.)

'You will compel me?' she asked hesitatingly.

Giuseppe nodded.

'Or else I don't give you the bottle,' he murmured.

Cecca drew the little silver image with well-simulated reluctance from inside her plaited bodice. 'What am I to swear?' she asked petulantly.

'Say the words after me,' Beppo insisted. 'I swear by the mother of God, Madonna della Guardia of Monteleone, and all holy saints, that I will not touch or hurt or harm the tall English lady with the military father. And if I do may the Madonna forget me.'

Cecca repeated the words after him, severally and distinctly. It was very necessary that she should be quite precise, lest the Madonna should by inadvertence make any mistake about the particular person. If she didn't make it quite clear at first that the oath only regarded Gwen, the Madonna might possibly be very angry with her for poisoning Minna, and that of course would be extremely awkward. It's a particularly unpleasant thing for any one to incur the displeasure of such a powerful lady as Madonna della Guardia at Monteleone.

'You may have the bottle now if you like,' Beppo said, handing it back to her carelessly.

Cecca pouted once more. 'What's the use of it now?' she asked languidly. 'Except, of course, to poison the cat with!'

Beppo laughed. To the simple unsophisticated Calabrian mind the whole episode only figured itself as a little bit of Cecca's pardonable feminine jealousy. Women will be women, and if they see a rival, of course, they'll naturally try to poison her. To say the truth, Beppo thought the fancy pretty and piquant on Cecca's part rather than otherwise. The fear of the Roman police was to him the only serious impediment.

'I may come and see you again next Sunday, Cecca?' he asked as he took up his bundle to leave the room. 'You owe me a little courtesy for this.'

Cecca smiled and nodded in a very gay humour. There was no need for deception now she had got the precious bottle securely put away in the innermost pocket of her model's kirtle. 'Yes,' she answered benignly. 'you may come on Sunday. You have deserved well of me.'

But as soon as Beppo had left the room Signora Cecca flung herself down upon the horsehair mattress in the corner (regardless of her back hair), and rolled over and over in her wild delight, and threw her arms about, as if she were posing for the Pythoness, and laughed aloud in her effusive southern joy and satisfaction. 'Ha! ha!' she cried to herself gaily, 'he thought it was that one! He thought it was that one, did he? He's got mighty particular since he came to Rome, Beppo has— afraid of the police, the coward; and he won't have anything to do even with poisoning a poor heretic of an Englishwoman. Madonna della Guardia, I have no such scruples for my part! But he mistook the one: he thought I was angry with the tall handsome one. No, no, she may do as she likes for all I care for her. It's the ugly little governess with the watery eyes that my Englishman's in love with. What he can see to admire in her I can't imagine, a thing with no figure, but he's in love with her, and she shall pay for it, the caitiff creature; she shall pay for it, I promise her. Here's the bottle, dear little bottle! How bright and clear it dances! Cecca Bianchelli, you shall have your revenge yet. Madonna della Guardia, good little Madonna, sweet little Madonna, you shall have your candles. Don't be angry with me, I pray you, Madonna mia, I shall not break my oath; it's the other one, the little governess, dear Madonna! She's only a heretic, an Englishwoman, a heretic; an affair of love, what would you have, Madonna? You shall get your candles, see if you don't, and your masses too, your two nice little masses, in your own pretty sweet little chapel on the high hill at Monteleone!'

CHAPTER XXXVII

CECCA AND MINNA

It was Tuesday afternoon at Colin Churchill's, and Minna had got her usual weekly leave to go and visit her cousin at his own studio. 'I find her devotion admirable,' said Madame, 'but then, this cousin he is young and handsome. After all, there is perhaps nothing so very extraordinary in it, really.'

Cecca was there, too, waiting her opportunity, with the little phial always in her pocket: for who knows when Madonna della Guardia may see the chance of earning her two promised masses? She is late this afternoon, the English governess; but she will come soon: she never forgets to come every Tuesday.

By and by, Minna duly arrived, and Colin kissed her before Cecca's very eyes, the miscreant! and she took off her bonnet even, and sat down and seemed quite prepared to make an afternoon of it.

'Cecca,' Colin cried, 'will you ask them to make us three cups of coffee? You can stop, Minna, and have some coffee, can't you?'

Cecca didn't understand the English half of the sentence, of course, but she ran off quite enchanted to execute the little commission in the Italian bent of it. A cup of coffee! It was the very thing; Madonna della Guardia, what fortune you have sent me!

Colin and Minna sat talking within while the coffee was brewing, and when it was brought in, Cecca waited for her opportunity cautiously, until Minna had taken a cup for herself, and laid it down upon the little bare wooden table beside her. It would never do to put the medicine by mistake into the cup of the Englishman; we must manage these little matters with all due care and circumspection. So Cecca watched in the background, as a cat watches a mouse's hole with the greatest silence and diligence, till at last a favourable chance occurred: and then under the pretence of handing Minna the biscuits which came up with the coffee, she managed cleverly to drop half the contents of the phial into the cup beside her. Half was quite enough for one trial: she kept the other half, in case of accident, to use again if circumstances should demand it.

Just at that moment a note came in from Maragliano. Could Colin step round to the other studio for a quarter of an hour? A wealthy patron had dropped in, and wanted to consult with him there about a commission.

Cohn read the letter through hastily; explained its contents to Minna; kissed her once more: (Ha, the last time, the last time forever! he will never do that again, the Englishman!) and then ran out to see the wealthy patron.

Minna was left alone for that half-hour in the studio with Cecca.

Would she drink the coffee, now? that was the question. No, as bad luck and all the devils would have it, she didn't seem to think of tasting or sipping it. A thousand maledictions! The stuff would get cold, and then she would throw it away and ask for another cupful. Blessed Madonna of Monteleone, make her drink! Make her drink it! Bethink you, unless she does, dear little Madonna, you do not get your candles or your masses!

Still Minna sat quite silent and motionless, looking vacantly at the beautiful model, whom she had forgotten now to feel angry or jealous about. She was thinking, thinking vacantly; and her Italian was so far from fluent that she didn't feel inclined to begin a conversation off-hand with the beautiful model.

Just to encourage her, then (there's nothing like society), Ceeca drew up her three-legged stool close beside the signorina, and began to sip carelessly and unconcernedly at her own cup of coffee. Perhaps the sight of somebody else drinking might chance by good luck to make the Englishwoman feel a little thirsty.

But Minna only looked at her, and smiled half-unconsciously. To her great surprise, the Italian woman perceived that two tears were slowly trickling down her rival's cheeks.

Italians are naturally sympathetic, even when they are on the eve of poisoning you; and besides one is always curious to know what one is crying for. So Cecca leaned forward kindly, and said in her gentlest tone: 'You are distressed, signorina. You are suffering in some way. Can I do anything for you?'

Minna started, and wiped away the two tears hastily. 'It is nothing,' she said, 'I didn't mean it. I—I fancied I was alone, I had forgotten.'

'What! you speak Italian!' Cecca cried, a little astonished, and half anxious to enjoy her triumph by anticipation. 'Ah, signorina, I know what is the matter. I have guessed your secret: I have guessed your secret!'

Minna blushed. 'Hush,' she said eagerly. 'Not a word about it. My friend may return. Not a word about it.'

But still she didn't touch her coffee.

Then Cecca began to talk to her gently and soothingly, in her best soft Italian manner. Poor thing, she was evidently very sad. So far away from her home too. Cecca was really quite sorry for her. She tried to draw her out and in her way to comfort her. The signorina hadn't long to live: let us at least be kind and sympathetic to her.

For, you see, an Italian woman is capable of poisoning you in such a perfectly good-humoured and almost affectionate fashion.

At first, Minna didn't warm very much to the beautiful model: she had still her innate horror of Italian women strong upon her; and besides she knew from her first meeting that Cecca had a terrible vindictive temper. But in time Cecca managed to engage her in real conversation, and to tell her about her own little personal peasant history. Yes, Cecca came from Calabria, from that beautiful province; and her father, her father was a fisherman.

Minna started. 'A fisherman! How strange. And my father too, was also a fisherman away over yonder in England!'

It was Cecca's turn to start at that. A fisherman! How extraordinary. She could hardly believe it. She took it for granted all along that Minna, though a governess, was a grand English lady; for the idea of a fisher man's daughter dressing and living in the way that Minna did was almost inconceivable to the unsophisticated mind of a Calabrian peasant woman. And to wear a bonnet, too! to wear a bonnet!

'Tell me all about it,' Cecca said, drawing closer, and genuinely interested (with a side eye upon the untasted coffee). 'You came to Rome then,' jerking her two hands in the direction of the door, 'to follow the Englishman?' 'Signora Cecca,' Minna said, with a sudden vague instinct, in her tentative Italian, 'I will trust you. I will tell you all about it. I was a poor fisherman's daughter in England, and I always loved my cousin, the sculptor.' Cecca listened with the intensest interest. Minna lifted her cup for the first time, and took a single sip of the poisoned coffee.

'Good!' thought Cecca calmly to herself. 'If she takes a first sip, why of course in that case she will certainly finish it.'

Then Minna went on with her story, shortly and in difficulty, pieced out every here and there by Cecca's questions and ready pantomime. Cecca drank in all the story with the deepest avidity. It was so strange that something should just then have moved the Englishwoman to make a confidante of her. A poor fisherman's daughter, and neglected now by her lover who had become a grand and wealthy sculptor! Mother of God, from the bottom of her heart, she really pitied her.

'And when he came to Rome,' Cecca said, helping out the story of her own accord, 'he fell in with the grand English ladies like the one with the military papa; and they made much of him; and you were afraid, my little signorina, that he had almost forgotten you! And so you came to Rome on purpose to follow him.'

Minna nodded, and her eyes filled with tears a second time.

'Poor little signorina!' Cecca said earnestly.

'It was cruel of him, very cruel of him. But when people come to Rome they are often cruel, and they soon forget their lovers of the province.' Something within her made her think that moment of poor Giuseppe, who had followed her so trustfully from that far Calabria.

Minna raised the cup once more, and took another sip at the poisoned coffee. Cecca watched the action closely, and this time gave a small involuntary sigh of relief when Minna set it down again almost untasted. Poor little thing! after all she was only a fisherman's daughter, and she wanted her lover, her lover of the province, to love her still the same as ever! Nothing so very wrong or surprising in that! Natural, most natural.... But then, the Englishman, the Englishman! she mustn't be allowed to carry off the Englishman.... And Giuseppe, poor Giuseppe.... Well, there, you know; in love and war these things will happen, and one can't avoid them.

'And you knew him from a child?' she asked innocently.

'Yes, from a child. We lived together in a little village by the sea-shore in England; my father was a fisherman, and his a gardener. He used to go into the fields by the village, and make me little images of mud, which I used to keep upon my mantelpiece, and that was the first beginning, you see, of his sculpture.'

Mother of heaven, just like herself and Giuseppe! How they used to play together as children on the long straight shore at Monteleone. 'But you were not Christians in England, you were pagans, not Christians!'

For the idea of images had suggested to Cecca's naïve mind the notion of the Madonna.

Minna almost laughed, in spite of herself, at the curious misapprehension, and drew out from her bosom the little cross that she always wore instead of a locket. 'Oh yes,' she said simply, without dwelling upon any minor points of difference between them; 'we are Christians—Christians.'

The girl examined the cross reverently, and then looked back at the coffee with a momentary misgiving. After all, the Englishwoman was very gentle and human-like and kind-hearted. It was natural she should want to keep her country lover. And besides she was really, it seemed, no heretic in the end at all, but a good Christian.

'When people come to Rome and become famous,' she repeated musingly, 'they do wrong to be proud and to forget the lovers of their childhood.' Giuseppe loved her dearly, there was no denying it, and she used to love him dearly, too, down yonder on the shore at Monteleone.

Minna raised her cup of coffee a third time, and took a deeper drink. Nearly a quarter of the whole was gone now; but not much of the poison, Cecca thought to herself, thank heaven; that was heavy and must have sunk to the bottom. If only one could change the cups now, without being observed! Poor little thing, it would be a pity, certainly, to poison her. One oughtn't to poison people, properly speaking, unless one has really got some serious grudge against them. She was a good little soul, though no doubt insipid, and a Christian, too; Madonna della Guardia, would the bargain hold good, Cecca wondered silently, seeing the Englishwoman had miraculously turned out to be after all a veritable Christian. These are points of casuistry on which one would certainly like to have beforehand the sound opinion of a good unprejudiced Calabrian confessor.

'You think he makes too much of the tall signorina!' Cecca said lightly, smiling and nodding. (Cecca had, of course, an immense fund of sympathy with the emotion of jealousy in other women.)

Minna blushed and looked down timidly without answering. What on earth could have possessed her to make so free, at this particular minute, with this terrible Italian model woman? She really couldn't make it out herself, and yet she knew there had been some strange unwonted impulse moving within her. (If she had read Von Hartmann, she would have called it learnedly the action of the Unconscious. As it was, she would have said, if she had known all, that it was a Special Providence.)

So wishing merely to change the subject, and having nothing else to say at the moment, she looked up almost accidentally at the completed clay of the Nymph Bathing, and said simply: 'That is a beautiful statue, Signora Cecca.'

Cecca smiled a majestic smile of womanly gratification, and showed her double row of even regular pearl-white teeth with coquettish beauty. 'I posed for it,' she said, throwing herself almost unconsciously into the familiar attitude. 'It is my portrait!'

'It is a splendid portrait,' Minna answered cordially, glancing quickly from the original to the copy, 'a splendid portrait of a very beautiful and exquisitely formed woman.'

'Signorina!' Cecca cried, standing up in front of her, and roused by a sudden outburst of spontaneous feeling to change her plan entirely, 'you are quite mistaken; the master does not love the tall lady. I know the master well, I have been here all the time, I have watched him narrowly. He does not love the tall lady: she loves him, I tell you, but he does not care for her; in his heart of hearts he does not love her; I know, for I have watched them. Signorina, I like you, you are a sweet little Englishwoman, and I like you dearly. Your friend from the village in England shall marry you!' ('Oh, don't talk so!' Minna cried parenthetically, hiding her face passionately between her hands.)

'And if the tall lady were to try to come between you and him,' Cecca added vigorously, 'I would poison her, I would poison her, I would poison her! She shall not steal another woman's lover, the wretched creature. I hate such meanness, signorina, I will poison her.'

As Cecca said those words, with an unfeigned air of the deepest and most benevolent sympathy, she managed to catch her long loose scarf as if by accident in the corner of the light table where Minna's half-finished cup of coffee was still standing, and to upset it carelessly on to the floor of the studio. The cup with a crash broke into a hundred pieces.

At that very moment Colin entered. He saw Minna rising hastily from the settee beside the overturned table, and Cecca down on her knees upon the floor, wiping up the coffee hurriedly with one of the coarse studio towels. Cecca looked up in his face with a fearless glance as if nothing unusual had happened. 'An accident, signor,' she cried: 'my scarf caught in the table. I have spilt the signorina's cup of coffee. But no matter. I will run down immediately and tell them below to make her another.'

'Cecca and I have been talking together, Colin,' Minna said, replacing the fallen table hastily, 'and, do you know, isn't it strange, she's a fisherman's daughter in Calabria? and oh! Colin, I don't believe after all she's really half such a bad sort of girl as I took her to be when I first saw her. She's been talking to me here quite nicely and sympathetically.'

'Italians are all alike,' Colin answered, with the usual glib English faculty for generalisation about all 'foreigners.' 'They'll be ready to stab you one minute, and to fall upon your neck and kiss you the very next.'

Going out of the studio to order more coffee from the trattoria next door, Cecca happened to meet on the doorstep with her friend Giuseppe.

'Beppo,' she said, looking up at him more kindly than had been her wont of late: 'Beppo, I want to tell you something, I've changed my mind about our little difference. If you like, next Sunday you may marry me.'

'Next Sunday! Marry you!' Beppo exclaimed, astonished. 'Oh, Cecca, Cecca, you cannot mean it!'

'I said, next Sunday, if you like, you may marry me. That's good ordinary sensible Calabrian, isn't it? If you wish, I'll give it you in Tuscan: you can understand nothing but Tuscan, it seems, since you came to Rome, my little brother.'

She said the words tenderly, banter as they were, in their own native dialect: and Beppo saw at once that she was really in earnest.

'But next Sunday,' he exclaimed. 'Next Sunday, my little one! And the preparations?'

'I am rich!' Cecca answered calmly. 'I bring you a dower. I am the most favourite model in all Rome this very moment.'

'And the Englishman, the Englishman? What are you going to do with the Englishman?'

'The Englishman may marry his sweetheart if he will,' the girl replied with dogged carelessness.

'Cecca! you did not give the.... medicine to the Englishman?'

Cecca drew the half-empty bottle from her pocket and dashed it savagely against the small paving-stones in the alley underfoot. 'There,' she cried, eagerly, as she watched it shiver into little fragments. 'See the medicine! That is the end of it.'

'And the cat, Cecca?'

Cecca drew a long breath. 'How much of it would hurt a human being, a woman?' she asked anxiously. 'Somebody has drunk a little by mistake, just so much!' And she measured the quantity approximately with the tip of her nail upon her little finger.

Giuseppe shook his head re-assuringly, shrugged his shoulders, and opened his hands, palms outward, as if to show he was evidently making no mental reservation. 'Harmless!' he said. Quite harmless. It would take a quarter of a phial at least to produce any effect worth speaking of.'

Cecca clasped her silver image of the Madonna ecstatically. 'That's well, Beppo,' she answered with a nod. 'I must go now. On Sunday, little brother! On Sunday. Beppo, Beppo, it was all a play. I love you. I love you.'

But as she went in to order the coffee the next second, she said to herself with a regretful grimace: 'What a fool I was after all to waste the medicine! Why, if only I had thought of it. I might have used it to poison the other one, the tall Englishwoman. She shall not be allowed to steal away the little signorina's lover!'

CHAPTER XXXVIII

GWEN HAS A VISITOR

In the gardens of the Villa Panormi, Gwen Howard-Russell was walking up and down by herself one morning, a few days later, among the winter flowers (for it was now January), when she saw a figure she fancied she could recognise entering cautiously at the main gate by the high road to the Ponte Molle. Why, yes, she couldn't be mistaken. It was certainly the woman Cecca, the beautiful model down at Mr. Colin Churchill's studio! How very extraordinary and mysterious! What on earth could she be coming here for?

Gwen walked quickly down to meet the girl, who stood half hesitating in the big central avenue, and asked her curiously what she wanted.

'Signorina,' Cecca answered, not unrespectfully, 'I wish to speak with you a few minutes in private.'

Gwen was surprised and amused at this proposal, but not in the least disconcerted. How deliciously Italian and romantic! Mr. Churchill had sent her a letter, no doubt, perhaps a declaration, and he had employed the beautiful model to be the naturally appropriate bearer of it. There's something in the very air of Rome that somehow lends itself spontaneously to these delightful mystifications. In London, now, his letter would have been delivered in the ordinary course of business by the common postman! How much more poetical, and antique, and romantic, to send it round by the veritable hands of his own beautiful imaginary Wood Nymph!

'Come this way,' she said, in her imperious English fashion; 41 will speak with you down here in the bower.'

Cecca followed her to the bower in silence, for she resented our brusque insular manners: and somewhat to Gwen's surprise when she reached the bower, she seated herself like an equal upon the bench beside her. These Italians have no idea of the natural distinctions between the various social classes.

'Well,' Gwen asked, after a moment's pause. 'What do you want to say to me? Have you brought me any message or letter?'

'No, signorina,' the girl answered somewhat maliciously. 'Nothing: nothing. I come to speak to you of my own accord solely.'

There was another short pause, as though Cecca expected the English lady to make some further inquiry: but as Gwen said nothing, Cecca began again: 'I want to tell you something, signorina. You know the little English governess, the master's cousin?'

'Yes, I know her. That is to say, I have met her.'

'Well, I have come to tell you something about her. She is a fisherman's daughter, as I am, and she was brought up, far away, in a village in England, together with the master.'

'I know all about her,' Gwen answered somewhat coldly. 'She was a servant afterwards at a house in London, and then she became a teacher in a school, and finally a governess. I have heard all that before, from a friend of mine in England.'

'But I have something else to tell you about her,' Cecca continued with unusual self-restraint for an Italian woman. 'Something else that concerns you personally. She was brought up with the master, and she used to play with him in the meadows, when she was a child, where he made her little images of the Madonna in clay; and that was how he first of all began to be a sculptor. Then she followed him from her village to a city: and there he learned to be more of a sculptor. By-and-by, he came to Rome: but still, the little signorina loved him and wished to follow him. And at last she did follow him, because she loved him. And the master loves her, too, and is very fond of her. That is all that I have to tell you.'

She kept her eye fixed steadily on Gwen while she spoke, and watched in her cat-like fashion to see whether the simple story was telling home, as she meant it to do, to Gwen's intelligence. As she uttered the words she saw Gwen's face grow suddenly scarlet, and she knew she had rightly effected her intended purpose. She had struck the right chord in Gwen's pride, and Minna now would have nothing more to fear from the tall Englishwoman. 'Safer than the poison,' she thought to herself reflectively, 'and as it happens, every bit as useful and effectual, without half the trouble or danger.'

Gwen looked at her steadily and without flinching. 'Why do you say all this to me?' she asked haughtily.

'Because I knew it closely concerned you,' Cecca replied, in her coolest tone: 'and I see from your face, too, signorina, whatever you choose to say, that I was not mistaken.'

And indeed, in that one moment, the whole truth about Minna and Colin, never before even suspected by her, had flashed suddenly across Gwen's mind with the most startling vividness. She saw it all now, as clear as daylight. How could she ever have been foolish enough for a moment not to have understood it? Colin Churchill didn't make love to her for the very best of all possible reasons, because he was already in love with another person: and that other person was nobody else but the little governess with the old-fashioned bonnet. She reeled a little at the suddenness of the revelation, but she managed somehow or other to master her confusion and even to assume externally a careless demeanour.

'But what interest have you in telling me this?' she asked again of Cecca haughtily.

'Because I like the little signorina,' Cecca answered quite truthfully, 'and I was anxious to do anything on earth I could to serve her.'

After all, except for her casual little provincial leaning towards the use of poison (quite pardonable in a pretty Calabrian), Cecca was really not a bad sort of girl at bottom, as girls go in this strange and oddly blended universe of ours.

'Is that all you have to say to me?' Gwen enquired after another short pause, with ill-affected languor, of the beautiful model.

'That is all, signorina. I see you understand me. Good morning.'

'Stop!' Gwen said, taking out her purse uneasily. 'You have done me, too, a service, my girl. Take that for your trouble in coming here.'

Cecca drew herself up proudly to her full height. She was an Italian peasant woman, and yet she could resist an offer of money. 'No, no, signorina,' she answered as haughtily as Gwen herself. 'I want no reward: I am rich, I am the queen of the models. I did it for love of the little lady.' And she walked with a stately salute out of the bower and down the solid marble steps of the great garden.

When she was gone, Gwen buried her face in her hands for a moment, and cried bitterly. It was not so much the disappointment that she felt, though she had really been very much in love with Colin Churchill, as the humiliation of knowing that Cecca had discovered both her secret and her disappointment. And indeed, Cecca's short disclosure had given a sudden death-blow to all Gwen's dearest and most deeply-rooted projects. In the inmost depths of her proud heart, Gwen Howard-Russell felt with instinctive unquestioning resolution that it would be impossible now under any circumstances for her to marry Colin Churchill. If it had been any other woman in the world save only little simple Minna, Gwen might have taken a sort of keen delight of battle in winning her sweetheart's love cleverly away from her. She might have fought her for her lover all along the line with feminine strategy, and enjoyed the victory all the better in the end because she had had to struggle hard for it. For though our hypocritical varnished civilisation is loth to confess it, in Europe at least it is always the women who are competing covertly among themselves for the small possible stock of husbands. How can it be otherwise when for every 'eligible' man in our society there are usually about half a dozen marriageable women? But the moment Gwen knew and realised that Colin was in love with Minna, or even that Minna was in love with Colin, she felt immediately that the game was now rendered absolutely impossible; for Minna had once been a servant, a common servant, a London parlour-maid, and Gwen Howard-Bussell could not for one moment bring down her proud head to treat a servant as even a conceivable rival. Oh, no, as soon as she thought it possible that Minna might even in her own heart aspire to marry Colin Churchill, there was nothing on earth left for her but to retire immediately from the utterly untenable position.

She could have married Colin himself, of course, in spite of all his past, as humble even as Minna's, for he had genius; and in a man genius is universally allowed to atone for everything. A woman may stoop to marry a man below her own position in the social scale by birth, if it is generally understood that she does it as a graceful and appreciative tribute to literary, scientific, or artistic greatness. But to put herself in rivalry as it were with a woman, not even a genius, and born beneath her, in a struggle for the hand of such a man, who ought rather of course to receive hers gratefully, as a distinguished favour, why, the whole thing is obviously an absolute impossibility. So Gwen dried her eyes as well as she was able, with her little dainty cambric pocket-handkerchief, and settled with herself at once and finally that the Colin Churchill day-dream was now at last dispelled for ever.

He was in love with the little governess, the little governess with the old-fashioned bonnet! And the little governess had been a parlour-maid in London! And she herself, Gwen Howard-Russell, had been on the very verge of putting herself in unworthy rivalry with her! She shuddered to think of it, actually shuddered even to think of it. The very idea was so horribly repugnant to her. And how many women of her own social status are there in this realm of England who would not have sympathised therein with Gwen Howard-Russell? Our pride is so much stronger than our Christianity, and in this case, oddly enough, the one power brought about pretty much the same practical result in the long run as the other.

As Gwen rose with red eyes and flushed cheeks, to make her way back to her own bedroom, she saw, as she passed along the shrubby orache hedge that separated the garden from the high-road, a wistful face looking anxiously and eagerly from outside, in the direction of the great villa. She knew in a moment whose it was: it was Hiram Winthrop's. He had stolen away from his studio and the Capture of Babylon, to come out that morning to the dusty roads of the suburbs, and see if he could catch a passing glimpse anywhere of Gwen Howard-Russell. His face was pale and anxious, and Gwen saw for herself in a second that he was wasted with his eagerness in waiting for her deferred answer. Her heart went forth for the moment to that sad devoted expression. 'Poor fellow,' she muttered to herself compassionately, 4 he's very much in love with me, very much in love with me. I wish to goodness I could only have given him a favourable answer.'

CHAPTER XXXIX

GWEN'S DECISION

There were five days yet to run before the expiration of the fortnight which Gwen had promised to give to the consideration of Hiram's proposal, and in the course of those five days Gwen met her Yankee admirer again, quite accidentally, on two separate occasions, though both times in company with other people. Half insensibly to herself, since the sudden collapse of that little bubble fancy about Colin Churchill, she had begun to take a somewhat different view of poor Hiram's earnest entreaty. Of course she didn't in the least intend to say yes to him at last, in spite of Cecca's timely disclosures; she wasn't the sort of girl to go and throw herself into the arms of the very first man who happened to ask her, for no better reason in the world than merely because she had just met with a first serious disappointment; but still, she couldn't help reflecting to herself how deeply the young American was in love with her, and contrasting his eager, single-hearted, childlike devotion with the English sculptor's utter insensibility and curious indifference. Ah, yes, there could be no denying that much at any rate, that Hiram Winthrop was most profoundly and desperately in love with her. Love at first sight, too! How very romantic! He had carried away her image for ever with him through all these long weary years, ever since the day when he first met her, so long ago, by the merest accident, beside the Lake of the Thousand Islands.

A first serious disappointment, did she say? Well, well, that was really making a great deal too much, even to herself, of a girl's mere passing maidenly fancy. She had never herself been actually in love, not to say exactly in love, you know, with Mr. Colin Churchill. Oh, no, she had never gone so far as that, of course, even in her most unguarded moments of self-abandoned day-dreaming. Girls will have their fancies, naturally, and one can't prevent them; you think a particular young man is rather nice, and rather handsome, and rather agreeable; and you imagine to yourself that if he were to pay you any very marked attentions, don't you know, well there, one can't help having one's little personal preferences, anyhow, now can one? But as to saying she was ever really in love with Mr. Churchill, why, how can you possibly ever be in love with a man who never for a single moment takes as much as the slightest notice of you? And yet—how odd!—men and women must certainly be very differently constituted in these respects, when one comes to think of it; for that poor little Mr. Winthrop had been madly in love with her for years and years, almost without her ever even so much as for one moment discovering it or suspecting it!

Oh, no, she had never been in the least in love with Mr. Colin Churchill. And even if she had been (which she hadn't, but only—well, what you may call rather struck with him, he was such a very clever sculptor, and she was always so fond of artists' society)—but still, even if she had been (just to put the case, you know), she couldn't think of going on with it any further now, of course, for it wouldn't be Christian to try and entice that poor little governess girl's lover away from her, even if it hadn't been the case that she had been once upon a time a common servant. Poor little thing! though it was a pity that Mr. Churchill should ever think of throwing himself away on such an utter little nonentity as she was, still it would be very hard on her undoubtedly, if, after she had taken the trouble to raise herself as much as she could into his position in life, she should go and lose her lover after all, that she had so long been looking up to. Yes, in its own way it was a very proper arrangement indeed that Mr. Churchill should end at last by marrying the poor little dowdy governess.

And yet he was a very great sculptor, to be sure, and she, Gwen, had always had a wonderful fancy for marrying an artist.

But Mr. Winthrop's landscapes were really very beautiful too; and after all, painters are so very much more human in the end than those cold, impassive, marble-hearted sculptors. And what a lonely life Mr. Winthrop had always led! and how he seemed to yearn and hunger and thirst, as he spoke to her, for warm living and human sympathy! He had never had a sister, he said, and his mother, crushed and wearied by hard farm life and his father's religious sternness, had died while he was still a mere schoolboy. And he had never known anybody he could love but Gwen, except only, of course, dear Mr. Audouin; and after all, say what you will of it, a man, you know, a man is not a woman. Poor fellow, in her heart of hearts she was really sorry for him. And what a rage papa would be in, too, if only she were to accept him!

Papa would certainly be in a most dreadful temper; that was really quite undeniable. Gwen hardly knew herself, in fact, what ever he would do or say to her. He had a most unreasoning objection to artists in the concrete, regarding them, in fact, as scarcely respectable, and he had a still more unreasoning objection to all Americans, whom he hated, root and branch, as a set of vulgar, obtrusive, upstart nobodies. To be sure, Mr. Winthrop, now, was by no means obtrusive: quite the contrary; nor was he even vulgar, though he did certainly speak with a very faint American accent; and as to his being a nobody, why, if it came to that, of course it was papa himself who was really the nobody (though he was a Howard-Russell and a colonel in the line), while Mr. Winthrop was a very clever and interesting artist. So in fact, if, just to put the case again, she ever did decide upon accepting him, she wasn't going to stand any nonsense of that sort from papa, you know, and that was just the long and the short of it.

With a girl of Gwen's high-spirited temperament it is probable that Hiram could hardly have had a better ally in his somewhat hopeless suit than this dim hypothetical consciousness on her part of the colonel's decided objection to Hiram as a possible husband.

If you want very much to marry a girl like Gwen, suggest to her incidentally, as you make your offer, that her parents will of course be very much opposed to a marriage between you. If that doesn't decide her to take your view of the matter, nothing on earth will, you may depend upon it.

And so the fortnight sped away, and at the end of it, Hiram Winthrop came up, as if by accident, one morning early to the Villa Panormi. The earl and the colonel were having a quiet game, with their after-breakfast cigars, in the billiard-room, and Hiram and Gwen had the big salon entirely to themselves for their final interview.

As Hiram entered, hardly daring to hope, and pale with restrained passion, Gwen had already made up her mind beforehand that she must say no to him: but at the very sight of his earnest face and worn eyelids her resolution suddenly faltered. He was desperately in love with her:—that was certain; she could hardly find it in her heart to dismiss him summarily. She would delay and temporise with him just for the moment. Poor fellow, if she blurted it out to him too bluntly and hastily, it might almost stun him. She would break her refusal to him gently, very gently.

'Well, Miss Russell,' he said to her eagerly, taking her hand as he entered with a faint hesitating pressure, 'you see I have come back for my answer; but before you give it to me, for good or for evil, there are one or two matters yet that I want to talk over with you very particularly.'

Gwen trembled a little as she seated herself on the big centre ottoman, and answered nervously, 'Well, Mr. Winthrop, then let me hear them.'

'I ought to plead for myself,' Hiram went on in a feverish voice, looking down on the ground and then up in her face alternately every half second. 'I ought to plead for myself with all my power, and all my soul, and all my energy, Miss Russell; for though to you this is only a matter of saying yes or no to one more suitor, and no doubt you have had many, to me it is a matter of life and death, for I never in my life for one moment imagined that I loved or could love any other woman; and if you refuse me now, I never in my life shall love another. If you refuse me, I shall lose heart altogether, and throw up this foolish painting business at once and for ever, and go back again to drive the plough and cut the corn once more in my own country. To that I have made my mind up irrevocably; so I ought to plead for myself, seeing how much is at stake, with all my heart and soul and energy.'

Gwen crumpled up the corners of the oriental antimacassar in her tremulous fingers as she answered very softly, 'I should be sorry to think you meant to do anything so unwise and so unjust to the world and to yourself on my account, Mr. Winthrop.'

'I ought to plead for myself, and to plead only,' Hiram went on, like one who has got a message to deliver and feels impelled to deliver it without heed of interruptions. 'I ought to say nothing that might in any way interfere with any faint chance I may possibly possess of winning your favour. I know how little likely I am to succeed, and I can't bear to make my own case seem still weaker and feebler to you. But, Miss Russell, before you answer me, and I'm not going to let you answer me yet, until you have heard me to the end fully, there are one or two things more I feel constrained to say to you. I want to make you understand exactly what you will have to do and to put up with if by any chance you promise to marry me.' (Gwen blushed slightly at the word, so seriously spoken, but could not take her eyes away from his earnest face as he still went on rapidly speaking.) 'In the first place, I am a very poor painter, and I have nothing on earth but my art to live upon.'

'If that were all,' Gwen said, unconsciously taking his part, as it were, 'I don't think that to be an artist's wife, however poor he may be, is a life that any woman on earth need be anything but proud of.'

'Thank you,' Hiram said fervidly, looking up at her once more with a sudden gleam of newborn hope upon his pale worn countenance. 'Thank you, thank you. I know you are one of those who can value art at its true worth, and I was sure before I spoke that that at least need be no barrier between us. And as I am an American, and as proud of my old Puritan New England ancestry as any gentleman in old England could possibly be of his Norman forefathers or his broad acres, I won't pretend to apologise to you on the score of birth, or connections, or social position. That is a thing, if you will excuse my saying so, Miss Russell, that no American can under any circumstances stoop to do. Your father is proud, I know; but every descendant of the New England pilgrims is indeed in his own democratic way a great deal prouder.'

That was a point of view that, to say the truth, had never struck Gwen before as even possible; still, as Hiram said it, so boldly and unaffectedly, she felt in her heart that it was really nothing more than the truth, and though she couldn't quite understand it or sympathise with the feeling, she respected him for it, and admired his open manliness in saying it so straightforwardly.

'But while I think nothing of what your own relations would doubtless consider the disparity in our positions,' Hiram went on earnestly, 'I do think a great deal of this, that I have at present absolutely no means of my own upon which to marry. If you consent, as I begin to hope you will consent, to be my wife, sooner or later, we may have to wait a long long time, perhaps even for years, before we can marry. I have risked everything upon my success as a painter. I have eaten up my capital to keep myself alive through my student period. I can find no purchasers now for the pictures I am painting. And I don't know whether the public will ever care to buy them at all, because I can't make up my own mind, even, whether I really am or am not a tolerable painter.'

'Upon that point, Mr. Winthrop,' Gwen said decidedly, 'I haven't myself the very slightest doubt or hesitation. I know you are a painter, and a very touching one; and I'm sure the world must find it out some day, sooner or later.'

Quite unconsciously to himself, Hiram was playing his own game in the very surest possible manner by seeming to take sides for the moment against himself, and so compelling Gwen, out of the mere necessities of the conversation, to argue the case for the defence with all a woman's momentary impetuosity.

'But I ought to have thought of all this before I ever spoke to you at all,' he went on earnestly. 'I ought to have reflected how cruel it was of me to ask you for a promise when I couldn't even tell whether I might ever be in a position to enable you to perform it. It was wrong of me, very wrong; and I felt angry with myself for having been led into doing it, the minute after I left you. But I was betrayed into my confession by the accidents of the moment. You must forgive me, because I had loved you so long, and so silently. I wouldn't have spoken to you even then if I hadn't imagined, it was ever so wrong and foolish of me, but still I imagined, that you seemed just then to be a little more interested than before in my work and my future. Oh, Miss Russell, I have loved you desperately; and I ventured, therefore, in a moment of haste to tell you that I loved you. But if you say yes to me to-day, it may be years and years, perhaps, before we can marry. I can't say when or how I may ever begin to earn my livelihood at all by painting pictures.'

'If I really loved a man, Mr. Winthrop,' Gwen answered in a lower voice, 'I shouldn't be afraid to wait for him as long as ever circumstances compelled it, if I really loved him. And apart altogether from that question, which you say I am not at present to answer, I can't believe that the world will be much longer yet in discovering that you have genius, yes, I will say genius. Mr. Churchill himself declares he is quite certain you have real genius.

Hiram smiled and shook his head incredulously. 'Still,' he said, 'it is at least some comfort to me to know that, putting the matter in its most abstract form, you have no absolute objection to a long engagement. If you loved a man, you would be ready to wait for him. I knew you would, indeed, like every brave and true woman. I didn't doubt that you could be steadfast enough to wait; I only doubted whether it would be just of any man to beg you to wait under such more than doubtful circumstances. But, remember, Miss Russell, I have this excuse to plead in my own case, that it wasn't the passing fancy of a moment, but a love that has grown with me into my very being. There is only one more consideration now before I go on to ask you that final answer to my question, and it is this. You must reflect whether you would be willing to brave the anger of your father. I can't disguise from myself the fact that Colonel Howard-Russell would be very ill satisfied at the idea of your waiting to marry a penniless unknown American painter.'

Gwen looked at him proudly, almost defiantly, as she answered in a clear bold tone, 'If I loved a man really, Mr. Winthrop, I would marry him and wait for him as long as I chose, even if my father cast me off for it for ever the very next minute. If ever I marry I shall marry because I have consulted my own heart, and not because I have consulted my father.'

'I knew that too,'Hiram answered, with just a touch of triumph in his trembling voice. 'I only spoke to you about it because I thought it right to clear the ground entirely for my final question. Then, Gwen, Gwen, Gwen, I will call you Gwen for this once in my life, if I never call you Gwen again as long as I live here; I have thought of you as Gwen for all these years, and I will think of you so still, whatever comes, till my dying minute, oh, Gwen, Gwen, Gwen, I ask you finally, and all my life hangs upon the question, can you love me, will you love me, do you love me?'

Gwen let him fold her passionately in his arms as she murmured twice, almost inaudibly, 'I love you! I love you!'

Yes, yes, she couldn't any longer herself withstand the conviction. She loved him. She loved him.

As for Hiram, the blood thrilled through his veins as though his heart would burst for very fulness. The dream of his existence had come true at last, and he cared for nothing else on earth now he had once heard Gwen say with her own dear lips that she loved him, she loved him.

CHAPTER XL

AFTER THE STORM

When Gwen told the colonel the very same evening that she had actually gone and got herself engaged to that shock-headed Yankee painter fellow, the colonel's wrath and grief and indignation were really something wonderful to observe and excellent to philosophise upon. The colonel raved, and stamped, and fretted; the colonel fumed in impotent rage, and talked grimly about his intentions and his paternal authority (just as if he had any); the colonel even swore strange Hindustani oaths at Gwen's devoted head, and supplemented them by all the choicest and most dignified military expletives to be found in the vocabulary of his native language. But Gwen remained perfectly unmoved by all the colonel's threats and imprecations; she flatly remarked that his testamentary dispositions were a subject in no way interesting or amusing to her, and stuck firm to her central contention, that it was she who was going to marry Hiram, and not her father, and that therefore she was the only person whose tastes and inclinations in the matter ought to be taken into any serious consideration. And though the colonel persisted in declaring that he for his part would never allow that Gwen was in any proper sense engaged to Hiram, Gwen herself stood to it stoutly that she was so engaged; and after all, her opinion on the subject was really by far the most important and conclusive of any.

In fact, the more the colonel declaimed against Hiram, the more profoundly convinced did Gwen become in her own heart that she thoroughly loved and admired him. And the final consequence of the colonel's violent opposition was merely this, that at the end of three weeks or so Gwen was as madly in love with her American painter fellow as any woman on this earth had ever yet been with a favoured lover.

As for poor Hiram, he was absolutely in the seventh heaven for the time being, and though a little later on he began to reproach himself bitterly at times for having tied down Gwen so prematurely to his own exceedingly doubtful fortunes, he could think as yet of nothing on earth but his delight at having actually won the love of the lady of his one long impassioned daydream.

On the day after Gwen had accepted Hiram's timid offer, Colin Churchill met Miss Howard-Russell accidentally in the Corso.

'Oh, Miss Russell,' he said, 'will you come on Sunday next to see my model, Cecca, married to her old Calabrian lover? She's very anxious you should come and assist, and she begged me most particularly to invite you. She says you're a friend of hers, and that the other day you did her and her lover a good service.'

'Tell her I'll be there, Mr. Churchill,' Gwen answered, smiling curiously, 'and tell her too that I have acted upon her advice, and she will understand you. Where's the wedding to be, and when must I be there?'

'At ten o'clock, close by our house, at Santa Maria of the Beautiful Ladies. She was to have been married a fortnight ago quite suddenly; but she changed her mind in a hurry at the last moment, because she hadn't got all her things ready. It'll be a dreadful loss to me, of course; for when once a model marries, you can never get her to sit again half as well as she used to do; but Cecca had a lover, it seems, who had followed her devotedly to Rome all the way from Monteleone; and she played fast-and-loose with him at first and rode the high horse, on the strength of her being so much admired and earning so much money as a model; and now she's seized with a sudden remorse, it appears, and wants to make it all up with him again and get married immediately.'

Gwen smiled a silent smile of quiet comprehension. 'I see,' she said. 'One can easily understand it. I shall be there, Mr. Churchill; you may depend upon me. And your cousin the, the Miss Wroe, I mean, will she be there also?'

'Oh yes,' Colin answered lightly, 'Minna's coming too. She and Cecca have most mysteriously struck up quite a singular and sudden friendship.'

'I shall be glad to meet her again,' Gwen said simply. Somehow, when once one has settled firmly one's own affections, one feels a newborn and most benevolent desire to expedite to the best of one's abilities everybody else's little pending matrimonial arrangements.

So on Sunday Cecca was duly married, and the colonel and the earl were induced by Gwen to be present at the ceremony; though the colonel had his scruples upon the point, for, like most old Anglo-Indians of his generation, he was profoundly evangelical in his religious views, and regarded a Roman Catholic church as a place only to be visited under protest, by way of a show, with every decent expression of distaste and irreverence. Still, he knew his duty as a father; and when Gwen declared that if he didn't accompany her she would take Cousin Dick alone, and go without him, the colonel reflected wisely that she would probably meet that shock-headed Yankee painter fellow after the ceremony, and have another chance of talking over this absurd engagement she imagined she'd contracted with him. So he went himself to mount guard over her, and to give that Yankee fellow a piece of his mind if occasion offered.

And when the wedding was over, the whole party of guests, including Hiram and Audouin, adjourned for breakfast to the big room at Colin Churchill's studio, which had been laid out and decorated by Cecca and Minna and the people at the trattoria the evening before for that very purpose. And the Italian peasant folk sat by themselves at one end of the long wooden table, and the English excellencies also by themselves at the other. And Colin proposed the bride's health in his very best Tuscan: and Giuseppe made answer with native Italian eloquence in the nearest approach he could attain to the same exalted northerly dialect. And everybody said it was a great success, and even Cecca herself felt immensely proud and very happy. But I'm afraid my insular English readers will still harbour an unworthy prejudice against poor simple easy-going Calabrian Cecca, for no better reason than just because she tried, in a moment of ordinary Italian jealousy, to poison Minna Wroe in a cup of coffee. Such are the effects of truculent Anglo-Saxon narrowness and exclusiveness.

When Gwen and Minna went into Cecca's dressing-room to take off their bonnets (for Colin insisted that they should make a day of it), Gwen was suddenly moved by that benevolent instinct aforesaid to make a confidante of the pretty little governess, who, by the way, had got a new and more fashionable bonnet from a Roman Parisian milliner expressly for the happy occasion. Poor little thing! after all, it was very natural she should be dreadfully in love with her handsome clever sculptor cousin. 'I myself very nearly fell in love with him once, indeed,' Gwen murmured to herself philosophically, with the calm inner confidence of a newly-found affection. So she said to Minna with a meaning look, after a few arch little remarks about Colin's success as a rising sculptor, 'I have something to tell you, Miss Wroe, that I think will please you. I tell it to you because I know the subject is one you're much interested in; but, if you please you must treat it as a secret, a very great secret. I'm—well, to tell you the truth, Miss Wroe, I'm engaged to be married.'

Minna's face turned pale as death, and she gasped faintly, but she answered nothing.

Gwen saw the cause of her anxiety at once, and hastened eagerly to reassure her.

'And if you'll promise not to say a word about it to anybody on earth, I'll tell you who it is, it's your cousin's American friend, Mr. Hiram Winthrop.'

Minna looked at her for a second in a transport of joy, and then burst suddenly into a flood of tears.

Gwen didn't for a moment pretend to misunderstand her. She knew what the tears meant, and she sympathised with them too deeply not to show her understanding frankly and openly. After all, the little governess was really at heart just a woman even as she herself was. 'There, there, dear,' she said, laying Minna's head upon her shoulder tenderly; 'cry on, cry on; cry as much as ever you want to; it'll do you good and relieve you. I know all about it, and I was sure you mistook me for a moment, and had got a wrong notion into your head, somehow; and that was why I took the liberty of telling you my little secret. It's all right, dear; don't be in the least afraid about it. Here, Cecca, quick; a glass of water!'

Cecca brought the water hastily, and then looking up with a wondering look into the tall Englishwoman's clear-cut face, she asked sternly, 'What is this you have been saying to the dear little signorina?'

Gwen laid Minna down in a chair, after loosening her bonnet, and bathing her forehead with water; and then taking Cecca aside, she whispered to her softly, 'It's all right. Don't be afraid that I had forgotten or repented. I was telling her something that has pleased and delighted her. I am, I am going to be married, too, Cecca; but not to the master, to somebody else—to another artist, who has loved me for years, Signora Cecca; only mind, it's a secret, and you mustn't say a word for worlds to anybody about it.

Cecca smiled, and nodded knowingly. 'I see,' she said with a perfect shower of gestures. 'I see. It is well, indeed. To the American! Felicitations, signorina.'

'Hush, hush!' Gwen cried, putting her hand upon the beautiful model's mouth hastily. 'Not a word about it, I beg of you! Well now, dear, how are you feeling after the water? Are you better? are you better?'

'Thank you, Miss Russell; it was only a minute's faintness. I thought—It's all right now. I'm better, Miss Russell, I'm better.'

Gwen looked at her tenderly as if she had been a sister. 'Your name's Minna, dear, I think,' she said; 'isn't it?'

Minna nodded acquiescence.

'And mine, I dare say you know, is Gwen. In future let us always call one another Gwen and Minna.'

She held out her arms caressingly, and Minna, forgetful at once of all her old wrath and jealousy of the grand young lady, nestled into them with a childlike look of unspeakable gratitude. 'It's very kind of you,' she cried, kissing Gwen's lull red lips two or three times over, 'so very, very kind of you. You can't tell how much you've relieved me, Miss Russell. You know, I'm so very fond, so very fond—so very fond of dear Colin.'

Gwen kissed her in return sympathetically.

'I know you are, dear,' she answered warmly.

'And you needn't be afraid; I'm sure he loves you, he can't help loving you. You dear little thing, he must be a stone indeed if he doesn't love you. Cecca says he does, and Cecca's really a wonderful woman at finding out all these things immediately by a kind of instinct. But if ever you dare to call me Miss Russell again from this very minute forward, why, really, Minna, I solemnly declare I shall be awfully angry with you.'

Minna smiled and promised cheerfully. In truth, at that moment her heart was full to overflowing. Her rivals, both of her real or imaginary rivals, were at last safely disposed of, and if only now she could be perfectly sure that Colin loved her! Gwen said so, and Cecca said so, but Colin didn't. If only Colin would once say to her in so many words, 'Minna, I love you. Will you marry me?' Oh, how happy she would be, if only he would say so!

CHAPTER XLI

AUDOUIN'S MISTAKE

Lothrop Audouin walked round a little tremblingly to the Villa Panormi. He wasn't generally a shy or nervous man, but on this particular afternoon he felt an unwonted agitation in his breast, for he was bound to the Villa on a very special errand; and he was glad when he saw Gwen Howard-Russell walking about alone in the alleys of the garden, for it saved him the necessity of having to make a formal call upon her in the big salon. Gwen saw him coming, and moved towards the heavy iron gate to meet him.

She gave him her hand with one of her sunniest smiles, and Audouin took it, as he always did, with antique Massachusetts ceremoniousness. Then he turned with her, almost by accident as it were, down the path bordered by the orange-trees, and began to talk as he loved so well to talk, about the trees, and the flowers, and the green-grey lizards, that sat sunning themselves lazily upon the red Roman tiles which formed the stiff and formal garden edging.

'Though these are not my own flowers, you know, Miss Russell,' he said at last, looking at her a little curiously. 'These are not my own flowers; and indeed everything here in Rome, even nature itself, always seems to me so overlaid by the all-pervading influence of art that I fail to feel at home with the very lilies and violets in this artificial atmosphere In America, you know, my surroundings are so absolutely those of unmixed nature: I lead the life of a perfect hermit in an unsophisticated and undesecrated wilderness.'

'Mr. Winthrop has told me a great deal about Lakeside,' Gwen answered lightly, and Audouin took it as a good omen that she should have remembered the very name of his woodland cottage. 'You live quite among the primæval forest, don't you, by a big shallow bend in Lake Ontario?'

'Yes, quite among the primæval forest indeed; from my study window I look out upon nothing but the green pines, and the rocky ravine, and the great blue sheet of Ontario for an infinite background. Not a house or a sign of life to be seen anywhere, except the flying-squirrels darting about among the branches of the hickories.'

'But don't you get very tired and lonely there, with nobody but yourself and your servants? Don't you feel dreadfully the want of congenial cultivated society?'

Audouin sighed pensively to hide the beating of his heart at that simple question.

Surely, surely, the beautiful queenly Englishwoman was leading up to his hand! Surely she must know what was the natural interpretation for him to put upon her last inquiry! It is gross presumptuousness on the part of any man to ask a woman for the priceless gift of her whole future unless you have good reason to think that you are not wholly without hope of a favourable answer; but Gwen Howard-Russell must certainly mean to encourage him in the bold plunge he was on the verge of taking. It is hard for a chivalrous man to ask a woman that supreme question at any time: harder still when, like Lothrop Audouin, he has left it till time has begun to sprinkle his locks with silver. But Gwen was evidently not wholly averse to his proposition: he would break the ice between them and venture at last upon a declaration.

'Well,' he answered slowly, looking at Gwen half askance in a timid fashion very unlike his usual easy airy gallantry, 'I usen't to think it so, Miss Howard; I usen't to think it so. I had my books and my good companions, Plato, and Montaigne, and Burton, and Rabelais. I loved the woods and the flowers and the living creatures, and all my life long, you know, I have been a fool to nature, a fool to nature. Perhaps there was a little spice of misanthropy, too, in my desire to fly from a base, degrading, materialised civilisation. I didn't feel lonely in those days;—no, in those days, in those days, Miss Russell, I didn't feel lonely.'

He spoke hesitatingly, with long pauses between each little sentence, and his lips quivered as he spoke with girlish tremulousness and suppressed emotion. He who was usually so fluent and so ready with his rounded periods, he hardly managed now to frame his tongue to the few short words he wished to say to her. Profoundly and tenderly respectful by nature to all women, he felt so deeply awed by Gwen's presence and by the magnitude of the favour he wished to ask of her, that he trembled like a child as he tried to speak out boldly his heart's desire. It was not nervousness, it was not timidity, it was not diffidence; it was the overpowering emotion of a mature man, pent up till now, and breaking over him at last in a perfect inundation through the late-opened floodgates of his repressed passion. For a moment he leaned his hand against the projecting rockery of the grotto for support; then he spoke once more in a hushed voice, so that even Gwen vaguely suspected the real nature of his coming declaration.

'In those days,' he repeated once more, with knees failing under him for trembling, 'in those days I didn't feel lonely; but since my last visit to Rome I have felt Lakeside much more solitary than before. I have tired of my old crony Nature, and have begun to feel a newborn desire for closer human companionship. I have begun to wish for the presence of some kind and beautiful friend to share its pleasures with me. I needn't tell you, Miss Russell, why I date the uprising of that feeling from the time of my last visit to Italy. It was then that I first learned really to know and to admire you. It is a great thing to ask, I know, a woman's heart, a true noble woman's whole heart and affection; but I dare to beg for it, I dare to beg for it. Oh, Miss Russell, oh, Gwen, Gwen, will you have pity upon me? will you give it me? will you give it me?' As he spoke, the tall strong-knit man, clutching the rock-work passionately for support, he looked so pale and faint and agitated that Gwen thought he would have fallen there and then, if she gave him the only possible answer too rudely and suddenly.

So she took his arm gently in hers, as a daughter might take a father's, and led him to the seat at the far end of the orange alley by the artificial fountain. Audouin followed her with a beating heart, and threw himself down half fainting on the slab of marble.

'Mr. Audouin,' Gwen began gently, for she pitied his evident overpowering emotion from the bottom of her heart, 'I can't tell you how sorry I am to have to say so, but it cannot possibly be; it can never be, never, so it's no use my trying to talk about it.'

A knife struck through Audouin's bosom at those simple words, and he grew still paler white than ever, but he merely bowed his head respectfully, and, crushing down his love with iron resolution, murmured slowly, 'Then forgive me, forgive me.' His unwritten creed would not have permitted him in such circumstances to press his broken suit one moment longer.

'Mr. Audouin,' Gwen went on, 'I'm afraid I have unintentionally misled you. No, I don't want you to go yet,' she added with one of her imperious gestures, for he seemed as if he would rise and leave her; 'I don't want you to go until I have explained it all to you. I like you very much, I have always liked you; I respect you, too, and I've been pleased and proud of the privilege of your acquaintance. Perhaps in doing so much, in seeking to talk with you and enjoy your society, I may have seemed to have encouraged you in feelings which it never struck me you were at all likely to harbour. I—I liked you so sincerely that I never even dreamt you might fancy I could love you.' 'And why, Miss Russell?' Audouin pleaded earnestly. 'If you dismiss me so hopelessly, let me know at least the reason of my dismissal. It was very presumptuous of me, I know, to dare to hope for so much happiness; but why did you think me quite outside the sphere of your possible suitors?'

'Why, Mr. Audouin,' Gwen said in a low tone, 'I have always looked upon you rather as one might look upon a father than as one might look upon a young man of one's own generation. I never even thought of you before to-day except as somebody so much older and wiser, and altogether different from myself, that it didn't occur to me for a single moment you yourself wouldn't feel so also.' Audouin's despairing face brightened a little as he said, 'If that is all, Miss Russell, mayn't I venture to look upon your answer as not quite final; mayn't I hope to leave the question open yet a little, so that you may see what time may do for me, now you know my inmost feeling? Don't crush me hopelessly at once; let me linger a little before you utterly reject me. If you only knew how deeply you have entwined yourself into my very being, you wouldn't cast me off so lightly and so easily.'

Gwen looked at him with a face full of unfeigned pity. 'Mr. Audouin,' she answered, 'I know how truly you are speaking. I should read your nature badly if I didn't see it in your very eyes. But I cannot hold you out any hope in any way. I like you immensely; I feel profoundly sorry to have to speak so plainly to you. I know how great an honour you confer upon me by your offer; but I can't accept it, it's quite impossible that I can ever accept it. I like you, and respect you more than I ever liked or respected any other person, except one; but there is one person I like and respect even more, so you see at once why it's quite impossible that I should listen to you about this any longer.'

'I understand,' Audouin answered slowly. 'I understand. I see it all now. Colin Churchill has been beforehand with me. While I hesitated, he has acted.'

Gwen's lips broke for a moment into a quiet smile, and she murmured softly, 'No, not Colin Churchill, Mr. Audouin, not Colin Churchill, but Hiram Winthrop. I think, as I have said so much, I ought to tell you it is Hiram Winthrop.'

Audouin's brain reeled round madly in grief and indignation at that astonishing revelation. Hiram Winthrop! His own familiar friend; his dearest ward and pupil! Was it he, then, who had stolen this prize of life, unseen, unsuspected, beneath his very eyesight? If Gwen had never fancied that Audouin could fall in love with her, neither could Audouin ever have suspected it of Hiram Winthrop. If Gwen had looked upon Audouin as a confirmed old bachelor of the elder generation, Audouin had looked upon Hiram as a mere boy, too young yet to meddle with such serious fancies. And now the boy had stolen Gwen from him unawares, and for half a second, all loyal as he was, Audouin felt sick and angry in soul at what he figured to himself as Hiram's cruel and ungrateful duplicity.

'Hiram Winthrop!' he muttered angrily. 'Hiram Winthrop! How unworthy of him! how unkind of him! how unjust of him to come between me and the one object he ever knew me set my heart upon!'

'But, Mr. Audouin,' Gwen cried in warmer tones, 'Hiram no more dreamt of this than I did; he took it for granted all along that you knew he loved me, but he never spoke of it because you know he is always reserved about everything that concerns his own personal feelings.'

The marble seat reeled and the ground shook beneath Audouin's feet as he sat there, his brow between his hands, and his elbows upon his knees, trying to realise the true bearings of what Gwen was saying to him. Yes, he saw it all plainly now; it dawned upon him slowly: in his foolish, selfish, blind preoccupation, he had been thinking only of his own love, and wholly overlooking Gwen's and Hiram's. 'What a short-sighted fool I have been, Miss Russell!' he cried, broken-spirited. 'Yes, yes; Hiram is not to blame. I only am to blame for my own folly. If Hiram loves you, and you love Hiram, I have only one duty left before me: to leave you this moment, and to do whatever in me lies to make you and Hiram as happy as I can. No two people on this earth have ever been dearer to me. I must try to change my attitude to you both, and learn that I am old enough to help even now to make you happy.' In his perfect loyalty, Audouin almost forgot at once his passing twinge of distrust for Hiram, and thought only of his own blindness. He rose slowly from the marble seat, and Gwen noticed that as he rose he seemed to have aged visibly in those few minutes. The suddenness and utterness of the disappointment had unmistakably crushed him. He staggered a little as he rose; then in a faltering voice he said, 'Good-bye, good-bye, Miss Russel.' Gwen turned away her face, and answered regretfully, 'Good-bye, Mr. Audouin.'

He raised his hat, with a touch of old-fashioned courtesy in his formal bow, and walked away quickly, out of the garden, and back towards the hotel where he had been then stopping. For some time his disappointment sat upon him so heavily that he could only brood over it in a vague, half unconscious fashion; but at last, as he passed the corner of the big piazza a thought seemed to flash suddenly across his dazzled brain, and he turned round at once, in feverish haste, pacing back moodily towards the Villa Panormi. 'How selfish of me!' he said to himself in angry self-expostulation, 'how selfish and cruel of me to have forgotten it! How small and narrow and petty we men are, after all! In my dejection at my own disappointment, I have quite overlooked poor Hiram. Love may be all that the poets say about it, I don't know, I can't say, how should I, a lonely wild man of the woods, who know not the ways of women? But one thing I do know: it's a terrible absorbing and self-centring passion. A man thinks only of him and her, and forgets all the rest of the world entirely, as though he were a solitary savage wooing in the gloom his solitary squaw. And yet they write about it as though it were the very head and front of all the beatitudes!'

He walked, or almost ran, to the Villa Panormi, and looked anxiously for Gwen in the alleys of the garden. She wasn't there: she had gone in evidently. He must go to the door and boldly ask for her. Was the signorina at home, he enquired of the servant. Yes, the signorina had just come in: what name, signor? Audouin handed the man his card, and waited with a burning heart in the long open salon.

In a minute Gwen sent down word by her English maid: she was very sorry; would Mr. Audouin kindly excuse her?—she was suffering from headache.

'Tell Miss Russell,' Audouin answered, so earnestly that the girl guessed at once something of his business, 'that I must see her without delay. The matter is important, immediate, urgent, and of more interest to her than even to me.'

He waited again for fully ten minutes. Then Gwen sailed into the room, queen-like as ever, and advanced towards him smiling; but he saw she had been crying, and had bathed her eyes to hide it, and he felt flattered in his heart even then at that womanly tribute of sympathy to his bitter disappointment. 'Miss Russell,' he said, with all the sincerity of his inner nature speaking vividly in his very voice, 'I am more sorry than I can say that I'm compelled to come back so soon and speak with you again after what has just happened. We may still be always firm friends, I'm sure; I shall try to feel towards you always as an elder brother: but I know you would have liked a day or two to pass before we met again on what is to me at least a new footing. Still, I felt compelled to come back and tell you something which it is of great importance that you should know at once. Miss Bussell, you mustn't on any account breathe a word of all this in any way to Hiram. Don't think I'm speaking without good reason. As you value your own happiness, don't breathe a word of it to Hiram.'

Gwen saw from his exceeding earnestness that he had some definite ground for this odd warning, and it piqued her curiosity to know what that ground could possibly be. 'Why, Mr. Audouin?' she asked simply.

'Because it would cause you great distress, I believe,' Audouin answered evasively. 'Because it would probably prevent his ever marrying you. Oh, Miss Russell, do please promise me that you'll say nothing at all to him about it.'

'But I can't promise, Mr. Audouin,' Gwen answered slowly. 'I can't promise. I feel I ought to tell him. I think a woman ought to tell her future husband everything.'

'Miss Russell,' Audouin went on, still more solemnly than before, 'I beg of you, I implore you, I beseech you, for the sake of your own future and Hiram's, don't say a word to him of this.'

'But why, why, Mr. Audouin? You give me no reason, no explanation. If you won't explain to me, you'll only frighten me the more into telling Hiram, because your manner seems so excited and so mysterious. I can't promise or refuse to promise until I understand what you mean by it.'

'I had rather not explain to you,' Audouin went on hesitatingly. 'I should prefer not to have told you. Indeed, unless you compel me, I will never tell you. But from my own knowledge of Hiram's character I feel sure that if you let him know about this he will never, never marry you. He is so unselfish, so good, so delicately self-sacrificing, that if he hears of this he will think he mustn't claim you. I have known him, Miss Russell, longer than you have; I can count better on what he would do under any given circumstances. Most men are selfish and blind in love; I was so just now: I have been all along, when in my personal eagerness to win your esteem I never noticed what was indeed as clear as daylight, that Hiram must have been in love with you too. But Hiram is not selfish and blind, even in love; of that I'm certain. He would never marry you if he thought that by so doing he was putting himself in rivalry with me.'

'And why not?' Gwen asked, with her large eyes looking through and through Audouin's to their very centre. 'Why not with you in particular?'

'Because,' Audouin answered, faltering, and trying to withdraw his gaze from hers, but unsuccessfully, for she seemed to mesmerise him with her keen glance, 'because, Miss Bussell, if you force me to tell you, I have been of some little service at various times to Hiram, and have placed him under some slight obligations, whose importance his generous nature vastly overestimates. I am quite sure, from what I know of him, that if he thought I had ever dreamt of the possibility of asking you to put up with my poor little individuality, he would never feel himself at liberty to marry you; he would think he was being unfriendly and (as he would say) ungrateful. I dare say you will fancy to yourself that I am making him out but a cold lover. I am not, Miss Russell; I am giving him the highest praise in my power. I feel confident that, though he loved you as the apple of his eye, he wouldn't sacrifice what he thought honour and duty even for your sake.'

Gwen looked at him steadily, and answered in a trembling voice, 'I will say nothing to him about it, Mr. Audouin, nothing at all until after we are married. Then, you know, then I must tell him.'

'Thank you,' Audouin said gently. 'That will do sufficiently. Thank you, thank you. If it hadn't been a matter of such urgency I wouldn't have troubled you with it now. But as I went along the road homeward, heavy at heart, as you may imagine, it struck me like a flash of lightning that you might speak to Hiram about it this very day, and that Hiram, if he heard it, might withdraw his pretensions, so to speak, and feel compelled to retire in my favour. And as he loves you, and as you love him, I should never have forgiven myself if that had happened, had even momentarily happened. You will have difficulties and perplexities enough in any case without my adding my mite to them, I feel certain. And I was so appalled at my own wicked selfishness in having overlooked all this, that I felt constrained to come back, even at the risk of offending you, and set the matter at rest this very afternoon. I won't detain you a moment longer now. Good-bye, Miss Russell, good-bye, and thank you.'

Gwen looked at him again as he stood there, with his face so evidently pained with the lasting pain of his great disappointment, utterly oblivious of self even at that supreme hour in his thought for his friend, yet reproaching himself so unfeignedly for his supposed selfishness, and she thought as she looked how truly noble he was at heart after all. The outer shell of affectation and mannerism was all gone now, and the true inner core of the man lay open before her in all its beautiful trustful simplicity. At that moment Gwen Howard-Russell felt as if she really loved Lothrop Audouin, loved him as a daughter might love a pure, generous, tender father. She looked at him steadily for a minute as he stood there with his hand outstretched for hers, and then, giving way to her natural womanly impulse for one second, she cried, 'Oh, Mr. Audouin, I mustn't love you, I mustn't love you; but I can't tell you how deeply I respect and admire you!' And as she spoke, to Audouin's intense surprise and joy, yes, joy, she laid both her hands tenderly upon his shoulders, drew him down to her unresisting, and kissed him once upon the face as she had long ago kissed her lost and all but forgotten mother. Then, with crimson cheeks, and eyes flooded with tears, she rushed away, astonished and half angry with herself for the audacious impulse, yet proudly beautiful as ever, leaving Audouin alone and trembling in the empty salon.

Audouin was too pure at heart himself not to accept the kiss exactly as it was intended. He drew himself up once more, ashamed of the fluttering in his unworthy bosom, which he could not help but feel; and saying in his own soul gently, 'Poor little guileless heart! she takes me for better than I am, and treats me accordingly,' he sallied forth once more into the narrow gloomy streets of Rome, and walked away hurriedly, he cared not whither.

CHAPTER XLII

A DISTINGUISHED CRITIC

It was a very warm morning in the Via Colonna, for many weeks had passed, and May was coming on: it was a warm morning, and Hiram was plodding away drearily by himself at his heroic picture of the Capture of Babylon, with a stalwart young Roman from the Campagna sitting for his model of the Persian leader, when the door unexpectedly opened, and a quiet-looking old gentleman entered suddenly, alone and unannounced. This was one of Hiram's days of deepest despondency, and he was heartily sorry for the untimely interruption. 'Mr. Churchill sent me to look at your pictures.' the stranger said in explanation, in a very soft, pleasant voice. 'He told me I might possibly see some things here that were really worth the looking at.'

Poor Hiram sighed somewhat wearily. 'Churchill has too good an opinion altogether of my little attempts,' he said in all sincerity.

'I'm afraid you'll find very little here that's worthy your attention. May I venture to ask your name?'

'Never mind my name, sir,' the old gentleman said, with a blandness that contrasted oddly with the rough wording of his brusque sentences. 'Never you mind my name, I say, what's that to you, pray? My name's not at all in question. I've come to see your pictures.'

'Are you a dealer, perhaps?' Hiram suggested, with another sigh at his own excessive frankness in depreciating what was after all his bread and butter, and a great deal more to him. 'You want to buy possibly?

'No, I don't want to buy,' the old gentleman answered flatly, with a certain mild and kindly fierceness. 'I don't want to buy certainly. I'm not a dealer; I'm an art-critic.'

'Oh, indeed,' Hiram said politely. The qualification is not one usually calculated to endear a visitor to a struggling young artist.

'And you, I should say by your accent, are an American. That's bad, to begin with. What on earth induced you to leave that cursed country of yours? Oh generation of vipers, don't misinterpret that much-mistaken word generation; it means merely son or offspring, who has warned you to flee from the wrath that is?'

Hiram smiled in spite of himself. 'Myself,' he said; 'my own inner prompting only.'

'Ha, that's better; so you fled from it.

You escaped from the city of destruction. You saved yourself from Sodom and Gomorrah. Well, well, having had the misfortune to be born an American, what better thing could you possibly do? Creditable, certainly, very creditable. And now, since you have come to Rome to paint, pray what sort of wares have you got to show me?'

Hiram pointed gravely to the unfinished Capture of Babylon.

'It won't do,' the old gentleman said decisively, after surveying the principal figures with a critical eye through his double eyeglass. 'Oh, no, it won't do at all. It's painted, I admit that; it's painted, solidly painted, which is always something nowadays, when coxcombs go splashing their brushes loosely about a yard or two of blank canvas, and then positively calling it a picture. It's painted, there's no denying it. Still, my dear sir, you'll excuse my saying so, but there's really nothing in it, absolutely nothing. What does it amount to, after all? A line farrago of tweedledum and tweedledee, in Assyrian armour and Oriental costume, and other unnatural, incongruous upholsterings, with a few Roman models stuck inside it all, to do duty instead of lay figures. Do you really mean to tell me, now, you think that was what the capture of Babylon actually looked like? Why, my dear sir, speaking quite candidly, I assure you, for my own part I much prefer the Assyrian bas-reliefs.'

Hiram's heart sank horribly within him. He knew it, he knew it; it was all an error, a gigantic error. He had mistaken a taste for painting for a genius for painting. He would never, never, never make a painter; of that he was now absolutely certain. He could have sat down that moment with his face between his hands and cried bitterly, even as he had done years before when the deacon left him in the peppermint lot, but for the constraining presence of that mild-mannered ferocious oddly-compounded old gentleman.

'Is this any better?' he asked humbly, pointing with his brush-handle to the Second Triumvirate.

'No sir, it is not any better,' the relentless critic answered as fiercely yet as blandly as ever. 'In fact, if it comes to that, it's a great deal worse. Look at it fairly in the face and ask yourself what it all comes to. It's a group of three amiable sugar-brokers in masquerade costume discussing the current price-lists, and it isn't even painted, though it's by way of being finished, I suppose, as people paint nowadays. Is that drawing, for example,' and he stuck his forefinger upon young Cæsar's foreshortened foot, 'or that, or that, or that, or that, sir? Oh, no, no; dear me, no. This is nothing like either drawing or colouring. The figure, my dear sir, you'll excuse my saying so, but you haven't the most rudimentary conception even of drawing or painting the human figure.'

Hiram coincided so heartily at that moment in this vigorous expression of adverse opinion, that but for Gwen he could have pulled out his pocket-knife on the spot and made a brief end of a life long failure.

But the stranger only went coolly through the studio piece by piece, passing the same discouraging criticisms upon everything he saw, and after he had finally reduced poor Hiram to the last abyss of unutterable despair, he said pleasantly in his soft, almost womanly voice, 'Well, well, these are all sad trash, sad trash certainly. Not worth coming from America to Rome to paint, you must admit; certainly not. Who on earth was blockhead enough to tell you that you could ever possibly paint the figure? I don't understand this. Churchill's an artist; Churchill's a sculptor; Churchill knows what a human body's like, he's no fool, I know. What the deuce did he send me here for, I wonder? How on earth could he ever have imagined that those stuffed Guy Fawkeses and wooden marionettes and dancing fantoccini were real living men and women? Preposterous, preposterous. Stay. Let me think. Churchill said something or other about your trying landscape. Have you got any landscapes, young man, got any landscapes?'

'I've a few back here,' Hiram answered timidly, 'but I'm afraid they're hardly worth your serious consideration. They were mostly done before I left America, with very little teaching, or else on holidays here in Europe, in the Tyrol chiefly, without much advice or assistance from competent masters.'

'Bring them out!' the old gentleman said in a tone of command. 'Produce your landscapes. Let's see what this place America is like, this desert of newfangled towns without, any castles.'

Hiram obeyed, and brought out the poor little landscapes, sticking them one after another on the easel in the light. There were the Thousand Island sketches, and the New York lakes, and the White Mountains, and a few pine-clad glens and dingles among the Tyrolese uplands and the lower Engadine. The stranger surveyed them all attentively through his double eyeglass with a stony critical stare, but still said absolutely nothing. Hiram stood by in breathless expectation. Perhaps the landscapes might fare better at this mysterious person's unsparing hands than the figure pieces. But no: when he had finished, the stranger only said calmly, 'Is that all?'

'All, all,' Hiram murmured in blank despair. 'The work of my lifetime.'

The stranger looked at him steadily.

'Young man,' he said with the voice and manner of a Hebrew prophet, 'believe me, you ought never to have come away from your native America.'

'I know it, I know it,' Hiram cried, in the profoundest depth of self-abasement.

'No, you ought never to have come away from America. As I wrote years ago in the Seven Domes of Florence—'

'What!' Hiram exclaimed, horror-stricken.

'The Seven Domes of Florence! Then—then—then you are Mr. Truman?'

'Yes,' the stranger went on unmoved, without heeding his startled condition. 'My name is John Truman, and, as I wrote years ago in the Seven Domes of Florence—'

Hiram never heard the end of his visitor's long sonorous quotation from his former self (in five volumes), for he sank back unmanned into an easy-chair, and fairly moaned aloud in the exceeding bitterness of his disappointment.

John Truman! It was he, then, the great art-critic of the age; the man whose merest word, whose slightest breath could make or mar a struggling reputation; the detector of fashionable shams, the promoter of honest artistic workmanship, it was he that had pronounced poor Hiram's whole life a miserable failure, and had remitted him remorselessly once more to the corn and potatoes of Geauga County. The tears filled Hiram's eyes as he showed the great man slowly and regretfully out of his studio; and when that benevolent beaming face had disappeared incongruously with the parting Parthian shot, 'Go back to your woods and forests, sir; go back immediately to your woods and forests,' Hiram quite forgot the very presence of the decked-out Persian commander, and burst into hot tears such as he had not shed before since he ran away to nurse his boyish sorrows alone by himself in the old familiar blackberry bottom.

How very differently he might have felt if only he could have followed that stooping figure down the Via Colonna and heard the bland old gentleman muttering audibly to himself, 'Oh, dear no, the young barbarian ought never to have come away from his native America. No castles, certainly not, but there's nature there clearly, a great deal of nature; and he knows how to paint it too, he knows how to paint it. Great purity of colouring in his Tyrolese sketches; breadth and brilliancy very unusual in so young an artist; capital robust drawing; a certain glassy liquid touch that I like about it all, too, especially in the water. Who on earth ever told him to go and paint those incomprehensible Assyrian monstrosities? Ridiculous, quite ridiculous. He ought to have concentrated himself on his own congenial lakes and woodlands. He has caught the exact spirit of them, weird, mysterious, solemn, primitive, unvulgarised, antidemotic, titanic, infinite. The draughtsmanship of the stratification in the rocks is quite superb in its originality. Oh, dear no, he ought never to have come away at all from his native natural America.

CHAPTER XLIII

THE SLOUGH OF DESPOND

Mr. Audouin,' Hiram cried, bursting into his friend's rooms in a fever of despair, three days later, 'I've come to tell you I'm going back to America!'

'Back to America, Hiram!' Audouin cried in dismay, for he guessed the cause instinctively at once. 'Why, what on earth do you want to do that for?'

Hiram flung himself back in moody dejection on the ottoman in the corner. 'Why,' he said, 'do you know who has been to see me? Mr. Truman.'

'Well, Hiram?' Audouin murmured, trembling.

'Well, he tells me I've made a complete mistake of it. I'm not a painter, I can't be a painter, and I never could possibly make a painter. Oh, Mr. Audouin, Mr. Audouin, I knew it myself long ago, but till this very week I've hoped against hope, and never ventured fully to realise it. But I know now he tells the truth. I can't paint, I tell you, I can't paint, no, not that much!' And he snapped his fingers bitterly in his utter humiliation.

Audouin drew a chair over softly to his friend's side, and laid his hand with womanly tenderness upon the listless arm. 'Hiram,' he said in a tone of deep self-reproach, 'it's all my fault; my fault, and mine only. I am to blame for all this. I wanted to help and direct and encourage you; and in the end, I've only succeeded in making both of us supremely miserable!'

'Oh, no,' Hiram cried, taking Audouin's hand warmly in his own, 'not your fault, dear Mr. Audouin, not your fault, nor mine, but nature's. You thought there was more in me than there actually was, that was kindly and friendly and well-meant of you. You fancied you had found an artistic genius, an oasis in the sandy desert of Geauga County, and you wanted to develop and assist him. It was generous and noble of you; if you were misled, it was your own sympathetic, appreciative, disinterested nature that misled you. You were too enthusiastic. You always thought better of me than I have ever thought of myself; but if that's a fault, it's a fault on the nobler side, surely. No, no, nobody is to blame for this but myself, my own feeble self, that cannot rise, whatever I may do, to the difficult heights you would have me fly to.' Audouin looked at him long and silently. In his own heart, he had begun to feel that Hiram's heroic figure-painting had turned out a distinct failure For that figure-painting he, Lotlirop Audouin, was alone responsible. But, even in spite of the great name of Truman urged against him, he could hardly believe that Hiram would not yet succeed in landscape. 'Did Truman see the Tyrolese sketches?' he asked anxiously at last.

'Yes, he did, Mr. Audouin.'

'And what did he say about them?'

'Simply that he thought I ought never to have come away from America.'

Audouin drew a long breath. 'This is very serious, Hiram,' he said slowly. 'I apprehend certainly that this is very serious. Truman's opinion is worth a great deal; but, after all, it isn't everything. I've led you wrong so long and so often, my poor boy, that I'm almost afraid to advise you any farther; and yet, do you know, I can't help somehow believing that you will really do great things yet in landscape.'

'Never, never,' Hiram answered firmly.

'I shall never do anything better than the edge of the lake at Chattawauga!'

'But you have done great things, Hiram,' Audouin cried, warming up with generous enthusiasm, just in proportion as his protégés spirits sank lower and lower. 'My dear fellow, you have done great things already. I'll stake my reputation upon it, Hiram, that the lake shore at Chattawauga's a piece of painting that'll even yet live and be famous.' Hiram shook his head gloomily. 'No, no,' he said; 'I mean to take Mr. Truman's advice, and go back to hoe corn and plant potatoes in Muddy Creek Valley. That's just about what I'm fit for.'

'But, Hiram,' his friend said, coming closer and closer to him, 'you mustn't dream of doing that. In justice to me you really mustn't. I've misled you and wasted your time, I know, by inducing you to go in for this wretched figure-painting. It doesn't suit you and your idiosyncrasy: that I see now quite clearly. All my life long it's been a favourite doctrine of mine, my boy, that the only true way of salvation lies in perfect fidelity to one's own inner promptings. And how have I carried out that gospel of mine in your case? Why, by absurdly inducing you to neglect the line you naturally excel in, and to take up with a line that you don't personally care a pin for. Now, dear Hiram, my dear, good fellow, don't go and punish me for this by returning in a huff' to Geauga County. Have pity upon me, and spare me this misery, this degradation. I've suffered much already, though you never knew it, about this false direction I've tried to give your genius (for you have genius, I'm sure you have): I've lain awake night after night and reproached myself for it bitterly: don't go now and put me to shame by making my mistake destroy your whole future career and chances as a painter. It need cost you nothing to remain. I misled you by getting you to paint those historical subjects. I see they were a mistake now, and I will buy the whole of them from you at your own valuation. That will be only just, for it was for me really that you originally painted them. Do, do please reconsider this hasty decision.' Hiram rocked himself to and fro piteously upon the ottoman, but only answered, 'Impossible, impossible. You are too kind, too generous.'

Audouin looked once more at his dejected dispirited face, and then, pausing a minute or two, said quietly and solemnly, 'And how about Gwen, Hiram?'

Hiram started up in surprise and discomfiture, and asked hastily, 'Why, what on earth do you know about Gwen, about Miss Russell, I mean, Mr. Audouin?'

'I can't tell you how I've surprised your secret, Hiram,' Audouin said, his voice trembling a little as he spoke: 'perhaps some day I may tell you, and perhaps never. But I've found it all out, and I ask you, my boy, for Gwen's sake, for Miss Russell's sake, to wait awhile before returning so rashly to America. Hiram, you owe it as a duty to her not to run away from her, and fame and fortune, at the first failure.'

Hiram flung himself down upon the ottoman again in a frenzy of despondency. 'That's just why I think I must go at once, Mr. Audouin,' he cried, in his agony. 'I only know two alternatives. One is America; the other is the Tiber.'

'Hiram, Hiram!' his friend said soothingly. 'Yes, yes, Mr. Audouin, I know all that, I know what you want to say to me. But I can't drag down Gwen, born and brought up as she has been, I can't drag her down with me to a struggling painter's pot-boiling squalidness. I can't do it, and I won't do it, and I oughtn't to do it; and the kindest thing for her sake, and for all our sakes, would be for me to get out of it all at once and altogether.'

'Then you will go, Hiram?'

'Yes, I will go, Mr. Audouin, by the very next Trieste steamer.'

He rose slowly from the ottoman, shook his friend's hand in silence, and went away without another word. Audouin saw by his manner that he really meant it, and he sat down wondering what good he could do to countervail this great unintentional evil he had done to Hiram.

'Lothrop Audouin,' he said to himself harshly, 'a pretty mess you have made now of your own life and of Hiram Winthrop's! Is this your perfect fidelity to the inner promptings, this your obedience to the unspoken voice of the divine human consciousness? You poor, purblind, affected, silly, weak, useless creature, I hate you, I hate you. Go, now, see what you can do to render happy these two better lives that you have done your best to ruin for ever.'

If any other man had used such words of Lothrop Audouin, he would have shown himself a bitter, foolish, short-sighted cynic. But as Lothrop Audouin said it himself, of course he had a full right to his own opinion.

Yet some men, not wholly bad men either, might have rejoiced at the thought that they would thus get rid of a successful rival. They would have said to themselves, 'When Hiram is gone, Gwen will soon forget him, and then I may have a chance at least of finally winning her favour.' In this belief, they would have urged Hiram, in a halfhearted way only, not to return to America; and if afterwards he persisted in his foolish intention, they might have said to themselves, 'I did my best to keep him, and now I wash my hands forever of it.' All's fair, says the proverb, in love and war; and many men still seem to think so. But Audouin was made of different mould; and having once frankly wooed and lost Gwen, he had no single shadow of a thought now left in his chivalrous mind save how to redress this great wrong he conceived he had done them, and how to make Gwen and Hiram finally happy.

He sat there long, musing and wondering, beating out a plan of action for himself in his own brain, till at last he saw some gleam of hope clear before him. Then he rose, took down his hat quickly from the peg, and hurried round to Colin Churchill's studio. He found Colin working away busily at the moist clay of Agamemnon and Clytemnestra.

'Churchill,' he said seriously, 'you must put away your work for an hour. I want to speak to you about something very important.'

Colin laid down his graver reluctantly, and turned to look at his unexpected visitor.

'Why, great heavens, Mr. Audouin,' he said, 'what can be the matter with you? You really look as white as that marble.'

'Matter enough, Churchill. Who do you think has been to see Winthrop? Why, John Truman.'

'Oh, I know,' Colin answered cheerfully. 'I sent him myself. And what did he say then?'

'He said that Winthrop ought to go back to America, and that he would never, never, never make a decent painter.'

Colin whistled to himself quickly, and then said, 'The dickens he did! How remarkable! But did Winthrop show him the landscapes?' 'Yes, and from what he says, Truman seems to have thought worse of them than even he thought of the figure pieces.'

'Impossible!' Colin cried incredulously. 'I don't believe it; I can't believe it. Truman knows a landscape when he sees it. There must be some mistake somewhere.'

'I'm afraid not,' Audouin answered sadly. 'I've begun to despair about poor Winthrop myself, a great deal of late, and to reproach myself terribly for the share I've had in putting his genius on the wrong metals. The thing we've got to do now is to face the actuality, and manage the best we can for him under the circumstances. Churchill, do you know, Hiram threatens to go back to America by the next steamer, and take to farming for a livelihood.'

Colin whistled low again. 'He mustn't be allowed to do it,' he said quickly. 'He must be kept in Rome at all hazards. If we have to lock him up in jail or put him into a lunatic asylum, we must keep him here for the present, whatever comes of it. I'm sure as I am of anything, Mr. Audouin, that Hiram Winthrop has a splendid future still before him.'

'Well, Churchill,' Audouin said calmly, 'I want you to help me in a little scheme I've decided upon. I'm going to make my will, and I want you to be trustee under it.'

'Make your will, Mr. Audouin! Why, what on earth has that to do with Hiram Winthrop? I hope you'll live for many years yet, to see him paint whole square yards of splendid pictures.'

Audouin smiled a little sadly. 'It's well to be prepared against all contingencies,' he said with a forced gaiety of tone: 'and I want to provide against one which seems to me by no means improbable. There's no knowing when any man may die. Don't the preachers tell us that our life hangs always by a thread, and that the sword of Damocles is suspended forever above us?'

Colin looked at him keenly and searchingly. Audouin met his gaze with frank open eyes, and did not quail for a moment before his evident curiosity. 'Well, Churchill,' he went on more gravely, 'I'm going to make my will, and I'll tell you how I'm going to make it. I propose to leave all my property in trust to you, as a charity in perpetuity. I intend that you shall appoint some one young American artist as Audouin Art Scholar at Home, and pay to him the interest on that property, so long as he considers that he stands in need of it. As soon as he, by the exercise of his profession, is earning such an income that he feels he can safely do without it, then I leave it to him and you to choose some other American Art student for the scholarship, to be enjoyed in like manner. On that second student voluntarily vacating the scholarship, you, he, and the first student shall similarly choose a third incumbent; and so on for ever. What do you think of the plan, Churchill, will it hold water?'

'But why shouldn't you leave it outright to Winthrop?' Colin asked, a little puzzled by this apparently roundabout proceeding. 'Wouldn't it be simpler and more satisfactory to give it to him direct, instead of in such a complicated fashion?'

'Who said a word about Winthrop being the first scholar?' Audouin answered with grave irony. 'You evidently misunderstand the spirit of the bequest. I want to advance American art, not to make a present to Hiram Winthrop. Besides,' and here Audouin lowered his voice a little more confidentially, 'if I left it to Hiram outright, I feel pretty confident he wouldn't accept it; he'd refuse the bequest as a personal matter. I know him, Churchill, better than you do; I know his proud sensitive nature, and the way he would shrink from accepting a fortune as a present even from a dead man, even from me, his most intimate friend and spiritual father. But if it's left in this way, he can hardly refuse; it will be only for a few years, till he gets his name up; it'll leave him free meanwhile to live and marry (if he wants to), and it'll be burdened with a condition, too, that he should go on studying and practising art, and that he should assist at the end of his own tenure in electing another scholar. That, I hope, would reconcile him (if the scholarship were offered to him) to the necessity of accepting and using it for a few years only. However, I don't wish, Churchill, to suggest any person whatsoever to you as the first student; I desire to leave your hands perfectly free and untied in that matter.'

'I see; I understand,' Cohn answered, smiling gently to himself. 'I will offer it, should the occasion ever arise, to the most promising young American student that I can anywhere discover.'

'Quite right, Churchill; exactly what I wish you to do. Then you'll accept the trust, and carry it out for me, will you?

'On one condition only, Mr. Audouin,' Colin said firmly, looking into his blanched face and straining eyeballs. 'On one condition only. Let me be quite frank with you—no suicide.'

Audouin started a little. 'Why, that's a fair enough proviso,' he answered slowly after a moment. 'Yes, I promise that. No suicide. We shall trust entirely to the chapter of accidents.'

'In that case,' Colin continued, reassured, 'I hope we may expect that the trusteeship will be a sinecure for many a long year to come. But I fail to see how all this will benefit poor Winthrop in the immediate future, if he means to sail for New York by the next steamer.'

'The two questions ought to be kept entirely distinct,' Audouin went on sharply, with perfect gravity. 'I fail myself to perceive how any possible connection can exist between them. Still, we will trust to the chapter of accidents. There's no knowing what a day may bring forth. We must try at least to keep Wintlirop here in Rome for another fortnight. That's not so very long to stay, and yet a great deal may be done in a fortnight. I'll go and look out at once for an American lawyer to draft my will for me. Meanwhile, will you just sign this joint note from both of us to Winthrop?'

He sat down hurriedly at Cohn's desk, and scribbled off a short note to poor Hiram.

'Dear Winthrop,—Will you as a personal favour to us both kindly delay your departure from Rome for another fortnight, by which time we hope we may be able to make different arrangements for you?

'Lothrop Audouin.'

He passed the note to Colin, and the pen with it. Colin read the doubtfully worded note over twice in a hesitating manner, and then, after some mental deliberation, added below in his clear masculine hand—'Colin Churchill.'

'Remember, Mr. Audouin,' he said as a parting warning. 'It's a bargain between us. No suicide.'

'Oh, all right,' Audouin answered lightly with the door in his hand. 'We trust entirely to the chapter of accidents.'

CHAPTER XLIV

THE CHAPTER OF ACCIDENTS

Next day, after seeing the American lawyer (caught by good luck at the Hôtel de Russie), and duly executing then and there his will in favour of Colin Churchill as trustee, Audouin sauntered down gloomily to the San Paolo station, and took the train by himself to a miserable little stopping place in the midst of the dreary desolate Campagna. It was a baking day, even in the narrow shaded streets of Rome itself; but out on the shadeless scorched-up Agro Romano the sun was pouring down with tropical fierceness upon the flat levels, one vast stretch of silent slopes, with lonely hollows interspersed at intervals, where even the sheep and cattle seemed to pant and stagger under the breathless heat of the Italian noontide. Audouin got out at the wayside road, gave up his ticket to the dirty military-looking official, passed the osteria and the half dozen feverish yellow-washed houses that clustered round the obtrusive modern railway, and turned away from the direction of the mouldering village on the projecting buttress of rock towards the mysterious, melancholy, treeless desert on the other side. It was just the place for Audouin to walk alone on such a day, with his whole heart sick and weary of a generous attempt ill frustrated by the unaccountable caprice of fate. He had tried to do his best for Hiram Winthrop, and he had only succeeded in making himself and his friend supremely unhappy. Audouin had never cared much for life, and he cared less for it that day than ever before. 'After all,' he said to himself, 'what use is existence to me? I had one mistress, nature: I have almost tired of her: she palled upon me, and I wanted another. That other would not take my homage; and nature, it seems, in a fit of jealousy, has revenged her slighted pretensions upon me, in most unfeminine fashion, by making herself less beautiful in my eyes than formerly. How dull and gloomy it all looks to-day! What a difficult world to live in, what an easy world to leave; if we had but the trick to do it!'

He walked along quickly, away from the hills and the village perched on an outlying spur of the distant Apennines, on to the summit of a rolling undulation in that great grassy sea of wave-like hillocks. Not a sound stirred the stagnant air. Away in front, towards the dim distant Mediterranean, the flat prairies of Ostia steamed visibly in the flickering sunlight; a low region of reeds and cane-brake, with feathery herbage unruffled by any passing breath of wind, and barely relieved from utter monotony by the wide dry umbrella-shaped bosses of the basking stone-pines of Castel Fusano. The malaria seemed to hang over it like a terrible pall, blinking before the eye over the heated reach of sweltering pasture lands. Yonder lay Alsium, Palo they call it nowadays, a Dutch oven of pestilence, breeding miasma in its thousand foul nooks for the inoculation of all the country round. In truth a sickly, sickening spot; but here, Audouin whispered to himself half apologetically, with self-evident hypocrisy, here on the higher moorlands of the Campagna, among the shepherds and the sheep, beside the shaggy briar and hillocks, a man may walk and not hurt himself surely. Colin Churchill had said, 'No suicide;' and that was a bargain between them; yet suicide was one thing, and a quiet afternoon stroll through the heart of the country was really another.

He had bought a flask of 'sincere wine' at the osteria, and had brought some biscuits with him in his pocket from Rome. He meant to lunch out here on the Campagna, and only return late to the hotel for dinner. When a man feels broken and dispirited, what more natural than that he should wish to escape by himself for a lonely tramp in the fields and meadows, where none will interrupt his flow of spleen and the run of his solitary meditations?

It would be quite untrue to say that Lothrop Audouin had come into the Campagna by himself that day on purpose to catch the Roman fever. Nothing could be more unjust or unkind to him. Wayward natures like his do not expect to have their actions so harshly judged by the unsympathetic tribunal of common-sense. They seldom do anything on purpose. Audouin was only tempting nature. He was trusting to the chapter of accidents. A man has a right to walk over the ground (if unenclosed and unappropriated) whenever he chooses; there can be nothing wrong in taking a little turn by oneself even among the desolate surging undulations of the great plain that rolls illimitably between Rome and Civita Vecchia. He was exercising his undoubted rights as an American citizen; he could go where he chose over those long unfenced slopes, where you may walk in a straight line for miles ahead, with nothing to hinder you save the sun and the fever. And the fever! Well, yes; he did perhaps have some slight passing qualms of conscience on that head, when he thought of his promise to Colin Churchill; but then of course that was straining language, interpreting it in non-natural senses. A man isn't bound to make a mollycoddle of himself simply because he has promised a friend that he won't commit suicide.

He sat down in the eye of the sun on a bit of broken rock, or at least it looked like rock, though it was really a fragment from the concrete foundations of some ancient villa, with his legs dangling over the deep brown bank of pozzolano earth, and his hat slouched deeply above his eyes to protect him from the penetrating sunlight. Dead generations lay beneath his feet; the air was heavy with the dust of unnumbered myriads. Lothrop Audouin took out his flask and drank his wine and ate his biscuits. An old contadino came up suspiciously to watch the stranger; Audouin offered him the remainder of the wine, and the man drank it off at a gulp and thanked his excellency with Italian profuseness.

Would his excellency buy a coin, the contadino went on slowly, with the insinuating Roman begging whine. Audouin looked at the thing carelessly, and turned it round once or twice in his fingers. It was a denarius of Trajan, apparently; he could read the inscription, Avg. Ger. Dac. p.m. Tri. pot. Cos. vii., and so forth. It might be worth half a lire or so. He gave the man two lire for it. Suicide indeed! Who talks of suicide? Mayn't a bit of a virtuoso come out on to the Campagna, quite legitimately, to collect antiquities?

The fancy pleased him, and he talked awhile with the contadino about the things he had found in the galleries that honeycomb for miles the whole Campagna. Yes, the man had once found a beautiful scarabæus, a scarabæus that might have belonged to Cæsar or St. Peter. He had found a lachrymatory, too, a relic of an ancient Christian; and many bones of holy martyrs. How did he know they were holy martyrs? The most illustrious was joking. When one finds bones in a catacomb, one knows they must have been preserved by miraculous interference.

Much ague on the Campagna? No, no, signor; an air most salubrious, most vital, most innocent. In the Ptfntine Swamps? oh there, by Bacchus, excellency, it is far different. There, the people die of fever by hundreds; it is a most desolate country; encumbered with dead and rotting vegetation, it procreates miasma, and is left to stagnate idly in the sun. The bottoms are all soft slime and ooze, where buffaloes wallow and wild boars hide. Nothing there save a solitary pot-house, and a few quaking, quavering, ague-smitten contadini, a bad place to live in, the Pontine Marshes, excellency. But here on the Agro Romano, high and dry, thanks to the Madonna and all holy saints, why, body of Bacchus, there is no malaria.

Or if any, very little. Towards nightfall, perhaps; yes, just a trifle towards nightfall; but what of that? One wraps one's sheepskin close around one; one takes care to be home early; one offers a candle now and then to the blessed Madonna; and the malaria is nothing. Except for foreigners. Ah, yes, foreigners ought always to be very sure not to stop out beyond nightfall.

Audouin let the man run on as long as he chose, and when the contadino was tired of conversation, he lay back upon the dry yellow grass, and thought bitterly to himself about life and fate, and Gwen and Hiram. What a miserable, foolish, impossible sort of world we all lived in after all! He had more money himself than he needed; he didn't want the nasty stuff, filthy lucre, filthy indeed in these days; dirty bank-notes, Italian or American, the first perhaps a trifle the dirtier and racrgeder of the two. He didn't want it, and Hiram for need of it was going to the wall; and yet he couldn't give it to Hiram, and Hiram wouldn't take it if he were to give it to him. Absurd conventionality! There was Gwen, too; Gwen; how happy he could make them both, if only they would let him; and yet, and yet, the thing was impossible. If only Hiram had those few wretched thousand dollars, scraps and scrips, shares and houses, Audouin didn't know exactly what they were or what was the worth of them; a lawyer in Boston managed the rubbish, if only Hiram had them, he could take to landscape, marry Gwen, and undo the evil that he, Lothrop Audouin, had unwittingly and unwillingly wrought in his foolish self-confidence, and live happily ever after. In fairy tales and novels and daydreams everybody always did live happy ever after, it's a way they have, somehow or other. The whole course of individual human history for the great Anglo-American race, in fancy anyhow, seems always to end with a wedding as its natural finale and grand consummation. Yet here he was, boxed up alone with all that useless money, and the only way he could possibly do any good with it was by ceasing to exist altogether. No suicide! oh, no, certainly not. Still, if quite accidentally he happened to get the Roman fever, nobody would be one penny the worse for it, while Gwen and Hiram would doubtless be a good deal the better.

The afternoon wore away slowly, and evening came on at last across the great shifting desolate panorama. The dirty greens and yellows began to flush into gold and crimson; the misty haze from the Pontine Marshes began to creep with deadly stealth across the Agro Romano; the grey veil began to descend upon the softening Alban hills in the murky distance; the purples on the hillside hollows began to darken into gloomy shadows. A little breeze had sprung up meanwhile, and rain was dropping slowly from invisible light drifting clouds upon the parched Campagna. The malaria is never so dangerous as after a slight rain, that just damps the dusty surface without really penetrating it; for then the germs that lie thick among the mouldering vegetation are quickened into spasmodic life, and the whole Campagna steams and simmers with invisible eddies of vaporous effluvia. But Audouin sat there still, moodily pretending to himself that his headache would be all the better for a few cooling drops upon his feverish forehead. Even the old contadino was on his way back to his wretched hut, and as he passed he begged his excellency to get back to the railway with the most rapid expedition. 'Fa cattivo tempo,' he cried with a warning gesture. But his excellency only strolled slowly towards the yellow-washed station, dawdling by the way to watch the shadows as they grew deeper and blacker and ever longer on the distant indentations of the circling amphitheatre of hills.

The sunset glow faded away into ashen greyness. The air struck cold and chill across the treeless levels. The wind swept harder and damper over the malarious lowland. Then the Campagna was swallowed up in dark, and Lothrop Audouin found his way alone, wet and steaming, to the tiny roadside station. The train from Civita Vecchia was not due for half an hour yet; he stood on the platform under the light wooden covering, and waited for it to come in with a certain profound internal sense of despairing resignation. His limbs were very cold, and his forehead was absolutely burning. Yes, yes, thank heaven for that! the chapter of accidents had not forsaken him. He felt sure he had caught the Roman fever.

When the English doctor came to see him at the hotel that evening, about eleven, the work of diagnosis was short and easy. 'Country fever in its worst and most dangerous form,' he said simply; 'in fact what we at Rome are accustomed to call the perniciosa.'

CHAPTER XLV

HOVERING

Acute Roman fever is a very serious matter. For seven days Audouin lay in extreme danger, hovering between life and death, with the crisis always approaching but never actually arriving. Every day, when the English doctor came to see him, Audouin asked feebly from his pillow, 'Am I getting worse?' and the doctor, who fancied he was a nervous man, answered cheerfully, 'Well, no, not worse; about the same again this morning, though I'm afraid I can't exactly say you're any better.' Audouin turned round wearily with a sigh, and thought to himself, 'How hard a thing it is to die, after all, even when you really want to.'

Colin Churchill came to see him as soon as ever he heard of his illness, and sitting in the easy-chair by the sick man's bedside, he said to him in a reproachful tone, 'Mr. Audouin, you don't play fair. You've broken the spirit of the agreement. Our compact was, no suicide. Now, I'm sure you've been recklessly exposing yourself out upon the Campagna, or else why should you have got this fever so very suddenly?'

Audouin smiled a faint smile from the bed, and answered half incoherently, 'Chapter of accidents. Put your trust in bad luck, and verily you will not be disappointed. But I'm afraid it's a terribly long and tedious piece of work, this dying.'

'If you weren't so ill,' Colin answered gravely and sternly, 'I think I should have to be very angry with you. You haven't stood by the spirit of the contract. As it is, we must do our best to defeat your endeavours, and bring you back to life again.'

Audouin moved restlessly in the bed. 'You must do your worst, I recognise,' he said; 'but I don't think you'll get the better of the fever for all that: she's a goddess, you know, and had her temple once upon the brow of the Palatine. Many have prayed to her to avoid them; it must be a novelty for her to hear a prayer for her good company. Perhaps she may be merciful to her only willing votary. But she's long about it; she might have got through by this time. Anyhow, you mustn't be too hard upon me, Churchill.'

As for Hiram, Audouin's illness came upon him like a final thunderclap. Everything had gone ill with him lately; he had reached almost the blackest abyss of despondency already; and if Audouin were to die now, he felt that his cup of bitterness would be overflowing. Besides, though he knew nothing, of course, of Audouin's interview with Colin Churchill, he had a grave suspicion in his own mind that his friend had egged himself into an illness by brooding over Truman's visit and Hiram's own proposals for returning to America. Of course all that was laid aside now, at least for the present. Whatever came, he must stop and nurse Audouin; and he nursed him with all the tender care and delicacy of a woman.

Gwen came round often, too, and sat watching in the sick-room for hours together. The colonel objected to it seriously, so very extraordinary, you know; indeed, really quite compromising; but Gwen was not to be kept away by the colonel's scruples and prejudices; so she watched and waited in her own good time, taking turns with Hiram in day and night nursing. It was all perfect misery to Audouin; the more he wanted to die for Gwen's and Hiram's convenience, the more utterly determined they both seemed to be to keep him living somehow at all hazards.

On the seventh day, the crisis came, and Audouin began to sink rapidly. Gwen and Hiram were both by his bedside, and Colin Churchill and Minna were waiting anxiously in the little salon alongside. When the doctor came, he stopped longer than usual; and as he passed out, Colin asked him what news this morning of the poor patient. The doctor twirled his watch-chain quietly. 'Well,' he said, in his calm professional manner, 'I should say it was probable he would get through the night; but I doubt if he'll live over Sunday.'

'Then there's no hope, you think?' Minna asked with tears in her eyes.

'Well, I couldn't exactly say that,' the doctor answered. 'A medical man always hopes to the last moment, especially in acute diseases. The critical point's hardly reached yet. Oh yes, he might recover; he might recover, certainly; but it isn't likely.'

Colin and Minna sat down once more in the empty salon, and looked at one another long, without speaking. At last there came a knock at the door. Colin answered 'Enter,' and a servant entered. 'A card for Signor Vintrop,' he said, handing it to Colin. 'The bringer says he must see him on important business immediately.'

Colin cast a careless glance at the card. It was that of a well-known Roman picture-dealer, agent for one of the largest firms of fine art auctioneers in London. 'How very ill-timed,' he said to Minna, handing her the card. At any other moment, Hiram would have been delighted; but it's quite impossible to trouble him with this at such a crisis.

'Does he want to buy some of Mr. Winthrop's pictures, do you think, Colin?' Minna asked anxiously.

'I'm sure he does; but it can't be helped now. Tell the gentleman that Mr. Winthrop can't see him now, if you please, Antonio. He's watching by the side of the American signor who is dying.'

Antonio bowed and went out. In a minute he returned once more. 'The person can't wait,' he said; 'the affair is urgent. He wishes to give Signor Vintrop an important commission. He wishes to buy pictures, many pictures, immediately. He has come from the studio, hearing that Signor Vintrop was at the hotel, and he wishes particularly to speak with him instantaneously.'

Colin looked at Minna and shook his head.

'This is very annoying, really, Minna,' he said with a sigh. 'At any other time, it would have been a perfect godsend; but now, one can't drag him away from poor Audouin's bedside. Tell the gentleman, Antonio,' he went on in Italian, 'that Mr. Winthrop can't possibly see him. It is most absolutely and decidedly impossible.'

Antonio went away, and for half an hour more Colin and Minna conversed together in an undertone without further interruption. Then a knock came again, and Antonio entered with a second card. It bore the name of another famous Roman picture-dealer, the agent for the rival London firm. 'He says he must see Signor Vintrop without delay,' Antonio reported, 'upon important business of the strictest urgency.'

Colin hesitated a moment. 'This is really very remarkable, Minna,' he said slowly, turning over the card in great perplexity. 'Why on earth should the two principal picture-dealers in Rome want to see Hiram Winthrop so very particularly on the same morning?'

'I can't imagine,' Minna answered, looking at the card curiously. 'Don't you think, Colin, you'd better see the man and ask him what's the meaning of it?'

Colin nodded assent, and went to the door to speak to the dealer. As he did so, a second servant stepped up with yet another card, that of a Manchester picture-agent in person.

'What do you want to see Mr. Winthrop for in such a hurry?' Colin asked the Italian dealer. 'How is it you all wish to buy his pictures the same morning? He's been in Rome a good many years now, but nobody ever seemed in any great haste to become a purchaser.'

'I cannot tell you, signor,' the dealer answered blandly; 'but I have my instructions from London. I have a telegram direct from a most illustrious firm, requesting me to buy up the landscapes, and especially the American landscapes, of Signor Vintrop.'

'And if Mr. Winthrop's too ill himself to come and show me his studio,' the Manchester agent put in, in English, 'perhaps, sir, you might step round yourself and arrange matters with me on his behalf.'

Colin hesitated a moment. It was an awkward predicament. He didn't like to go away selling pictures when Audouin was actually dying; and yet, knowing what he knew, and taking into consideration Audouin's particular mental constitution, he saw in it a possible chance of saving his life indirectly. Something or other had occurred, that was clear, to make a sudden demand arise for Hiram's pictures. If the demand was a genuine one, and if he could sell them for good prices, the effect upon Audouin might be truly magical. The man was really dying, not of fever, of that Colin felt certain, but of hopeless chagrin and disappointment. If he could only learn that Hiram's landscapes were meeting with due appreciation after all, he might perhaps even now recover.

Colin went back to Minna for a few minutes' whispered conversation; and then, having learned from Gwen (without telling her his plans) that Audouin was no worse, and that he would probably go on without serious change for some hours, he hurried off to the studio between the two intending purchasers.

As he got to the door, he saw a small crowd of artistic folk, mostly agents or dealers, and amongst them he noticed a friend and fellow-student at Maragliano's, the young Englishman, Arthur Forton. 'Why, what on earth's the meaning of this, Forton?' he asked in fresh amazement. 'All the world seems to have taken suddenly to besieging Winthrop's studio.'

'Ah, yes,' Forton answered briskly; 'I thought there was sure to be a run upon his bank after what I saw in Truman's paper; and I happened to be at Raffaele Pedrocchi's when a telegram came in from Magnus of London asking him to buy up all Winthrop's landscapes that he could lay his hands upon at once, and especially authorising him to pay up to something in cypher for Chattawauga Lake or some such heathenish Yankee name or other. So I came round immediately to see Winthrop, and advise him not to let the things go for a mere song, as Magnus is evidently anxious to get them almost at any price.'

Colin listened in profound astonishment. 'Truman's paper!' he cried in surprise. 'Why, Winthrop positively assured me that Truman told him he ought to go back at once to America.'

'So he did, no doubt,' Forton replied carelessly. 'Indeed, he tells him so in print in Fortuna Melliflua. Here's the cutting: I cut it out on purpose, so that Winthrop might take care he wasn't chiselled, as you were, you know, over "Autumn and the Breezes."'

Colin took the scrap of paper from the little pamphlet from Forton's hands, and read the whole paragraph through with a thrill of pleasure.

'And yet from this same entirely damned land of America,' ran Mr. Truman's candid and vigorous criticism, 'some good thing may haply come, even as (cynical Nathaniel to the contrary notwithstanding) some good thing did indubitably come out of Nazareth of Galilee. The other day, walking by chance into a certain small shabby studio, down a side alley from the Street of the Beautiful Ladies at Rome, I unearthed there busily at work upon a Babylonian Woe one Hiram Winthrop, an American artist, who had fled from America and the City of Destruction to come enthusiastically Romeward. He had better far have stopped at home. For this young man Winthrop, a God-sent landscape painter, if ever there was one, has in truth the veritable eye for seeing and painting a bit of overgrown rank waterside vegetation exactly as nature herself originally disposed it, with no nice orthodox and academical graces of arrangement, but simply so, weeds and water, no more than that; just a tangled corner of neglected reeds and waving irises, seen in an aerial perspective which is almost stereoscopic. Strange to say, this American savage from the wild woods can reproduce the wild woods from which he came, in all their native wildness, without the remotest desire to make them look like a Dutch picture of the garden of Eden. Moreover, he positively knows that red things are red, green things green, and white things white; a piece of knowledge truly remarkable in this artificially colour-blind age of dichroic vision (I get my fine words from a scientific treatise on the subject by Professor Stilling of Leipzig, to whose soul may heaven be merciful). There was one picture of his there—Chattawauga Lake I think he called it, which I had it in my mind to buy at the moment, and had even gone so far as to purse up my lips into due form for saying, "How much is it?" (as we price spring chickens at market), but on deeper thought, I refrained deliberately, because I am now a poor man, and I do not want to buy pictures at low rates, being fully of opinion, on good warranty, that the labourer is worthy of his hire. So I left it, more out of political than personal economy, for some wealthier man to buy hereafter. Yet whoever does buy Chattawauga Lake (the name alone is too repellant) will find himself in possession, I do not hesitate to say, of the finest bit of entirely sincere and scrupulous landscape that has ever been painted since Turner's brush lay finally still upon his broken palette. And young Mr. Hiram Wintlirop himself, I dare predict, will go back to America hereafter and give us other landscapes which will more than suffice to wash out the Babylonian woes whereupon he is at present engaged in sedulously wasting a most decisive and categorical genius.'

Colin took the scrap of paper in his hands, and went with Forton into the disorderly studio.

'May I take it to show Winthrop and Audouin?' he asked.

Forton nodded.

They turned to the pictures, and Chattawauga Lake having been duly produced, Colin found himself at a moment's notice turned into a sort of amateur auctioneer, receiving informal bids one after another from the representatives of almost all the best picture firms in the whole of England.

He had soon got rid of Chattawauga Lake, and before an hour and a half was over, the agents had almost made a clean sweep of the entire studio. Even the Babylonian Woe was bought up at a fair price by one enthusiastic person, on the ground that it had been immensely enhanced in value by being mentioned, although unfavourably, in a note of Truman's. The great critic had simply made Hiram Winthrop's fortune; people were prepared to buy anything he might paint now, on the strength of Truman's recommendation.

As soon as Colin had got rid of the more pressing purchasers, he left Forton in charge of the studio, and ran back hastily to Audouin's hotel. Would the good news be in time to save the dying man's life? that was the question. Colin wondered what he could make of it, and turned over the matter anxiously in his own mind, as he went back to Minna, Gwen, and Hiram.

CHAPTER XLVI

AUDOUIN SINKS OR SWIMS

Colin entered the little salon once more with bated breath and eager anxiety. 'Is he alive yet, Minna?' he asked in a low tone, as she came to meet him, pale and timid.

'Alive, Colin, but hardly more. The fever's very serious, and Miss Russell says he's wandering in his mind terribly.'

'What's he saying, Minna? Did Miss Russell tell you?'

'Oh, yes, poor girl; she's crying her eyes out. She says, Colin, he's muttering that he has ruined Mr. Winthrop, and that he wished he was dead, and then they'd both be happy.' Colin went in without another word to the sick-room, and stood awhile by the bedside, listening anxiously to poor Audouin's incoherent mutterings. As he caught a word or two of his troubled thoughts, he made up his mind at once as to what he must do. Taking Hiram by the arm, he drew him quietly without a word into the salon. 'Winthrop,' he said, 'I have something to explain to you. You must listen to it now, though it sounds irrelevant, because it's really a matter of life and death to Mr. Audouin. I've just sold your Chattawauga Lake for seven thousand five hundred lire.

Hiram started in surprise for a moment, and then made a gesture of impatience. 'What does that matter, my dear fellow,' he cried, 'when Mr. Audouin's just dying?'

'It matters a great deal,' Colin answered; 'and if you'll wait and hear, you'll see it may be the means of saving his life for you.'

Hiram sat down and listened with blanched face to Colin's story. Then Colin began at the beginning and told him all he knew: how Audouin had lost heart entirely at Hiram's want of success; how he had made a will, practically in Hiram's favour; and how he had gone out quite deliberately upon the Campagna, and caught the perniciosa, on purpose to kill himself for Hiram's benefit. At this point Hiram interrupted him for a moment. His lips were deadly pale, and he trembled violently, but he said in his usual calm voice, 'You do him an injustice there, Churchill. He didn't do it on purpose. I know him better than you do. Whatever he did, he did half unconsciously by way of meeting fate half way only. Mr. Audouin is quite incapable of breaking his promise.'

Colin heard him and nodded acquiescence. It was no time, indeed, for discussing the abstract points of Audouin's character. Then he went on with his story, telling Hiram how the picture-dealers had come to him that morning, how he had sold Chattawauga Lake and several other of his pieces for excellent prices, and how the influx had been wholly due to a single paragraph in Truman's 'For-tuna Melliflua.' As he spoke he handed Hiram the cutting to read, and Hiram read it rapidly through with an unwonted sense of relief and freedom 'I don't know, Churchill,' he said when he had finished. 'I can't feel sure of it. But I think it has come in time to save his life for us.'

They concerted a little scheme shortly between them, and then they went into the sick-room once more, where Audouin was now lying somewhat more quietly with his eyes half open. Hiram held up his head and gave him a dose of the mixture which had been ordered for him at moments of feebleness. It seemed to revive him a little. Then they sat down by the bed together, and began talking to one another in a low tone, so that Audouin could easily overhear them. He was less feverish, for the moment, and seemed quite sensible; so Colin said in a quiet voice, 'Yes, I sold Chattawauga Lake to old Focacci, who acts as agent, you know, for Magnus of London.'

Audouin evidently overheard the words, and took in their meaning vaguely, for his eye turned towards Colin, and he seemed to listen with some attention.

'How much did you sell it for?' asked Hiram. He hated himself for even seeming to be thus talking about his own wretched pecuniary business when Audouin was perhaps dying, but he knew it was the only chance of rousing his best and earliest friend from that fatal torpor.

'Seven thousand five hundred lire,' answered Colin.

'How much is that in our money?'

'In English money, three hundred pounds sterling,' Colin replied, distinctly.

There was a little rustling in the bed, an attempt to sit up feebly, and then Audouin asked in a parched voice, 'How many dollars?' 'Hush, hush, Mr. Audouin,' Colin said gently, pretending to check him, but feeling in his own heart that their little ruse had almost succeeded already. 'You mustn't excite yourself on any account.'

Audouin was silent for a moment; then he said again, in a somewhat stronger and more decided manner, 'How many dollars, I say: how many dollars?'

'Five into seven thousand five hundred' Hiram reckoned with a slight shudder, 'makes fifteen hundred, doesn't it, Churchill? Yes, fifteen hundred. Fifteen hundred dollars, Mr. Audouin.'

Audouin fell back upon the pillow, for he had raised his head slightly once more, and seemed for a while to be dozing quietly. At lust he asked again, 'Who to, did you say?'

'Focacci of the Piazza di Spagna, agent for Magnus and Hickson of London.'

This time, Audouin lay a long while ruminating in his fevered head over that last important disclosure. He seemed to take it in faintly bit by bit, for after another long pause he asked even more deliberately, 'How did Magnus and Rickson ever come to hear of you, Hiram?'

Colin thought the time had now come to tell him briefly the good news in its entirety, if it was to keep him from dying of disappointment. 'Truman has written very favourably about Winthrop's abilities as a landscape painter,' he said gently, 'in his "Fortuna Melliflua," and a great many London dealers have sent telegrams to buy up all his pictures. I have been round to the studio this morning, and sold almost all of them at high prices.

Truman has spoken so well of them that there can be very little doubt Winthrop's fortune is fairly made in real earnest.'

They watched Audouin carefully as Colin spoke, for they feared the excitement might perhaps have been too much for him: it was a risky card to play, but they played it in all good intention. Audouin listened quite intelligently to the end, and then he suddenly burst out crying. For some minutes he cried silently, without even a sob to break the deathlike stillness. The tears seemed to do him good, too; for as he cried, Gwen, hanging over him eagerly, noticed that little beads of moisture were beginning to form faintly upon his parched forehead. In their concentrated anxiety for Audouin's life, neither she nor Hiram had yet found time adequately to realise their own good fortune; they could only think of its effect upon the crisis of that terrible fever.

Audouin cried on without a word for ten minutes, and then he asked once more, in a weak voice, 'What did Truman say? Have you got "Fortuna?"'

Colin took out the paragraph once more and read it all over, omitting only the Babylonian Woe, which he feared might have the effect of distressing Audouin. When he had finished, Audouin smiled, and answered, smiling faintly, with a touch of his wonted self, 'Then, like Wolfe, I shall die happy;' and after a moment he added, in a feebly theatrical fashion, 'They run. Who run? The Philistines, to buy his pictures. Then I die happy.'

'No, no, Mr. Audouin,' Gwen cried passionately, lifting his white hand to her lips and kissing it fervidly. 'You mustn't die. For our sakes, you must try to live and share all our happiness.'

Audouin shook his head slowly. 'No, no,' he said; 'the fever has got too strong a hold upon me. I shall never, never recover.'

'You must, Mr. Audouin,' Colin Churchill said resolutely. 'If you go and die after all, I shall never forgive you. You've got nothing to die for now, and you mustn't think of going at last and doing anything so wicked and foolish.'

Audouin smiled again, and turning over on his side, began to doze off in a feverish sleep. He slept so long and so soundly that Gwen was frightened, and insisted upon sending for the doctor. When the doctor came, it was growing dark, and Audouin lay still and peaceful like a child in the cradle. The doctor felt his pulse without awakening him. 'Why,' he cried in surprise, 'he seems to have been very much excited, but his pulse is decidedly fuller and slower than it was this morning. Something unexpected must have occurred to make an improvement in his condition. I think the crisis is over, and he'll get round again in time with good nursing.' Gwen and the hired nurse sat up all that night with him.

CHAPTER XLVII

ALL'S WELL THAT ENDS WELL

Audouin's recovery was slow, of course; but, he did recover; and as soon as he was safely out of all danger, Gwen and Hiram, now fairly on the road to fortune, proposed that they should forthwith marry. The colonel had almost given up active opposition by this time; he knew that that girl's temper was absolutely ungovernable; and besides, they said the shock-headed Yankee fellow was beginning to make quite a decent livelihood out of his painting business. So the colonel merely answered when Gwen mentioned to him the date she had fixed upon, 'You'll go your own way, I suppose, Miss, whatever I choose to say to you about it,' and threw no further obstacles in the way of the ceremony.

'And, Gwen,' Hiram said to her, as they walked together down the path by the Casca-telli at Tivoli a few days before the wedding, 'we'll take the Tyrol, if you'd like it, for our wedding tour, darling.'

'Yes,' Gwen answered, 'we will, and we'll never come back again to Rome, to live I mean, Hiram, but go to Switzerland, or Wales, or Scotland, or America. You must go, you know, where you can find what you most want to paint, your own beautiful delicate landscapes. I always knew that that was what you could do best; and I always told you that there at least you had real genius.' Hiram's answer was of a sort that cannot readily be put down in definite language; and yet Gwen understood it perfectly, and only murmured in a low soft tone, 'Not here, Hiram, not here, there's a dear good fellow.'

The bushes around were fairly thick and screening, to be sure, but still, in the open air, you know, and in a place overrun with tourists, like Tivoli, well, it was certainly very imprudent.

When Colin Churchill heard that Hiram and Gwen had definitely fixed the day for their own wedding, he put on his hat and went round to the English quarter to call for Minna. They walked together up from the Piazza del Popolo, by the Pincian and Esquiline, towards the straggling vineyards on the Colian Hill. There the young vines were coming into the first fresh leaf, and the air was thick with perfume from the jonquils and lilacs in the neighbouring flower gardens.

'Minna darling,' Colin began quietly, and Minna flushed crimson and thrilled through to her inmost marrow at the sound of the words, for Colin had never before called her 'darling.' She looked at him full of tender surmise, and her bursting heart stood still for a moment within her bosom, waiting to know whether it was to bound again with joy, or flutter feebly in disappointment. After all, then, Colin Churchill really loved her!

Colin noticed the evident tokens of suspense upon her dark cheek, with the hot blood struggling red through the rich gipsy complexion, and wondered to himself that she should feel so deeply moved by the simple question he was going to ask her. Had they not always loved one another, all their lives long, and was it not a mere question of time and convenience, now, the particular day they fixed upon for their marriage? He could hardly understand the profoundness of her emotion, though he was too practised an observer of the human face not to read it readily in her flushed features: for, after all, it was nothing more than settling the final arrangements for a foregone conclusion.

'Minna darling,' he said once more, watching her narrowly all the time, 'Win-throp and Miss Howard-Russell are going to be married on Thursday fortnight. I was thinking, dearest, that if you could arrange it with your people so soon, it'd be a good plan for us to have our wedding at the same time, for I suppose you don't think a fortnight too short notice after such a long engagement?'

Minna trembled violently from head to foot as she answered, with a little tremor in her voice, 'Then Colin, Colin, oh Colin, you really love me!'

Colin caught her small round hand tenderly in his and said, with a tone of genuine surprise, 'Why, you know perfectly well, my own darling little Minna, I've always loved you dearly. All my life long, darling, I've always loved you.'

It was well that Colin held the round brown hand tight in his, that moment, for as Minna heard those words, those words that her heart had longed so long to hear, and whose truth she had doubted to herself so often, she uttered a little loud sharp cry, and fell forward, not fainting, but overcome with too sudden joy, so that her head reeled, and she might have dropped unconscious, but that Colin caught her, and pressed her in his arms, and kissed lier, and cried to her in surprise and self-reproach, 'Why, Minna, Minna, darling Minna, my own heart's darling, you knew I loved you; you must have known I always loved you.'

Minna's heart fluttered up and down within her bosom, and heaved and swelled as though it would burst asunder that tight little plain black bodice. (Why do not dressmakers allow something for the natural expansiveness of emotion, I wonder.) It was so sweet to hear Colin say so; and yet even now she could hardly believe her life-long daydream had wrought out at last its own fulfillment. 'Oh, Colin, Colin,' she murmured through her tears, for she had found that relief, 'you never told me so; you never, never told me you loved me.'

'Told you, Minna!' Colin cried with another kiss upon the trembling lips (and all this on the open Colian too); 'told you, Minna darling! Why, who on earth would ever have dreamt of deliberately telling you. But you must have known it; of course you must have known it. Haven't we been lovers together, darling, from our babyhood upward?'

'But that was just it, Colin,' Minna answered, brushing away her tears, and trying to look as if nothing extraordinary at all had happened. 'We had always known one another, of course, and been very fond of one another, like old companions, and I wasn't sure, with you, Colin, whether it was love or merely friendship.'

'And with yourself, Minna?' Cohn asked, taking her soft wee hand once more between his own two; 'tell me, darling, which was it, which was it?'

Minna's face gave her only answer, and Colin accepted it silently with another kiss.

There was a minute's pause again (the Colian is really such a very awkward place for lovemaking, with all those horrid prying old priests poking about everywhere), and then Minna began once more: 'You see, Colin, you seemed so cold and indifferent. You were always so wrapped up in your marble and your statues, and you didn't appear to care a bit for anything but art, till I almost grew to hate it. Oh, Colin, I know the things you make are the most beautiful that ever were moulded, but I almost hated them, because you seemed to think of nothing on earth but your clay and your sculpture. I was afraid you only liked me; I didn't feel sure whether you really loved me.'

'Minna,' Colin said soberly, standing up before her and looking full into those bright black eyes straight in front of him, 'I love you with all the love in my nature. I have loved you ever since we were children together, and I have never for one moment ceased from loving you. How could I, when you were Minna? If I ever seemed cold and careless, darling, it was only because I loved you so thoroughly and unquestioningly that it didn't occur to me to waste words in telling you what I thought you yourself could never question. My darling, if I've caused you doubt or pain, I can't tell you how sorry I am for it. I have worked for you, and for you only, all these years. Don't you remember, little woman, long ago at Wootton, how I always used to make images for Minna?

Well, I've been making images for Minna ever since. I never for a moment fancied you didn't know it. But now, as I love you, and as you love me, tell me, darling, will you marry me on Thursday fortnight? Don't say no, or wait to think about it, but answer me "yes" at once; now do'ee, Minna, do'ee.'

That half-unconscious, half-artful return on Colin's part to the old loved familiar dialect of their peasant childhood was more than Minna's bursting little heart could ever have resisted, even if she had wanted to—which she certainly didn't. With the tears once more trickling slowly down her cheek, she answered softly, 'Yes, Colin;' and Colin pressed her hand a second time in token of the completed contract. And then the two turned slowly back towards the great city, and Minna tried to dry her eyes and look as though nothing at all out of the way had happened against her return to the Via Clementina.

Gwen and Hiram Winthrop, in their little cottage in North Wales, are within easy reach of many wild bits that exactly suit Hiram's canvas. His natural genius has full play now, and at the Academy every year there are few pictures more studiously avoided by the crowd, and more carefully observed by the best judges, than Mr. Winthrop's, the famous American landscape painter's. Now and then he pays a short visit to America, and sketches unbroken nature, as he alone can sketch it, in the Adirondacks, and the White Mountains, and the Upper Alleghanies; but for the most part, as Gwen simply phrases it, 'Wales and Scotland are quite good enough for us.' Once a year, too, he runs across for a month or six weeks to Rome and Florence, where Colin and Minna are always glad to give him and his wife a hearty welcome. Even the colonel has relented somewhat in a grim official Anglo-Indian fashion, and as he jogs Gwen's youngest boy upon his knee to the tune of some Hindustani jingle about Warren Hastings, he reflects to himself that after all that shockheaded Yankee painter fellow isn't really such a bad sort of person by way of a son-in-law.

And Audouin? Audouin has sold Lakeside, and flits to and fro uneasily between Europe and America in a somewhat vague and purposeless fashion. Sometimes he stops with Colin Churchill at Rome (on a strict pledge that he won't go out alone without leave to stroll upon the Campagna), and sometimes he wanders by himself, knapsack on back, among the Swiss or Tyrolese mountains; but most often he gravitates towards Bryn-y-mynydd, on the slopes of Aran, where Gwen still greets him always in most daughterly fashion with a kiss of welcome. Gwen's little boys are firm as a rock upon one point, that except daddy, there isn't a man in the world at all to be compared for starting a squirrel or scaring a pine marten to Uncle Audouin. But what his precise claim to uncleship may be is a genealogical question that has never for a moment troubled their simple unsophisticated little intellects. They hold ingenuously that a rocking-horse apiece upon their birthdays, and a bright new gold half-sovereign on every visit, is quite sufficient guarantee for that naïf and expansive title of kinship.

Grant Allen – A Short Biography

Charles Grant Blairfindie Allen was born on February 24th, 1848 at Alwington, near Kingston, Canada West (now part of Ontario). He was the second son of the Rev. Joseph Antisell Allen, a Protestant minister from Dublin, Ireland and Catharine Ann Grant, the daughter of the fifth Baron of Longueuil.

Grant was educated at home until he was thirteen at which time the family moved, initially to the United States, then France and finally settling in the United Kingdom.

Whilst growing up the family background was obviously religious but Grant developed his own views on life and the world and turned to agnosticism and socialism.

He was educated at King Edward's School in Birmingham and Merton College in Oxford. After graduating, Grant studied in France and also taught at Brighton College. By 1870, still only in his mid-twenties, he became a professor at Queen's College, a black college in Jamaica.

Whilst in Jamaica Grant met and married his first wife Ellen Jerrard in 1873 and they produced a son five years later; Jerrard Grant Allen, who grew up to become a theatrical agent/manager.

In 1876 Grant and his family left Jamaica to return to England with both the talent and ambition to become a writer.

He quickly turned to writing essays, gaining a reputation for his work on science and literary works. An early article, 'Note-Deafness' a description of what is now called amusia, was published in 1878 in the learned journal Mind and was cited approvingly by Oliver Sacks very recently.

From essays in magazines and journals he now turned to books, initially on scientific subjects. These include Physiological Æsthetics 1877 and Flowers and Their Pedigrees 1886.

His first major influence was associationist psychology, as then expounded by Alexander Bain and Herbert Spencer, the latter is often considered the most important individual in the transition from associationist psychology to Darwinian functionalism. In Grant's many articles on flowers and perception in insects, Darwinian arguments now replaced the old Spencerian terms.

On a personal level, a long friendship that started when Grant met Herbert Spencer on his return from Jamaica, turned eventually to one of unease over its long course. Grant was to write a critical and revealing biographical article on Spencer that was published after Spencer was dead.

In the early 1880's Grant began to assist Sir W. W. Hunter in his Gazeteer of India. It is at this time that Grant now turned his full attention away from the factual and towards the world of imagination and fiction.

Between this shift to fiction in 1884 and his death fifteen years later Grant was to write about 30 novels.

Many were adventure novels which were very common in the late Victorian period as writers turned their literary talents to the voracious appetites of the weekly or monthly serial magazines.

Some however were to cause quite a stir. For instance in 1895 Grant took the subject of children born out of wedlock as his subject matter. The result was The Woman Who Did, that suggested, indeed pushed, for its time, certain quite startling views on marriage and related areas. In keeping with his then glowing reputation it became a bestseller despite it being seemingly at odds with society's unease at its provocative subject matter.

Interestingly Grant wrote novels under female pseudonyms. One of these was the short novel The Type-writer Girl, which he wrote under the name Olive Pratt Rayner.

Another work, The Evolution of the Idea of God 1897, propounding a theory of religion on heterodox lines, has the disadvantage of endeavoring to explain everything by one theory. This "ghost theory" was often seen as a derivative of Herbert Spencer's theory. However, at the time, it was well known and brief references to it can be found in a review by Marcel Mauss, Durkheim's nephew, in the articles of William James and in the works of Sigmund Freud. The young G. K. Chesterton wrote on what he considered the flawed premise of the idea, arguing that the idea of God preceded human mythologies, rather than developing from them. Chesterton said of Grant Allen's book on the evolution of the idea of God "it would be much more interesting if God wrote a book on the evolution of the idea of Grant Allen".

From this and other instances, it can be seen that his work was in debate and whether agreed with or not could always ensure a lively discussion.

Grant also helped to pioneer science fiction, with the 1895 novel The British Barbarians. This book, was published at about the same time as H. G. Wells was to publish The Time Machine. The plots are quite different but both describe time travel. A few years later his short story The Thames Valley Catastrophe (published 1901 in The Strand magazine) describes the destruction of London by a massive volcanic eruption. Whilst the premise now may seem outlandish, at the time genuine panic and concern set in as, like his contemporary, Jules Verne, much of great science fiction writing is rooted in a plausibility that is set out very convincingly.

In detective fiction too his works include female detectives, very much an innovation in the young genre and his gentleman rogue, Colonel Clay, is seen as a forerunner to other, perhaps more famous characters, by other later writers.

In 1881 he had settled at Dorking, where he took great delight in botanical walks in the woods and sandy heaths. He never enjoyed particularly good health and so almost every winter he would depart for milder climes, to winter in the south of Europe, usually at Antibes, though occasionally as far as Algiers and Egypt.

In 1892 he bought land almost on the summit of Hind Head, and built himself a charming cottage which he called the Croft. Here he found that it was possible to endure the vagaries of the English winter and in landscape more beautiful and wilder than at Dorking and that his long scientific training could better appreciate.

His growing re-discovery and interest in art in the later part of his life allowed him to blend together literature, art and history in a series of guide books on Paris, Florence, Venice, and the cities of Belgium.

On October 25th 1899 Grant Allen died at his home in Hindhead, Haslemere, Surrey, England. He died just before finishing Hilda Wade. The novel's final episode, which he dictated to his friend, doctor and neighbour Sir Arthur Conan Doyle from his bed appeared under the appropriate title, The Episode of the Dead Man Who Spoke in the Strand Magazine in 1900.

Grant Allen is rarely heard of today, although an occasional short story can be heard on the radio or reprinted among magazine enthusiasts but in his time he did much to entertain the masses and push several genres along a richer journey they are still proceeding on today.

Grant Allen – A Concise Bibliography

Physiological Æsthetics. 1877
The Colour-Sense: Its Origin and Development. 1879
Evolutionist at Large. 1881
Vignettes from Nature. 1881
The Colours of Flowers. 1882
Colin Clout's Calendar. 1883
Flowers and Their Pedigrees. 1883
Philistia. 1884
Strange Stories. Short Stories. 1884
Babylon. A novel in 3 volumes. 1885
For Mamie's Sake. 1886

In All Shades. 1886
The Beckoning Hand & Other Stories. 1887
This Mortal Coil: A Novel. 1888
Force and Energy. 1888
The Devil's Die. 1888
The White Man's Foot. 1888
Falling in Love. 1889
The Tents of Shem. 1889
Wednesday the Tenth. 1890
The Great Taboo. 1890
Dumaresq's Daughter. 1891
What's Bred in the Bone. 1891
The Duchess of Powysland. 1892
The Scallywag. 1893
Michael's Crag. 1893
The Lower Slopes. 1894
Post-Prandial Philosophy. 1894
The British Barbarians. 1895
At Market Value. 1895
The Story of the Plants. 1895
The Desire of the Eyes. 1895
The Woman Who Did. 1895
The Jaws of Death. 1896
A Bride from the Desert. 1896
Under Sealed Orders. 1896
Moorland Idylls. 1896
An African Millionaire. Colonel Clay's novel. 1897
The Evolution of the Idea of God. 1897
Paris. 1897
The Type-writer Girl. (as Olive Pratt Rayner) 1897
Tom, Unlimited. (as Martin Leach Warborough) 1897
Flashlights on Nature. 1898
The Incidental Bishop. 1898
Venice. 1898
The European Tour. 1899
A Splendid Sin. 1899
Miss Cayley's Adventures. 1899
Twelve Tales: With a Headpiece, a Tailpiece, and an Intermezzo. 1899
Hilda Wade (finished by Arthur Conan Doyle). 1900
Linnet. 1900
The Backslider. 1901
Sir Theodore's Guest & Other Stories. 1902
Evolution in Italian Art. 1908
The Hand of God. 1909
The Plants. 1909

Short Stories
The Empress of Andorra. 1878
My New Year Among the Mummies. 1878
Lucretia. 1879

My Circular Tour. 1880
A Ballade of Evolution. 1880
Ram Das of Cawnpore. 1880
The Chinese Play at the Haymarket. 1880
The Senior Proctor's Wooing. 1881
Pausodyne. 1881
Caribbean Twelve Per Cents. 1882
An Episode in High Life. 1882
Mr Chung. 1882
Isadine and I. 1883
The Backsider. 1883
The Reverend John Creedy. 1883
The Foundering of the Fortuna. 1883
The Third Time
The Gold Wulfric
My Uncle's Will. 1884
Carvalho. 1884
The Mysterious Occurence in Piccadilly. 1884
Dr Greatex's Engagement. 1884
Hugh Portledown's Return from Normandy. 1884
The Child of Phalanstery. 1884
The Curate of Churnside. 1884
John Cann's Treasure. 1884
Olga Davidoff's Husband. 1884
The Search Party's Find. 1885
The Two Carnegie's. 1885
Professor Milliter's Dilemma. 1885
In Strict Confidence. 1885
The Beckoning Hand. 1885
The Third Time. 1886
Harry's Inheritance. 1886
The Gold Wulfric. 1886
Mr Pierpoint's Repentance. 1886
Claude Tyack's Ordeal. 1887
Leonard's Recovery. 1887
A Social Difficulty. 1887
Dr Palliser's Patient. 1888
My Christmas Eve at Marzin. 1888
The Sultan's Sister. 1888
His First Crime. 1889
The Mayfield Mystery. 1889
Andre Canivet's Curse. 1890
Old Margaret. 1890
My One Gorilla. 1890
Dick Prothero's Luck. 1890
A Deadly Dilemna. 1891
Jerry Stokes. 1891
Selwyn Utterton's Nemesis. 1891
General Passavant's Will. 1891
The Briefless Barrister. 1891
Melissa's Tour. 1891

Karen – A Canadian Romance. 1891
The Prisoner of Assiout. 1891
The Abbe's Repentance. 1891
Masie Bowman's Fate. 1891
Naomi's Christmas Eves. 1891
That Friend of Sylvia's. 1892
The Conscientious Burglar. 1892
The Minor Poet. 1892
The Governor's Story. 1892
The Pot Boiler. 1892
The Great Ruby. 1892
Ewen Murray's Swim. 1892
Ivan Greet's Masterpiece. 1892
Pallinghurst Barrow. 1892
Langalula. 1893
The Assasin's Knife. 1893
The Artist and the Penny-a-Liner. 1893
A Casual Conversation. 1893
How To Succeed in Literature. 1893
Torrigiano. 1893
A Modern Sibyl: A Florentine Sketch. 1893
Nemesis Wins. 1894
Cecca's Lover. 1894
A Self Respecting Servant. 1894
Passiflora Sanguinea. 1894
An Excellent Match. 1894
Major Kinfaun's Marriage. 1894
Grateful Joe. 1894
An Idyll of the Ice. 1894
Criss Cross Love. 1894
Poor Little Soul. 1894
Amour de Voyage. 1894
The Dynamiter's Sweetheart. 1894
A Triumph of Civilisation. 1894
Dr Wardroper's Lie. 1894
The Miraclous Explorer. 1894
Leon and Leonie. 1895
A Comic Emotion. 1895
Joe's Rascality. 1895
Evelyn Moore's Poet. 1895
Frasine's First Communion. 1895
TheDead Man Speaks. 1895
A Study From the Nude. 1895
Cecca's Choice. 1895
The Desire of the Eyes. 1895
The Making of a Poet. 1895
The Man From Cumbrae. 1895
Fogo Skerries. 1895
The Great Californian Heiress. 1895
Cap'n Tom Woolley. 1895
The Girl at the Fair. 1895

Love's Old Dream. 1895
A Modern Pygmalion. 1895
A Bride From the Desert. 1895
The Practical Test. 1896
A Confidential Communication. 1896
The Great Temperance Preacher. 1896
A Day on the River. 1896
The Episode of the Mexican Seer. 1896
A Midsummer Episode. 1896
The Episode of the Diamond Links. 1896
Omar at Marlow. 1896
A Mere Matter of Standpoint. 1896
Fair Exchange. 1896
The Cowardly Dynamiter. 1896
The Episode of the Old Master. 1896
The Episode of the Tyrolean Castle. 1896
Janet's Nemesis. 1896
Entirely Accidential. 1896
The Episode of the Drawn Game. 1896
Wolverden Tower. 1896
The Episode of the German Professor. 1896
The Episode of the Arrest of the Colonel. 1896
The Episode of the Seldom Gold Mine. 1897
The Camisard's Bride. 1897
The Episode of the Japanned Dispatch Box. 1897
Llanfihangel Skerries. 1897
The Episode of the Game of Poker. 1897
The Episode of the Bertillon Method. 1897
A Lady of Florence. 1897
The Episode of the Old Bailey. 1897
A British Verdict. 1897
A Domestic Tragedy. 1897
A College Charm. 1897
A Freak of Memory. 1897
The Judge's Cross. 1897
The Thames Valley Catastrophe. 1897
The Great Oriental Seer. 1897
The Adventures of the Cantankerous Old Lady. 1898
The Adventure of the Supercilious Attache. 1898
The Pirate of Cliveden Reach. 1898
The Adventure of the Amateur Commission. 1898.
The Adventure of the Impromptu Mountaineer. 1898
Joe's Wife. 1898
The Adventure of the Urbane Old Gentleman. 1898
The Adventure of the Unobtrusive Oasis. 1898
The Adventure of the Pea Green Patrician. 1898
Isenberg's Regiment. 1898
The Adventure of the Magnificent Maharajah. 1898
A Woman's Hand: A Story. 1898
The Adventure of the Cross Eyed QC. 1898
The Christmas Eve Concert. 1898

The Adventure of the Oriental Attendant. 1899
Joseph's Dream. 1899
The Adventure of the Unprofessional Detective. 1899
Hobbling Mary. 1899
The Episode of the Patient Who Disappointed Her Doctor. 1899
The Episode of the Gentleman Who Had Failed For Everything. 1899
The Episode of the Wife Who Did Her Duty. 1899
The Episode of the Man Who Would Not Commit Suicide. 1899
A Regrettable Error. 1899
Peace-At-Any-Price Bill. 1899
The Episode of the Letter with a Basingstoke Post-Mark. 1899
The Episode of the Stone That Looked About It. 1899
His Ways Inscrutable. 1899
The Episode of the European With A Kaffir Heart. 1899
The Episode of the Lady Who Was Very Exclusive. 1899
The Episode of the Guide Who Knew the Country. 1899
Luigi and the Salvationist. 1899.
A Christmas Adventure. 1899.
The Episode of the Officer Who Understood Perfectly. 1900
Meriel Stanley, Poacher. 1900
The Episode of the Dead Man Who Spoke. 1900
A Question of Colour. 1900
Fra Benedett's Medal: A Story. 1900
The Temple of Fate: A Fable. 1900
The Way to Keronan. 1902
Lucy Lockett. 1902
Spencerian. 1904

Articles

1878. Hellas and Civilization, Gentleman's Magazine, Vol. CCXLIII
1878. Nation-making: A Theory of National Characters, Gentleman's Magazine, Vol. CCXLIII
1878. The Origin of Fruits, in Popular Science Monthly Volume 13
1879. Why Do We Eat our Dinner? in Popular Science Monthly Volume 14
1879. A Problem in Human Evolution, in Popular Science Monthly Volume
1879. Pleased with a Feather, in Popular Science Monthly Volume 15
1880. Why Keep India? The Contemporary Review, Vol. XXXVIII
1880. The Growth of Sculpture, The Cornhill Magazine, Vol. XLII
1880. The English Chronicle, Gentleman's Magazine, Vol. CCXLV
1880. The Venerable Bede, Gentleman's Magazine, Vol. CCXLIX
1880. The Dog's Universe, Gentleman's Magazine, Vol. CCXLIX
1880. Evolution and Geological Time, Gentleman's Magazine, Vol. CCXLIX
1880. Geology and History, in Popular Science Monthly Volume 17
1880. Aesthetic Feeling in Birds, in Popular Science Monthly Volume 17
1880. Aesthetic Evolution in Man, in Popular Science Monthly Volume 18
1881. The Story of Wulfgeat, Gentleman's Magazine, Vol. CCLI
1882. An English Shire, Gentleman's Magazine, Vol. CCLII
1882. The Welsh in the West Country, Gentleman's Magazine, Vol. CCLIII
1882. The Colours of Flowers, The Cornhill Magazine, Vol. XLV
1882. An English Weed, The Cornhill Magazine, Vol. XLV
1882. Sir Charles Lyell, in Popular Science Monthly Volume 20

1882. Hyacinth-Bulbs, in Popular Science Monthly Volume 20
1882. Who was Primitive Man? in Popular Science Monthly Volume 22
1883. The Pedigree of Wheat, in Popular Science Monthly Volume 22
1883. From Buttercups to Monk's-Hood, in Popular Science Monthly Volume 23
1883. Honeysuckle, Gentleman's Magazine, Vol. CCLV
1884. The Garden Snail, Gentleman's Magazine, Vol. CCLVI
1884. Our Debt to Insects, Gentleman's Magazine, Vol. CCLVI
1884. Idiosyncrasy, in Popular Science Monthly Volume 24
1884. The Ancestry of Birds, in Popular Science Monthly Volume 24
1884. The Milk in the Cocoa-Nut, in Popular Science Monthly Volume 25
1884. Our Debt to Insects, in Popular Science Monthly Volume 25
1884. Hickory-Nuts and Butternuts, in Popular Science Monthly Volume 25
1884. Queer Flowers, in Popular Science Monthly Volume 26
1885. Food and Feeding, in Popular Science Monthly Volume 26
1885. Concerning Clover, in Popular Science Monthly Volume 28
1886. A Thinking Machine, Gentleman's Magazine, Vol. CCLX
1886. Fish Out of Water, in Popular Science Monthly Volume 28
1886. A Thinking Machine, in Popular Science Monthly Volume 28
1886. Thistles, in Popular Science Monthly Volume 30, November 1886
1887. A Mount Washington Sandwort, in Popular Science Monthly Volume 30
1887. Among the Thousand Islands, in Popular Science Monthly Volume 31
1887. The Progress of Science from 1836 to 1886, in Popular Science Monthly Volume 31
1887. American Cinque-Foils, in Popular Science Monthly Volume 32
1888. Gourds and Bottles, in Popular Science Monthly Volume 33
1888. A Living Mystery, in Popular Science Monthly Volume 33
1888. Evolving the Camel, in Popular Science Monthly Volume 34
1889. From Africa, Gentleman's Magazine, Vol. CCLXVII
1889. Genius and Talent, in Popular Science Monthly Volume 34
1889. Plain Words on the Woman Question, in Popular Science Monthly Volume 36
1890. The Girl of the Future, Universal Review, Vol. VII.
1891. Democracy and Diamonds, The Contemporary Review, Vol. LIX
1892. A Desert Fruit, in Popular Science Monthly Volume 41
1893. Ghost Worship and Tree Worship I, in Popular Science Monthly Volume 42
1893. Ghost Worship and Tree Worship II, in Popular Science Monthly Volume 42
1897. Spencer and Darwin, in Popular Science Monthly Volume 50
1898. The Romance of Race, in Popular Science Monthly Volume 53
1898. The Season of the Year, in Popular Science Monthly Volume 54

Poetry

Grant Allen wrote various poems published in many magazines etc. We have not listed them here but hope to record some of them in the future.